APOSTLE PAUL

APOSTLE PAUL

A Novel

JAMES CANNON

ZOLAND BOOKS
an imprint of
STEERFORTH PRESS
HANOVER, NEW HAMPSHIRE

For information about permission to reproduce
selections from this book, write to:
Zoland Books / Steerforth Press L.C., 25 Lebanon Street
Hanover, New Hampshire 03755

The Library of Congress has cataloged the hardcover edition of this title as:

Cannon, James.
   Apostle Paul : a novel of the man who brought Christianity to the Western world / James
Cannon.— 1st ed.
      p. cm.
   ISBN 1-58642-094-1 (alk. paper)
   1. Paul, the Apostle, Saint—Fiction. 2. Church history—Primitive and early church,
ca. 30–600—Fiction. 3. Bible. N.T.—History of Biblical events—Fiction. 4. Christian saints—
Fiction. 5. Tarsus (Turkey)—Fiction. 6. Apostles—Fiction. I. Title.
   PS3603.A547A86 2005
   813'.6—dc22

                            2005010180

ZOLAND BOOKS TRADE PAPERBACK ISBN-10: 1-58195-220-1
                            ISBN-13: 978-1-58195-220-9

FIRST PAPERBACK EDITION

CONTENTS

This book, a fictional biography of Saint Paul, is based on the historical record. Major characters — notably Paul, Barnabas, Peter, John Mark, Timothy, Phoebe, Gamaliel, Aquila, and Prisca — and major events are drawn from the reporting of Luke and the letters of Paul. Others I invented.

In writing this historical novel I set out to narrate the known incidents of Paul's life factually, to tell the unknown parts of his life plausibly, and to show that Paul was not a myth but a man, a leader who redirected the course of civilization.

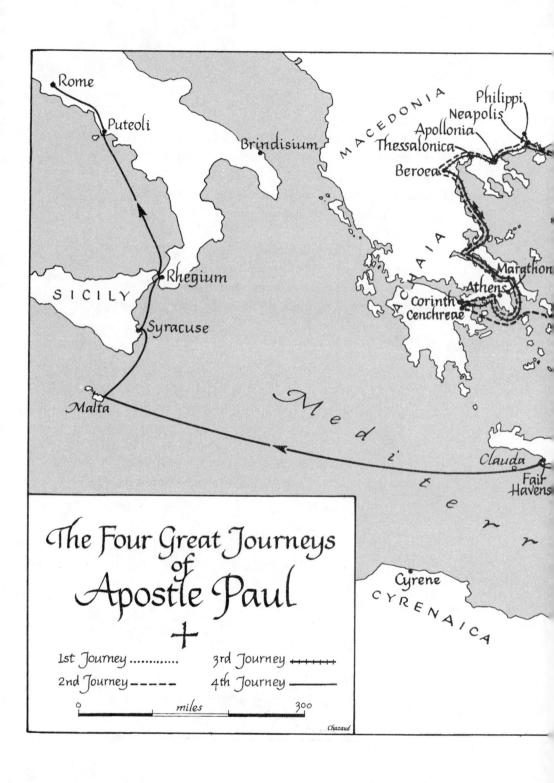

Rome

Puteoli

Brindisium

MACEDONIA

Philippi
Neapolis
Apollonia
Thessalonica
Beroea

SICILY

Rhegium

Syracuse

Marathon
Athens
Corinth
Cenchreae

Malta

Mediterr

Clauda
Fair
Havens

Cyrene
CYRENAICA

The Four Great Journeys
of
Apostle Paul
+

1st Journey ....   3rd Journey ++++++
2nd Journey -----   4th Journey ———

0   miles   300

Chazaud

THRACE

Black Sea

Byzantium

BITHYNIA

Troas   MYSIA

Assos

Mytilene

PHRYGIA

Ancyra

Pessinus

Pergamum
Thyatira
ASIA
Sardis   Philadelphia
Smyrna

Chios

GALATIA

Psidian Antioch

Iconium

CILICIA

Ephesus   Laodicea
Miletus   Colossae

Lystra

Samos

Derbe

Cilician
Gates

Issus

Cos

Attalia   Perga

Tarsus
Mersin

Antioch

Patara
Myra

Rhodes

Crete

Salamis
Paphos

Cyprus

Byblos

an   e a n   S e a

Damascus
Sidon
Tyre
Ptolemais

Caesarea

Joppa
JUDEA
Jerusalem

Alexandria

E G Y P T

N

I

BARGAIN

In the thirty-second year of the reign of Caesar Augustus, a cruel winter struck the lands and people of the eastern provinces. Snow filled the Cilician Gates, the only pass through the fortresses of the Taurus Mountains; there, traders and porters starved, and their camels and horses froze and died in harness. Drifts of snow blocked the Roman highway that wound southeast from the Gates through the foothills and across the fertile plain to the capital city of Tarsus. Rings of ice bound ships at their docks in the Cydnus River and closed the channel to the sea. The busy streets of Tarsus were silent, empty, for there was no food in the central market. Citizens of property doubled the guard outside their granaries. At the palace of the provincial governor, the imperial augur sacrificed a bull and cried out to the sky-god: "O Jupiter! End your terrible wrath. Bring back the sun to the heavens you rule."

In a clay hut in the quarter of the city set apart for Jews lived a rabbi and his daughter. Mordecai was bent with age but strong of spirit; Abigail was virginal, comely, and resolute as only a child reared in solitude can be. As they huddled by their meager charcoal fire one bleak Sabbath morning the daughter placed her hand on the old man's arm and pleaded: "Go not into this snow and cold, Father. You are ill."

Slowly the old man rose from his chair. "I will go to the synagogue," he said. "It is my duty to invoke the God of Israel to deliver my people from this prison of cold, to comfort them in this hour of peril. I must convince the fearful that this cruel tempest, like every storm of life, will soon pass."

In vain she shook her head, in the manner of the younger judging more wisely than the elder, but having less authority. "Then also will I go." So they wrapped themselves in their worn robes and began to make their way across the narrow street to the stone broadhouse where the Jews assembled

I

to honor their God. For the old man it was a struggle through the snow, a step, a breath, another step, another breath, all the while clutching his daughter's arm.

On the low platform before the Torah, the rabbi raised the ancient scrolls with trembling fingers. Hand to heaven, he beseeched the Lord to return the sun and its warmth to the land. To the anxious twoscore before him he entreated: "Endure the affliction of cold as since the olden time we, the chosen, the twelve tribes of Israel, have endured defeat, exile, and slavery. Remember the promise of God: 'Call upon me in the day of trouble; I will deliver thee.'"

As night clothed the city in a translucent shroud of freezing mist, father and daughter returned to their hut. Inside, to Abigail's surprise, Mordecai led her to the little room where he pored over his dusty scrolls and heavy books. With a nod he motioned her to the seat opposite him, and after a moment of silence he said, "Abigail, as I must fulfill my sacred duty to my people, so also must I fulfill my duty to you."

"What do you mean, Father?"

"Daughter, I have contracted for your marriage."

The young woman's full lips parted in astonishment at her father's words.

"This is against my will, Father." She spoke each word in deliberate measure, eye to eye with the old man, clenching her fists and striking the table, again, and then again.

Outside, the wind whispered at the eaves. The flame of the oil lamp, dancing in the drafts of the cold room, reflected in the young woman's dark eyes as tiny fires of anger.

Mordecai held out his bony hand to his daughter and in a grave voice tried to reason. "My dear Abigail, it is for your good that I do this."

Abigail watched the tears course along the web of wrinkles of her father's familiar cheek and into the thinning wisps of white beard. The old hand trembled. The once strong voice wavered in weakness and anguish. She was not moved.

"Why is this your choice, Father? Why am I not permitted to choose my own husband?"

"What do you know of men, my daughter?" His words were spoken not in scorn but sympathy. "What have you seen of men except for me and your brother Enoch?" He buried his face in his hands and murmured, "Woe! Had

2

your mother not died when you were born, it would be different now . . ." His voice broke, and he began to weep.

Abigail knew that her father spoke the truth. She had never talked with any man of her age. She had never been permitted to go alone to the nearby well, where custom allowed young girls filling their water jars to talk openly with each other, and with young men. Rarely had she been to the marketplace by herself. In a moment of sadness Abigail thought about her lonely childhood — a solitary small girl in a dark house dominated by the daily ritual, where bearded men intoned long prayers and endless recitations; and she, this child, attended by Danuta, her mother's handmaiden.

Memories bore Abigail away to a time past. She was five, sitting in this very room, attentive, absorbed, as her father first explained the marks on the page of a book. A new world opened in her mind, and still another when Enoch taught her Greek and brought her manuscripts from his school. Left to herself, Abigail had filled her days with scrolls and books, reading, copying, not only the Torah and the Prophets, but also Hammurabi and Homer and Sappho. With quill and papyrus she began in childhood to devote long hours to the journals of her meditations and dreams. She lived in her imagination; of the real world beyond her father's hut and synagogue, she caught only glimpses.

"Who is this man whose wife you would make me?" She made no effort to conceal her anger.

"He is Isaac the tentmaker," Mordecai said, his voice brightening. "He is the most able of his trade in this great city of Tarsus. He prospers by buying the finest Cilician wool and felting tents for travelers to east and west. He grows his own flax to weave sails for ships that travel the seas to Judea and Egypt. His leatherworkers make saddles and harness for the Roman legions that keep the peace of Caesar Augustus. So well has this Isaac served the Roman armies that the emperor has conferred on him, a Jew, the high status of citizen of Rome. Few of our tribe in this city have been so honored. Yet every Sabbath this Isaac comes to the synagogue. Every month he gives money; it was he who paid for the new roof to our building. He helps poor widows of our community. Daughter, no Jew in this city is more generous, or has more to give."

"So," Abigail said with a shiver, pulling her cloak more tightly around her shoulders, "like a tethered she-goat, I am to be sold to this old rich man."

"Rich he is, but not too old."

"How old?" she asked quickly.

"Not yet does he have forty years."

Abigail leaped to her feet. "Father! I am but eighteen. Why must I be imprisoned in another house of an old man?" She stopped, realizing she had hurt her father; but it was too late. She could not bring back her impulsive words, nor did she fully wish to.

"And why does this Isaac want to buy me?" she went on. "Danuta has told me that rich men can buy pagan virgins from Africa and Persia for a handful of shekels."

"Isaac wants a son," her father replied. "He wants a wife who can give him a son and heir. In this he is like all men. Long ago he spoke to me of his desire. He is of the House of Benjamin, as we are. He seeks a strong and healthy woman of our tribe who would favor him with a son. But no marriage broker has found him a woman he considers worthy."

"How came him to know about me?" Abigail asked.

The father hesitated, prompting her to guess what was to be his answer. "I speak in truth, daughter," he said. "Some time ago, I noticed Isaac looking at you in the synagogue as I read from the scrolls of the Torah. Sabbath after Sabbath I observed this. When next I saw Isaac alone I asked him if he had found a wife. He had not, and I told him that I had seen his eyes on my daughter."

"Thus you offered me for sale," Abigail said.

"I observed his interest," the father replied. "I saw that Isaac hesitated to speak to me, so I spoke to him."

"Would this Isaac the tentmaker pay you well for me?" She deliberately put an edge of cruelty into her voice. "What is the bride price you have set?"

The old man bowed his head. "Daughter, this marriage that I have arranged is the best I can do for you. I am a poor rabbi with no dowry to give you. Your brother is a struggling student of Torah and the Prophets; the meager bread on his table his wife earns at her potter's wheel. He cannot shelter you." He began to wheeze and cough, his cheeks drawn in and his eyes bulging as he struggled to get his breath. She waited in silence.

"You, Abigail, like all Jewish women, have a sacred obligation to bring children into the world. God expects you to give life to sons and daughters, to nurture them, to teach and train them so that our tribes may continue and flourish. Isaac is a good man who wants a son. He is worthy of you, as you are of him. He is generous and will provide well for you. I will have a contract of marriage drawn so that you will live a good life with a fine house and many servants and share all that he has."

"Chattel I am," she said bitterly. "To be sold for silver, like a lamb to be sacrificed."

Into the stillness of the room the north wind intruded, rattling the shutter secured against the cold of the night. "Why, Father, do you speak of marriage at this time, when you are ill and we are beset by this storm?"

Straightening in his chair, the old rabbi said calmly, "Because I am dying, Abigail —"

She rose from her chair, fell to her knees before him, and began to sob.

He brushed his hand over her shoulder. "My time is near. You know how long I have endured this pain that comes and goes in my chest. Now this bitter cold has brought on such an attack of asthma that every breath has become a struggle." He coughed deeply, as though he were strangling, then closed his eyes and hunched his back to regain his breath. "Any day now I will die — and I must know that someone will care for you."

She placed her hand on his forehead. "Father! You are burning with fever! O Father, Father, do not leave me." She rested her head on his knees, closed her eyes, and began to wail, her sobs ululating in despair.

"Weep not for me, my daughter, for my life has been good, and death I do not fear." He raised his head and with dimming eyes looked long into the lamplight. "In my youth I made a covenant to serve God. This I have done." His voice was low, little more than a whisper. "Here at our synagogue in this great city I was given knowledge of Torah. Here I taught the Commandments and statutes to our people, and here I lived as Torah decrees, in purity and simplicity. Here I have kept my covenant. And here my soul will be lifted into the heavens as Elijah ascended on God's chariot."

As the lamp burned low on the table beside them, father and daughter held each other in silence. Outside, the cold wind shrieked and moaned, intoning its own kaddish for the dead. At last Mordecai raised his head. "Help me to my bed, daughter. I must sleep now."

After she had helped her father to his cot and kissed him, Abigail walked slowly to her own room. She had long known that her father was ill. The hunched shoulders as he fought for breath, the fits of coughing she heard in the night, the feeble steps: She had watched the signs increase even as she denied the reality she must now confront. This fever, she had felt with her own hand. At one moment she was stricken with fear, fear of being alone, a spinster trying to survive on the pittance of alms given to poor Jews in the city; the next moment she cringed from another fear, of betrothal to an old stranger who would invade her body and command her life.

As she drew aside the curtain of her room she saw the glow of lamplight; there at the foot of the bed stood Danuta, her swarthy face all angles and shadows, her head and shoulders wrapped in a black shawl against the cold. She was pretending to rearrange the worn bedclothes.

"You know," Abigail said.

"Yes, child."

"How long will Father live?"

Danuta paused to reflect. "When will the storm end? Your father will cling to life until he has delivered his people from this wilderness of ice."

Abigail bowed her head, brushed the tears from her eyes with her sleeve, and rested her cheek on the handmaiden's shoulder. "O Danuta, why?"

"Change is destined," Danuta consoled her. "In the many books you have read to me, one chapter ends; a new chapter begins. So it is with life. Your father's mission in life ends so that yours may begin."

"Begin? Sold into bondage? How can you say that, Danuta? Sad as I am that Father is dying, I cannot overcome my anger that he has contracted for my marriage."

"He is bound by love and duty to provide for you," Danuta said.

Abigail began to pace back and forth, beating her hands against her breast, compressing her lips to hold back tears. "Why is it, in this enlightened age, that only a man can choose his course in life? In my heart I know that a woman is equal to a man, and often superior. But in reality a woman is treated as chattel, goods for sale." She struck her fists on her cot.

Danuta waited in silence.

"Long ago," Abigail continued, "I learned that by the Law given to Moses a father rules his child, but why must it be that he makes the choice when I am to become a wife?"

"It is a woman's lot to be chosen rather than to choose," Danuta said. "Women are blessed above men. God appointed us to create life, as he did

6

in the beginning. He did not trust men to carry out the sacred duty of giving birth to a new soul and being."

"What shall I do?" Abigail said. "My father says that this stranger, this Isaac, wants a son, and that he has chosen me to give him a son. To be the mare who delivers his colt."

"It is the way of all men to want a son," Danuta replied. She spoke carefully, for long ago the rabbi had told her that he hoped, when Abigail came of age, to arrange her marriage to the wealthy Isaac. Danuta had suggested a younger man of the community, a shipwright, but the father had replied, "No, Abigail is too learned. She is a woman of merit and promise. Poor, she was not meant to be." Then he told Danuta that she must play her part in bringing about a transaction for the family good.

Danuta put her hand on Abigail's shoulder. "Men believe themselves to be superior," Danuta said. "They fight for kingdoms, but every king kneels before a woman who may give him a son."

Impulsively Abigail put her arm around the servant. She remembered how the sage and strong-willed Danuta had mothered her as a child, beguiled her with tales of the Sea People who were Danuta's ancestors, consoled her when she first came to be in the way of women, and counseled her in all things. Now she must ask Danuta the question she had never before dared ask.

"What is it like to be with a man?" Abigail's eyes were intent, searching. "Is it painful?"

"At first it is, yes," Danuta said. After a moment of reflection she continued: "But if a man is strong and at the same time gentle, it can bring great pleasure to the woman as well as to the man. Remember always, always, that giving pleasure brings pleasure."

Again Danuta paused before she spoke again. "Our secret as women is to give pleasure to accomplish an end. I was a young slave in Byblos when my master first took me into his bed. I was little more than a child, yet I learned quickly. I found it useful to become my master's favorite concubine. Give a man joy in the night and he is your slave in the day. When, after some years, my master came to favor a younger girl, I entreated him to permit me to earn my freedom by initiating his oldest son and heir into the wonders of a woman in the night. Once that was done, he handed me a purse of gold and signed the parchment that set me free."

"Must we be slaves before we can be free?" Abigail asked.

"All women are slaves to circumstance," Danuta replied. "Yet each of us can earn the freedom we most want, if we will it." She paused, looked into Abigail's eyes, and repeated: "If we will it."

Abigail folded her arms and began to pace the floor again. "What do you know of this Isaac?" she asked.

Taking care not to reveal the inquiries she had made for the rabbi, the maidservant said casually, "I have seen his servants buying in the market and I have walked past his shops and fine house. A mansion it is. He must have great riches."

"And is he tall and handsome?" Abigail asked, her voice filled with scorn.

"No," Danuta replied. "He is not so tall as you; but then, you are tall for a woman. Nor is he fat. The front of his head is bald as a melon, but the back is thick with black hair. He has no beard. He is not like most merchants, plain of dress, for this Isaac is always arrayed in a toga of fine white linen, as befits his standing as a citizen of Rome. Yet pompous he is not." She stopped for a moment before she continued: "When I have seen him, he appears to be ever in a hurry, speaking rapidly, constantly waving his arms as he bargains."

Abigail was silent, swiftly creating in her imagination a merchant of the streets, busy, voluble, coarse, and unlearned. Would so rich a merchant be greedy and stingy, or — as her father said — generous? What would it be like to dwell in a mansion, to have many warm clothes and even silks and jewelry? If this tentmaker was so busy with his shops and workers, perhaps she could do as she pleased in his fine house.

Danuta interrupted Abigail's thoughts. "We cannot know what kind of husband this Isaac would be for you, whether kind and warm, or cold and mean. But it is good, child, for a woman to know comfort and have wealth. Given those, she can endure much."

Abigail stared into the darkness but said nothing. Except for a new warm robe for her father, she could not think of anything she would buy if she had money to spend. Books, perhaps, many books.

Again Danuta broke the silence. "This son. This son for whom Isaac yearns, remember that he is first and always your son. It is the mother who sets the course of life for every child." Danuta took the hand of the younger woman. "Remember, as it is given to us to bring forth a son, so also is it given to us to make of the son what we will. It is you who will lead your son to become reaper or poet, conqueror or philosopher."

Abigail sat on her cot and looked into the darkness. At last she said, "If I were to go to this Isaac's house, Danuta, would you go with me?"

"Yes, child, I would go with you," Danuta said, relieved that she had been asked, certain that the marriage would provide her a home when she became too old to cook and wash and mend.

For a long time neither woman spoke. "A son," Abigail whispered, as though speaking to herself. "My son. *My* son." Memory brought back and made vivid a continuing daydream of girlhood. She had imagined, and written in her journal, that she would grow up to bear a son and a daughter. In her fancy she had resolved to name her son Saul, after the great warrior whom God had chosen to be the first king of Israel. Her daughter would be Rachel, for the favorite wife of the patriarch Jacob and mother of the indomitable Joseph and Abigail's own ancestor Benjamin. In the prayers of her budding womanhood Abigail had made a covenant with God: She would be to her son and daughter the mother she had never had. Now the dream she had long ago set down in her journal might come true.

Abigail lay back on her bed and pulled a blanket of rough wool around her shoulders. "Good Danuta, now I am weary. I will sleep." The hand-maiden smoothed the bedclothes and put out the lamp as the rabbi's daughter huddled in the darkness.

Abigail dreamed: She was running, running free over wide sands beside a great blue sea, running toward a distant figure stretching forth his arms to receive and embrace her. She had never seen him before but he was not a stranger, a warrior of great strength with a bearing more splendid and a face more handsome than she had ever imagined. And as they came together the warrior's strong arms swept her up and took her to a waiting ship. They were borne away to a distant island kingdom where they walked in the sunshine, sang joyful songs and laughed together, bathed in a clear pool and climbed to a mountaintop where they could see great winding rivers and vast valleys of grain fields and orchards. And there was a child, their son, slender of form and dark-eyed as she was. The young child she bore was suddenly transformed into a handsome prince. A thousand trumpets sounded and the king's prophet appeared and summoned the young prince and bade him speak, and a great multitude of all races and tongues gathered, Roman and Greek, African and Asian. The many assembled there listened, entranced by the words of the prince. Suddenly there appeared on the sea a tall ship with many-colored sails billowing in the breeze, and the king's prophet commanded the prince to begin a journey. The prince raised aloft a flaming torch, boarded the great ship, and sailed away.

The next morning Abigail rose to find Danuta and recount the dream to her. "How am I to interpret this dream?" she asked. "Is it an omen?"

Danuta put down the worn spoon with which she stirred the barley for their breakfast and took the hands of the young woman. "The trumpets of destiny sound. You will have a son favored by king and conqueror, by people of all nations. The ship signifies that your son will travel afar; the torch, that he will light a path unto the whole world."

Abigail turned away and walked to her room, head lowered. Her fears of the night before, the fear of marriage to a stranger, of going to an unfamiliar house, of entering a new life — all the fears were there but diminished, overcome in part by a quickening excitement. She would bring a son into the world and fill his life with knowledge, with learning, with all that was good and strong so that he would become a great leader, as the dream foretold. She was ready for the bargain.

She went immediately to her father. "Father, if I consent to betrothal to this Isaac, will I share equally his property and possessions?"

"Yes, daughter. So Isaac has proposed, and so can it be written in the marriage contract."

"Then I will be his bride," she said. "I will bear him a son. I will bear a son who will bring honor to our House of Benjamin and to all Israel. My son will change the world."

The old rabbi wept with joy. His last mission was accomplished. He could die at peace with himself. And on that day in the city of Tarsus and across the valley of the Cydnus, the sun returned to the land.

II

CHOICE

Through the streets of the old city the youth ran with Olympian grace, his head high, his black curls flying in the summer wind. The wizened grain seller of the ghetto saw him coming, snatched his baskets from the paving stones, and stood back as the athlete in his fine linen tunic raced by. With a final burst of speed, the runner turned the corner and charged through the high wooden gate of his father's compound. He was late. Again.

Inside the gate the youth stopped to catch his breath. What would he tell his mother? The truth, he supposed. The morning races, the baths, the tutorial with Callicles on Pindar's Encomium for Alexander, the summons from Zagoreos: So much to do, and he had forgotten the time. His mother would be angry, but she would forgive him. She always did.

Dashing up the broad steps of her pavilion in the south wing of the family mansion, the youth reached for her door — then stayed his hand at the sound of raised and angry voices. Father and Mother were quarreling again.

". . . days of idleness must end!" Today his father's voice carried greater vehemence than usual: "I say to you it is time that the boy cease this indolence, cease to parade his learning, and come to work with me like a dutiful son."

"My son Saul is a scholar." His mother's voice was calm and resolute, as always.

"I need him! Now!" Abruptly the voice stopped. After a silence his father spoke again, not in anger but with order and reason. "There are important events, Abigail. Tiberius, fearing assassination, has fled to Capri. Sejanus, ruling as imperial proconsul in Caesar's absence, has ordered a new expedition against the Persians. Six legions will stage in Tarsus for this campaign; that will bring me tenscore new orders for saddles, tents, and sails. The royal procurer arrives this afternoon. With the boy's help to oversee the new workers I must hire, I can double our profits."

"Saul's education must come before profit, Isaac. Training my son's mind is more important than having him bend over your loom or bathe animal skins in your foul-smelling tannery vats."

Hiding and listening, Saul shook his head in dismay: The never-ending differences between his mother and father converged, more and more, on his future. Why did they not let him decide what to do with his life?

Through the door Saul could hear the tapping of the shepherd's crook that his father carried to support his back, the spare old body bent from forty years over needle and bench. Saul imagined the scene inside — his father, bald head reddening with rage, hobbling back and forth in his toga, waving his arms, entreating one moment, abusing the next. With a fond smile Saul pictured his mother: as composed as in a painting, reclining on her raised Roman couch, her striking face and womanly form set, as on a stage, against the elegant sandalwood paneling of her parlor. She would be wearing a peplos, the white silk draped over her full breasts and belted with gold. With her dark eyes, dark as a winter midnight, she would be watching his father, ready to sense and exploit any sign of weakness in the old man.

The tapping of the cane stopped. Now his father's voice was choked and guttural with wrath. "You, Abigail, you and Saul wear silk and gold only because of my looms and tannery. It was our bargain that I would provide you a fine house and servants, which I have faithfully done, and you would give me a son and heir. Now that the boy is eighteen, he must come to me." There was a silence for a moment, and the father's tone changed to pleading. "I grow old, Abigail. My eye dims. I cannot wait longer to claim my heir. Before my wit goes and my step falters, I must teach Saul all the skills that I know, teach him to buy and sell, to be a master of trade as I am."

"My son was not born to be made a street merchant." His mother's voice was curt. "When we signed the marriage contract twenty-one years ago, I was to give you a son, not another weaver, nor another saddler. I kept my bargain. He will continue your name and your line of the House of Benjamin."

Saul wondered if she had rehearsed her words; she always thought through an important conversation in advance.

"Yes, you bore me a son," Isaac replied, his voice bitter. "And when he was a child your brother's synagogue school was not enough; you filled my boy's mind with books and scrolls and dreams of glory. And when I needed him in my shops, you turned him over to Greek pedants who disdain toil with their hands. You encouraged him to play useless games with Greek companions who practice strange ways and worship false gods. Now that he becomes a man you would deny my son to me."

"My son Saul was born to be a leader of men," Abigail said. "I know that God has a special purpose for him. When he was in my womb I had a vision of his future. I resolved to make that vision a reality. Isaac, I know what must be. It is God's will."

"Your scheme for Saul breaks the bargain of our marriage," Isaac said. "I, too, dreamed that you would give me a son, and this son would work by my side, learn my craft, and inherit my shops and all else that I have."

Saul heard his father lower his voice to an angry musing. "From nothing I built this great house. A child of the Tarsus streets I was, wretched and hungry, and I vowed that I would not always be poor. I toiled. By the skill of these two hands I myself fashioned the finest tents and strongest sails in all Cilicia. I built workshops. I taught others my skills. I trained my workers to be fine weavers. I bartered for the finest wool. I bought fields of flax to be certain I would have the strongest linen. The great Caesar Augustus sent his procurer to my door to buy tents for his legions, and for my service Augustus decreed that I should become a citizen of the Roman Empire. Now I serve Tiberius with equal honor and profit. No other Jew in Tarsus has prospered as I have. All this I earned. All this I dreamed of bestowing on my son and heir."

"You speak of an heir," Abigail replied quickly, "but in truth what you seek is an indentured servant. I know your ways, Isaac. You will dominate every worker and drive every bargain until your last breath. Your trade is your way of life, but it is not Saul's way. Yours is the life of the hand, of the coin; his is of the mind." Saul had never heard such open defiance in his mother's voice; usually she gained her way with more subtlety. Her next words were spoken as a command. "Saul will go to Jerusalem. It is settled. He will study there at the academy of the eminent Gamaliel."

Saul stepped away from the door. Jerusalem! Was he hearing right? Was his mother sending him away from home? He clapped hands to head in alarm, his astonishment interrupted by a shout from his father: "No! I will not give you the money for school in Jerusalem."

There was a moment of silence before his mother replied. "It will be paid from my equal share of our wealth, Isaac, as set forth in the marriage contract my father negotiated with you." She spoke as though issuing a decree.

Except for the tapping of cane on marble as his father walked to and fro, Saul could hear nothing. In his mind he could see his father confronting his mother. "Abigail, in my trade and in my house a man keeps his word. I gave my word to share equally all my possessions. I have kept my word. But you withhold my share of our son."

"Isaac," Abigail said at last, "which is of greater importance: increasing the ample wealth we have, or sending forth into the world a son who will become a leader of our people?"

"Abigail, what is this dream of greatness? You live in fancy. I live in reality."

"The reality, Isaac, is that Saul was born to lead. And God help me, so it must be."

All that could be heard was the sound of the cane, back and forth. "I must take account of the fact that you dispossess me of my son and heir, Abigail. Thus you force me to an action I have been reluctant to take but now find necessary."

Saul could hear no response from his mother. Then the tapping of his father's cane sharpened as he approached the door. Saul stepped quickly into an alcove and out of sight. As soon as his father had hobbled down the stairs, Saul quietly crept down behind him, then turned and noisily raced back up to enter his mother's pavilion.

It was empty.

Saul looked about. Every chair, every book, the Cycladic figurine in its niche, the light rose scent of his mother's perfume — all were familiar; all stirred memories. How often had he run up to this room. Here in his mother's lap he first heard the fables of Aesop and the poems of Horace. Here she taught him the alphabets of Hebrew and Greek, and to count in decimals and in the Sumerian twelves. He had raced up to this room to tell her when he won first prize in recitations in Uncle Enoch's synagogue. Every new idea that engaged him at the Academy — philosophy, mathematics, *politika* — he had brought it here to her so they could examine it together.

Looking across the broad pavilion, Saul observed that the figs were almost ripe in the glazed urns that his mother had imported from Attica to frame the balcony. He looked beyond, through the breadth of the opening to the south and over the tiled roofs of the city, to count seven ships riding at anchor in the Cydnus estuary. Near the wharves were the warehouses and stables, and then the mud huts of the city's poor, and close by the stone houses of wealth, none finer than this house of his father the tentmaker Isaac.

Shading his eyes Saul looked west to the Acropolis and beyond to the peaks of the Taurus Mountains, an irregular wall of blue and snowy white standing against the clear horizon. How he loved this splendid place, this city, its merchants haggling in the noisy streets, the peal of the hammer-smiths working their iron and brass, the dark-faced strangers leading their camel caravans down from the mountain passes to bring silk and spices to the agora. Beyond the market he could pick out the gymnasium where he had practiced with the javelin, and the stadium where he won his laurels in the long footraces. Nearby stood the columns and gardens of the Greek Academy, where Zagoreos and Callicles and the other masters had challenged his mind and taught him to think with logic and speak with skill and confidence.

He remembered how in his first days there he had been taunted as the only Jew in his classes, and how he had hated the young Greeks and Romans who mocked his narrow shoulders and bowed legs. Only after Saul demonstrated his swift foot in the stadium and his skill in mnemonics and rhetoric did any gentile become a friend. In time his Greek comrades accepted him, calling him *Paulos*, their translation of his Hebrew name.

The better he came to know his Greek classmates, the more Saul admired their spirit, their cheerful optimism, their ability to express their imaginative ideas in clear language, their physical grace and open sensuality, the way they trained their vigorous minds and muscular bodies to excel. The full life the Greeks sought had become his; he could see that now. And the pleasures of learning and competing had so filled his four years at the Academy that he had given no thought to an end, until now.

Behind him Saul heard the sound of a curtain being pulled aside.

Saul turned to watch his mother enter. Proud and poised as always, she walked with studied grace from her chamber into the open pavilion. Taller by a head than her husband, she had skin of burnished copper, a prominent nose curved like a scimitar, and fine black hair braided and pinned in the Greek style with slender rods of ivory. She was, he thought, a caryatid come to life.

The moment she saw her son, Abigail raised her arms and they came together in close embrace, more woman and man than mother and son. She kissed him on each side of his face, on his mouth, then held him close again. She leaned her head back to look down into his sad, long face, so like her own, ran her fingers through his black curls, and caressed his bare, muscular arms. Her pride in his lithe grace and sturdy form masked her disappointment that he had grown no taller than his father. To her, he had matched the vigor and resolve of his Jewish forebears with the self-esteem of the Greeks. She kissed him again, murmuring, "My beloved. My beloved son."

The fervor of his mother's embrace and the warmth of his mother's body sent an emotional surge through Saul's being, as they always did. He knew he loved her inordinately, and she him. They teased each other, she by telling him of a dream that Zeus transformed her into a young maiden who became his bride, he by promising she would ever be the only woman in his life.

With a long sigh Abigail took her son by the hand and led him to the couch. "Here, my beloved," she said. "Sit close to me."

Abigail looked into her son's dark eyes. This was the day she had long dreaded; this the day she had many times postponed. She lived through her son, through his felicitous life in Tarsus. His delight in the Greek way became her delight; his happiness was her happiness. Now it must end.

"I heard your sandals outside the door," she said, "so you must have listened to my discussion with your father."

"Yes, Mother, I did." Suddenly he could hold back no longer. "Must I go to Jerusalem?" He blurted out the words. "I want to be here with you, with my friends, in my school. Here I have the best of life. Why do you make me give up all this?"

"O Saul," she said, as she struggled to hold back the tears. Impulsively she clutched her son's hand. "How it will empty my hours when you go, my son. Yet there is no choice. It is necessary. Indeed, it is imperative."

"Why?" It was a cry of dismay and anguish. "Why must I go?"

"If you remain in Tarsus," she said, deliberating on each word, "your father will find a way under Roman law to force you into his shops. Isaac is clever, and determined. You heard his threat to take action. He has Roman friends of great power. Now that you are eighteen, I can no longer sustain my claim that you are too young for the loom and needle."

Abigail rose from her couch, paced back and forth, and then stopped to confront her son. "I will not permit you to be trapped in your father's trade, Saul. My father ruled my life. But your father shall not rule yours." She took both his hands in hers. "You were born to lead, Saul. Greatness is in your blood — I have always known this."

Saul shook his head in anger. "But Mother, I have not yet completed my studies at the Academy."

"That do I understand," she said. "But your father has already taken steps to terminate your studies. Immediately. Often in the past he has tried, and I cannot forever thwart him."

Saul looked at his mother, his lip trembling, his arms raised in appeal. "My classes ended? Only today I won a prize and ran here to tell you."

"Another laurel, another award?" Her face lit with a smile. "Tell me of your new prize, Saul."

"I was awarded first laurel for my essay on the Socratic method of discourse. Zagoreos brought me to his podium before the class to accept the laurel." Saul put his arm around his mother and pleaded, "Mother, let me go to Father and beg him to give me another year at the Academy. Or even half a year."

"To what end?" Abigail stepped back to confront her son, her jaw set, her eyes burning with anger. "Saul! Do you not remember that day after you completed your studies at the synagogue, when I lay ill and your father first put you at the loom?"

Saul remembered well: Sitting as a boy among the sallow gray men fingering dirty wool and scraping flesh from animal skins, he was overcome with disgust. His open disdain for the work provoked his father's rage; old Isaac retaliated by forcing his son to perform the lowest menial's task of cleaning the tannery vats. When his mother recovered and learned what was happening she interceded, took Saul out of the workshop, and enrolled him in the Greek Academy. Later, in remorse for humiliating his son, his father apologized, tried to make amends, and solicitously encouraged Saul to learn the higher skill of tentmaking. But Saul, with the connivance of his mother, found ways to evade his father's plan. The incident wounded the family; the wound festered into hostility that separated not only son from father, but also father from mother.

Abigail spoke again. "Saul, in any bargain with your father you will lose.

To remain in Tarsus, you must accept your father's terms, train your hand to the needle and shuttle, make a covenant to succeed him, and spend your life sweating in the workshop and haggling in the marketplaces. And yes, in time you would become a merchant of wealth on your own. That is one choice."

She paused and took her son's arm. "Or," she said, her eyes alight with fervor, "you can serve the cause of God and Israel and all our people. Saul, God gave you such gifts of mind and reason and voice that multitudes will follow you. You are of royal seed; in your veins flows the blood of kings. Go now to Jerusalem, to the city of King David from whom you descend, to the center of the universe for our Hebrew people, for there you will become a leader. I know in my soul, my beloved son, that in Jerusalem you will fulfill your destiny."

A long silence rose like a wall between them. At last Saul lifted his head and turned to his mother: "When would you have me leave?"

"You are to sail two days hence, on the early-morning tide."

"Two days? Two days!" Saul's eyes burned; his face turned red. He began to walk away, but she caught his shoulder.

"Wait, Saul. Hear me. Brief the time is, yes, but any delay will risk an intervention by Isaac through the Roman governor — you know that old Pleminius is in his pay. Thus, Saul, you must take the first ship. Not an hour can we waste."

Saul felt his knees tremble. To steady himself, he put both hands on the parapet and closed his eyes. "Does Father know that I sail so quickly?"

"I have not told him," Abigail whispered. "He may find out. By good fortune there is a ship in the harbor loading wool for Seleucia and Caesarea. It is the *Pegasus*, and her captain is Targon, a Phoenician, the most skilled of sailors. Danuta knew his grandfather in Byblos. I would entrust you to none but the best. I took care to send Alida to pay for your passage; she and Danuta are the only servants I can trust. However, as you know, nothing in Tarsus is secret for long. If fortune continues to favor us, you will be at sea before Isaac can maneuver a Roman magistrate to block us."

Abigail had been struggling to maintain her composure and knew she had reached her limit. "Now go and prepare for your journey," she said abruptly. "Our farewells we shall say on the morrow, here at noon." With that she turned away and walked into her bedchamber without looking back.

Saul watched her go, then slowly headed down the steps of the pavilion and across the courtyard, shaking his head in consternation at how swiftly the splendor of life had been shattered. All seemed unreal, as in a dream.

In his room he dropped heavily to his bed. Exile, a descent into darkness. What could he do? Impulse spurred Saul to rise and go to his writing table; the stylus always clarified his mind. As he unrolled the vellum of his journal and picked up his pen, he wondered about Jerusalem, distant and strange, a city he knew only through the eyes of his uncle Enoch. He supposed that Jerusalem, so remote an outpost of the Roman Empire, was narrow-minded and provincial, and probably lacked the beauty and order imposed by Greek architects. Uncle Enoch had spoken of Gamaliel, of the brilliant mind of this master rabban, of his profound knowledge and understanding of the history of the Jews. Saul assumed that Gamaliel, like his uncle, and father, would scorn the Greeks' openness and their enthusiasm for ideas that were new and different from their own.

His thoughts wandered to the familiar faces of his Greek friends. "No more afternoons of sunshine and philosophy at the Stoa," Saul wrote. "No more footraces in the gymnasium. And no more my warm embraces with Phoebe." She had been only a child when he first saw her in the house of his classmate Alcmaeon, and he had watched her grow up to become a buxom young woman of independent spirit and passionate nature. "My love, my friends, my good life, all I must leave." He dipped his pen in the inkwell and continued. "Life is unjust. I am to lose everything."

Pondering his next words, Saul realized that his breathing was becoming labored, and he was unconsciously bending over his writing table to ease the tightness in his chest. He tried to sit erect. Concentrating his mind and muscles, he inhaled slowly, deeply, drawing as much air as possible into his lungs, holding it as long as he could, and exhaling slowly, leaning his shoulders forward to force the air out before his next breath. The effort made him wheeze and cough, cough again and again.

Since childhood Saul had endured asthma, suffered its mysterious onsets and disappearances, the wheezing, the struggle for breath, the constriction of unseen bindings pressing his chest like ropes taut against the billowing sails of a ship in a gale. His first memory of life was being taken into a room where a strange old man pressed his ear to Saul's bare chest and back. His mother had written down the diagnosis of the physician Nicomedes: "Asthma. Not curable. If the child survives to ten years he will have an enlarged heart and brilliant mind. The disease appears to expand the brain. Build up his body with strenuous physical exercise. Yield to the boy's wishes. Give him his way, for Hippocrates advises, 'The asthmatic must guard against anger.'"

After he began his studies at the Stoa, Saul had better accepted his inexplicable malady when he and Musonius, a tutor crippled since birth, had become friends. "Learn to repress emotion," Musonius instructed him. "Practice indifference to pain. There is no tragedy that courage cannot conquer." Saul did practice, but in the first hours of every attack of asthma, gasping for air dominated his mind and consumed all his energy.

"In tragedy, courage." Bent over with pain, Saul whispered Musonius' words aloud as he struggled for breath. "Soon it will be over," he repeated. The paroxysms of the first two or three hours were always the worst. Now he must press his wrists against his diaphragm to force out the air for another breath.

When a gentle tap sounded on the door, Saul did not respond. Struggling for breath made it impossible to speak.

A woman entered and said softly, "I heard your cough." It was Alida, his mother's maidservant, bearing a bowl of water and a linen cloth. Since he had been a small child, Alida had attended him when the asthma came. Older by ten years, she was an island girl, the plump and sun-browned daughter of a Phoenician ship captain from Cyprus who had taught his daughter to read Greek before he indentured her to Abigail. Strong, intelligent, and cheerful of spirit, she had asked Abigail to let her take care of the five-year-old Saul when he fell ill. Abigail was reluctant. She insisted it was her duty to comfort her son; still, his seizures, his gasping for breath, provoked her to panic. Danuta convinced Abigail that her uncontrolled weeping during Saul's asthma attacks frightened the boy and always made him worse.

As a young woman Alida would come to the small child's room with her bowl of cool water and cloth of linen at the onset of the asthma. As little Saul lay on his bed and struggled to breathe, she would kneel beside him to bathe his forehead, gently rub the muscles of his chest and back, and murmur quiet words of assurance until he fell asleep. During his most severe attacks of asthma, she would sleep on the floor of Saul's room. By her devotion and competence, Alida made herself a favorite of the child's mother and father.

Over the years the symbiosis of child and servant turned into bonds of affection and companionship: She trained and disciplined the boy in building his chest and leg muscles; he taught her to read Aramaic and Latin. She beguiled her charge with stories about the myths and gods of Cyprus; with her tales of sailing with her father, she engendered in the boy a love of the sea. Playmates, companions, they became like brother and sister. One night after Saul suffered a mild attack of asthma and Alida had bathed and comforted him until he breathed more easily, she put aside her bowl and cloth, walked close to his bed, and let her robe fall to the floor. She stood naked before the youth, entered his bed, and wrapped her muscular legs around his body. Saul, for the first time in his fourteen years, felt a surge of energy in his loins that ended with boy and woman being consumed in pleasure. Often, since that first time, she had found a reason to come into Saul's room.

In despair on the afternoon that overturned his life, Saul did not welcome Alida. He wanted to be alone, to resume meditating on his plight and its consequences. But the pain of breathing took command of his senses, forcing him to go to his bed and rest until the asthma passed.

Sensing Saul's distance, Alida said nothing. She took the moist linen from the bowl and bathed his forehead and arms. When she saw him become drowsy, she put away her cloth and sat on the floor beside him until the easier sound of his breathing told her he was asleep.

Some hours later she heard him stir. Not yet fully awake, Saul muttered to Alida that he had not eaten since morning and asked her to bring him food. She returned with a tray of bread, goat's milk, cheeses, pomegranates, and dates. He ate slowly, saying nothing. When he had finished, he lay back on his bed and slept. After an hour he stirred and opened his eyes. For a long moment his eyes met Alida's and he stretched out his arm. She went to him.

III

SECRET

The first crow of a distant cock woke Saul. Rising early was a self-imposed ritual. He stood at the window, stretching his arms and observing the first light of dawn breaking over the rooftops to the east. His mind was alert, his muscles taut with energy. He was always intrigued by how strong and exuberant he felt on the morning after the debilitating paroxysms of asthma.

At his desk he read the last entry in his journal and closed the book. "The time for despair has passed," he said to himself. An apothegm of Zagoreos came to mind: *Deliberate with reason. Plan with logic. Act with order.* He would run to clear his mind, then find Zagoreos: Perhaps they could devise a way to postpone his exile to Jerusalem.

Making his way down the stairs in darkness, Saul left the family compound by the side gate and walked rapidly to the gymnasium. The stadium was empty, almost dark, except for the marble seats on the westward rise, which were brushed with the first crimson of sunrise. On the oval track the comb marks of the rakes in the dirt showed no footsteps; Saul always ran better on fresh earth. He stripped and tossed his linen tunic on the dewy grass beside the track. Naked and free, he began running, slowly at first, then faster and faster until he completed his regular long-distance course, twenty-four laps. Sweating and blowing hard, he picked up his clothes and ran on to the tiled baths. Only two sleepy attendants were there. At the brimming fountain pool Saul filled a polished copper amphora and poured cool water over his head, filled it again and doused shoulders and torso, then poured another over his legs, repeating the process until he felt clean and refreshed. As he sat in the morning sun to dry his body and cropped black curls, he outlined in his mind the points he would make to Zagoreos. That done, Saul called an attendant to bring him a fresh tunic, dressed, and walked along the porch of the academy classrooms until he reached Zagoreos' corner.

Zagoreos was there, filling the entire room. Tall as a praetorian, fat as a merchant, and bald as marble, the teacher raised a mammoth hand in greeting. "Paulos! My friend. You come early. Let us break the fast of night and begin the day."

From long experience Saul knew that Zagoreos would consider no discourse until after he had eaten his fill. "No wisdom comes on an empty belly," the tutor liked to say.

So Zagoreos summoned his slave, who brought loaves of wheat bread, barley cakes, cheese, cucumbers, almonds, dates, figs, and a well-formed pottery jar of goat's milk. Tutor and pupil ate with both hands, filling their mouths, drinking from the common jar, and wiping their faces with moist towels brought by the slave.

When Zagoreos had finished, he removed his sandals, reclined on the couch specially made for his length, and folded his hands across his vast stomach.

"Speak, Paulos."

Saul began by recounting how by chance he had overheard a dispute between his parents, with his father demanding that he quit school to help him fill orders for Sejanus' expedition into Persia, and his mother insisting that he go to Jerusalem to study at the Hebrew Academy of Gamaliel. "It is my wish to remain here," Saul said, "to remain here at your academy, learning from you and my other tutors, to enjoy my friends and the pleasures of this good life in Tarsus. But my mother warns that if I remain in Tarsus, my father will force me to toil like a common drudge in his shops. You know the Jewish law: An heir is a slave until he is freed by his father. Thus, Master, what shall I do?"

For long moments Zagoreos said nothing, but lay quietly on the couch with his eyes closed. Then he slowly sat up, rested his chin on his fingertips, and looked steadily at Saul, musing that the god of the Jews had given this prize pupil the short and spare stature of his father, the handsome cheekbones and luminous eyes of the mother, and the intuitive mind of the Hebrew Prophets.

"Now," Zagoreos said slowly, "let us suppose that Zeus or your God came to you and said, 'Paulos, I have a gift for you. You may choose your future in life. Ten years hence, what would you be?'"

Saul slowly shook his head. "I do not know."

Zagoreos rocked back and folded his arms. "And does your ignorance stem from the inability to select between choices, or from the lack of thought?"

"In truth the latter," Saul said. "Until yesterday I gave not a thought to my future."

"A common thing for the young," Zagoreos said amiably. "And for many who are no longer young."

Saul interrupted: "I know what I do *not* want to be. I will not demean myself to toil at a loom or bargain for money." He paused to reflect. "It is learning that I love most. Could I become a teacher?"

"You have the mind to teach, Paulos, but not the patience. And you do not tolerate any intellect inferior to your own."

"How does a person choose his course in life?" Saul asked.

"Logic," Zagoreos said. "First, know thyself. This, you will remember, was the first precept of the oracle at Delphi; worthy counsel it remains. Second, make a conscious choice. Study, examine, contemplate, then decide. Third, plan how to go from where you are to where you want to be. Fourth, act. Carry out your plan."

"It sounds simple," Saul said.

"Simple to say, difficult to accomplish," Zagoreos replied quickly. "To begin with, few of us study ourselves with any measure of objectivity. Or make a conscious choice. In the main we are carried along on the sea of life by the winds of circumstance, or an event, or a tragedy, or an opportunity."

Saul listened in silence, wondering where the dialogue was headed.

"Paulos, what is the highest good in life?"

Saul considered the possibilities. "To search for truth?"

"A good answer!" Zagoreos said. "Now, when we find the truth, what should we do?"

"Reveal it," Saul replied. "Teach it, and live it."

"Turn that around," Zagoreos said. "Live the truth, then teach it." Suddenly Zagoreos stood up. "Come. Let us walk." He led Saul to the edge of the porch overlooking the gardens and fountains, the colonnades of the Academy and the adjoining Stoa. Waving his arm at their surroundings, Zagoreos asked: "What do you see?"

"Harmony. Proportion." Saul thought for a moment. "I see beauty of form, the symmetry of Ionic columns, graceful pediments."

"Now look below and tell me what you see."

"Plinth stones. Foundation blocks," Saul said.

"Exactly," Zagoreos said. "A man is like a building. If he is to rise, it must be on a foundation that endures all seasons. Look to these foundations; so wisely planned they were, so carefully put down when Cicero governed here seventy-five years ago, that no earthquake has moved one of them." He turned to look at his pupil. "All we have given you here, all we can give you, Paulos, is the plinth stone. It is you who must build on this foundation."

Zagoreos led the way back to his room. "You ask for my counsel. To begin, consider the action of the vain and ambitious Sejanus as a stroke of magnificent fortune. Zeus has intervened. Or perhaps it was your God who brought you to this time of decision." He faced Saul and raised his great hand as tutor instructing pupil.

"Now, Paulos, what is the choice before you? Define the problem."

"I must choose: to study, or to toil."

"Precisely: to advance the mind or to fatten the purse."

"And my desire is to study here, Master, at this academy."

"Is that realistic? If you remain in Tarsus, Paulos, do you doubt that your father will relegate you to the workbench?"

Saul shook his head.

"Now, Paulos, consider this: Here in Tarsus you have excelled in the center of Greek learning second only to Athens. There is little more that you will ever learn from us, or from our brothers at the Stoa. It is time for you to proceed to the center of Judaic learning, and I am told there is no finer academy in Jerusalem than that of Gamaliel. To him you must go."

For long moments Saul sat in silence: He had come hoping to find a way to remain in the Academy; now his favorite tutor was telling him he must leave Tarsus, and he could not contest the master's logic.

Zagoreos turned to his table, poured two goblets of wine, and handed one to Saul. In a voice at once grave and sympathetic, he said: "Paulos, what will you make of your life? That is the question. And only you can find the answer." After a pause, Zagoreos smiled, lifted his cup, and said warmly, "I drink to you, Paulos, to the end of your youth. I honor a beginning, the setting forth of a young man of noble promise on what is likely to be a magnificent journey. Destiny has summoned you, Paulos. I foresee that your life will be a quest, an unending search for the ultimate question, the secret that eludes each of us: *Who am I? Why am I on earth?*"

He put aside his goblet and, broad countenance intent, proclaimed: "Paulos, look inward to find your purpose. That is the starting point of the great race that we know as life. Then follow that goal and conquer, as the young Alexander did. You, too, have great power, not of arms but of the power to speak, to write, to persuade. Experience a new world. Examine the philosophy and laws of your own Jewish race. You Hebrews crafted rules for living and governing a thousand years before Solon initiated democracy in Athens. Now, regrettably, many of your Hebrew leaders have closed minds. Perhaps you can open them." He stopped and again clapped his huge hands on Saul's shoulders. "Paulos, you are ready. Begin your journey. Go. Lift your spirits and go. Run the race. Press on to the prize. Press on."

With a clasp of right hands, Saul said farewell and left his tutor's room. He walked slowly along the familiar porch, intent on finding a scholar's cubicle. He wanted to be alone, to absorb the wisdom of Zagoreos' arguments, to weep, perhaps, but accept the reality that he must give up his good life and go to a distant and unknown land.

Head down, preoccupied with his thoughts, Saul stepped back in alarm when suddenly a tall and masked figure in a black cloak leaped from behind a marble column. Saul instinctively raised his hands in defense, and immediately the figure swept off an actor's tragic mask and replaced it with a comedy mask. Saul laughed.

It was his friend and classmate, Pan. His full name was Panaeus Scipio Marcellus, but his goatish hedonism and merry face had prompted the schoolname of the god of music and love. Handsome as a statue of Apollo, he was the only child of the richest man in Cilicia, an enterprising Greek who had amassed a fortune from copper and iron mines, adopted a Roman name, and drifted into early senility after his wife died. Pan made enough of an effort at learning to remain at the Academy, but his first interest was revelry. Saul had often joined the festivals at the Scipio family estate in the hills west of Tarsus, where Pan — with his father hidden away and attended by eunuchs — reigned as a carefree satyr. Nymphs lounged in his pools. Actors, clowns, jugglers, and musicians performed in his theater. Pan feted his classmates in an edifice copied from the Parthenon of Athens, with each guest attended and entertained by an almond-eyed *hetaira* of his choosing.

"My good Paulos," Pan said, "the news has reached me that you are to be banished to provincial Jerusalem. Say not! Say not!"

Saul was not completely surprised that his friend knew he must leave. Pan loved gossip, both benign and harmful; everyone at the Academy believed he paid spies to report on their personal lives.

"Pan, I sail tomorrow for Seleucia and Caesarea," Saul said. "I am to study with Rabban Gamaliel in Jerusalem."

Pan took Saul by the arm and said earnestly: "O you must not leave us. You belong in Tarsus. Your friends are here. You are our most eminent scholar. You set the mark for us to reach. Come instead to live at my modest palace. I shall make you my resident scholar and pay you well. Together we will learn and take our pleasures. Who knows — perhaps we can abduct your fair Phoebe and imprison her at my palace. Will you say yes?"

Saul clapped his friend on the shoulder. "Pan, if only I could. But the fates decree another course."

The two youths walked in silence along the porch of the academy until Saul gestured toward a stone bench under an ancient hemlock, a favorite place for dialogue between teacher and pupil.

After they were seated, Pan turned to his friend. "Tell me, Paulos, why are Jews such a grim and somber people?"

Saul tilted his head in thought before replying. "We differ, you and I," he said. "A Greek, from birth, delights in life. From birth, we Jews worry. You inquire. You explore. To you, the new is always attractive. We look to the past. We seek truth in tradition; the more ancient it is, the more we venerate it. You enthusiastically broaden your minds; we narrow ours. You admire beauty, ideas, learning. Optimism is part of your nature. Fear is part of ours. This anxiety is instilled in us, bred into us by two thousand years of persecution and slavery. We have been forced into exile so many times that it has become our most enduring legacy."

"But here there is no persecution," Pan said.

"Yes, some Jews, like me, live well," Saul replied. "Yet we are strangers here. Greeks belong to their islands and mountains, and their lands belong to them. Jews have no homeland. We are nomads, wandering people of the desert, making our lives for a time in one city or another, never secure, never certain that tomorrow will not bring another pogrom, another exodus. We live in a state of peril. How can we not be grim and somber?"

"What will you learn in Jerusalem?" Pan asked.

"Rabban Gamaliel is a scholar of our history and a masterful teacher, so my uncle says. As does Zagoreos. I know nothing more of Gamaliel, or of the nature of life at his academy. My choice lay between the hateful and the unknown. This hour I resolved the matter. I will go to Jerusalem."

"O by the mighty Zeus, I shall miss our dialogues," Pan said. "And our games and" — he rolled his eyes — "our pleasures."

"And I shall miss your cheerful spirit, my friend."

"A certain *hetaira* will shed tears upon hearing this news," Pan said. "What shall I tell the warm-blooded Aspasia?"

Saul smiled. "That I shall return, and she must wait for me." He looked up to the position of the sun. He must leave quickly; there would be just enough time to say farewell to Phoebe before he met his mother at noon. "Farewell, faithful comrade. I return to my race, to my Hebrew people. I put Plato aside; I open the scrolls of the Torah. Yet I know that a part of my spirit is and will always be Greek. For that I am ever in debt to you and my fellows in this academy."

It was a short run to the house of Epicrates, father of Phoebe. The Ethiopian slave who managed the household led Saul into the garden. Pacing back and forth, Saul tried to invent an easy way to tell her he must go away. When Phoebe appeared like a svelte goddess in the doorway, Saul thought for a moment that he could not and would not leave her, whatever the consequences. She ran to him, embraced him, drawing her body to his and whispering, "O my love, my love."

Saul pushed her away. "I must go to Jerusalem," he said, his voice abrupt and angry. He dropped his head to hide his tears. "I must leave tomorrow." He choked on the words. "It is my mother's will, and I cannot deny her."

The young girl stepped back and placed a tender hand on his cheek. "Dear Paulos, I will go with you to Jerusalem," she said calmly. "I will go with you anywhere, across the seas, to the ends of earth and time. Take me! Take me with you, my beloved." She put her arms around him and looked into his dark eyes. "I remember the words from the book you gave me, 'Whither thou goest I will go; and where thou lodgest, I will lodge: thy people shall be my people, and thy God my God.' Dear Paulos, I must go with you to Jerusalem."

"If only I could take you with me, precious Phoebe." Saul shook his head sadly. "But my mother would never permit it."

"So strong a mother you have, and I have no mother to order my life," she said. "But why must you go?"

"My mother has convinced me that if I do not leave Tarsus, my father will force me to slavery in his workshops. So I am to be sent away, to school in Jerusalem, to the academy of Rabban Gamaliel. All my good life here is ended. I am cursed."

The young woman faced him and took both his hands in hers. "How long will you be away?" she asked.

"At least a year, I suppose," Saul said. "It may be longer."

Phoebe gently took Saul by the arm. "I, too, have momentous news," she said, and led him to a bower of flowers enclosing a marble bench. When they were seated she reached out her hand, cupped Saul's cheek in her slender fingers, and said, "I believe I am with child, Paulos. Your child. I beg you not to leave me."

Saul looked at her, his eyes widening with astonishment. Was Phoebe jesting? But the quiver in her voice and the grave look in her blue eyes told him this was no jest. How could this be? And instantly he knew the answer. Innocent children they were at first, hiding among the flowers and playing a game of Chase and Catch. Their trysts in their secret corner of Epicrates' garden led to young love, young love that quickened and swelled to passion and overpowered all restraints. Suddenly Saul could see that he had been so swept up in their youthful romance that not once had he paused to consider the consequences. He envisioned the rebuke and condemnation he would suffer from his mother. And for his dear Phoebe? The innocent daughter of the senior Roman magistrate of the city would be disgraced. Raising his hand and striking his forehead in woe, Saul said, "It is my fault. I am to blame for this."

"O Paulos, do not regret our love," she said, "for I shared equally in our passion and pleasure." She took him in her arms and kissed him; Saul felt the warmth of her body and sensed the desire in her kisses, but the image of his mother's face loomed over his thoughts.

Curious, desperate to know more but not wanting to offend, Saul said hesitantly, "How can you be certain?"

Phoebe's face turned crimson and she looked away. "For two months I

29

have not been in the way of women," she said. "I thought it my secret until the old handmaiden who washes my clothing took me aside and confided her concern for me."

Saul tried to focus his mind, to calculate what he should say. He wanted to think logically, but confusion took command of his thoughts. Phoebe had walked aside and was examining a white narcissus she had plucked from the garden. "Last night I dreamed," she said softly, "and in my dream I gave birth to our son. When the morning came, I saw that I had bled in the night and I wondered if I had lost our child." She turned to Saul. "Dear lover, I want to bear your son as a symbol of our love. This morning I prayed to the goddess Diana that I will have a son. Our son, Paulos, our son."

"But I am being sent away to Jerusalem —"

Phoebe put two fingers over his mouth. "Say no more," she said. "The whims of the gods — Zeus, Eros, and your Lord — rule our lives. I am not afraid. Yes, my father will be angry, but I shall tell him that I am proud that I gave my virgin body to the man I love and shall always love. And when I appear in the market and my form betrays the truth, the gossips will laugh and point. Let them. I know my love. And when you return from Jerusalem, you shall come to me and our son."

Saul was silent, still stunned by her revelation that he had fathered her child. In his heart he did not share her joy, but he must not betray his alarm. He glanced at the angle of the sun and knew he must leave at once for his appointment with his mother.

"Dear Phoebe," he said, taking her hand. "Your words are of such moment that my tongue is stilled. Yes, the gods rule our lives. Could I overcome circumstances, you and I would betroth this day, and I would be at your side in this time ahead, and rejoice with you at the birth of our child."

With tears of joy, Phoebe turned to Saul. "Paulos, your words fill my heart with gladness." She touched her hand to his cheek and said softly, "Come, my love. Let us play our game. We will run once more to our secret place in the garden before you go."

For one brief moment Saul hesitated, fearing to be late for his mother; but in that same moment he felt in his throat the voluptuous taste of lust; and in that instant ardor conquered fear.

After their hour in the garden, they joined hands and walked slowly through the courtyard to the door. "Farewell, dear Paulos," Phoebe said.

"Patience I lack, as you know; yet I will wait, and wait, and wait, until I shall see you once more. Deep in my heart I know that you will return to me and our son."

"Know thee also, dear Phoebe, and know thee well, that my love for you will abide forever."

On the street outside Saul looked up at the decline of the sun. It was well past noon. His mother would be concerned by his absence, but he must take time to think. What should he tell her? Stopping by the wayside in the shade of an old cedar, he swiftly examined his situation. "First," he said to himself, "I have made my choice. Zagoreos is right. I should not remain in Tarsus and follow my father's trade, but go to Jerusalem to advance my studies. Better to learn than to slave. That issue is resolved, and needs no more to be debated. I sail tomorrow on the early-morning tide. Therefore, I will begin by speaking to my mother with enthusiasm about my journey.

"Second, if Phoebe is indeed with child, it is better for her, and for myself, if I am beyond the reach of her father. If she has lost the child, as she suspects, neither her father nor my mother need ever know. Therefore, the answer is clear. I shall say nothing of Phoebe, nothing at all. This is my secret. There will be anguish enough in parting from Mother; it would be cruel to make it worse."

His decision made, Saul raced to the family compound.

IV

PARTING

Abigail paced from salon to terrace, balustrade to couch, sunlight to shadow on her pavilion, and back again. During the first hour of waiting her vexation turned to hurt, then hurt to anger: How could Saul be so late for their final appointment before he sailed? She had so much to say; she wanted so much to encourage him, to lift his spirits, to reassure her own.

In the second hour after noon her anger changed to alarm. Had something happened to him? Had he run away, taken refuge with one of his Greek friends in order to miss the boat? No, he would protest a disagreeable task, vehemently, but even as a child he had always met his responsibilities. She wondered if Isaac had contrived to have him detained. No, Isaac could be devious in business, but never with his family. She looked up at the sun; it was almost three hours after noon. Where could he be? She walked back in, sat down heavily on her couch, and felt the first tears come to her eyes.

At that moment she heard footsteps on the stairs.

Saul burst in and saw his mother bent over, her head bowed in grief. For the first time in his life he thought she looked defeated, even old.

"I am sorry. I —"

"It's all right." She rose from the couch, stood with her head high, and opened her arms to her son. "You are here now. Though I did worry that something had happened."

Saul clasped his arms around her and felt her body shudder with anguish. He closed his eyes, pressing his eyelids together tightly to hold back his own tears.

Abigail stepped back and said gently, "We are both too strong to permit our emotions to rule."

"I know, for so you have taught me," Saul said. "Yet I must tell you, Mother, that all my being cries out against leaving you, but I shall follow your wishes."

Saul smiled at his mother, took both her hands, and said in a firm voice: "Now, Mother, you shall know my change of heart. Yesterday, when you first told me that I must go to Jerusalem, I was filled with wrath and dismay. I was desperate to change your mind. And believed I could. In the hours since, I have come to see the wisdom of your plan. You are right, Mother, as always. I will go to Jerusalem. Today I am ready for the journey."

"O Saul, how you gladden my heart and soul." She kissed him, and raised her hands together as though in prayer as she looked in his eyes. "And how fortunate you are. I have longed to stand within the gates of Jerusalem since my father told me of King David's city when I was a small child. He would cite a Hebrew proverb: *Of the ten measures of beauty that God gave the world, he gave Jerusalem nine.* Now my beloved son will go in my place. And in Jerusalem you shall fulfill my vision that you will lead our people."

Arm in arm, mother and son walked out to the terrace and stood side by side in the sunshine. After a long silence Saul asked: "Has Father's anger lessened?"

"Your father knows you are leaving, Saul, and will make no effort to deter you."

"Then I must see him before I go."

Abigail turned to look gravely at her son. "He will not see you, Saul."

"But surely I can bid him farewell."

Abigail spoke slowly and deliberately. "Isaac said to me, 'I no longer have a son.'"

Trying to hold back his tears, Saul put his head on his mother's shoulder and clutched his fingers in the folds of her gown. Abigail held her son close and stroked the black curls crowning his head. At last she said, "Grieve no more, dear son. It is done. Young and old, each of us must live with the consequences of our actions."

Saul raised a hand as if in warning. "If Father is so angry with me, will he not take revenge against you after I have gone?"

Abigail shook her head. "I have no fear of that. Isaac needs me, as I need him. Yes, he is bitter now, but time may heal his wounds. And what cannot be changed must be endured." She hesitated. "One thing does disturb me, Saul. Danuta, ever sharp of ear, overheard this morning that Isaac will appoint Malech to help him oversee his shops."

"Malech?" Saul's face turned red with dismay and anger. "Malech! He cannot be trusted. He connives like a palace eunuch."

Only months earlier this stranger with sly words and cunning eyes had appeared, hungry and in rags. Isaac had taken pity on Malech and let him sleep in a corner of a storage shed.

"Yes, Malech," Abigail said. "By his constant flattery, he has beguiled your father. He begged Isaac to instruct him at the loom, and I must admit an apt apprentice Malech is. Not every young man of twenty learns to handle the shuttle and frame so quickly. Although we know nothing of Malech's origins, or how he came to be in Tarsus, your father trusts him — even though there are older and more loyal men in the shops."

"That is not like Father."

"Yes, strange it is, for Isaac is always suspicious of everyone. Yet he allows Malech to help him count the money after a trade. I myself have witnessed the glitter in Malech's eye when he fingers the coins."

Abigail lowered her voice. "The servants always try to listen," she whispered. "Saul, so long as your father has the wit to bargain and manage, no great harm will come. Yet given your father's wrath and disappointment, and Malech's ambition, it is a danger." She closed her hand and shook her fist. "If necessary, I will intervene."

A chill came over Saul as he realized for the first time the peril to his mother, to her love of this elegant mansion, and to her splendid life — and all because he rejected his father's trade. For a moment he wondered if he should capitulate, go to his father and accept his terms.

Sensing her son's thoughts, Abigail put her hand on his arm. "No, Saul, there is no turning back. It is done. Fear not for me. I am a strong woman, and I shall manage." From her writing desk she took a bulging leather pouch and handed it to her son. "In this purse I have placed two hundred Roman denarii of silver. At my direction Alida fashioned a belt in which she sewed one hundred shekels of gold. These sums should be more than enough for your first year in Jerusalem."

"Am I to return then?"

After a pensive moment, Abigail said softly, "Time must pass, Saul. Let us decide in a year." She took both of her son's hands in hers and smiled. "The time of your departure is at hand. Put the strife of this house behind you. You have become a man. You have chosen the right course. Go in confidence. Hold fast to what is true and right, good and just. Never compromise when you know what is right. Never. I know that you will triumph. I believe in you. I know not how, yet I am certain that you will leave your mark on the world."

She opened her arms. "May God be with you always," she whispered. She drew back and looked deep into Saul's eyes. "Henceforth I will be alone, yet you will ever be with me."

Saul's parting words came quickly, not by design but from the heart. "Mother, so also will you ever live within me. No day of my life will dawn when I do not remember all that you taught me. It was you who spurred me to excel. It was you who inspired me to achieve, to reach higher and always higher for the prize, to seek and strive, to be a leader. Your belief in me brought me to believe in myself. My faith is whole, complete, a gift from you. Faith, and love — these are the bonds that will bind us together, mother and son, for all of time. There will be no hour of my life when I do not think of your love for me and my love for you. Your dream shall become my dream. With your blessing and your inspiration, to Jerusalem I go." Once more they embraced; then Saul turned and left.

Head high, resolved to control his emotions, he walked slowly across the courtyard. In the corner of his eye he noticed his little sister reading beside a fountain, and sat down on the stone bench beside her. Instantly Rachel grimaced in anger and clutched her book. "I hate you," she said, and began to cry. "Poor Father. He does not eat or speak. He does not leave his shop. I tried to console him but he sent me away." She began to stammer, then said slowly: "May God punish you for what you have done."

Taken aback by the vehemence of her words, Saul watched her as she ran. His sister was only seven. He hoped that in time she would forget what he had done. All at once a wave of remorse swept over him. "I stand guilty of destroying my family," he said bitterly to himself. Somehow he must make amends. On an impulse he decided to write his father a letter of apology and contrition, to affirm his fidelity and regret their differences. By reaching out a hand, he was sure his father would see him, and perhaps forgive him.

Quickly he bounded up the stairs to his room; even before he sat down at his table and unrolled a fresh sheet of parchment, he had fashioned his words.

Saul, the son of Isaac and Abigail of the House of Benjamin, brother to Rachel. To my beloved Father: By whom I was brought to life, for whom I have the greatest love and respect. From you I learned the merits of honor, industry, and perseverance. From you I learned to speak plainly, to deceive neither others nor myself. From you I learned the difference between good and evil, to know right and to do right, to avoid evil thoughts and evil actions. May I, in my life, attain the esteem and reputation that you earned and so well deserve.

Now, for all that you have given to me and all that you mean to me, I affirm my gratitude. I regret the differences that drove us apart. I ask that you forgive any and all things I have done that cause you sorrow and pain. It is my greatest wish that we may reconcile our differences. It would lift the burden from my heart to clasp your strong hand once more and to hear your blessing. Yet if that cannot be, know this: My love for you will never end. Farewell, noble and dear Father, farewell.

Saul put his wax seal on the parchment, rolled and tied it with a strip of linen. Glancing out his window, he saw that the sun was within an hour of setting. There was still time to have a servant find his father in his shop and put the letter in his hands. For a messenger, Saul could trust no one but Alida. Opening the door into the corridor, he found her waiting there, sensing that he would need her.

"Alida, bear this scroll to my father. Let nothing deter you. Choose a moment when he is alone to give it to him. I will await you here."

Alida's usually merry eyes were anxious as she searched her master's face and whispered, "I understand."

The act of writing and dispatching the letter lifted Saul's spirit. He was sure that common blood and bonds of affection, which old Isaac felt but rarely expressed, would impel his father to summon him for a farewell embrace and blessing.

His mind now at rest, Saul turned to prepare for his journey. The essentials: first, stylus, ink, and papyrus. He picked out four new reed pens and fitted them into a wooden pen case given him by his mother when he was four and learning to write. No longer than his hand, and half as wide, the case was carved from olive wood and inset with two oval bronze cups to hold gum and soot for ink. The cover, also of olive wood, was made to slide over the base and fit snugly for travel. Rubbing his thumb along the polished wood, Saul said to himself, "I shall keep this as a memento of Mother; it will be my talisman of good fortune."

Papyrus might be hard to find in Jerusalem, he guessed, so he selected two new rolls from his cabinet, rolled them together, and set them on his desk beside his pen case. For warmth he chose his favorite traveling cloak, made of brown cloth from the finest Cilician wool, loomed and tailored by his father. Saul spread the heavy cloak out on his bed, folded a linen tunic and a woolen tunic, placed them in the center of the cloak, and arranged the pen case, papyrus roll, and purse on top. Beside his bed he saw his sandals, lined up in a neat row by Alida. He decided to take two extra pairs for his journey. Carthas, Isaac's oldest and best saddler, had made the sandals especially for Saul, doubling the hard-tanned horsehide on the sole and attaching double-wide goatskin straps to hold the sandals firmly for walking on rough ground. Food and water, Alida would supply.

Where was Alida? Was his father too busy to read it? Could he have gone? Saul began to pace back and forth. After a long time he heard the brush of leather on stone as Alida climbed the stairs. When she entered her hands were empty.

"Your father did not want to take the letter."

"Then where is it?" Saul asked impatiently.

"At last he did take it," Alida said quietly.

"What did Father say? I must know."

"When I went into the shop, I saw that he was talking with a Roman centurion. I waited quietly, and when the stranger left I walked to Master Isaac's bench, took the letter from my sewing, and held it out to him. 'What is that?' he asked. 'A letter from your son,' I said. 'I have no son,' he said, without looking at me. I replied, 'My good Master Isaac, Saul is your son, and he sends this letter of respect and affection to you by my hand.' For a moment your father said nothing, then he looked at the letter, and at me, and said, 'I will not take it. I do not wish to read words of betrayal.' So I stood without moving for a moment, and I observed workers lifting their heads from their looms and benches to cast furtive glances at us.

"'Sir,' I said, keeping my voice low, 'my master Saul ordered me to give this to you, only you, and I fear his wrath if I fail. I must stand here until you accept this letter.' So I did wait by his bench, and waited, and waited. Suddenly he said in an angry voice, 'Give me the letter and go.'"

Saul listened intently, weighing the significance of his father's behavior. Yes, his father would have measured in advance the enormity of the act of telling a servant that he had no son. Workers in the shop would surely have overheard him. *I will not despair*, he thought. *Father will not cast me out of his life. He will read my letter and forgive me.*

Turning toward Alida, Saul said, "You have done well. You persisted, and I am grateful." Then he took her hand. "Alida, from my earliest memories, you have been at my side, as friend, sister, healer, teacher, and lover, as well as wise and loyal servant. When I leave on the morning tide, I shall leave with gratitude to you, and love for you."

As Saul spoke, Alida lowered her head to hide her tears. "Good Master Saul, as you remember me, so shall I remember you." Wiping her eyes on her sleeve, she added quickly, "Now I must bring food and water for your journey."

Alone in his room, Saul felt empty, dispirited. The sun was down. He was sure that Isaac, Abigail, and Rachel were at the family's evening prayers, each bowing by the lamplight in the warm chamber where all had gathered for as long as he could remember. He wondered how long it might be before the family met together again. Happy memories, many of them, but now he must look ahead. Saul walked over to his window and looked out at the clear night sky, trying to pick out the stars and constellations that Targon would use in navigating their course to Seleucia and Caesarea.

Footsteps approached his door, and Alida returned with a reed basket of food for his journey and a belt of supple horsehide lined with chamois pockets that contained coins. "Buckle it," she said. "Make sure it fits."

Saul swung the belt around his tunic and fastened it. It was heavy but comfortable. "By this belt I shall be bound to you and Mother on my journey as I have been bound to you in this house."

His words seemed to sadden her. "When my father next sails into Tarsus," she said, "I shall return with him to Cyprus."

Saul looked at her and frowned. "Return to Cyprus?" he asked. "Why? Next to Danuta, you are my mother's favorite."

"You know my devotion to Mistress Abigail," she replied, "but once you are gone, I do not wish to live in this house."

"But why?"

She moved closer. "Malech covets me," she whispered. "He boasts that he will become master of this house and then make me his wife."

Saul looked at her in astonishment. "Alida, you are far too wise to believe such rubbish. Malech is a fool. You and I know the strength and resolve of my mother. She will protect you, as I will when I return. A year, two years, it will not be so long."

"Master Saul," Alida said evenly, "you will not return to this house."

"What are you saying?" Saul's voice rose in anger.

Alida looked directly at Saul. "The oracle of the sacred oak by the mirror lake on Mount Cebros prophesies that Saul of the House of Benjamin will never return to the house of his father Isaac in Tarsus."

Saul knew that a cult of pagans in Tarsus consulted the three priestesses who lived in a log hut by a spring on the mountain north of the city. The trio worshiped Cebros, a son of Zeus; for a coin, they would present a question to the oracle and bring back his answer.

"None can ignore the prophet Cebros," Saul said, "but I am certain that I shall return to Father and Mother and this house and this room." He smiled and took her hand. "When I return from Jerusalem, you must be here. Now, Alida, I must sleep. The *Pegasus* sails with the tide at first light, so I must leave this house at cock-crow. Will you come at midnight and wake me?"

"I will, Master Saul," she said as she departed.

Saul knew Cebros was no prophet, but he could not put out of his mind Alida's new evidence of Malech's ambition. The dread of danger to his mother returned to plague his thoughts. Through the window Saul looked long at his city in the starlight, fixing in memory the look of the mountains against the night glow on the far horizon to the west and north. At last he turned away, stretched out on his bed, and immediately fell asleep.

In his dream Saul was running, faster than he had ever run before, across the sand from the leaky old Roman boat that had brought him back to Tarsus, past the street beggars and prostitutes by the docks, past the busy stalls of copper pots and smoking charcoal; faster and faster he was running, through the familiar streets, past the stadium, past the Academy, his eyes straining for the first sight of home, his hands eager to open the wooden gate that would lead him into the atrium, up the broad steps to his mother's pavilion, and across the court to his own room. He was getting closer, and closer; *here, it should be here, this is the street, this is the corner. No, no, it's not the same.* Where was the wall, where was the gate, where was his mother's house, where was his father's shop? Everything was different. Did the House of Isaac burn while he was gone? Was there an earthquake? Was he on the right street? Yes. Yes. But all was so strange. Up and down the familiar street he ran, going off in one direction then another, looking, searching, making sure he was not lost. "No, no," he cried aloud, "the houses of my neighbors stand as I remember them." But in the place where his home stood there was only the ruin of a house, crumbling bricks and empty windows. To a favorite neighbor's door he ran, pounded desperately, to be confronted by a stooped and wrinkled old woman he did not recognize. "The House of Isaac! Where is it?" he asked. The old woman looked at him, shook her head, and drew away. "Isaac! The tentmaker," Saul heard himself shouting. "Abigail, his wife. Where are they?" With a toothless grin, the old woman croaked, "Long have I lived here. No Isaac have I known, nor Abigail." Cackling with laughter, she closed the door. Saul ran back to where he thought his home had been, saw all in ruins, cried out in anguish and fell to the ground weeping and beating his breast.

His cry in the night, or footsteps in his room, awakened Saul. He was sweating and at the same time shuddering from cold. "It was only a dream, a nightmare," he tried to tell himself. Confused, half awake, he wondered for a moment if it was also only a dream that he must go to Jerusalem.

He felt the touch of Alida's hand. "It is almost midnight by the stars," she whispered. "I brought food and fresh water."

"Yes, water," he said. He drank it down as Alida cooled his face and shoulders with a fresh linen cloth.

At her touch Saul sensed the god Priapus calling him again. Not yet fully awake, and still anxious from the terror of his dream, he wondered if it would be sinful to lie with Alida one last time. He loved Phoebe; yet he loved Alida as well.

After that moment of hesitation Saul placed his arm around Alida's waist and drew her close. She put aside the cloth and, without taking her eyes from Saul, removed the clips holding her peplos. He took her hand and brought her to him.

Later they heard the crow of the cock at the same moment. "It is time," Saul said quietly. He dressed quickly, buckled on his new belt, and fastened the straps of his running sandals. Alida slipped into her peplos, lifted Saul's bundle of clothing and food by the two thongs, and placed it by the door. "Meet me at the front gate," Saul said.

Alone, Saul looked around his room one last time. Suddenly, impulsively, he raised his hands and prayed aloud: "O Lord of grace and power, sovereign of all the earth and heavens above, I call upon thee to bear me safely on this journey. As my forefathers made a covenant with you, O Lord, so do I now. Show me the purpose for which I go to Jerusalem. Reveal to me your vision for my life. Guide me to find truth. Grant me, now and always, the wisdom to know your will and the courage to follow it. When I fall into danger, protect me. When I am in distress, strengthen me. When I sorrow with longing for my family and home, comfort me. Restore accord to this house, I beseech you; preserve my mother, my father, and my sister from enemies known and unknown. May they forgive me for the hurt and anguish I have brought upon them. Go with me, O Lord, across the seas, through the valleys, across the mountains, on all my travels; return me to this city, to this my home, to my beloved family. In you, O Lord, I place my trust." Slowly he repeated the words: "In you, O Lord, I place my trust."

As Saul ended his prayer a sense of resolution and confidence came over him, and he felt excited about this journey to Jerusalem, this passage into the unknown. Swinging his pack over his right shoulder, the waterskin over the left, he marched out of his room, down the steps, and to the gate. Facing Alida, he clapped his hands on her shoulders and in a strong voice said, "Be here when I return to Tarsus."

With a cheerful smile that brought a glow to her face, Alida nodded vigorously. Saul looked up at his mother's pavilion; a lamp glowed in one window. She might be watching, so he raised his arm in farewell, turned quickly, and set off at a run along the dark street. Alida watched him go, then slowly closed and barred the gate.

At the docks Saul found the *Pegasus* and climbed over the rail. Watching him was a stout figure, dark of skin, with a black beard trimmed squarely below the chin. He was clothed in purple — cloak, sash, and turban. His eyes were slits below a brooding brow.

"I am Targon, master of the *Pegasus*. Be you Saul?" His voice was deep, his Greek measured, distinct, with the accent of Phoenicia.

"I am Saul. A passenger aboard your ship."

Targon looked at the lean body and muscular legs. "Have you been to sea before?" he asked brusquely. Saul shook his head. Targon frowned. "My strongest deckhand was killed last night in a drunken brawl," he said. "You will replace him. We have no choice. You will take an oar of the longboat until we clear the harbor. At sea, you will join the riggers who man the halyards to raise the sails. Now we load goods and provisions for the journey. Put your pack in my cabin. Move quickly. The tide turns just before the day breaks."

Saul ran to Targon's small cabin, stowed his belongings in a corner, and hurried back to help with the loading. With all goods aboard, a giant ruffian with one good eye, and an empty socket where the other had been, beckoned. He was Pilum, master of the oars. He looked at Saul's soft hands and grimaced with disgust as he led the way down a swaying rope ladder into the longboat.

"The stern oar sets the pace," Pilum said gruffly. "You sit in the bow and follow the others." Saul took his seat and lifted the long oar, getting the feel of the thick pine worn smooth by callused hands. In the darkness the other crew members were huddled forms and shadowy silhouettes. Saul resolved to show them his arms were strong, strong enough to match theirs.

The *Pegasus* was slipping her lines, getting ready to sail. Saul could hear the planking grind and creak against pilings as the tide began to ebb. Suddenly there was a shout — Targon's voice — and Saul heard his name called. "On deck, Saul! Quickly! A messenger for you."

Saul shipped his oar and scrambled up the rope ladder to the deck of the *Pegasus*. In the dim light he saw a tall unkempt man standing on the dock. "Is it . . . ? Is it . . . ?" he said to himself. "Yes, it is Malech." There he was, menacing, smug, triumphant; Malech, holding an object in his hand, holding it out to Saul. Was it a letter from his father? Wary, Saul paused for a moment, then put out his hand: He felt cloth, and weight. Saul recognized the Cilician tent cloth, a scrap woven by his father's hand from the look and feel of it. Holding his breath, Saul opened the cloth.

There was no letter; it was a broken fragment of stone. With a sense of dread, Saul saw that it was an *ostraka*, the Greek symbol of banishment in disgrace. Turning the fragment of stone in his hand, Saul saw one word in black ink on the stone — his name, and beside it the Roman numeral X. The handwriting was his father's. All was instantly clear. Isaac had given Saul an answer to his letter. Exile. Banishment for ten years.

When Saul looked up the messenger had disappeared, and the *Pegasus* had slipped her last ropes. He felt the ship moving with the tide, felt himself being borne away, away from all that he had known, away from his past and into a new life.

V

PASSAGE

With bare feet braced on the highest yardarm and his right elbow crooked firmly around the tapered mast of weathered pine, Saul shaded his eyes from the brilliance of the sun rising in the clear morning sky. Turning his head slowly, he searched the horizon to windward and leeward, to port and starboard, searching for some interruption, however slight, in the unbroken line that defined sea and sky. Saul feared heights, but the captain of the *Pegasus* had dismissed his protests and ordered Saul aloft as lookout for the dawn watch. "Call out only if you see land," Targon said, "not a hippocampus, nor a passing cloud."

As the youngest and least experienced seaman aboard, Saul resolved to conquer the mast. Locking his legs around the slippery pine, blistering his soft hands on the halyards, he pulled himself up, never once looking down as he climbed. Once aloft, he chanced to see the mast swaying over blue water fifty feet below and closed his eyes in terror, clutching his arms around the mast. Taking a deep breath, he repeated to himself, "No one can help me. I must prove my courage." As Saul calmed himself, fear yielded to his determination not to risk the laughing scorn of his fellow seaman by a false report.

Diligently he searched, observing how the light changed on the sea and the horizon line as the sun mounted, one finger, two fingers, a handbreadth above earth. "There, off the port quarter, is that a thunderhead towering in the far distance?" He looked again. "Or is it the peak of Mount Atchana that rises to the north of Seleucia?" He closed his eyes, then peered intently toward the eastern horizon. Against the deep blue of the sky he could make out a distinct shape, an irregular cone of a different and darker shade of light, the outline of a peak that could only be land. Yet he must be certain. Again he searched the edge of the great bowl of the heavens; again he saw the change of form and light. It was no illusion. Maintaining his firm grip on the mast, Saul turned his body and head toward the stern of the boat, located the purple figure of Captain Targon standing by the helmsman, and called out: "Land! Off the port bow."

Targon took the tiller and motioned Bokaar, the helmsman, forward and aloft. With one arm tight to the mastpole and the other hand clinging to a halyard, Saul carefully moved to one side of the yardarm to make room for Bokaar, now nimbly climbing the rigging.

With a skeptical glance at Saul, Bokaar balanced his stout legs easily on the yardarm and looked in the direction where he pointed. "Eye good," he growled, then turned and bellowed to the deck below: "Land ho! Atchana. Port bow."

At midday the *Pegasus* stood well inside the harbor of Seleucia. With a calm sea and gentle breeze, just enough to maintain steerage, Targon used the tide to bring his ship directly to the dock. Admiring the captain's practiced hand, Saul studied the ship's response to force of wind and touch of tiller. Once sails were secured and the ship tied fast, Saul joined the crew in lifting the heavy bales of Cilician wool from the hold and taking them ashore. With Targon keeping count, the crew brought aboard new cargo, jute bags of barley and wheat, rough castings of bronze, and great pottery jars of fresh water for the next leg of the voyage.

As the tide ebbed, the *Pegasus* was ready for the sea again. In the longboat Saul tugged with the nine other oarsmen, slowly towing the ship past the stone breakwater at the harbor entrance. In the open sea the oarsmen clambered aboard and Targon commanded the sails to be raised. As the canvas filled and the ship moved briskly over the blue water, Saul found a seat by the captain's stand near the helm to observe and learn.

"Long ago, the People of the Sea discovered that an offshore wind comes up off Seleucia as the sun descends," Targon said to Saul. "From voyages past, I also know that if my crew goes ashore at night in Seleucia, I will lose at least three to prostitutes and drunken brawls. Thus, safer we are at sea than ashore."

"What course do we now follow, Captain Targon?" Saul asked. "And how, in this great open sea, do you find the port of Caesarea?"

"By day we follow the coast," Targon replied. "By night certain constellations show the way, depending on the time of year. Close to shore the winds usually hold constant in this season. With sails trimmed and taut, in two days we will come abreast of Byblos, the city of my Phoenician ancestors. There from ages past we have trained the best of shipwrights and launched the finest of ships and sailors. My grandfather was an ironsmith, my father well known as the best of caulkers. His ships never leaked. On the third day we will be off Sidon — Sidon of the twin harbors. The island city of Tyre is but half a day south of Sidon. By the fifth day, if we are not becalmed, we shall see the great fortress and city that Herod the Great built and called Caesarea Maritima as a tribute to Augustus."

He shaded his eyes, squinted at the set of the sails, and seemed satisfied. "Now Saul, stand at the helm by Bokaar. I have told him to train you at the tiller. Knowing how to keep a ship on course is a useful skill."

Saul jumped forward eagerly, and Bokaar, after showing Saul how to grip the tiller, stepped aside. In the first hours Saul could not keep the boat from weaving back and forth, prompting sailors lounging on deck to taunt him with snakelike hand motions. By noon, with Bokaar's guidance, Saul had learned to watch the swells on the windward quarter and anticipate how much pressure to put on the tiller to keep a steady course.

Thus were Saul's first days filled aboard the *Pegasus*, studying the sea and the winds and his fellow seaman, cheerfully accepting every task Captain Targon assigned. Saul relished the sailor's life. Always, he had scorned toil at his father's loom or harness bench; now, to his surprise, he delighted in the physical challenge of pulling an oar and hoisting sail. He resolved to prove to these rough and robust strangers that he could match their brawn and skills and stamina.

Indeed, so bound up was Saul in the endless tasks of seafaring that he gave less and less thought to home and Tarsus, to the pleasures and easy days he had left behind. The feel of the helm pulling at his arms and shoulders, the contest to gauge wave and wind and maintain a steady track on the sea, the strenuous work of pulling on coarse hemp and lifting tackle, the unaccustomed stiffness from the salty deck that was his bed — all these new experiences stirred his spirits, all brought a new sense of learning and adventure and invoked his desire to meet a challenge, to excel.

On the fourth night out of Seleucia, Saul finished his watch, found a space on deck away from the dark forms of sleeping crew, and lay on his back looking up at the vast vault of the shimmering heavens. He thought of his mother. He pictured her standing alone in the darkness on her pavilion, looking up at the same stars he saw now. He imagined that at that moment in time she was thinking of him. So close did she seem that a sense of peace came over Saul, and the gentle roll of the ship lulled him to sleep.

Hours later a change in the motion of the ship awakened him; or was it the pounding of running feet? He leaped up from the deck. The *Pegasus* was pitching, plunging, tossing like a chip over the dark sea through the black night. The stars had disappeared, and in the darkness Saul could make out great waves breaking over the bow of the ship, sending a salt spray over the foredeck and drenching the ghostly forms of men hauling down the sails. The billowing sheets seemed alive, angry, defiant.

Instinctively Saul struggled across the wet deck toward the helm. He had taken no more than a few steps when the deck tilted sharply to port, and he lost his balance. Sliding across the slippery boards he spread his legs and reached out both arms, hoping desperately to catch a rope or stanchion to break his plunge toward the sea. Moments passed, moments that seemed to stretch to eternity, until finally his foot struck the outer rail, and he grasped a cleat and held on with desperation. A wave swept over him, lifting him, propelling him toward the rail and filling his chest with cold brine. Terrified, he forced himself to cough and gag and expel the water from his lungs. Locking both hands around the cleat, he held on until the ship finally righted itself. With the deck almost level, Saul rose to his knees and ran, low and stooping, toward the helm.

A sudden skyburst of lightning half a mile off the starboard beam pierced the darkness, and Saul could make out Bokaar braced at the helm, his feet planted wide, his huge arms wrestling the tiller to hold the bow into the waves. On the captain's stand Targon stood like a statue, arms folded, face erect, looking to the mast and searching the stormy sky. His purple robe, wet and darkened, was pressed by the wind against his skin. Suddenly over the howl of the tempest came the crunch of splintering wood, and Saul saw Bokaar fall backward with the tiller loose and crashing on his chest. "Rudder post — broken!" Bokaar shouted.

In an instant the wind swept the *Pegasus* broadside to the waves, and the ship rolled to port, perilously, the rail under green water, hanging there forever, it seemed to Saul as he held on to a stanchion. Again the lightning struck, closer, closer, repeatedly, immediately bringing drumrolls of thunder that caused the stoutest crossbeams to tremble. In the vivid flashes the ship seemed to be caught at the bottom of a vast canyon of stormcloud, with menacing cliffs churning, twisting, towering to port and starboard above the now small and fragile craft.

Then all was darkness, with the wind shrieking in the rigging and the waves beating against and breaking over the hull, the ship rising, falling, yawing, twisting helplessly on the sea. Crouching by the stanchion, Saul could make out Bokaar, fixed like a stone with the tiller in his arms, and Captain Targon, standing with his feet set wide as he bent his knees windward to keep his balance, arms still folded, calmly studying wave and sky as his ship rolled and tossed.

As suddenly as it had arrived, the storm ended. Lightning still streaked in the distance off the port beam, but the rumbles of thunder that followed seemed to be moving away. "The squall has passed," Targon said. "Come, Saul. We must find what damage lies forward."

The mainsail, lashed to the lower spar, was intact, but the topsail was ripped down the middle as though cut by a knife. Targon stepped easily over a tangle of rope and pulleys rocking to and fro on the deck and inspected the mast. It stood like a great lone tree rising toward the night. Pilum had counted the crew: one missing, an old Egyptian. Targon shook his head. Pilum shrugged.

Belowdecks the cargo was still dry, the bags of grain still in place. The bronze castings, wedged low amidship, had served as ballast. The planking had held. "A brave vessel," Targon murmured. As they climbed out of the hold and returned to the helm a waxing half-moon broke through racing tendrils of clouds.

All was silent except for the waves crashing intermittently over the starboard rail and the creaking of timbers. The wind had dropped, and the first evanescence of light suggested the dawn to come. Targon stood easily and seemed to be listening, intently. After a time he nodded to Bokaar, and then Saul heard it, too: surf, waves breaking over rocks.

Targon motioned for Saul to follow him. On the foredeck the captain found the oarmaster. "Pilum!" he commanded. "Take every able man you can fit into the longboat. We drift near a reef. You will tow us around the rocks to a safe beach. It is our only chance to save the ship. And our lives."

Ten men lifted and launched the longboat. "Pull!" Pilum commanded from the bow. As the towline tightened and arrested the random wallowing of the *Pegasus*, Saul, muscling the big oar from his forward seat, could hear the surf crashing on the reef to his right. "Pull!" Slowly the ship began to move, a foot at a time. "Pull!" The first good light before sunrise revealed the danger, a line of jagged rocks, long as a stadium but no higher than a hut, barring the ship from the beach beyond. Slowly, inexorably, the remnants of the storm wind carried the *Pegasus* toward the reef; slowly, man and oar tugged the ship forward.

"Pull!" Every seaman bent his back, braced his legs, pulled with arms and muscles and every sinew of his being. Targon stood on the bowsprit of the *Pegasus*, pointing with his arm to the opening in the reef. Saul felt blisters on his hands, thirst in his mouth, pain in his arms; still he pulled, each long stroke putting him almost prone on the narrow seat, holding to the rhythm, lifting the oar, pushing it forward, taking the blade deep, and pulling with the other nine in the boat. "Pull!" The sound of wave breaking on rock came closer. "Pull!" Faster and faster Pilum shouted above the waves until at the last moment the stern of the *Pegasus* cleared the end of the reef by no more than the length of the longboat.

Once the ship had passed the rocks Targon signaled a new course toward the beach. Inside the reef the sea calmed, and Pilum steered the longboat directly toward shore. When the longboat grounded all ten oarsmen leaped out into the waves and tugged the *Pegasus* through the surf. At that moment good fortune intervened: A great wave lifted the ship and dropped her bow firmly on the sand.

Targon climbed down a rope ladder and strode through the waves to the beach. He motioned for the crew to gather around him, and spoke with respect as well as authority. "Good seamanship, all of you. You have done well." He paced the beach for a moment, then turned again to the crew.

"Pilum: Have the men build a fire to dry their clothes. Bring water and food ashore and feed the crew well. Bokaar: When all have eaten, take the ship's carpenter and an ax up the hill into that forest and cut a stout pine or a young oak for a new rudder post. Saul: Assist the sailmaker in patching the topsail. All others: Heat pitch and caulk stem to stern. Fill all joints, inside and out, that may have loosened."

Within three days the ship's carpenter, benefited by a low tide, had cut, chiseled, fitted, and replaced the rudder post. Saul, fingering a needle for the first time in years, had fashioned stitches as strong, if not as neat, as the sailmaker's. Caulkers had finished their work and put away their blades. The *Pegasus* was ready for the sea. Yet struggle as they did, the crew could not budge the ship. Her knee and forward keel rested firmly in the sand.

At Targon's direction the crew shifted cargo aft. They cut long logs as levers to push against the stem. Ten oarsmen in the longboat pulled at the stern. Still the bow of the *Pegasus* did not move.

That evening Targon summoned Saul to his cabin. As they sat by a small lamp, Targon took off his cap and looked at his young passenger. "How do you like your first taste of life at sea?"

Saul clapped his hands on his thighs with a boyish smile." "The sea is exciting, an endless adventure," he said, pounding a knee for emphasis. "Before, I knew the physical challenge of games; now I know the contest for life itself."

"Were you afraid during the storm?"

"At first, yes," Saul replied. "Then so many things happened so quickly that I did not have time to be afraid."

Beaming assurance, Targon nodded.

"I was sure I would not drown," Saul continued, "not even when the wave swept me to the rail. Something flashed in my mind that I would be saved, and in an instant my hand felt that cleat. And in the longboat I was sure we would clear the reef and bring the *Pegasus* to the sand."

"It was close," Targon said.

After a moment, curiosity impelled Saul to ask: "Captain Targon, how do you maintain such calm in a storm?"

Targon rested his chin on his palm and reflected. "If the leader loses his head in crisis, Saul, all go down. The master of a ship must, in every situation, know what he will do next. He must be calm and show himself to be calm. He must think with logic and quickness. He must command with order and dignity. Otherwise he fails as a leader."

"You saved our lives," Saul said, "and I shall forever be grateful."

With a wave of his hand Targon brushed the compliment aside. "Duty, no more." He rubbed his beard for a moment. "Now, Saul, we are stranded for at least ten days. We must wait until the high tide of a full moon floats the ship. We stand south of Tyre. The Via Maris, the main Roman highway along the coast to Caesarea Maritima, lies not far beyond the hills to the east. I calculate you could walk to Caesarea in a day. Tomorrow you may wish to find that road and proceed on your journey."

Saul was surprised. "You wish me to go?"

Targon laughed. "You earned your passage, Saul. You are welcome to remain aboard and sail with us into Caesarea. I am obligated to tell you, however, that your mother, in her note to me arranging passage, asked that I expedite your journey to Jerusalem."

Saul was silent. He had come to like being on the ship. "Captain Targon, I shall give you my answer in the morning."

He left the cabin, found a quiet place on deck, and wrapped himself in his cloak. He wanted to stay with the ship, with Targon, the crew. Always before he had scorned physical work for his father, but climbing the mast, hoisting the sails, wrestling the tiller — each was a test not only of his brawn but also of his spirit. He knew he had done well; Targon had said so. Yet he also knew he must leave his ship and carry out his promise to his mother. He should not wait for a full moon. It was more important that he go on to Jerusalem and enter the school of Gamaliel without delay.

At daybreak he put on his heavy sandals and went to Targon's cabin.

"So sure was I of your decision that I prepared for your departure," Targon said. He pulled a heavy wooden box from under his cot and brought out a leather pouch. "Your mother's servant brought a purse of gold for your journey. My instructions were to give this money to you upon landing in Caesarea. Take it now."

"But she provided me with money before I left," Saul said, gesturing toward the pack and money belt he had stowed in the corner of the captain's cabin.

"This purse belongs to you," Targon said firmly. "Take it. And this, too, the money paid for your passage."

"But I owe you for my lessons."

Targon shook his head. "It is yours. Take it." Leaning forward in his chair he again addressed his passenger. "The highway is patrolled by Roman soldiers and presents no danger. However, the hills between this shore and the road may hold brigands. Bokaar asked that he accompany you to the highway."

"No better guide could I have, at sea or ashore," Saul replied.

"Now, take heed: When you reach Caesarea, look for the north wall of the fortress. Follow the cobbled path along the shore to the synagogue. Seek there the best route for a Jew walking to Jerusalem. Earlier passengers on my ship say the journey is three days at most, two for a man with strong legs. There are wells along the road, but it is wise to carry a skin of fresh water."

Both men stood, and Targon put his arm on the younger man's shoulder. "An able seaman you have become, Saul."

"I shall find no finer master at sea, ever," he replied.

Armed with a quarterstaff that reached above his head, Bokaar bounded through the forest with the purpose of a foraging boar. With Saul at his heels, the two men climbed the hills, crossed a high ridgeline, and found the Roman highway within two hours. For a few minutes they sat on a boulder, watched a camel caravan plod past, and drank from the waterskin in silence.

Saul stood. It was time to go. When he grasped Bokaar's mammoth hand, he found it difficult to speak. "The sea has bound us in brotherhood," Saul said.

Bokaar struck his hand on Saul's chest and then his own. "Sometime. Sail together again." With a hearty clasp of arms the two men parted, and Bokaar disappeared in the brush.

The sun above was high, the sky clear. The brown grass by the roadside indicated a light wind from the northwest — a good day for a journey. Settling his pack comfortably on his back, Saul looked around and sensed that he had been here before. It was the Roman road that was so familiar: Exactly like the Roman highways leading from Tarsus, it was constructed of heavy stones laid down by Caesar's military engineers and now worn smooth by foot and hoof.

On Saul's last overland journey, months earlier, he had hiked from Tarsus westward on just such a road, the Roman highway that followed the old Silk Road through the foothills of the Taurus Mountains to the Roman fort at the entrance to the Cilician Gates. There he had visited the legate Tullus Sertorius, a friend of Saul's father who commanded the troops guarding the pass. Saul wondered if his father had repented; but, no, it was not Isaac's nature to change his mind or so soon forgive. His mother had been right when she had said, "It is done."

Adapting his long stride to the rapid marching pace he had learned from the Roman soldiers, Saul walked on, and by afternoon he reached a hilltop that commanded a view of Caesarea. Drinking from his waterskin, he identified the landmark Targon had described — Strato's Tower, a pinnacle of stone at the shoreline, with pitch flaming and smoking at the peak, a beacon light to ships at sea. He could pick out other storied monuments Herod the Great had built to Caesar: distant arches of aqueducts bringing water into the city, a Roman amphitheater rising against a hillside, the breakwater of enormous blocks of stone creating the anchorage. Overlooking the harbor was the vast fortress King Herod had built for himself.

Inside the walls of the fortress stood a magnificent marble palace, pavilions and gardens, massive houses of stone along symmetrical broad streets, stables and workshops, a marketplace, a city within a city. Never had Saul seen such a grandiose monument, such edifices to self. Shaking his head in amazement, he remembered that Uncle Enoch had told him the story of the warrior Herod, and how he defeated and put to death the last of the Maccabee kings, and how Caesar Augustus appointed Herod to be king of the Jews and to rule over all Judea. After Herod died twenty-four years ago, the kingdom had sundered. Now Herod's son, Antipas, ruled only the backwater of Galilee. But the fortress stood, and the Roman procurator, Pontius Pilate, reigned from the palace and lived in its myriad splendor.

Curious, Saul hurried down the hill. Just outside the city wall a naked corpse hung by the arms from a crossbar on a pole set into the earth beside the highway. The legs had been twisted and broken. Rivulets of fresh blood dripped onto the earth. Mingling with a crowd of onlookers, Saul asked a camel driver why the man had been crucified. "He was caught trying to rob a traveler on a Roman highway," said the cameleer.

From Caesarea to Joppa the Roman highway ran wide and straight across a level plain, close to the sea and paralleling the coast, turning at times around low hills, crossing a broad valley, fording a brook, stretching on and on to the horizon. As he passed milestone after milestone, Saul marveled at the numbers and variety of humans and animals trudging the paving stones of the road: lean fishermen with their catch strung on long canes, shepherds driving fat sheep to market, toothless old women, ragged children with faces pinched and eyes hollowed from hunger, wheeled carts drawn by gray donkeys with tall black ears flopping at each step, camels lifting their heads in haughty disdain. In midafternoon a breeze rose from the west, cooling Saul's brow and so speeding his pace that he reached Joppa sooner than he expected.

At the inn of the widow Tabitha, Saul dropped his pack and waterskin on a bench, removed his belt, and stretched out on the cot. He was almost asleep when Tabitha brought a small bowl of fish and lentils. It was all she had. When he finished he was still hungry, but he unrolled his journal, inked his stylus, and began to write.

> Far have I come. The Great Sea and its deep blue waters have I crossed. A storm-tossed night of danger have I survived. Caesar's highways have I walked. This night I sleep in ancient Joppa, in a rude inn where the floor is bare earth and my bed a cot of fraying hemp looped over a broken wood frame. Far have I come, both in miles and in circumstance. No longer is my bed soft, my table plentiful. Comfort has turned to necessity, abundance to essentials. The familiar is absent, lost. Every footstep takes me more deeply into a strange and different world. It is a world hard, poor, filled with misfortune, empty of hope. In this universe I am a stranger, a nomad, a wanderer. In little more than a week I have become unknown to myself. Here alone in this strange room, I wonder who I am.

"Awake, pilgrim, awake. Dawn is near." From the restlessness of sleep in an unfamiliar place Saul heard Tabitha's voice. He rose from the cot, splashed his face and arms from the bowl of water she had brought, and quickly buckled chiton and sandals. With bread and the directions she had given him, Saul set forth.

His stride was long, his pace steady. The road began to rise and the lush green land of the coastal plain gave way to a forest of pine and cedar, then to bare hills, empty except for an occasional flock of sheep on a patch of sparse grass. The road narrowed, steepened, emptied. How, Saul wondered, could these bleak mountains be the glorious Promised Land, the "land of wheat and barley and vines and fig trees, olive oil and honey" that Moses had described?

Never stopping to rest, Saul pressed on until he reached a pass, and a magnificent view opened before him, a scape of soaring peak and brilliant sky. Across a steep ravine and high above stood a city of dun blocks of stone and baked mud that seemed to have risen from the earth itself. It could only be Jerusalem, those crenellated parapets rambling along hillsides and enclosing twisting narrow streets, close-packed houses, bluffs and olive trees. He remembered his mother's long-ago story of King David's ascent to power, and how David had created Jerusalem to stand forever as the earthly expression of the preeminence of God and his chosen people. To her, the Jerusalem she loved from afar was "the beating heart of the eternal body of the Hebrew peoples." To Saul, it was disappointing.

The renowned city was surprisingly small. Within its walls — no more than a mile long from north to south and even less in width — the rough land was divided, cleft by a vale. On the nearer plateau rose a gray and gloomy stone palace with three lookout towers. That, Saul assumed, must have been the palace of long-dead King Herod, but now it bore no pennant of royalty. On the farther plateau was a vast porch — a long rectangle, or was it a trapezoid? — framed by double rows of Roman columns. There in its very center had been erected an edifice three hundred feet long with walls of white marble crowned by a roof that glittered with gold in the bright sun of the summer afternoon. That could only be the Temple, which Herod had begun reconstructing and embellishing fifty years earlier to gain the favor of the Hebrew people. Uncle Enoch had once remarked that Herod neither finished the Temple nor won over the Jews. Yet there it stood, against bleak earth and drab rooftop, like a jewel lost from its setting.

He walked on; he had promised his mother he would go to the Temple in his first hour in Jerusalem. At the Joppa Gate a Roman soldier pointed out the street of David that led to the Temple Mount. With a somber feeling Saul walked slowly through the West Gate of the Wall into the Court of the Gentiles, as noisy as a marketplace, with pilgrims haggling at tables to change money and buy goats and lambs for sacrifice.

From the Beautiful Gate, Saul entered the Women's Court, where all was quiet except for the brush of his own sandals on the marble floor. On through the Nicanor Gate he walked, and into the Court of Israel. It, too, was empty, silent. He stood still, expecting to be awed, wondering if he would feel the presence of God. He waited, but felt nothing.

His mother would expect him to pray, so he lifted his face and hands to the heavens: "Blessed are you Lord God king of the universe, who has sustained me and enabled me to live to see this season." He added words he remembered from songs of David: "Our feet shall stand within thy gates, O Jerusalem . . . Whither the tribes of the Lord give thanks unto the name of the Lord . . . Great is the Lord, and exceedingly to be praised in the city of our God . . ."

His promise kept, Saul left the Temple as the sun was setting. A money changer in the Court of the Gentiles pointed the way to the school of Gamaliel — out the double gate of the Royal Portico to the Street of Herod, then south, down the hill, for half a mile. Saul hurried past beseeching shopkeepers to the Lower City. Near the Pool of Siloam he found the school, a wide building of rough stone, its whitewash peeling with age and inattention. Looking up at the neglected wall, Saul longed for the sight of the lofty columns of the Academy and the sunny porches of the Stoa. In Tarsus the architecture and gardens had been as inspiring as the teachers.

Gritting his teeth in resolve, Saul pushed open the heavy cedar door and stepped into an empty corridor. Slowly he made his way down a dark hall until he reached the end, where a door stood open into a cluttered study. There in a great oak chair with a high arched back sat a man writing by the light of a blackened pottery lamp.

To Saul he was too old to be a student, too young to be a master. His face was without a wrinkle, his rusty brown hair combed neatly, and his beard trimmed close. On the table beside him was a neat stack of scrolls, and at his right hand was an odd hat, a truncated cone of black silk turned upside down and tapering to a square flat top. Upon noticing Saul, the man raised an eyebrow in surprise.

"I am Saul of Tarsus. I seek Rabban Gamaliel."

The man in the chair nodded once. "I am Gamaliel."

Saul tried to conceal his astonishment; he had expected the revered Gamaliel to be a stooped graybeard. This stocky man, with his heavy arms and stout legs, could have been a stonecutter. After a moment Saul said: "I am here to enter your school, Rabban Gamaliel."

Gamaliel leaned back, rested his chin on his hand, and examined his visitor, studying the angular face, the dark, intense eyes. He observed the lean frame of the youth, the fine clothes, the neat pack, the new waterskin, the heavy sandals. After a long silence he said quietly: "Why?"

Saul decided he must speak the truth; any teacher of this eminence would surely detect any attempt to delude. "It is my mother's desire," he replied. "My father wanted to take me from my studies at the Greek Academy in Tarsus and teach me to make tents, a profession that has made him rich. My mother rejected his plan and sent me here to study."

Gamaliel gently stroked his neatly trimmed beard. "I commend your honesty." He paused and lifted a hand. "The aspiration of a mother is not without importance. But the question is" — he pointed a finger at Saul — "do *you* wish to study here?"

"I have no choice," Saul said.

Gamaliel pondered for a moment. His large brown eyes, with their glints of gold, seemed to twinkle with bemusement. "We do," he said.

It had never occurred to Saul that he might not be accepted in the school. "I have money to pay," he said quickly, pointing to his pack.

Gamaliel looked at Saul and spoke with cold disdain. "A coin of the purest gold will never be the key to the door of this school of Torah."

The rebuke provoked Saul. "Then I have a greater asset," Saul said quickly. "I excel. All my life I have been taught to excel at whatever I attempted, be that a challenge to mind or body. If you permit, I will excel here. I come here to be taught."

Gamaliel pursed his lips. "Very little do we rabbis teach. In this school it is up to the student to learn."

"Then I will learn to be a scholar."

"So ambitious you are!" Gamaliel smiled. "The teachings say that a priest must have twenty-four qualities; a monarch, thirty; and a scholar, forty-eight. Do you know the forty-eight attributes of a scholar?"

"I do not," Saul replied. "But I will learn what they are."

"It is not enough to list these attributes." Gamaliel opened his palms and gestured toward Saul. "You must live these attributes. The true scholar must not only understand and interpret Torah; he must live Torah. In essence the scholar and Torah are synonymous." He paused. "What do you know of Torah?"

"I can recite from the Law, the Prophets, and the Writings," Saul boasted.

"A child can recite," Gamaliel said, not unkindly. "A scholar understands."

Fixing his eyes intently on Saul, he sat forward. "The Law says that if one is hungry one has to eat. And one can take an egg from a bird that is not a bird of prey. One can take the egg so long as it is not done in front of the mother, for one cannot openly hurt the mother.

"There was a very, very good boy who was very hungry. He saw a tree, and in the tree a nest, and in the nest a bird and an egg. He waved his arms and caused the bird to fly away so that she could not see what he was about to do. He climbed the tree to the nest, looked around to make certain the mother could not be seen, and took the egg, whereupon he fell from the tree, broke his neck, and died.

"Another boy was hungry, and spotted a nest with a bird and egg. He climbed the tree, seized the mother by the neck, took the egg, and put her back in the nest. Then and there, in front of the mother, he ate the egg, satisfied his hunger, and climbed down the tree.

"Tell me, Saul of Tarsus, is there justice?"

Saul thought for a moment before he constructed his reply. "Under God there is always justice. Not always do we see his purpose or comprehend his wisdom. But we believe — indeed, we know — that God is just. Surely the good boy is in heaven, seated next to Abraham. In your parable I see the abundant mercy of God that surpasses all understanding."

After Saul's reply, Gamaliel leaned back in his chair. This youth could envision a broader concept of justice than could most of his age. "Where in Tarsus did you study?"

"I learned to read at my mother's knee. She was taught by her father and older brother, both rabbis. I attended synagogue school, and then the splendid Greek Academy of Tarsus and simultaneously the Stoa. In all I excelled."

Gamaliel rested his cheek on his hand, the palm covering a smile. "Who is the greater, Achilles or Odysseus?"

Saul scratched his black curls in thought. "To me, *Iliad* is a celebration of man's courage; *Odyssey* an account of man's wits. I learned from both."

Gamaliel studied the applicant standing before him. "What else did you learn from the Greeks?"

"To think. To reason. To question." Saul paused. "And to create."

Gamaliel slowly nodded. "A beginning," he said. "A beginning." Closing his eyes, he brought his fingertips together and rocked back and forth in his chair for what seemed to Saul an unnecessarily long time. At last he spoke, and with formality: "Saul of Tarsus, I hereby admit you to this school — on probation. You may begin in the lowest of the three orders here. Time will reveal your capability. You show promise but have much to learn." With a gentle nod of dismissal, Gamaliel picked up his pen and began to write on the scroll before him.

Saul had more questions, but it was clear that his interview was over. Outside in the corridor a tall, well-formed young man waited to speak to Saul. There was a dignity and grace about this stranger until he opened his mouth to speak; then his face flushed with awkwardness. He tried to say something to Saul, but no word came forth. Saul realized that he stammered.

"I-I am Barnabas of Cyprus," he said at last. "I, too, am a new student on probation. I arrived here four Sabbaths ago, and I have rooms and servants nearby that I will share with you if you wish." Barnabas, standing outside the door listening to the discussion between Rabban Gamaliel and Saul, had concluded that this Tarsian with such a keen and lively mind could help him with his studies and recitations.

Saul contemplated the stranger with his copper-red hair and matching freckles who, even as he stammered, spoke in the Greek of an educated Cypriot. The fine linen chiton and tooled-leather sandals on his unusually large feet suggested that he came of wealth; his broad muscular shoulders could have been those of a discus thrower. Saul liked his ready smile and deferential manner. From the earnest tone in his voice and the entreating look in his eyes Saul inferred that the young man was looking for a friend in this new and strange place.

Saul, too, would need a friend. And he had no other place to go. "Barnabas of Cyprus," he said, drawing himself up and looking the stranger in the eye, "I accept your offer."

VI

SCHOLAR

On a brisk midwinter morning, Saul left the house he shared with Barnabas at daybreak to stride quickly down Herodian Street to school. No longer did he run with youthful joy through the streets; in Jerusalem a naked limb was considered an unseemly public display.

Pushing through the heavy cedar door, Saul strode briskly down the corridor to the students' discussion room. He treasured the quiet of early morning in the classroom; the hour and place were ideal for study. And he felt sure the tutors would note his diligence.

As Saul expected, Rabban Gamaliel was there alone, sitting in his commanding chair of fine Bashan oak, right elbow on his desk, beginning his day by studying the scrolls and meditating. Always, Rabban Gamaliel was there early on the fourth day of the week, the special day when he presided over a full morning of spirited inquiry and debate for all forty-eight students of the school. Taking care to make no noise, Saul moved to his favorite place at the front of the classroom and seated himself on the floor at the feet of the master.

Gamaliel could not have failed to observe the entry of this clever and contentious student, but he did not lift his head or in any way acknowledge Saul. He reminded himself to counsel Saul privately, to suggest that in and out of the classroom he talk less, listen more, and develop a mite of humility.

From the pocket of his rough woolen student's gown, Saul took out his pen case. He had a lesson to write, but for a moment he paused and rubbed his thumb across the polished wood. Touching this childhood gift from his mother always reminded him of her. In his mind he could see her now, strolling out into her sun-filled pavilion like a princess, beautiful, composed, confident, her dark eyes glistening with amusement. It had been two years, three months, and nineteen days since he had left Tarsus; he kept a count in his journal. And more than twenty months had passed since a friend of Uncle Enoch, walking the long trek from Tarsus to celebrate Passover in Jerusalem, had brought Saul a purse of two hundred shekels of gold for his second year in school, and a letter from Abigail.

It was a warm letter, full of her love for him. She confided that sometimes her longing for him prompted her to go alone to his room, to touch his books and laurels, to feel his presence, and to recall their delightful times together. That week she had taken Rachel to the theater and there seen Zagoreos, who had asked about Saul's progress in Jerusalem. The household was unchanged, except that Alida had returned to Cyprus. She said nothing about Phoebe; had there been a scandal, she would surely have said so. She was cryptic about his father and the family business. "Remain in school," she had written in closing. "It is best for all."

Saul had immediately written back, telling her how he longed for her, for the sound of her voice and the warmth of her bosom, yet he recognized her wisdom in sending him to study in Jerusalem. The House of Study was the most formidable challenge he had ever faced, he wrote. Rabban Gamaliel was surely the wisest teacher he had ever experienced: He intuited the capability of each student, required each to do his best, and rewarded merit. After Saul had written a treatise on the rights of the poor in civil suits, Gamaliel had invited him to the Sanhedrin to observe how a court would consider and rule on such a dispute.

In his letter Saul also described his schooldays, how classes began an hour after sunrise, with mornings spent in recitation and dialogue and afternoons reserved for reading, study, and preparation for the next day's discussions. He told her he had his own room in a comfortable house he shared with his classmate and new friend Barnabas. He confessed that he had not visited the Temple as often as he had promised, but would try to do better. It was a lengthy and thoughtful report, and Saul was pleased when he finished it. But he had never dispatched the letter, for the Tarsian pilgrim had disappeared in the Passover crowds in the city. So Saul put his mother's letter and his reply away for safekeeping with his journal.

Sitting on the cold stone floor of the classroom, he tried to focus on the lesson he must prepare, but he was distracted. He missed his mother. He thought of the things he would tell her if she could come to see him in

Jerusalem. She would be proud of his success in school. He had set out to excel and had succeeded: first in his class in his first year, first in his second year. She would expect that; indeed, nothing less would she accept. She would be pleased, and perhaps amused, to see how older students would often gather around when Saul expounded on some casuistic form of the Covenant Code. She, too, had studied the Law, and he could imagine how she would speak with confidence and authority during a spirited debate in the class — if women were permitted in Gamaliel's school.

She would like Barnabas. In an hour she would know all about him — that he was innocent of guile, uncommonly warm, and generous — and she would quickly perceive why this tall and handsome young Cypriot and her son had become like brothers. She would admire Barnabas' determination to realize his childhood dream of becoming a rabbi, and sympathize as he struggled to recite without stammering and master the complexity of the Law and statutes. She would put a reassuring arm around his shoulder and say, "God does not give you more work than your mind and your hand can accomplish." Then she would quietly encourage Saul to continue to tutor his friend.

When Saul and his mother were alone, she might look at him and say, with a frown, that he was too thin and order a feast prepared. She would not be pleased at the frequency with which Saul and Barnabas drank too deeply of wine and sometimes visited a house where prostitutes were known to live. She would not so much rebuke Saul as insist that he meditate on his actions and ask himself whether such debauchery was fitting for a young man of his intellect and other gifts. Yes, reprove she would, but she understood the impulses of youth. She had all the many gifts of woman — insight and wisdom, resolve and infallible judgment — so many that Saul wondered why God at the Creation had subordinated woman to man.

The rustle of sandal and scroll brought Saul back to the present moment and place. His fellow novices of the Gimmel order were seating themselves on the floor near Saul as the Bets, the second order, found their places on four low benches at the front of the room. The eleven members of the first order, the Aleths, stood in the back at the high desks that held their books and writings. Saul picked up his papyrus tablet and quickly finished his lesson for the day. When all forty-eight students were present in the classroom, Gamaliel put away his scroll and set his cap of black silk firmly on his head. All fell silent as Gamaliel methodically surveyed the faces of his students, then called on a pale and constantly worrying Aleth who had raised his right palm to his shoulder to seek recognition.

"Jonathan of Alexandria, what question do you bring before us?" Gamaliel said.

"Rabban, in the village of Gibeon where last week I took alms to the needy, a poor man complained that if he could not drive his cart to the market on the Sabbath, he and his family would starve. What should I have told him?"

"What does the Law say, Jonathan?"

"The Law says we shall keep the Sabbath holy. And through the prophet Isaiah, God said that each of us should refrain from pursuing our own interests on his holy day."

"What do the elders say?" Gamaliel asked.

"They say that anything that would be involved with the building of the Ark must be defined as work. Transporting material by cart qualifies as work. Therefore, the elders say, transporting goods cannot be performed on the Sabbath day."

"Then how will you counsel this poor man?" Gamaliel asked.

"I will tell him that he cannot drive his cart to the market on the Sabbath," Jonathan replied.

"Yet consider his family," Gamaliel said. "Is this poor man's wife healthy? Do they have a sick child? A new baby whose life might be in danger if the mother has no food?"

"I failed to ask those questions, Rabban."

"Inquire diligently," Gamaliel said, "for only if we understand all relevant circumstances can we reflect the wisdom of God and offer wise counsel. The rules of Halakah state that a father or mother may break the Sabbath to save a sick child. The reasoning is thus: On the infant's behalf, a father may desecrate one Sabbath so that the child may live to observe many Sabbaths."

Gamaliel then addressed an Aleth at a back-row desk. "You may speak, Merari of Gaza."

All students, young and older, turned to listen. Merari was no quiet scholar. He was a slight man who made up in voice what he lacked in size. His long face held eyes that pierced like knives; his tawny beard was wild and unkempt. He cultivated the look of a prophet and relished being the firebrand of the school, the leader of the six zealots who openly championed rebellion against the Roman occupation.

"I rise to speak against oppression," Merari said. "Israel is the land that God promised to our fathers. Now it is ruled by Rome. Must this continue? Must we permit these foreigners to trespass on our soil and desecrate our God? As God's people, Rabban, don't we have a responsibility to drive the heathen Romans from this blessed land of God?"

Saul always felt stirred by the vigor of Merari's arguments but had little sympathy for his cause. Saul had no quarrel with Rome. He had been free, growing up as the son of a Roman citizen in one of Rome's great provincial capitals. His father had prospered from Rome's legions. Roman law protected his father's house and business in Tarsus. Comfortable though he was under Roman rule, Saul admired the courage of his senior classmate.

"Since this has come to hand, let us say something about it," Gamaliel said. His voice was calm, deliberate. He looked directly at Merari and said quietly: "I ask you, as a future leader of Jews in this and other lands, what is your first responsibility?"

"To do God's work," Merari replied, raising his fist. "To follow and teach the Law and traditions of our forefathers. But do I not also have a duty as a teacher and leader to free this Promised Land? Shammai teaches: 'No compromise.' I believe that one Roman soldier in this Holy City of Jerusalem is an abomination."

"Is our present plight worse than that of our forefathers in Egypt, or in Babylon?" Gamaliel asked.

Merari started to speak, but Gamaliel raised his hand to silence him. "And did not our forefathers triumph in the end?"

He leaned back in his chair and folded his hands across his chest. "A judgment on the question before us must rest more heavily on fact than on passion. So let us examine our situation. Merari, how many Roman soldiers are in Jerusalem?"

"The Hierosolyma Legion is six thousand," Merari said. "And we Jews number more than ten times as many as they."

"And how many spears and horses and chariots do we have?" Gamaliel asked.

"None, so we must seize the Roman arms," Merari replied. Again he raised his fist; again he struck his desk.

"And if we attempted to seize their arms, how many Jews would die?" Gamaliel asked.

"Many would die, but all in a good cause," Merari said.

"Many, and many more," Gamaliel said, "for we know the skill and cruelty of the Roman soldier. Here in this city, only thirty-two years ago, a minority of Jews publicly protested against Caesar Augustus and refused to pay the Roman tax. Archelaus, then the ethnarch for Rome, brought legions into the streets to put down the rebellion; in retaliation, he then ordered two thousand of our finest to be crucified." The expression on Gamaliel's face was grave, his voice subdued. "Surely we must contemplate that if we struck against this Caesar, vengeance could bring him to kill all Jews — not only here in Israel but throughout the Roman Empire." He opened his arms in appeal. "And if all Jews die in one great battle, who will sanctify the name of God by our teachings and by our good works?"

As Gamaliel paused, another student spoke up: "I challenge the premise of Merari of Gaza! Are we not commanded, 'Thou shalt not kill'?" The speaker was Stephen of Athens, oldest of the Aleths and the outstanding scholar of the school. Ardent in belief and conviction, Stephen had once been imprisoned for coming to the aid of a poor farmer being beaten by Roman soldiers; in prison he had written a masterful treatise on early Jewish leaders.

"A relevant question, Stephen of Athens," Gamaliel said. "The answer is this: In war we may take lives, as we have done throughout our history. The Sixth Commandment that God handed to Moses was intended to deny any man the right to murder his neighbor in sudden anger or for revenge. But Halakah teaches that Jews may kill in war. Or stone to death a man convicted of heresy or certain other crimes, such as the rape of a betrothed maiden. The reasoning is this: A community of God's people may decide that war is necessary, or that an execution is in the common interest. On his own a Jew may not kill, except in one circumstance: to defend himself." Gamaliel paused. "Mark you well, each of you, as you go into the world to lead our people: Every life is precious to God. As God gives life, so he alone may end life."

Gamaliel turned back to Merari. "Who among us is not moved by your fervor? This land is ours, granted by the Covenant with God. With fervor equal to your own we pray that we shall restore the House of David to rule over Israel."

"But when?" Merari asked.

"That is known only to God," Gamaliel replied. "In this time, as in the days of old, we are a people in conflict. We tread a narrow path, through the world that is and the world we hope for, pray for — that free and peaceful land flowing with milk and honey that God promised."

Gamaliel stood and paused to focus attention: "Are we oppressed? Yes. Are we slaves? No. By perseverance we have won from Caesar the right to worship the one true God, not the Roman idols. Within limits we govern ourselves: The Sanhedrin writes and enforces the civil and property laws under which Jews live and prosper. Now, as in the times of Joseph, Moses, and David, we must hold to the faith that God will in his good time restore our kingdom on earth. Meanwhile we must be patient. No empire of arms lasts forever."

He raised his right hand as if in blessing. "To die nobly is an honor," he said, his voice measuring out every word with care. "To live nobly, and to do God's work on earth, is a greater honor. That is why you are here."

After he took his seat again he looked to the benches of the second order and selected the school jester, Obadiah of Antioch. "Rabban, it is true that once in Ptolemais you bathed in a pool before an idol, and if so, how do you reconcile this with the Law?" The senior students laughed, and Gamaliel joined them.

"Yes, I did bathe in the pool of a stream in Ptolemais, and while in the pool someone pointed out to me that downstream and not far away the Greeks had erected an unclothed statue of their river princess Daphne. How did I reconcile this? Well, the pool was there first. The pool does not honor the idol; the idol honors the pool."

Others of the second order sought recognition. One asked for an interpretation of the requirement that Jews afflict the soul at Yom Kippur, another for the reason why a game bird and milk may not be eaten at the same meal, another about the damage due the owner after the death of a borrowed ox.

"Why," asked Gershon of Philadelphia, "can a Hebrew man take two or three wives but a Hebrew woman only one husband?"

"The early sages favored men," Gamaliel replied. "They wrote the rules that still favor men. But customs are changing, although slowly. Until recent times a husband could divorce his wife simply by writing her a note stating place, date, and 'I divorce you, Sapphira.' Now a bill of divorcement can be written and granted only by the court. There are some among the seventy-one members of the Sanhedrin — and I am one among them — who contend that a wife should be given the equal right to divorce a husband. But Caiaphas, our current high priest, has yet to agree to this change."

When all of the first and second orders had spoken, Gamaliel turned to the third-order students sitting on the floor before him. Saul, impatient for his opportunity to speak, immediately lifted his palm for recognition.

"Rabban, we know that in the Torah there are six hundred and thirteen Commandments, three hundred and sixty-five Thou-shall-nots, and two hundred and forty-eight Thou-shalls. I can recite them all, but try as I might, I cannot observe all commandments and shall-nots and shalls every hour of the day. What is my standing with God?"

Gamaliel observed to himself that his bumptious prodigy was showing off again. He was gratified, however, to observe how Saul was changing: In two years his voice had developed timbre and authority; his face had lost the bloom of boyishness, with the new beard emphasizing the lean, strong jaw. "Why, Saul of Tarsus, did God create the world?"

"To bring order out of chaos," Saul replied. "And then to create man and woman in God's image."

"And why did God create Israel?"

"To guide the world along the path of truth and righteousness," Saul replied.

"Why did God give us the Commandments?"

"To know how to carry forward our responsibility to lead the world."

"God gave us the Commandments because he loved us — all of us," Gamaliel said, raising his arms as though embracing his students. "He instructs us so to conduct ourselves that our lives will be not only dutiful, but also joyful to God and to ourselves. Living by the Commandments should bring us joy."

Turning back to Saul, he said: "You have yet to answer your first question. Where do you stand with God?"

Before class, Saul had written out and memorized the answer to his own question. "I believe that God has assigned to me, as he does to all men, a purpose in life. Not yet do I know this purpose. When God reveals to me what I am to do with my life, I will commit mind and body and soul to that mission. Where I stand with God will depend on how well I carry out his purpose for me."

Gamaliel observed his promising pupil with gratification, but made no comment; school custom held that no tutor would compliment or criticize a student before the others. Gesturing for Saul to take his seat, Gamaliel addressed the class: "Surely God does have a mission for each of us, but do not — any of you — stand idle and wait for a heavenly message. Your purpose in life is to be discovered only by searching within, through diligence and perseverance. Search within."

Gamaliel set his cap aside. "The hour you await has come," he said, bringing glad faces to all. Twice yearly Gamaliel dispatched his students into the countryside for a fortnight to go among the people and practice what they had learned in school. For the students it was at once a serious apprenticeship and a welcome respite from the long days and weeks of recitation and study.

"Go now into the villages and listen to poor and rich alike," Gamaliel said. "Hear their joys and sorrows. Comfort them. Share your bread, and your faith."

Saul, gathering up his scrolls, felt a sense of elation. He was sure he had done well before the class. Outside, Barnabas said: "C-come with me to the house of my aunt Mary. Her steward has brought new wine from her vineyard. We will feast and plan our journey." It had turned into a beautiful day, unusually warm for winter, the sunshine pleasant, the air benign.

With the aimless joy of two boys freed from the schoolroom, Saul and Barnabas rambled through the noisy streets of the Old City to the door of the compound of Mary, close by the Zion Gate. Through the archway of cut stone the two entered, and the housekeeper led them through the courtyard and upstairs to the reception chamber where Mary rose from her marble chair to greet Saul and Barnabas.

Often a visitor here, Saul had come to admire this widow with the commanding presence, a stout figure with a massive head and broad cheeks dominated by symmetrical lines of wrinkles radiating from her green eyes and crowned with a halo of curls the color of molten bronze. Barnabas was devoted to his aunt and took pride in telling her story. She was the youngest daughter of Shem of Soli, who mined, refined, and shipped copper on the northern coast of Cyprus. At sixteen Mary had come to love Eliakim of Alexandria, a sharp-eyed dealer in gold, silver, and gemstones. They married, and Eliakim took her to Jerusalem. Six months after the birth of their son, John Mark, Eliakim drowned in a shipwreck, whereupon Mary took over his trade, matching and then exceeding the success of her husband. After she kept Eliakim's promise to supply the gold for the dome of the Temple of Herod, she entered the established order of political power in Jerusalem. She was generous, giving freely to widows and orphans of the city, and fearless. Once, when a ruffian tried to rob her in an alley, she seized his club and beat him senseless. Then she searched the thief, took the money from another purse he had stolen, and scattered it among the poor children of the streets who had gathered to watch the beating.

"Enter my humble house," Mary said to Barnabas and Saul, putting an ample arm around each of the students. Nodding in turn at her two guests, she said, "This is Shebnah, a priest of the Sanhedrin and confidant of Pilate. And this is Tullius, son of Quirinius and envoy from Caesar." To the older men she said, "These are my two boys, my nephew Barnabas, son of my brother Ezra of Cyprus, and his classmate Saul of Tarsus. Rabban Gamaliel tries to teach them the Law; I try to lighten their lives." To Barnabas she added, "We are discussing matters of state, so take you both into the library while we finish our business. John Mark is there. He will rejoice at seeing his favorite cousin."

In the library John Mark put down his pen and rose from his desk to clasp Barnabas in a boyish embrace. "Here," John Mark said, "look at this story of Hezekiah I am writing for school."

Barnabas and Saul leaned over the desk and began reading. Saul thought it impressive writing for a twelve-year-old.

"Cousin," Barnabas said, "it is done well. Now I am sure we have a scribe in the family."

John Mark looked at Saul with expectation.

"Yes, John Mark, a promising beginning," Saul said, affecting the grave mien of a tutor. "After you finish the story in Hebrew, write it in Greek. We think more deeply in Hebrew, but it is in Greek that we write with the greatest precision."

A servant summoned them to the dining room, and after they feasted on roast quail, cucumbers, leeks, leavened bread, and red wine, Mary pushed back her chair and said: "Saul, have you yet come to accept this hard life in Jerusalem, or do you still pine for the aimless hedonism of Tarsus?"

"Tarsus was pleasure; Jerusalem is challenge," Saul replied. "Yes, I came here surly with anger. Now I see more clearly. From Gamaliel I am coming to learn that life is responsibility. I am beginning to look inward."

"What do you see within yourself?" Mary asked.

"That I was more Greek than Jew when first I came to Jerusalem. Now I am more Jew than Greek."

"In what way do you remain Greek?" Mary asked.

"Curiosity about everything that is new — new ideas, new things, a new play," Saul said. "And the necessity to excel, to exceed my classmates in every way."

"Yet you say you are more Jew than Greek," Mary said.

"Here in Jerusalem I have come to have greater reverence for the past. Indeed, at the feet of Rabban Gamaliel I am discovering the depth and dimension of the history of our people. Studying the Torah; contemplating the deeds of Abraham, Isaac, Jacob, Joseph, Moses; reading the Early and Later Prophets; discoursing with Rabban Gamaliel and Zadok and the other masters — all these things have given me a powerful sense of what is to be a Jew. As a boy I lived as a Jew and was schooled as a Jew. As a youth I became Greek. Here, as a man, I have become a Jew again."

Mary looked at Saul for a long time. "The strongest ox is a hybrid," she said. "Fortunate you are to be both Jew and Greek. Preserve within yourself the best of both."

She rose from the table. "Now go I must to see Pilate. Rome would burden us with even more taxes. I will protest. Pilate will affect sympathy but obey Caesar. Stay and do what pleases you. There are books, food, wine — and yes, the baths have been made ready."

Saul stood up quickly. "Before you go, Mary, my curiosity about your meetings impels a question. Is it right that Caesar's procurator governs Jerusalem, or should the Sanhedrin rule?"

Mary lifted her eyebrows in surprise. "I am a practical woman in business," she replied. "I tithe to the Temple. I bribe Caiaphas. I send gold to Tiberius in tribute. I concern myself not with Jerusalem as I might wish it to be, but with things as they are." With a shrug she added: "What else can I do?"

After Mary had gone, Saul and Barnabas walked down the curving stair and through the courtyard to the tiled bathhouse, where they stripped and plunged into the warm water. "I-I am the better swimmer," Barnabas challenged, as the two raced back and forth. After a time they found thick towels and lay facedown in the warmth of the sun. "Barnabas," Saul said, "what better life could we wish for?"

Drowsing in the sun, Saul heard soft footsteps approaching. Turning to look, he saw that Barnabas had disappeared and a Nubian slave girl with fresh linens was entering the dressing room beside the pool. Saul had noticed her on a previous visit to Mary's house; she was young and comely, with skin that glistened like polished ebony.

Saul heard the unmistakable call of desire. Quickly he rose and entered the pool house. The slave girl turned to face him, her eyes wide with wonder. Saul touched her arm, then her face. Her hands trembled, but she said nothing. "Do not be afraid," Saul said quietly. He took her by the hand and led her to a low couch in the room. Still she made no cry, nor did she speak a word. Gently, slowly, Saul put his hand to the clasp of her gown. She closed her eyes and lowered her head. Saul released the clasp, and her gown fell away. He put one arm behind her back, the other behind her trembling knees, and lifted her to the couch.

Some time later the slave girl left and Saul saw that the couch was stained with blood. He closed his eyes and drifted into sleep. How long he slept he would never remember, but the sound of voices and running feet brought him instantly awake.

"Saul! Saul! Arise! Come quickly!" It was Barnabas calling, and another voice he could not recognize at first. When Saul sat up, he saw before him the anxious face of Johanan, clerk to Gamaliel.

"The rabban . . . ," Johanan gasped, ". . . sent me to find you . . . for hours I have searched . . . you are to come at once!"

"What is it?" Saul asked, seizing the clerk roughly by the arm. "What has happened?" He looked at Barnabas, and saw a face long and grave. "I will go with you," Barnabas said.

They began to run.

VII

TURNING

"Saul, your mother is dead." Gamaliel spoke with anguish, but his voice was firm, controlled. "A letter from your uncle Enoch reached me this afternoon. She was poisoned. God have mercy on her, and on you, her son."

Saul looked at the rabban, hearing but not hearing, feeling a great rush of heat to his head, hoping that what was happening was not real, that he was not here in the flesh but in a dream, in a nightmare of terror from which he could by sheer force of will bring himself awake.

"This cannot be," he whispered. He fell to his knees, raised his arms to the heavens, and cried out: "Please, God — I beg you: Do not let this be so!"

Gamaliel knelt beside Saul and put an arm around his shoulders.

Saul bowed his head and racked his body, wailing, "No! No! This cannot be . . ." Suddenly he turned to face Gamaliel. His voice choking, he said: "Let me see the letter. Is this a trick by my father?"

Saul took the folded papyrus, saw the wax seal of his uncle's synagogue, and opened the paper. It was the Aramaic of Enoch's hand; Saul recognized it immediately. The message was brief, and appeared to have been written in haste.

I, Enoch of Tarsus, rabbi in this city by the will of the Lord, to Gamaliel, Rabban of the House of Study in Jerusalem that bears his name: In sorrow I send this message to you for Saul, the one who is my nephew and your aspiring scholar. Abigail, mother of Saul, and my sister, is dead. She was found by a maid lying on her couch in her pavilion two mornings past. From the contortions of her face and body, the physician who was called to her aid judged that she had been poisoned. Her husband, Isaac, comprehends not. Many months ago his wits departed from him, and the fox of a

72

worker whom Isaac trusted has stolen his business and occupied his house. Rachel, sister of Saul, I have taken into my humble home. May the Lord preserve the soul of Abigail. May he attend to Saul in his sorrow. May we in our grief come to accept his mysterious ways. Peace to you, O most respected Rabban, and peace to your House of Study.

Saul stared at the letter, seeing the words dissolve into strange shapes and meaningless symbols. Yet while his eyes blurred, his mind pieced together a scenario: His father had lost his mind. The cunning Malech then contrived to rob Isaac of his shops and properties. When Abigail moved to stop Malech, he had schemed to poison her food.

"I have lost everything," he whispered, and handed the letter back to Gamaliel. He turned to Barnabas. "Take me home. I must be alone."

They walked quickly; neither spoke. As they neared their house, Saul stopped suddenly and raised his fists to the sky, shaking them, and shouting: "What kind of God would let my mother be killed? If this can happen, who is to believe in a just God?"

In his room Saul closed the door quickly and prostrated himself on the floor. He wept. He raged. He shrieked. He tore his robe, ripping away all his clothing until he stood naked. He beat his fists on the walls, then wiped the blood from his hands on his face. He shouted blasphemy: "There is no God. I deny God. I curse the name of God. I curse the God who took my mother from me. My mother, my mother," he cried out as tears streamed from his eyes. "Never again shall I see her face or hear her voice. Never again shall I feel the touch of her hand." He struck his forehead on the stone floor again and again until blood flowed.

He leaped up and pounded his fist against his chest. "Vengeance! I will kill Malech." He curled his fingers like talons. "With these hands I will break his neck. As my mother suffered and died, so will he."

Saul heard but ignored a soft knock at his door. "F-friend Saul," Barnabas said, "is there anything whatever that I can d-do for you?"

Saul shook his head. "It is my fault, Barnabas. All this is because of me. I deserve to be punished for what I have done. I cannot expiate my wrong, but penance I must pay. For three days I shall remain in this room, taking no food — only water to sustain life. After these three days I shall wash my garments and body; once cleansed, I shall make a sacrifice in the Temple to atone for my guilt."

Barnabas hesitated in the doorway. "S-Stephen asked that I journey with him to Capernaum to see and hear a new prophet who is said to perform miracles. I consented, and am to leave at dawn, but I will remain here with you if you so say."

"No. Go your way, Barnabas. Alone, with my wretched self, I must be."

That night as Saul lay prostrate on the stone floor, incidents returned in memory: He was four, and the marble squares of the floor where he was playing began to move. He heard rumbles like thunder, and he could see his mother running into the room, seizing him quickly, clasping him to her bosom and running down the steps to the open courtyard, where maids and cooks huddled in terror as the earthquake shook the cobblestones beneath their feet and nearby buildings collapsed in clouds of dust. "O God, spare my son," his mother had cried. The image was as vivid as if it had happened yesterday.

In his despair Saul was again a small boy, climbing into his mother's lap and asking her to read to him from her book. She was laughing and kissing him and running her fingers through his curls, then holding him close as she told him the story of brave Odysseus sailing over stormy seas, facing danger, surviving hardship and peril, never losing his indomitable spirit. Ever since, he had loved the sea. Another time, he was dressed for his first day at school, saying good-bye to his mother at the gate of the compound, taking the hand of the pedagogue who would walk him to the rabbinical academy in Tarsus, looking back at her standing by the heavy gate, beautiful as the breeze brushed her long hair.

His memories flowed on and on like a swift-running stream. He was standing at her knee as she sat in the sunshine on a marble bench on the porch of her pavilion. He had raced up the stairs to tell her the story of Moses he learned that day at the synagogue. She listened, eyes wide and bright with attention, as though she were hearing the story for the first time.

He was thirteen, home from his first day at the Greek Academy, weeping at his mother's knee because older Greek youths ridiculed him for being small and ugly and a Jew. He could still feel the comforting touch of her hand, the reassurance of her voice: "Not yet do they see your merit, but see it they will."

Twice he drifted toward sleep, and each time he roused himself, piercing his arm to inflict pain so intense that he would stay awake. At dawn he heard Barnabas close his door and depart on his journey. "Faithful Barnabas. Now he will never know my mother." He wept.

As the morning brought light through his window, Saul moved to his writing desk and picked up his pen, but he could not order his thoughts. Finding no word in any language to describe his sorrow, he put his head down on his desk and sobbed.

"It is all my fault. I, and I alone, am to be blamed. Had I followed my father's wishes, Mother would be alive. O that I might go back in time. O that I might change the path I took. How gladly would I give up my life to bring her back."

If only he had worked with his father. He would have been there to see his decline into dementia, and Saul would have taken command of the shops, and made certain they prospered. But he did not. He had refused his father, scorned his profession: He was responsible for the murder of his mother. For as long as he lived, he would carry this burden on his soul.

On the second night of his mourning Saul fell asleep against his will. In a dream he was suspended over a boiling vat in his father's tannery, with his hands slowly slipping on the rope that held him above the vile smells of the tanning oils. He was falling, falling, and wondering if his father, who wasted nothing, would turn his skin into leather and make of it a saddle for a Roman soldier.

On the morning of the third day Saul tried to compose his mind and examine the choices before him. Should he return to Tarsus? He could ask a Roman court to return the property stolen from his father. But Malech had surely contrived to make himself the legal heir under Roman law, and would use his father's money to bribe the magistrate. No, retribution would not come in a courtroom; a just reprisal would be Malech's death. "Life for life, eye for eye." These were God's words to Moses, so a dagger at Malech's throat would be justified.

Saul imagined himself plunging a heavy knife into the heart of his enemy. Yes, if he went back to Tarsus he would kill Malech. But then a Roman magistrate might order him executed. The more he thought, the more he hated

Tarsus. He would never return. No, he would sail away to some distant land and begin a new life.

Through that long day his mind roamed in disorder, confusion, uncertainty. Doubt turned to despair. At his desk he wrote:

> All is lost. My mother, my poor mother. My father lost, too, lost in madness worse than death. All that we owned, lost. I cannot remain here, for I have no money, nothing. School, opportunity, hope — all gone. My life is over.

Again he put his head on his desk and sobbed. After a time he fell asleep, and his pen fell to the floor. At midnight he woke hungry and thirsty, but he vowed to keep his fast and stumbled to his cot. Drifting from consciousness, he heard the clear, musical voice of his mother: "Do not grieve for me, Saul. I am in another place of such beauty as I never knew on earth. Rise, and live your life triumphant. Always I shall be with you; always I shall watch over you." For one fleeting fraction of time, he glimpsed her face, entreating and sad.

Awake, eyes wide with wonder, he lay still, hoping the vision would return. It was not to be, but he did hear her familiar voice, murmuring words that commanded his mind, his heart, his very soul: "Excel . . . stand first . . . make your mark . . . serve Israel . . . the blood of kings is in your veins . . . persevere . . . triumph . . . use your gifts . . . God means for you to lead . . ."

When Saul woke again he looked from his window for the first time in three days. The world had not changed. Curls of smoke rose from cooking fires. A peddler rearranged his clay lamps and vials of oil. An old woman struggled with her water jar. Life moved along as before, unaware of his sorrow. But he had changed: In his innermost being, he would never be the same.

He opened his door, but no servant was to be seen in the common room. On the table he saw that the cook had left bread, cheese, dates, and a pitcher of goat's milk. The sight of food made him ravenous, and he ate and drank — and pondered.

He had no mother, no father, no money — not a shekel. But his mother would counsel: Do not cower in defeat. Advance. Persevere. Never surrender, not to ill fortune, not to any enemy.

Suddenly he rose from the table and said in a loud voice, "I will go this hour to Rabban Gamaliel. He is the one person in the world I can trust now, and he will counsel me." Saul immersed himself in a bath to purify his body, put on fresh clothing, and set out for the House of Study.

"I have been hoping you would come, Saul," Gamaliel said. Once they were seated in the small room cluttered with books and scrolls, Gamaliel looked intently at Saul's face, studying the gaunt cheeks, the reddened eyes, the wound on his forehead, the trembling hands. "I mourn with you," he said quietly. "Tragedy is common to the old; to the young it strikes a heavier blow."

"Rabban, how came this letter from my uncle?" Saul asked.

"A legionnaire brought it," Gamaliel replied. "He said the Roman commander in Tarsus had ordered that it be included in the pouch of orders dispatched by military post to Fort Antonia."

"The messenger's journey by land would take at least four weeks," Saul said slowly.

Gamaliel nodded, and waited.

"I ask your counsel, Rabban. Should I return to Tarsus?"

"To what purpose?" Gamaliel asked.

"To avenge my mother's death, and to recover the wealth stolen from my father," Saul said.

"Would vengeance bring your mother back to life?" Gamaliel asked quietly. "Would wealth replace your loss?"

"It is unjust that this vile Malech, who poisoned my mother and robbed my father, should go unpunished."

Gamaliel saw the hatred in the young man's eyes and leaned forward. "You would repay evil with evil?" Gamaliel shook his head. "Saul, it is not man, but God, who must punish such sin."

Saul drew away. "Yet God commanded Moses, 'Life for life, eye for eye, tooth for tooth . . .' Under the Law, I can take the life of this murderer."

"Again I must ask, Saul: To what purpose?"

"It is my nature to act," Saul said, raising his fist. "To fight back. To right this wrong."

"Is it right for one man to take justice into his hands? As God spoke to Moses, so also did he speak long after to Isaiah and promise that he will punish the sinner and recompense the victim."

Saul shook his head. "Wait for God's retribution? No. No!" Tears of anger flooded his eyes. "I must confess this, Rabban: In my sorrow I doubted God. Indeed, in my rage and grief I cursed God. Even now, I cannot understand how God could permit this man of evil to take the life of so noble a being as my mother."

"Nor do I understand," Gamaliel said. "Yet surely my inability to see God's purpose should in no way affect my belief in God."

"How can I believe in anything with such torment in my soul?" Saul asked. "Yesterday I thought to lose myself in another country — Egypt, Cyrenaica, Spain. Or I thought I should become a sailor and forever wander the Great Sea —"

Gamaliel interrupted: "The very notion is folly. Surely we have learned that we cannot run away from ourselves."

Saul nodded and began to weep.

"God does not give us a greater burden than we can bear," Gamaliel said quietly.

"Her death is my fault," Saul sobbed. "O Rabban, if only time could heal my sorrow."

"It is not time that heals, but occupation, purpose, and resolution."

Saul looked up. "I had found my purpose in life, Rabban: To become a scholar in the Law. It was my mother's dream. And here in your House of Study it became my dream. But I can no longer remain here, for now I have no money. For months I have borrowed from Barnabas."

Gamaliel shrugged. "Barnabas, like his aunt, is generous."

"I expected to repay him when I received a purse from my mother for my third year," Saul said. "But no money arrived. Now none will."

"Saul, your friendship means more to Barnabas than gold." Gamaliel leaned on his arm and looked at Saul. "Surely you know that most here in this school are poor; they work and study."

"But I have no skill, Rabban."

Gamaliel replied: "God made gifts of mind and voice and energy to you. Use them."

"How? How?"

"The resolute find a way," Gamaliel said.

After a long silence the rabban continued: "Saul, coincident with your tragedy has come an opportunity — if you are prepared to accept certain conditions and rise to a challenge." He paused. "Two days ago the seventy-one members of the Sanhedrin elected Zadok to be a scribe of the court, and he proposes to make you his apprentice and clerk."

"Zadok! Work with Zadok?" Saul's eyes widened in surprise. In Gamaliel's school Zadok was recognized as a teacher of coruscating brilliance; yet he provoked fear in everyone as well. As a taskmaster he was irascible, demanding, never satisfied. Behind his back students called him the Ugly; his entire face was pocked from a childhood fever. Tall, commanding in presence and voice, Zadok was a Levite, the direct descendant of a dynasty of high priests, and ambitious. A frequent, if unofficial, adviser to Caiaphas the high priest, Zadok would now hold power in his own hands. And he wanted Saul to serve him.

For once Saul was mute. The twelve scribes of the Sanhedrin ranked just below Caiaphas and his two chief priests, and well ahead of the fifty-six elders. While the three priests determined religious policy, it was common knowledge that in day-to-day affairs it was the twelve scribes who governed Israel — and Zadok would surely contrive to become first among them.

As the dimension of this unexpected opportunity began to unfold, Saul said slowly, "A great honor this is, Rabban, but you said there are conditions."

"First, Zadok requires that you put no other work or study or activity before his. Day and night he drives himself, and so would he drive you. Second, all apprentices must live in the dormitorium, under the strict supervision of the chief clerk of the Sanhedrin. Third, you would be paid one shekel each week."

Gamaliel leaned back in his chair and raised a hand in warning. "There is another and fourth condition, Saul. You must cease your visits to the flesh-pots of this city. You know that fornication is sinful. We have been concerned over your behavior as a student. For one who serves a court scribe, such conduct would be unacceptable."

Saul looked at the floor, embarrassed that the rabban, and presumably others, knew about his vices. "Rabban, I confess to being tempted by pleasures of the flesh. Are you saying that I must take an oath to celibacy, like an Essene?"

"No," Gamaliel said. "The teachings recognize the nature and power of sexual desire. Indeed, they bind every Jewish man to take a wife. Halakah says, 'He who has no wife cannot be called a man.' What is required, before marriage, is that man and woman control their impulses and keep themselves chaste. It is known, Saul, that you do neither. And this is unworthy of you."

Saul could not bring himself to look his master in the eye. "I know I have sinned," he said.

"Saul, overcome your weakness. Make this tragedy a turning point in your life."

For a long time Saul sat in silence. Giving up sensual pleasure was not to be decided in an instant. The soft and yielding flesh of a woman created an excitement like no other. But he had felt debased after every encounter with a prostitute, and the impulsive deflowering of Aunt Mary's comely slave could never be separated from the swift-following shock of learning his mother was dead.

He stood, as Gamaliel said, at a turning point. He was in need, poor, orphaned, a circumstance he had never before known or even contemplated. Yet out of the bleakest of prospects had come the chance to play a part in the court of authority over all the Jewish people. Gamaliel was right: He must choose. At last he said, in a firm voice: "I have the power within me to change my ways, Rabban."

"I know that," Gamaliel said. "Now consider this challenge before you. Here in this school you have merely studied the Law. As a clerk of the court you will see how the Law is applied, made real; you will observe how it affects a man's life. In time, Saul, you may come to affect how justice is done."

"I accept the conditions, Rabban. And grateful I am to you and to Master Zadok. Here and now I make this covenant: to serve in this responsibility, to serve Zadok, to serve the Sanhedrin. I will faithfully serve the Law."

Gamaliel rose, and the two men clasped hands to affirm their agreement.

On his way home Saul walked with tingling excitement. He felt that he had been brought back to life. To be appointed a clerk for one of the three courts of the Sanhedrin — that was the prize most sought by students of all nine rabbinical schools in Jerusalem. He would have standing, responsibility, a future almost guaranteed. He would be in the place of the greatest power and authority. School, life, both would go forward. Faster and faster he walked. Perhaps Barnabas had returned from his journey; Saul could not wait to share his good news.

As Saul opened the door, he started to speak, but Barnabas interrupted. "I have seen a new prophet!" he exclaimed, his dark eyes bright with enthusiasm. "I have heard this man called Jesus. I saw him touch the eyes of a blind man and make him see. I witnessed this miracle. Truly, Saul, this Jesus is a messenger from God."

Saul laughed. "Have you gone mad?"

"No, Saul, I have seen a great truth." He paused, speaking slowly, measuring his words with care. "I say to you, Saul, that this Jesus is a prophet. He walks in light and speaks with authority. I am a witness. I know what I have seen. Stephen and I journeyed to Galilee and there by the waters we found Jesus teaching. We listened. We followed him into a synagogue, where the rabbis sought to ridicule him. Jesus answered in parables that confounded even the priests — yet the people understood. He is of David's line, as the prophet Samuel foretold the Messiah would be. Saul, I believe this Jesus *is* the Messiah."

"The Messiah?" Saul did not hide his scorn. "Barnabas, do not be a fool. This sorcerer has beguiled you. Your Jesus is no more than a rustic pretender. He cannot be the Messiah. Our traditions and teachings foretell that the Messiah will be a man of arms, a warrior of might and power who will defeat our enemies in battle. He will be a king greater than David, and he will rule over this Promised Land and the nation of Israel."

"Yes, so the ancients have predicted," Barnabas replied. "Yet I say to you that this man Jesus is a leader not of arms but of the spirit. He is a teacher such as I have never experienced — not in the House of Gamaliel, nor in the Great Temple of Herod, nor in the scrolls we study. Jesus needs no book or scroll for teaching. When he stands to speak, all fall silent. His voice is quiet, but it penetrates. His words seem to linger in the air and embed themselves in memory. He does not harry or accuse or point a finger at sinners. After I saw him heal a diseased woman, I heard him say to her, 'Daughter, your faith has made you well.' Saul, this Jesus says it is faith in God, and not Moses' Covenant with God, that brings salvation."

"I will hear no more of this," Saul said curtly. In his innocent attraction to an itinerant mystic, Barnabas was stepping close to blasphemy. "You are a Levite, Barnabas, born to the priesthood. For a Levite priest to question the Covenant and the Law is heresy. Surely you know this."

"Saul, you are my brother, my beloved brother, and far more brilliant a scholar than I. But you must hear what I say: In the rustic hills of Galilee that you disdain I have seen and heard a new prophet greater than Elijah and Jeremiah."

Saul shook his head. "Barnabas, throughout our history our tribes have been plagued with false Messiahs. So also in these times, when strange sects sprout like weeds. Healers, shouters — they suddenly appear by the road-side, live for a season, and disappear. The north country around Galilee is a particularly fertile seedbed for schisms. Each is false to the Law of Moses. So also with your Jesus."

"Hear me, Saul. Well does my Jesus — and I am proud to call him my Jesus — well does he know the text of the Law, far better than I, far better even than you. He has come, he says, not to abolish the Law and the Prophets, but to fulfill them. It is his message that the Kingdom of God is at hand."

"What does that mean?" Saul asked. "What does he say, Barnabas, that affects you and me as good Jews, and our duty to learn and teach the Law?"

"Jesus says it is more important to follow God than the Law."

Saul lifted his hands in exasperation. "How can there be a difference? God gave Moses the Law and the Law is God's will."

Saul's face reddened with anger. He had been cheated. Barnabas' mindless enthusiasm for a rustic imposter had afforded no opportunity to recount the exciting transformation of his own life. "Barnabas," he said as he closed his door, "to preserve our friendship, let us not speak of this Jesus again."

The next morning Saul rose before dawn, eager to have his first meeting with Zadok. He dressed quickly and was ready to walk out the door when he turned back to his desk. In haste he wrote, "Today I begin as clerk to Zadok in the Sanhedrin. Consequently, I am required to live in the *dormitorium*." He considered, but dismissed, any mention of his debt to Barnabas. He could not pay it now, perhaps not ever, so he would say nothing about it. "I will return for my belongings," he scribbled quickly, folded the note, and put it on the table in the common room.

Closing the front gate, he was surprised to be met by Johanan, out of breath and anxiously wringing his hands. "Counselor Zadok sent me. He awaits you at the Sanhedrin. He looked for you in the dormitorium, and threatened to flog me because you were not there."

Saul ran so fast that he was breathing hard when he reached the Sanhedrin, a hewn-stone building a mile to the north on a hillside west and immediately outside the Temple Wall. As he rushed in, Zadok stood waiting impatiently in an anteroom.

With a brusque gesture, Zadok handed Saul a sheet of papyrus. "Find the law on this issue. It is a dispute between two cousins over land in Jericho. I am to present the case to a court at noon."

In two hours Saul returned from the Sanhedrin library with his written reply. "Is this your best?" Zadok asked.

"Yes," Saul said firmly. "It is a precise summary of the written and oral laws and precedents. In this case, where the older cousin has tilled the land for three years, the burden is on the claimant — a younger cousin who lives elsewhere, in Bethany. Thus the claim of the absent cousin is inferior to that of the cousin who is present and possesses."

Zadok read the document, in an instant it seemed to Saul. He handed it back. "You did not cite the minor commentaries. Do so. Leave no detail open for any member of the court to question or criticize. Act quickly. When I appear at court, you will sit behind me in the place reserved for my clerk."

At noon Zadok placed a scarlet vesture over his linen robe, girdled it with an embroidered belt, and motioned for Saul to follow him. When they walked into the high-domed assembly room of the Sanhedrin, Saul looked about, taking care to suppress his feelings of excitement and expectation. Along the north wall three tiers of platforms, each smaller than the one below, were arranged so that from their benches the seventy-one members of the full court looked down on the square black stone where the witness stood. In the center of the highest platform was the chair of the high priest, unoccupied for this minor case. A bailiff struck his staff on the marble floor and led the members, all vested in scarlet, to their places.

Saul was pleased that Zadok presented the facts much as he had written them, but surprised as deliberations began. The less a member knew about the precedents, the longer and the more pompously he talked. The entire proceeding seemed more somber than the importance of the case or the facts in dispute. For two hours the seven judges of the property court debated esoteric points of claim and counterclaim, and finally ruled that the possessor of the land was the rightful owner.

With the dispute resolved, Saul followed Zadok back into his cluttered workroom. Zadok closed the door.

"What did you see and learn today?" he asked.

"Endless discussion of trivia and irrelevancies," Saul replied. "A Roman magistrate in Tarsus would have settled this dispute in five minutes."

Zadok stared at his new pupil.

"Gamaliel was right; you have no bridle on your tongue." He paused, continuing to stare at Saul. "Very well. I can profit by that." He leaned on his elbow and stroked his chin.

"Yes, the priests and elders of the Sanhedrin dwell as long on the unimportant as on the important. And many a decision turns not on fact, or precedent, but on a well-spoken sophistry. Yet this court, inept though it sometimes is, stands as the guardian of the Law. It is we in this highest of councils who are responsible to keep the statutes that God handed down to Moses in the Sinai thirteen hundred years ago. The seventy-one members of this Sanhedrin are the direct heirs to Moses, the patriarchs, the Prophets; we, and no others. It is we who preserve not only the Law but all the traditions and customs of all the Hebrew peoples; in this we are the supreme earthly authority. We govern Jews whoever they are and wherever they live. We are the chosen few to lead God's chosen people. We rule."

Zadok leaned back in his chair and fixed his cold black eyes on Saul. "Now, why have I brought you here? Because I believe you will be useful to me. Make no mistake about that."

Saul waited in silence.

"Before I say more," Zadok continued, "I require that you pledge to keep secret what I reveal to you."

"I do so pledge, Master Zadok."

"It is known to few that I was appointed to this court for a certain purpose. There are some among the members of this Sanhedrin who would soften the statutes. These members were weak. They would bend to the passing winds of change. Last year, as counsel to the court, I sought Caiaphas in his private chambers to warn him of this dangerous drift. He feared any strong move — it is his nature — and bade me to talk to Annas, his father-in-law. Even though Annas was deposed as high priest by that Roman puppet Valerius Gratus, by wile and ruse he continues to wield great power in this court. Over time I persuaded Annas that we must stiffen the spine of the Sanhedrin. Consequently, he directed Caiaphas to appoint me a senior scribe to the court, and to grant me the authority to reaffirm and restore the Pentateuchal laws. That is my mission."

Zadok paused and rocked back in his chair. "The court clerks offered to me are competent, but insufficiently engaged. I concluded it was necessary that I bring in my own apprentice clerk and train him to my ways. So I told Rabban Gamaliel that for the task ahead I wanted a young man with a quick head, loyal heart, and tireless nature. He placed your name first. You do know the Law; that I have seen in the classroom. Two questions remain." He stopped to look Saul in the eye. "First, can you measure up to this responsibility to be my clerk at court? From what I have seen and learned from Gamaliel, I believe the answer is yes. Second, do you wish to join me in this cause? Consider carefully before you answer. You will labor from dawn to midnight. You can have no other life. You will be enslaved to this mission to uphold and enforce the Law. My mission must become your mission."

"What of my classes at the House of Study?" Saul asked.

"You will be assigned to me," Zadok said. "You will have no time to attend classes. But you will discover that here at this court you will learn more in a day than you would learn in a month in the classroom."

Certainly that had been true for Saul on his first day. He had been intrigued by Zadok's deft performance. As the junior member of the court, he had presented with brevity and clarity the facts of the case, then sat back to let the graybeards talk, debate, ponder, preen their knowledge, or try to conceal their ignorance. When all had spoken, and at length, Zadok moved in with a final summary, deferentially citing a comment from each of his fellow members, and fashioned the ruling in words to which all could agree. He had demonstrated to Saul how a formidable mind and skill in rhetoric had accomplished an end. In a flash of comprehension, Saul saw Zadok as a rising star, a power in the court; and power in the Sanhedrin was power over the nation and all the tribes and people of Israel. Saul did not doubt that he would learn more from observing Zadok, and working with him as a junior partner, than he would in Gamaliel's House of Study.

A door had opened into a dominion of authority and power. Destiny beckoned. He could step inside that open door and join a political force on the ascent. Ambition, the lure of power, stirred within his soul. God was opening the path that could lead to his becoming a leader of the tribes of Israel; that had been his dead mother's dream.

"I will join your cause," Saul said.

Zadok reached out his right hand to seal the bargain. Eye met eye, and Zadok said, "We will go far together."

With a brisk nod Zadok turned to his desk to collect a stack of documents and scrolls. As he handed them to Saul, a stranger entered.

"You sent for me, sir." He spoke with officiousness, and the word of respect did not conceal a measure of disdain as he folded his arms and looked down his nose at the two younger men. He was corpulent, wide and thick, and dressed in a fine robe of Egyptian cotton filigreed with gold thread. "Is this the new clerk you intend to bring in?" the official continued, wrinkling his nose in distaste.

"It is," Zadok said curtly. "Saul, this is Hirudin, chief steward to the high priest. He oversees all clerks of the court. He will show you where you are to live. Take with you these three cases. The first concerns usury. Bring it here to me tonight, within the hour. The second involves two brothers disputing over whether one can free the slave they own together. The third is the appearance but not the proof of adultery. Meet me here at dawn with the second and third summaries."

As they walked through the corridor the chief steward looked at Saul and drew away. "It was reported to me that you appeared in court in a school garment. Such does not befit a clerk of the Sanhedrin." He shook his head and his jowls waggled. "The tailor will come to make you presentable in court."

"I have linen clothes in the house where I live," Saul replied. "I will go for them as soon as I have time."

"Fetching and erranding is for lackeys," Hirudin said. "I will send a servant for your belongings."

VIII

APPRENTICE

Eyes closed, listening to the rain beating against his window, Saul lay under the warm blankets one cold morning of late winter. For the first time in ten weeks he had a moment to reflect, and a full morning to himself. On the evening before, after Saul had turned in his cases, Zadok had mentioned — too casually, Saul thought — that court was suspended the next day for a closed meeting of Caiaphas' privy council of seven.

Stretching his arms and locking his fingers behind his head, Saul thought of how well everything had gone since he had come to the court. He had worked on disputes over water rights, land boundaries, fraud, usury, divorce, inheritances, the rights of a laborer, the ritual in a synagogue — so many cases that he had lost count. At first he had been studiously impartial in his mind and in his summaries, but he had quickly turned to forming an opinion, taking sides. Zadok responded affirmatively, sometimes by agreeing, more often by taking the same facts and transforming them into a line of reasoning that demolished Saul's point of view. At times Zadok would then turn back verbally and present Saul's position with better arguments than Saul had originated in his summary.

Every day was a challenge, an adventure that stirred Saul's competitive spirit. A young widow had come in to see him one day to ask that she be permitted to marry the younger brother of her dead husband rather than the oldest. Despite the precedents, Saul found a clause of compassion that enabled Zadok to win her case.

One day Saul was summoned by Jonathan, the high priest second only to Caiaphas. Jonathan's wealthy sister wanted to evade the Roman *fiscus iudaicus*, the "Jews' tax," on her prosperous valley farm in Gaza. Since all Jews considered Caesar's taxes nothing less than robbery at the point of a spear, the court unofficially sanctioned false oaths made to any Roman tax collector. Saul contrived for the sister an ambivalent declaration that so confused the collector, he granted the exemption.

Of all the trials in which Saul had taken part, the most exciting concerned an entire village. It was an idolatry case, and it required a decision by all seventy members of the Sanhedrin with High Priest Caiaphas presiding. The court brought to the witness stand a landowner in Lehi who repeatedly refused to take down a carved stone idol representing Abraham. After hearing the evidence that Zadok presented, the court unanimously condemned the people of the village as well as the landowner for idolatry. Saul was ordered to accompany Zadok and the Temple guards, who marched to Lehi, shattered the stone idol into rubble, burned all the houses, and salted the fields.

Zadok was not only a demanding taskmaster but an assiduous teacher as well. He took time to explain to Saul how he manipulated the court by playing to the egos of the priests as they contended for political power and by exploiting the weaknesses of the other scribes and elders. "Find a specific case you can win to establish the broader principle of law," Zadok said to Saul one day. "No issue is trivial if victory reveals your strength." After Zadok resolved a contentious dispute between the brother of a priest and a money lender, he reviewed the settlement with Saul and confided, "Take on the assignments others shun. You will be respected for your boldness, and a bold man is soon feared."

Saul was intrigued by how Zadok organized the Pharisees, the majority party in the Sanhedrin, and then provoked the more conservative Sadducees to create controversy on shades of belief and petty rules of conduct that enabled the majority to assert its strength in council meetings and thereby sustain itself in the majority. Serving as clerk to Zadok brought Saul his first understanding of how easily a few can acquire and hold authority over the many. He had begun as Zadok's pupil; after just a few weeks Saul began to look up to him as patron and leader. At times he found himself wishing Zadok were his father.

With the promise of a free morning, Saul elected to attend school again. It was the fourth day of the week, the day of Rabban Gamaliel's seminar, and Saul felt a welling up of excitement as he thought about listening again to the wise aphorisms of Gamaliel and seeing his friend Barnabas. He missed both. So he swept aside the blankets and stood for a moment on the warm stone floor. This was just one of the luxuries Saul enjoyed in his new residence, for the builders of the Sanhedrin court and dormitorium had — with the help of Roman engineers — constructed channels for heated water beneath the floors. Drawing in the warmth, Saul summoned a servant to bring him his favorite breakfast, emmer bread with butter of goat's milk, and pomegranates. His hunger satisfied, he pondered whether to appear at school as court clerk or student. Impulse made the choice: He would wear his new badge of office, a white cotton robe the Sanhedrin tailor had fashioned for him. Over it he put on his new woolen cloak, white with scarlet bands on the long sleeves.

The rain had stopped, and a gusty wind cleared the skies. On his way down the hill and along Herodian Street, Saul was pleased to see that shopkeepers, upon observing his attire, moved aside and bowed their heads as he approached. At the moment he entered the classroom, Rabban Gamaliel was putting on his cap of black silk to signal the beginning of discussion. Saul slipped quietly toward the back of the room and looked for a first-order desk where he could stand in his proper place; all were taken. Feeling slighted, he found a space by the wall, away from the others, and listened.

"Micah of Beersheba," Gamaliel said, "what question do you bring to this assembly?"

"A man and woman in a village of southern Judea agreed to betrothal, and subsequently, before the requisite ten witnesses, they did carry out their contract of marriage. One was a Jew, the other a gentile. Is their marriage legal?"

"Halakah does not recognize as marriage any joining of Jew and pagan," Gamaliel said.

"Then is any child born of such a union a bastard?" Micah asked.

"By our laws, the child is illegitimate."

"Is the child a Jew?" Micah said.

"The precedents tell us that if the mother in a mixed marriage is a Jew, the child is a Jew. But not if the father is the Jew." Gamaliel paused. "Can you tell us the reasoning for this, Micah?"

Micah tilted his head and scratched his forehead. "Could it be that, from suckling infant until puberty, every child is more often with the mother than the father? Therefore, it is the mother who is chiefly responsible to impart to the child the traditions and beliefs of Judaism?"

"The nature of the family is as you say," Gamaliel said. "Long ago, moreover, the patriarchs decreed that as the mother brings the child into the world, it shall be the mother who determines the religion of the child."

Gamaliel next recognized Stephen of Athens. "In the desert of Arabia, two men travel. One stumbles. The fall splits his waterskin and his water disappears into the sand. The other man has enough water for himself, but not enough to keep both alive until they reach a well. Is it the responsibility of the man with the water to share what he has?"

"The sages of old debated the very hypothesis you present," Gamaliel said. "They would not decide — could not decide — until they knew more about these two men."

"Let us suppose, then," Stephen replied, "that one is a weaver, and the other a scholar."

"Which has water?" Gamaliel asked.

"The weaver," Stephen replied, "but why does it make a difference?"

"As men are different, so are their responsibilities different," Gamaliel said. "The weaver may keep his water and survive. The reasoning is that for the common man, the first obligation is to preserve his own life. However, the sages concluded that if it is the scholar who possesses the water, he must share it with his companion, even though he knows that by his act, both will die."

"Is that a wise conclusion?" Stephen asked. "Surely the man of learning is of more value to the world than an ordinary weaver."

"The issue is not one of value, but of nobility," Gamaliel said. "The scholar is measured even more by his deeds than by his intellect. The highest of the forty-eight qualities that a scholar should possess is compassion. Thus it would be contemptible for a scholar to deny to a fellow man the water that sustains life, even for an hour, whatever the consequences to himself."

For hours the students of the first order, one after another, posed their questions. To Saul it was interesting but pedantic, far removed from actual events. At last it was time for the third order, and Saul was delighted when Rabban Gamaliel recognized Barnabas.

"To plow his field," Barnabas began, "a poor man of Bethlehem borrows an ox from a rich man with many herds. As he is returning the ox, it steps into a hole and breaks a leg. The judge for the village decrees that the poor man must pay the rich man for the ox. Is it just that the poor must give to the rich?"

"If laws are to be just, must they not bind all men equally?" Gamaliel asked.

"That I do understand," Barnabas replied. "And I know that Torah enjoins all judges, 'Thou shalt not favor the cause of a poor man.' Yet it does not seem fair that this poor man must take bread from his children to give to someone whose table groans with abundance."

"The law must not be perverted for rich or poor," Gamaliel said. "Yet the hand of mercy can balance the scales of justice. For the circumstance that you present, Barnabas of Cyprus, the fathers decreed that yes, the poor man must pay the damage to the rich man's property. Then, on his own, the rich man gives the money back to the poor man. The court, it must be said, does not require this recompense; it simply offers the opportunity for the rich man to rise above the letter of the Law and demonstrate his generosity."

"Thus charity can overcome the Law," Barnabas said.

"Indeed yes," Gamaliel said. "Remember the admonition that Hillel spoke some thirty years ago: 'Do not unto thy fellow men what is hateful to thee. This is the whole law; the rest is commentary.'"

Saul brought his hands together with ill-concealed delight. Barnabas had spoken well; not once, Saul realized, had his friend stuttered.

When the seminar ended at noon, Saul made his way to the front to greet Gamaliel. "Rabban, you should teach the Sanhedrin. There are members there who would benefit from your wisdom."

Taken aback by Saul's presumptuous criticism of the high court, Gamaliel frowned, then spoke bluntly: "The seventy-one members of the Sanhedrin reflect the Hebrew people — some sagacious, others foolhardy; some generous, others greedy. You, Saul, are there to employ your talents toward making the Sanhedrin a more just council." And with a glance at the younger man's flowing white robes Gamaliel added, "Take care that pride and position do not overcome your better judgment."

In the corridor outside Barnabas waited, and the two friends seized each other by the shoulders with warmth and affection. "Our house is empty without you," Barnabas said. "But every day I rejoice for your good fortune. Tell me of your life at court."

"Never have I worked so hard," Saul said, shaking his head. "Zadok is ambitious, tireless, and resolute. It is his goal to rise above lesser members and in time be chosen high priest. He deserves to be in command, for he embodies authority, discipline, clear direction — the qualities of a strong leader. I shall rise with him. Indeed, I benefit now. Except for the ambition that drives his soul, and in turn mine, never would I have come to understand the Law as now I do. I learn, good Barnabas. Every day, every hour, I learn. I relish the challenge. The demands are heavy, yes; yet the work has given me a sense of purpose — and brought me solace. I have no time to brood or mourn the loss of my mother."

Saul paused. "But tell me of yourself, my brother Barnabas. You spoke well today. Your question was one of the best."

"I improve at recitation but I still struggle with logic and reasoning," Barnabas replied. "Stephen has been helping me since you left." Barnabas grasped Saul's arms with fervor. "But you, Saul, you were better at explaining. You were the better teacher."

For a moment Saul was silent, then he frowned and said gravely, "Barnabas, not one of the first order welcomed me this morning, or offered me a place at a desk."

Barnabas hesitated before he spoke. "Surely you know there is great envy among them, brother Saul. You won the prize that all coveted."

"Did I not earn my place at court?"

"I know you earned your position, Saul. I know that you attained it by merit. But others are jealous, and some even say that you bought your position."

"Bought it?" Saul shook his head. "How could I? I have nothing." He waved his hands helplessly. "I owe you money I cannot pay."

"You owe me nothing," Barnabas said. "I was long since repaid by your friendship, encouragement, and mentoring. For these things I shall always remain indebted to you."

Saul did not reply. So it was envy that accounted for the enmity of his former classmates. Well, what did it matter? Except for Barnabas, he had no friend in school. If his elevation to responsibility at the Sanhedrin provoked jealousy, there was nothing he could do to diminish it. So be it. Merit had no need of friends. He had position. He had prestige. He had power.

"Barnabas, I must return to court. Will you come to visit me?"

"You must arrange it, Saul. You know a student cannot enter the court on his own."

"Arrange your visit I shall. That I promise." Taking Barnabas' right hand in his own, Saul said: "Farewell, good brother Barnabas. I shall not forget our happy days together."

"Nor will I," Barnabas replied. "My aunt Mary greets you and wishes you well in your new eminence."

Saul turned to walk up the hill toward the Sanhedrin. Listening in the classroom, he had realized he had already mastered more of the Law than he would ever learn in school. His four-hour visit had opened his eyes. Saul had never before realized that his former classmates were puerile, detached, irrelevant. He was glad he had gone to the school that day, but he would not go back again. He had expected that his fellow students would be proud of a colleague's attainments, would commend his success; instead they had turned their backs. The House of Study had been a useful chapter in life, but the page had turned. Rabban Gamaliel seemed as wise as ever, but passive, detached from the world, indolent compared with the energy and audacity of Zadok. Furthermore, Gamaliel, his beloved counselor, had criticized him, sharply, and it hurt.

Saul lifted his chin high. In his mind he knew he had reached another turning point. He had passed through the preparatory exercises of academia and embarked on a course in the real world. At school the statutes were the subjects of discussion, with endless variations and permutations, and answers rarely reached. In court there was an answer, a decision, and by that decision the court took from one man and gave to another. By giving and taking the court demonstrated its authority and carried out its power over the people of Israel. Zadok was right: The Sanhedrin ruled. Saul's knowledge of the Law would be his path to power.

"Sir! Sir!" Saul's thoughts were interrupted by a Sanhedrin messenger running toward him. "Zadok seeks you. Immediately!"

Saul gathered up the skirt of his new robes and hurried up the hill.

Zadok paced the floor of his working chamber, head down, hands clasped behind him, face pale. As soon as Saul entered, Zadok closed and latched the door, brought two chairs close together, and lowered his voice.

"You are to speak of this matter to no person but me." His eyes were as blazes of fire; his words, dark and foreboding. "Caiaphas informed me today that in the north country a mysterious heretic is making seditious speeches against the high priests of this Sanhedrin." He paused. "There is danger, Saul, great danger."

Saul lifted his eyebrows in surprise. Never before had Zadok been so secretive or so intense about any case.

"This is the dilemma," Zadok continued. "Some months ago, in villages near the Sea of Galilee, a self-appointed 'prophet' appeared out of nowhere to challenge, openly, the teachings and practices of our well-schooled rabbis. At first our rabbis ignored him, or scoffed at him as one possessed by demons. That was a mistake. For they came to realize that this stranger not only brought an appealing message but also exhibited undeniable qualities of charisma. His words and his manner began to attract followers, and soon more followers. So Caiaphas dispatched agents to watch and listen."

Zadok turned to his desk and held up a sheaf of documents.

"The reports of our agents reveal that his offenses are many, and deliberate. He eats with sinners and gentiles, openly. He breaks the Sabbath. One account here tells how his little band of attendants — he calls them 'disciples' — were seen gathering wheat on the Sabbath. When one of our rabbis admonished him, he replied that the poor and hungry are not bound by priestly rules.

"The most surprising reports here are that he appears to work miracles, and his skill at thaumaturgy accounts for much of his appeal. He waves a hand before these gullible Galileans and affects to cure a paralytic, a leper, an epileptic, a woman with a high fever. In Nain he commanded a young man given up for dead and lying on his bier to get up, and the man did. None of our agents has yet explained the method of his sorcery."

Zadok sat back, reflected for a moment, and then leaned forward again. "Though he is a Jew, he questions Temple ritual and worship, and even scorns the sacrifice." Zadok shook his head and ground his teeth. "How can any Jew disdain this symbolic act of mortal man communing with God? For two thousand years, since God stayed Abraham's knife, we have taken to the altar the best we have to expiate our sins and show our penitence. Yes, I know that opportunists profit on Temple grounds from selling the rams and doves to be killed, but someone must provide these gifts that manifest how each of us is one with God."

Saul broke in. "To question the sacrifice is to question the Covenant and the Law. 'You shall sacrifice your burnt offerings' were God's words as part of the Covenant."

Zadok nodded. "Yes, yes, of course. That was settled centuries ago. But now we have this presumptuous northerner. He says his intent is not to annul the Law or reject the Prophets, but to fulfill them. He goes so far as to claim that he speaks with greater authority on the Law than this court or the high priests of the Temple."

"Why not charge him with heresy?" Saul asked. "Once we prove before this high court that his teachings are false, his followers will abandon him."

Zadok shook his head. "It will not be so easy."

"What do we know of his origin?" Saul asked.

Zadok shrugged. "There is a myth that he was born of a virgin, Mary, a most common name, in Bethlehem, about thirty years ago. His father — or stepfather if one is to believe the virgin story — is Joseph, a carpenter in Nazareth. The parents are poor and illiterate, but the boy in some way educated himself. And very well. He knows the Law and the Prophets as well as any country rabbi, and usually better. He claims his teachings come directly from God and are thus superior to ours."

"Clearly, that is heresy," Saul said.

"Heresy is one possible charge," Zadok said. "Another is blasphemy, for he openly tells his audiences, 'I come in the name of the Lord.' But this man is too crafty to claim he is God. He calls himself 'the son of man.' One of his attendants calls him 'Lord,' and another, Andrew, a fisherman, was overheard saying, 'We have found the Messiah.' Still another, Nathanael, said to him: 'Rabbi, you are the son of God.'"

"Why can we not charge these attendants with blasphemy as a warning to their leader?" Saul asked.

"Take the cubs and not the lion? No, Saul, that will not eliminate the danger."

"If then," Saul said, "this false rabbi does not rebuke these illiterate attendants who call him 'Lord,' then I am certain that the charge of blasphemy can be brought against him. We would need only two witnesses, and there is surely an abundance of witnesses."

Zadok reflected for a moment and shook his head. "It may come to that," he said slowly, "but by such action, we could create more problems than we solve."

"How could that be?"

"This demagogue is popular. His believers are numerous and they increase. At first it was a handful of the curious; then it was to hundreds that he spoke. From Bethsaida our agents report that he addressed there an audience of five thousand."

"Five thousand? Surely that cannot be."

"Yes, five thousand, so we are told. And we must contend not only with the numbers of his listeners, but also their fervency. To the poor he promises rewards in heaven. To the hungry he gives bread. To the wretched he offers hope. Anyone who promises so much for so little is certain to become popular." Zadok opened his palms in dismay and shook his head. "We must be careful not to give the lowly a hero and martyr."

"How, then, do we silence this Jesus without creating resentment against the Sanhedrin?" Saul asked.

Zadok drew back in astonishment and stared at Saul. "How do you know his name?" he asked.

"I heard of this imposter at the House of Study," Saul replied quickly. "Several students journeyed to Galilee to hear him."

"Then his teachings have infected the school of Gamaliel." Zadok shook his head and glowered. "You should have told me earlier."

"I learned of it by chance," Saul said. With a shrug he added, "I thought a rustic pretender in the northern hills to be of no importance."

"Who in Gamaliel's school is a follower?" Zadok asked.

Saul stopped himself. He must protect Barnabas. "I believe the leader is Stephen of Athens."

"Aha! That Hellenist. Who else?"

Saul shook his head. "I know no others."

"But you just said several of your fellow students went to Galilee to see this Jesus."

Again Saul shook his head. "So I did overhear after a class one day. I know not who they were."

For a long time Zadok looked intently in Saul's face, his eyes narrowed in suspicion. Under the scrutiny Saul felt the sweat dripping down the back of his neck, but he made no move to brush it away.

At last Zadok leaned forward again. "We must silence this Jesus for another reason. We must act before Rome sees him as a threat, or we of this court are done."

"What do you mean?"

"Exactly that. Fear rules every Caesar, every Herod, every royal courtier. Now this Jesus speaks in the remote hills; what will happen when he comes to Jerusalem?"

"Why would he come here? He is safer in Galilee."

"He will come. He must come here because his ambition will drive him to this center of power. And when he comes, and Pilate learns that mobs in Galilee acclaim this Jesus as 'king of the Jews,' then Pilate may suspect that this self-appointed Messiah is leading a mass revolt of Jews against him, against his authority, against the Roman Empire itself. What will Pilate do? As procurator, he can order Caesar's legions stationed here to put down the threat of a rebellion. Out of fear he may also appeal to Rome for more soldiers. With Tiberius a recluse in Capri, that conniving praetorian Lucius Aeilius Sejanus would welcome the opportunity to put down a revolt here so that he — in Caesar's absence — might lead a victory parade through the streets of Rome.

"If that happens, we are finished. If there is any threat to the peace, Rome will rip asunder the concordat by which we lawyers and priests govern this province. We lose our power to administer, to impose justice. We lose our positions at court, our standing in the city, our fine houses, our comfortable way of life. And we lose the way we worship God. A vengeful Rome might even destroy the Temple and sack the city of Jerusalem — just as King Nebuchadnezzar did six hundred years ago before he enslaved us in Babylon." Zadok shook his head. "No, we must save Jerusalem, save our Temple — whatever the cost."

Saul waited, then asked quietly: "What do you wish me to do?"

Zadok lifted his head, looked into the distance, and said, "What is in the best interest of the nation of Israel? That is the issue. Our purpose is, and must always be, to preserve the Hebrew way of life. It is to make certain that we who know the great distinction of being Jews survive — not only survive but prosper. With that as our purpose, we must go for guidance to the Torah, to the eternal words that God spoke to Moses: 'Obey my voice . . . Keep my Covenant.' Eons have passed since God handed Moses the Law on Mount Sinai. That Law brought us to this place and this time.

"Yes, there is one force that binds our tribes together as a people, and that is the Law. That Law and the statutes and rituals the sages of the ancient time have handed down are the forces that guided us, strengthened us.

Through famine and travail and slavery, the Law preserved our unity as the chosen people, made us responsible beyond all other races of the earth. Others wrote laws to establish equity, accord, and purpose in their daily lives — Hammurabi, Alexander. And when they failed to keep their laws, their empires faded, perished. That must not happen here." He struck his fist into his right hand. "We must defend the Law against any and all, against any alien teaching, against any false god, and, yes, against any apostate Jew. It is the Law that is our heritage, our strength, our unique gift from God. It is the life and soul of Israel."

Zadok turned to face Saul. "Today Caiaphas asked, 'Will no one rid me of this problem?' Tomorrow I will go back to Caiaphas with the answer. I, Zadok, will silence this heretic."

Saul listened with intensity, taking care to remember every word of his master. He could see that the false prophet who called himself Jesus presented a profound threat to the Hebrew people. Saul judged Zadok's reasoning and arguments to be incontestable, and surmised that Zadok was testing the words he would use in a future oration before the full Sanhedrin.

Zadok turned and brought forth the documents again. "There may be another way," he said briskly. "We could show Pilate the evidence and contrive to have him move against this menace."

He brought out one sheet of papyrus and read from it. "Here, in the village of Gennesaret, this Jesus said, 'I bring fire to earth. Not peace but division, disorder.' We might convince Pilate that this is a case of treason against Rome. Against treason — *ius gladii* — Pilate has the 'right of the sword.' If we can show treason against Rome, Pilate has full power of immediate execution."

"Execution?" The word slipped out.

Zadok observed that Saul's face had turned pale. "You show some concern for this Jesus."

"No, it's not that," Saul replied. "It is just that I have not been involved in a capital case before, where someone may be put to death."

"Every individual must answer to the Law." Zadok's voice was stern, cold. "Do you know the penalty, Saul, for the prophet or dreamer who seeks to turn us away from God?"

"Of course," Saul replied. "It is written in the fifth book of the Torah: 'Thou shall stone him with stones, that he die.'"

Zadok placed a hand on Saul's shoulder and looked in his eyes. "If you are to rise in this court, if you are to become a leader, and I know this is in your heart, you must show the courage of our leaders of old. Reflect: Did Abraham hesitate to sacrifice Isaac? Did David shrink from striking at his own sons to preserve his kingdom? We have a duty to put down the rebellion that this false Messiah is fomenting. Are we to hide our faces from this blasphemy that is before our eyes?"

"I shall do as you say," Saul said.

"Here then are your instructions," Zadok said. "Go back through the centuries and write a summary of the Law and all precedents on heresy and blasphemy. Give that to me before nightfall. By dawn tomorrow, provide me a summary of the Roman law on sedition and treason, and a record on how the Herods ruled and acted on all such cases."

Saul worked through the night and delivered the final papers at dawn. Late in the afternoon, Hirudin, chief steward to the high priest, burst open his door. "Go at once to Zadok!"

Saul ran down the stairs, wondering if he had missed some crucial element in a summary. As soon as he entered, he stopped in alarm. Zadok stood with his feet planted wide, his face thrust forward and red with rage. He shook his fist in Saul's face. "You betrayed me. You concealed your comrades who follow Jesus. Such perfidy. Do you, too, follow this heretic in secret?"

Before Saul could answer, Zadok raged on. "You lied to me. We found seven followers of this Jesus in the school of Gamaliel. They were discovered after Caiaphas, at my insistence, ordered inquiries. On Caiaphas' order all seven were dismissed today. Your bosom friend Barnabas of Cyprus was one of their leaders. Why did you not reveal the truth — that you, until you came to this dormitorium, shared a house with Barnabas? Your classmates testified that you and Barnabas were like brothers. You frequented the house of his aunt who harbors the despicable sect in this very city. All of this you covered up. You said nothing of your collusion with the followers of this heretic. Just now Caiaphas called me before his advisers and rebuked me for bringing into this court a spy for the enemy. Such disloyalty I cannot accept. Such treachery I will not tolerate. You are dismissed as a clerk to this court. Turn in all your seals and cloaks of office and leave at once."

IX

RETURNING

The cold garret was livable, once Saul became accustomed to it. In despair after his dismissal, he had turned to Rabban Gamaliel, who bade him return to school and earn his bread by overseeing the scrolls and books of the library. For six years — far, far longer it seemed to Saul — he organized and indexed the tattered documents and yellowed parchment that Gamaliel had collected and preserved. And he read. All the Law, all the statutes, all the commentaries, every page in the school library he studied and stored in memory. To busy his nights he fashioned a desk from a battered door, found a broken but usable lamp, and copied on vellum the five books of the Torah. Gamaliel was delighted with the gift to the school.

As always, Saul rose early. He slept on a pallet of thin straw, wrapped in the now threadbare cloak his father had woven and tailored ten years earlier. He ate once a day in the kitchen with Gamaliel's cook, then took up his solitary post in the library. Sometimes he looked in on Gamaliel's weekly colloquium, but he never spoke. He listened, appraising the first-order students preening their learning and the third order stumbling through their recitations. Once or twice a week he would take a student into the library and show him where to find the material points of law and how to frame his proposition and arguments. Saul liked working with promising scholars; with the slow, he tried to be patient, but with little success. Otherwise he kept to himself. He accepted being friendless and alone, but inaction wasted him like a fever.

Most afternoons he would go alone to the Temple. Not for the rituals — he hated the odor of burning goat, and the acrid smoke sometimes brought on an asthma attack — but because he had discovered that the Temple was the place where he could best lose himself in thought and contemplation. There he would brood over his ill fortune. He would wonder why one mistake, one moment of compassion for his only friend, should have ended the bright promise then before him. Admittedly, he had not told the truth to Zadok, but he had been given no chance to testify that from the beginning he had warned Barnabas against the mystic of Galilee. Well, that was long past. Pilate had ordered Roman soldiers to execute Jesus for treason; thus they crucified the Nazarene outside the city walls on Skull Hill. With Jesus' death, his followers vanished.

Saul learned of these events later. On the day that Jesus overturned the tables of the money changers in the Temple, riots broke out in the streets of Jerusalem — provoking Gamaliel to lock his students and staff inside the school building to protect them from the bloodshed he feared would come.

One evening in midsummer, sheltered from the lightning and torrents of rain pouring off rooftops, Saul remained late in the library, absorbed in Jeremiah's account of Israel's kings. The story was one of Saul's favorites: Bathsheba persuading the dying King David to name their son Solomon as successor, and young King Solomon executing his rivals, expanding the empire, and reigning by devious politics and rough justice for forty years. As the lamp burned low, Saul fell asleep — until some time after midnight, when he woke with instant and total clarity. His mother had come to him in a dream: They were standing together, her face radiant, her voice clear and loving. "Despair not, my son." She stepped back; her manner and voice took on the nature of imperial command he had known so well. "You, too, have the blood of kings, Saul. Act. Act!" Then she disappeared.

In the darkness Saul tried to understand. How could he act? He had nothing. No money. No position. No expectations. Knowledge, yes; when a man cannot use it, however, knowledge only brings pain. Perplexed and weary, he wrapped his cloak around him and tried to sleep. But there in the darkness he kept wondering: What was his mother trying to tell him?

That afternoon — Saul marked it down in his journal as the fifteenth day of the month of Tammuz — he was on his way to the Temple when he chanced to glimpse himself in the polished copper mirror of a street vendor. He paused to look again at the image. His wispy beard showed the first streaks of gray. His black curls had receded; the front of his head was almost bald, like his father. His face was long, sallow, cheerless; his shoulders sagged, as had his father's. "I age," Saul said, shaking his head. He counted his years: Only twenty-seven, but his life was without promise.

In the Temple, as he brooded over his bleak prospects for the future, his mind turned again to his mother's words in the dream. The priest chanted from Psalms, but Saul barely listened. Suddenly the spoken words struck him as though heralded by the peal of a trumpet. ". . . Have mercy upon me; for I am desolate and afflicted . . . bring thou me out of my distresses. Look upon mine affliction and my pain; and forgive all my sins . . ."

Forgiveness: Like a great burst of light it came to Saul that he must ask to be forgiven. He closed a fist and whispered to himself, "If God could forgive the author of that Psalm for adultery and murder, surely Zadok can forgive me for one falsehood." His mind began to race: Torah decreed that forgiveness came after confessing and repenting. He could go to Zadok, confess, and ask to be forgiven.

Would Zadok and the court take him back? Perhaps not. But Saul could hope, and he must try. He wanted desperately to make his life meaningful again. His banishment had been unjust. And after six years in exile he was close to a breaking point. He could no longer endure the waste of his days. Life was aimless. There must be a way to return to court, to serve there again, to use his intellect constructively, and yes, to return to power. He would prove himself worthy of responsibility. Never again would he conceal the truth or be disloyal in any way. He had been a superior clerk of the Law; of that he was certain. His merit was recognized by scribes and priests alike. He was sure that Zadok had never found any other apprentice who could find the right statutes with such quickness and present them with such skill. He made up his mind. "I shall go to Zadok. But when?" For no more than a moment he reflected. "It is the end of the day. Zadok will be in his workroom. I shall go now."

Once outside the Temple porches, Saul walked swiftly to the entrance of the high court. The guard did not stop or question him. Saul strode down the corridor and opened the door to the familiar workroom.

Zadok was reading. Saul closed the door behind him and waited. Documents and scrolls lay about; the workroom was more cluttered than ever. Zadok had grown a full beard that masked the pockmarks and afforded him a look of sage distinction. After a few moments he said, without looking up from his book, "What have you to say?"

Saul fixed his eyes on Zadok and spoke firmly: "I sinned against the Sanhedrin when I failed to tell the whole truth. I have suffered. I am penitent. I ask forgiveness."

Zadok turned to look at Saul, but said nothing. In a great rush, in a torrent of words, Saul recounted the story of his return to the house that he and Barnabas shared, on the very day that Rabban Gamaliel had told of his assignment to Zadok. He related in full his dispute with Barnabas over the false Messiah, concluding with an oath that he had never again discussed it with Barnabas.

"I know," Zadok replied. "Rabban Gamaliel questioned Barnabas before he disappeared. Gamaliel then described the event and circumstances to the esteemed high priest himself. He also told Caiaphas that in all your years in Jerusalem, your commitment to the Law wavered not once. Caiaphas in turn informed me."

Instantly anger rose in Saul's heart. "Then why did you not send for me?"

Zadok studied Saul's face for a moment. "It was essential that you return on your own initiative. Or not at all."

Saul struggled to put down the fury within. How much time, how many long mornings and afternoons and nights had been wasted? Slowly and deliberately he said, "I have returned. I belong here in this court. It is my mission. Put away my mistake. I am ready to serve you and this high court. Only with you and through this court can I fulfill my destiny to serve the Law."

Zadok placed his fingertips together under his chin and looked directly at Saul. "I cannot forget that you misled me, and thereby placed in jeopardy the legitimacy of my position as chief counselor to this high court. But it is right to forgive, and I am prepared to offer you one more chance, to put you to the test."

Zadok stood and began pacing back and forth. "First, have you been informed of the continuing seditions of the Nazarene sect?"

"I know nothing of the sect," Saul said. "Since my dismissal I have been cloistered in the library of the academy of Gamaliel, reading, writing, studying, speaking only to him and to students about their assignments."

Zadok nodded. "We of this court assumed that after the death of Jesus, the threat would end. It has not been entirely so. Most leaders of the sect fled into the remote hills. Over time, however, those in thrall to this heretic returned to Jerusalem. The chief 'disciple,' the fisherman called Peter, and James, a half brother of the dead Jesus, hold secret meetings with their followers in one house, and then another, here in the city. Here they continue to worship the Nazarene as the appointed messenger from God. We estimate that in Jerusalem there may be two hundred members of the Way, as they now call their movement — not many in a city of more than one hundred thousand Jews. But our agents who infiltrated the movement report it is growing. Consequently, we have discussed their seditious actions with Pilate."

He grimaced in scorn. "Pilate will do nothing. Nor, ever fearful of a riot, will he permit the Sanhedrin to act against Peter or James — for their displays of sorcery purporting to heal the lame and ill have attracted public attention and popular support. More important, Pilate's wife, Procia, of all persons, found merit in Jesus' teachings and thought his execution an injustice. She is also superstitious, and complains to Pilate that his order to nail Jesus to the cross brought on a series of misfortunes that have beset the family ever since. Thus, we cannot depend on Pilate; we must circumvent him, and circumvent Roman law."

Zadok leaned forward and clenched his fists. "I have persuaded Caiaphas that his responsibility as high priest requires that the Sanhedrin must, on its own, take an action so naked and absolute that it will convince all Jews that we cannot and will not condone any Jew's worship of this false Messiah. We who comprise this court must demonstrate a will of iron." He pounded his fists on his table. "We will not tolerate heresy."

Listening to Zadok's words, the years of Saul's isolation began to fall away; he could feel his blood pumping. Once more there stirred within him the familiar sense of supremacy, of participating in decisions and actions that governed lives. "What is your plan?" he asked quietly.

"To conduct a campaign of repression that will purge this poison from Jewish blood. To begin, we will smite their young. We will arrest a little-known but important member of the sect, put him on trial before the full Sanhedrin for a crime against God, convict him, and execute him. By singling out one, we will warn the others."

"Then the charge will be blasphemy, or incitement to worship other gods, or both?" Saul asked.

"That is for you to determine," Zadok replied. "You will prepare the case that I will bring to trial. This will give you the opportunity to redeem yourself in this court, to affirm your commitment to the Law, to prove to all what the Romans call *bona fides*."

Saul tried to mask his elation. The door had reopened; in an hour his life had been transformed. He was to be given a chance to return, to be again inducted into the brotherhood that ruled over others. As calmly as he could, he said, "I welcome this opportunity. Am I to work with agents to determine the member of the sect to bring to trial?"

"That I have already done," Zadok replied. "He is young, favored within the sect for his learning and ardent nature, but otherwise unknown. He has just been chosen, an agent tells us, to organize and lead six other young Nazarenes in distributing alms to the poor of the sect." Zadok turned to look intently at Saul. "His name is Stephen," he said quietly. "Stephen of Athens."

So this was the beginning of Zadok's testing, and Zadok was watching his face to see if he flinched. He would not flinch. He would not pale. He had learned a hard lesson. Six years in exile had convinced him he must never again hesitate to take a life to enforce the Law of God. Saul looked Zadok in the eye and said in a firm and even voice: "When do I begin?"

"At once," Zadok replied. "I have delayed this case until your return. Bring your first summary to me by noon tomorrow."

Within the hour Saul was immersed in the scrolls and documents of the Sanhedrin library. He searched first in the Book of Moses honoring Levi, and there, on the worn scroll, he found: "And the Lord spake unto Moses, saying, . . . he who blasphemes the name of the Lord shall certainly be put to death. All the congregation shall certainly cast stones at him." Across the room Saul leafed through the papyrus codices of precedents until he found that scholars had defined *blasphemy* most concisely as "verbal contempt." Such a definition was so broad, he noted, that blasphemy could be any words that offended any priest or elder on the Sanhedrin. At least two witnesses to blasphemy would be necessary at the trial, and Zadok would, as always, recruit and instruct witnesses to prove his case.

Late that night, by the light of a refilled lamp, Saul came upon another part of the Law that struck him as prescient, as though written for this particular time and circumstance: "If your brother, or your son, or your daughter, or your wife, or your friend who is as your own soul, shall entice you secretly, saying 'Let us go and serve other gods,' you shall not consent to him nor listen to him, nor shall your eye have pity on him, nor shall you spare nor hide him. But you shall surely kill him; your hand shall be first upon him to put him to death, and the hand of all people last. And you shall stone him with stones, and he shall die, for he has sought to drive you away from the Lord your God."

Saul sat back to contemplate the full force of words from the second statutes God handed down to Moses in Moab more than a thousand years ago. To Saul the words were absolute, unmistakable: Keep God's Commandments and statutes, lest Israel perish. Could there be any question of God's will? The heirs to Moses whom God appointed must destroy the apostate and the blasphemer. It must be done. The court, its members, and he, Saul, in particular — all were being tested by God.

The Nazarenes served another god. They sought to drive Jews from God. The Law was specific: Show no pity. No friend, not even a brother, could be spared. Anyone who served Jesus must be brought to trial and stoned to death; that was the clear intent of the Law. Stephen was a Jew calling on his fellow Jews to serve another god. Therefore Stephen must be put to death.

But wait: Why should it end with Stephen? Any other Jew in the Nazarene sect who called on his fellow Jews to worship another god must also be put to death. How could the court justify executing one apostate, making an example of one person, then permitting other members of the sect to go free to continue to worship this false god? For the court to permit the Nazarene sect to survive at all would be failing the test of God.

Alone in the library late that night, Saul formed a new plan: Stephen would be only the beginning of a series of trials. Saul would mobilize the facts and precedents so well and present such a strong case against Stephen that the court would acknowledge its obligation to act with equal force against the other Nazarenes. Once Stephen was convicted and executed, then, Saul envisaged, he would go to Zadok and Caiaphas and persuade them that all members of the sect must be rounded up and brought to trial. It was right and just to carry out the letter of the Law, to destroy all Jews who served another god.

From the lamplight Saul turned to stare into the darkness as he thought through his course of action. He organized it in his mind, committed it to memory, and then began to draft his summary of the case against Stephen.

At noon Saul delivered the scrolls and books and documents to Zadok. As he read through the summary, Zadok paused from time to time to make a point or ask a question. "As this trial concerns a capital offense, the accused is permitted to speak, of course. From your knowledge of Stephen, will he deny the charges?"

Saul shook his head. "No. Craven he is not."

"Will he confess?" Zadok asked.

"I cannot say. Stephen prides himself on being an orator, so he will surely speak to the court with fervor, and even defiance. Thus, I believe that rather than confess previous acts of blasphemy, it is more likely that he will actually commit blasphemy before the court."

"Blasphemy before the court?" Zadok lifted his hands in surprise. "How could he be so rash? His guilt would be evident to all members of the Sanhedrin, and Caiaphas can immediately issue the verdict and order the Temple guards to take him outside the city walls to be stoned."

He turned to his desk and placed his hand on Saul's summary and notes. "The Law is even more explicit than I remembered, thus the case is stronger than I expected. I have retained three witnesses, all from distant provinces. Jerusalem dwellers fear retaliation when they are paid to testify."

Abruptly Zadok stood. "We must act quickly. This being the fourth day of the week, we must hold the trial tomorrow or be forced to wait until after the Sabbath. Come. We will see Caiaphas now."

Only once before had Saul been in the chamber of the high priest. Caiaphas sat on a high-backed throne of cedar and gold, at a table carved of ivory, all raised on a platform of imperial grandeur. The scarlet robe filigreed with gold, the crown of a white linen turban with its gold plate inscribed HOLY TO THE LORD, the galaxy of courtiers in the chamber, all seemed designed to accord Caiaphas the look of what he was: high prince of all Jews. But when he spoke, his reedy voice and halting words suggested a man of timidity, even fear.

With Zadok standing in the center before the throne and Saul at his left, the two looked up with appropriate respect.

"Most esteemed High Priest," Zadok began, "I appear before you to request that you consider a case of great and immediate importance to the highest court of the Sanhedrin."

"Proceed," Caiaphas replied. Zadok summarized the testimony he had collected against Stephen, briefly cited relevant sections of the Law, and concluded: "As chief counselor, I warrant that these acts of apostasy and heresy constitute an issue affecting the totality of the nation of Israel, and I propose that you call the full Sanhedrin into session at noon tomorrow to hear the case and judge this offense against the people."

Caiaphas moved his hands in a brief but helpless gesture and turned to his courtiers. With solemn faces they nodded. Saul sensed that Zadok had previously spoken with them.

"It will be done," Caiaphas said. "Master of clerks, summon all members of the court to attend the trial at noon on the morrow."

As Zadok and Saul turned to go, Caiaphas said. "A moment, Saul. You have returned, I see. You are here by the grace of the wise and eminent Rabban Gamaliel. Disappoint us not."

Saul raised his right hand. "Most esteemed High Priest, I do swear in your presence that I shall excel at serving you and this court. You will never be disappointed. May the Lord be my witness, you will never be disappointed. Never."

X

TRIAL

The great gathering room in the Hall of Hewn Stone was hushed as the members of the Sanhedrin came together for the trial of Stephen. The capital crime of heresy rarely came before the court. By midmorning men of worth and standing occupied all forty seats reserved for visitors. From his chair at the table of the prosecutor, Saul watched the beards and sages, all in black robes, all somber of mien, take their assigned places along the semicircles of tiered benches. When all seventy-one members were present, the court bailiff rapped his staff and opened the door to the private chamber of the high priest. Caiaphas, gowned and hatted in black silk, entered the chamber and solemnly took his seat high above the others.

Striking his podium with a wooden block, Caiaphas ordered the Temple guards to bring the accused before the court. To Saul's eyes, Stephen seemed transformed. Standing there on the black square for the accused, he was no longer a youth. His face was lined and drawn, but resolute. His eyes gleamed with the fire of a penned tiger. He wore the ragged cloak common among the hill people. The affectations of a scholar had been replaced by the contained but visible energy of a zealot. He stood with body erect, head high, and looked directly at Caiaphas. His hand did not tremble.

Zadok opened the trial with a summary of the charges, specifying apostasy and heresy, and cited from Saul's notes the relevant Law and statutes that detailed the punishment for those convicted. To Saul's surprise the first witness was a Cilician, Manoah of Tarsus. Pointing to Stephen, he said: "We have heard this man speaking blasphemous words against Moses and God." Hearing the Cilician accent stirred in Saul a memory of his mother, but he stopped his mind from wandering.

"Where did the accused speak these words?" Zadok asked.

The witness described a stone house in Jerusalem that could have been the home of Barnabas' Aunt Mary; for one brief moment Saul wondered whether, someday, Barnabas might also be found and summoned before the Sanhedrin. But he quickly closed off extraneous thoughts and listened to the next witness, a sailor of Cyrene with a stentorian voice. "We heard this man saying that his Jesus will bring down the Great Temple of Herod."

Zadok raised his hand to the witness. "Where did the accused make this threat to destroy the Temple?" Zadok asked.

"He spoke these words in the market square by the Antonia Tower, outside the very gates of the Temple."

The last witness, a coppersmith from Alexandria, confirmed the testimony of the others.

Zadok dismissed the three, turned to face the robed tiers, and spoke briefly, quietly. "Most esteemed High Priest and honorable members of this supreme court, you have heard the witnesses to the acts of apostasy and heresy committed by the accused. This is a crime against all Jews, against this court charged with the responsibility to be defender of our faith. Our duty is clear. We must act today, this hour, to rid ourselves of this menace to the people of Israel and to the Lord our God."

From his high place Caiaphas addressed Stephen. "You have heard the witnesses to your false teachings," he said in his thin voice. "Do you deny their testimony?"

"Men, brothers, and fathers!" Stephen began, sweeping his arm toward the semicircle of priests and elders. "The God of glory appeared to our father Abraham," he said, and went on to recite at length the condemnations of Abraham and Isaac and Jacob, eloquently citing the history of Jews continually rebelling against a new leader chosen by God to fulfill his promises. For a moment Saul was stricken with fear: Stephen's premise was correct; if his arguments were so persuasive that he won his freedom, Zadok would blame Saul for losing the case.

At that moment Stephen made an incomprehensible move that rescued Saul. In flagrant contempt of the court, Stephen turned from logic to scorn, beginning with the Temple itself: "God does not dwell in houses made by the hand of man." Suddenly Stephen's face darkened and he pointed toward the priests and elders. "O stiff-necked and uncircumcised in heart and in the ears: You always rebelled against the Holy Spirit. Which of the Prophets did your fathers not persecute?" As members of the court began to mutter oaths and grind their teeth, Stephen raised his voice, leveling an accusation against Caiaphas and the entire court: "You yourselves betrayed and murdered Jesus the Messiah, the son of God."

At this flagrant act of blasphemy, calling Jesus the Messiah, members cried out to Caiaphas: "Stop this outrage!" "Enough! Enough!" "Stone him! Stone him!"

To still the pandemonium Caiaphas pounded his block on the podium, his face reddening in shock and anger. Once order was restored in the hall he raised his hand to deliver his verdict.

But Stephen had lifted his arms to the heavens as though dismissing this court and appealing to a higher tribunal. In a voice serene and confident he proclaimed: "Behold! I see the heavens opened and Jesus the anointed one standing at the right hand of God."

At a signal from Caiaphas, Temple guards and visitors rushed forward from the gallery to seize Stephen and silence him by twisting a hemp rope across his mouth. With order restored, Caiaphas delivered the verdict: "Three witnesses have accused this man Stephen of blasphemy in this city of Jerusalem. Indeed, the accused has blasphemed the name of God before this very high court of priests and elders. Therefore, I now sentence the accused Stephen to be taken out of the city and stoned, as commanded by the Law given to Moses by God."

In the clatter of members stepping down from their places, Caiaphas summoned Zadok and Saul to his high bench. "Saul, I charge you, as clerk to the prosecutor, to represent this court as official executor. Go now with the guards and prisoner to the place of stoning. When it is finished, report to me in my chambers on where and how it was accomplished."

Saul quickly collected the three witnesses; the Law required that they must cast the first stones. Outside the court the mob that had gathered followed the guards and their manacled prisoner along the Street of Herod out the Tekoa Gate to a stony hillside of the Kedron Valley.

When the guards knocked Stephen to the ground, Saul leaped up to a high boulder where he could best witness the execution. It was warm in the midday sun, and the three witnesses laid their coats at Saul's feet and formed the arc of a circle around the condemned. Manoah the Cilician lifted a stone as big as a plowshare over his head and flung it, missing

Stephen's head but striking his chest. It caused him to gasp for breath, but his eyes remained open and alert. The Cyrenian followed with a stone that landed squarely on Stephen's cheek and jaw; the Alexandrite flung a jagged broken rock with such force that it brought a flow of blood from Stephen's mouth and forehead. At the sight of blood the crowd joined in the killing. Stone after stone, volley after volley rained down on Stephen.

Observing carefully for his report to Caiaphas, Saul could see blood streaming from Stephen's mouth and a wound in his side. The left leg was broken, exposing white bone. At one point Stephen looked up at Saul, and their eyes met for a long moment. Saul did not move, nor did he speak. Stephen closed his eyes and lay still. Thinking him dead, the crowd fell into silence. Then suddenly he opened his eyes and spoke in a voice firm and serene: "Lord Jesus, receive my spirit!" Blasphemy to the end. Lifting his head, he looked first at the crowd, then at Saul. "Lord," Stephen said, each of his last words clear and vibrant, "do not hold this crime against them." He closed his eyes. He was dead.

In an instant Saul was consumed by an ecstasy that he had never before experienced. Excited by the blood, elated with victory, he leaped into the air and pranced about on the hillside. Ravenous hunger and thirst seized him; he grasped a double handful of figs from a passing fruit seller and devoured them. Like one possessed, he snatched a water jar from a woman passing by and drank in great gulps, spilling it on his face and robe as he reeled in exaltation.

"What shall we do with the body?" The question from the captain of Temple guards broke the spell.

For a moment Saul looked in puzzlement, then regained his senses. "Set a watch over it," he said, relishing the power of knowing the guard was his to command. "And take the names of any in the sect who come to claim it."

With bold and measured steps of new authority, and a squad of Temple guards in train, Saul strode across the city to report to Caiaphas. At the entrance hall of the Sanhedrin, Zadok was waiting, and together they went into the princely chamber.

As Saul described in exact and extended detail the stoning and the victim's suffering and death, Caiaphas lost interest and began to look about as though annoyed. When at last Saul finished his report, Caiaphas impatiently turned to his courtier Baladan, proctor for the city. "Have there been riots?"

"No disorder has been reported, most esteemed High Priest," the proctor replied. "Word spread throughout the city that the accused Stephen committed an act of blasphemy before the high court. Therefore the people of Jerusalem not only accept your verdict as just and necessary, they also praise your courage and resolution."

Caiaphas turned to Saul. "You have redeemed yourself."

The high priest's compliment and Saul's ebullient sense of victory provoked him to act. There could be no better time to propose his plan. Of course it would have been proper to discuss it first with Zadok, but events had moved so swiftly that there had been no opportunity for that. This was the moment.

"Most esteemed High Priest," Saul said, "if I may speak further." Both Caiaphas and Zadok looked up in surprise.

"Today we carried out the Law," Saul blurted out, not waiting for recognition. "We put to death one born a Hebrew who, not by chance but after deliberation, chose to follow another god. How, most esteemed High Priest, can we justify executing one member of this sect and letting the others go free? I propose that you, as ruling prince, direct your Temple guards to arrest and bring to trial all in this city who belong to this sect. They betray the Law, the statutes, the patriarchs. They would drive us away from the Lord our God."

After a long silence Caiaphas said: "A pogrom? You advocate a pogrom against the Jesus sect?"

"Necessary action in defense of the Law," Saul replied. "'The Lord is One.' As that we proclaim, that we must enforce."

Caiaphas looked toward Zadok, who was staring at Saul in surprise. Had the sight of Stephen's blood created a thirst for more blood? Whatever Saul's motive, Zadok knew he could not appear less vengeful than his subordinate.

"Most esteemed High Priest," Zadok said slowly, "it had been my thought to consider this question and as your counsel present a formal proposal. Now that it has come before us, I believe a decision is proper and stands well within your authority. We must act swiftly, as on a battlefield, to consolidate our victory. If we are to purge Israel of our internal enemies, this day was the beginning, not the end. Therefore I favor, strongly, the proposal by your clerk Saul. Indeed, I consider such action not only prudent but imperative. There can be no better time. Thus I say, why wait, my prince? Why wait?"

Caiaphas lifted his hands in a gesture of helplessness and turned to his proctor. "Would such arrests create disturbances among the people? What of Fort Antonia?"

Baladan replied slowly and with care. "Most esteemed High Priest, when today I informed the legate Taius of the execution, he shrugged. If we maintain order among our people in the city, Pilate will wash his hands of our actions."

"Do you have the names of these Nazarenes? Do you know where to find them?" Caiaphas asked.

"We do," Baladan replied. "Long ago I instructed our secret police to infiltrate the sect, and we have a list of members."

Once more Caiaphas lifted his hands in uncertainty, and Zadok sought recognition. "In the streets and in the markets the people of Jerusalem applaud your action this day, most esteemed High Priest. Ride this wave of popular support. Act now. You hold full authority in your hands."

After a long hesitation, Caiaphas said, "Very well. If all present agree, I will sign the order."

Zadok spoke again. "With your consent, on the premise that a plan can best be executed by its originator, I shall assign Saul to oversee this pogrom."

"I have no objection," Caiaphas said, "but there must be no riots." He looked to each man in the room, shook his finger, and repeated: "No riots."

Marching at the head of a company of the Temple guards the next morning, Saul led them from the courtyard of their barracks within the Temple grounds out the gate and into the streets of Jerusalem. The tramp of boots on cobble sounded across the square. Shopkeepers and mendicants and small boys stopped to watch. Saul felt the return of the strange elation that had swept over him after the stoning. His head tingled with excitement; his throat filled with the taste of power.

In four days his world had been transformed from despair to victory. By his own will he had burst from obscurity to a position of consequence. He had been given a task of law and had excelled, showing a mastery of the statutes greater even than Zadok's. He had certified his position at court before the high priest himself. He had conceived and won the victory over a heretic. And now he had boldly advanced beyond the court counsel, beyond the high priest, and initiated a campaign to destroy the sect of the Nazarene and thereby carry out the will of God.

On Moab Street, at the first house on Baladan's list, he found a bewildered old man and his wife who denied that they belonged to the Jesus sect and professed only to have listened to a disciple in the market square on a distant day. Saul's order was clear: He must arrest everyone on the list. So he commanded the Temple guards to take the old people to prison.

In a doorway three houses away he confronted a young ironsmith who responded proudly: "Yes, I follow the Way." Saul arrested him, his wife, and two young sons. They went peacefully, and he heard the husband whisper to his wife, "Fear not. Have faith in Jesus, for he will protect us."

At the mud-walled house where Stephen had lived with Philip and the others who served the Jerusalem poor, the rude door was barred. The guards broke it down and entered, but found nothing except the half-eaten remains of bread. A stooped and toothless crone came from her house next door to lean on her stick and watch the excitement. "Gone two days ago," she croaked, going from one guard to another. "To the hills, to another country, nobody knows." The next four houses on the list, all on the same street and nearby, were also empty.

On Chain Street, Saul knocked at the door of a stone house and found six men and women in the act of discussing the teachings of Jesus. He ordered all sent to prison. In the quarter west of Hezekiah's Pool the guards arrested two families of silversmiths who had given money to Stephen for alms. In an alley nearby Saul saw three men and a woman loading an ass with grain and water. They readily admitted they were followers of Jesus. Under questioning, they revealed that upon the arrest of Stephen, many in the sect were fleeing to Antioch and Damascus for safety. Saul arrested the four, confiscated their provisions, and ordered them to prison.

Through Baladan's list, house by house, Saul and the captain of the Temple guards continued their search, knocking at a door, being met with silence, ordering the guards to break down the door with spear and club. More often than not the house would be empty. Altogether they found and arrested forty-seven men and women of the Way. The guards formed relays to take them to prison. To the surprise of the captain, and Saul, not one resisted arrest.

At last one name remained on Baladan's list: Mary, aunt of Barnabas. Duty was duty, and Saul knocked at her gate. In a moment he was confronted by the woman in whose house he had been often welcomed. There she was, the stout figure with the coppery freckles and the halo of bronze-red hair, glaring at Saul.

"I am here by the order of the most esteemed High Priest Caiaphas to arrest followers of the Way," Saul said in a loud voice.

"Hah!" Mary replied with great contempt. "So Caiaphas is being pushed to act by zealots in the court. How like him. I knew him as a boy. He was weak of spirit then, and now he has grown up to be the craven puppet of the coward Pilate." When the captain moved his spear, she turned and said: "Stay where you are, Captain. You will not frighten this old woman."

Turning back to Saul, she said: "Saul, I once thought well of you. Now I despair that you are in thrall to this cunning Zadok, who craves power as an infant thirsts for its mother's milk. An evil man, that Zadok, combining the mind of a scholar with the principles of a hyena. And you, Saul, presiding at the execution of a fellow scholar. How unworthy of you." She waved a hand at the company of guards. "You, all of you, are mad to think that you can force Jews to deny Jesus. From my grandfather Hillel I learned that Jews have minds that respond to reason and argument, not force. Yes, the sage Hillel knew the Law far better than those self-important expositors who today preen about the Temple in their gaudy robes. In his day the princes knew how to interpret the Law for the times, not as it was written a thousand years ago. You, Saul, studied under the wise Gamaliel. Did you not there learn tolerance?"

The captain of the guard was watching Saul, and Saul thought he must end the discussion and take Mary into custody. "It is my duty — " he began, when she interrupted.

"You are not going to arrest me, boy, not you and all your Temple guards. I am of the Way, yes, as is my son, John Mark, and my nephew, Barnabas. I sent them into hiding until reason shall again prevail in Jerusalem. This house of stone has sheltered many followers of Jesus, and will again. If you attempt to take me by force, I have arranged that my friends among the poor of this city will rush into the streets and provoke such a riot that Pilate must ask the legate Taius to call out his centurions and impose martial law in Jerusalem. Ask your ambitious Zadok how he will explain that to the elders of the Sanhedrin."

The captain of the guard drew Saul aside. "My orders are to make these arrests without creating any public disturbance," he said. Saul hesitated, not sure it was wise to try to make the arrest, and not certain that the captain would even follow such an order. Mary, observing Saul's ambivalence with scorn, closed her gate. Angered by the rebuke before the guards, Saul moved to knock again; but the captain stopped him and said firmly: "I will take responsibility for letting this woman remain in her home."

The city was deep in darkness by the time Saul returned to the Sanhedrin, where he found Zadok reading in his chamber. Saul reported on the arrests he had made, identified those on the list who had escaped, and told of his encounter with Mary. "The captain was right," Zadok said. "So many in this city are in her debt, and not only the poor. There are members of this court she could stir against this pogrom."

"My task goes unfinished," Saul said. "Less than half the sect did we arrest. More fled into the hills of Judea, and to Syria. Let us ask Caiaphas to give me companies of guards to go tomorrow and find them, wherever they are, and bring them to trial."

"I commend your zeal," Zadok said, putting aside his scroll. "However, an expedition of Temple guards would surely cause disturbances within the villages. Indeed, the havoc you have created here in the city has provoked, within the last hour, a warning from Pilate."

"But we must press on," Saul insisted. "We cannot rest. You yourself declared that the enemy, now routed, must be pursued and destroyed. If we cannot carry our campaign into the Judean villages, let us act outside Pilate's province."

Zadok lifted his eyebrows in surprise. "What do you propose?"

"Today we learned that many in the sect escaped to Damascus. Section Six of the Concordat with Rome specifically gives the high priest authority over Jews outside Judea, including the summary right of extradition. Send me, as executor of the Sanhedrin, to Damascus with Temple guards and instructions to arrest the Nazarenes there and bring them here to be tried before this high court."

Zadok sat back, folded his arms, and looked at Saul. Was this, he mused, an act by Saul to dramatize fidelity to the Law and the court? Or, more likely, had that first taste of raw power captured Saul's spirit? The proposal was clever, imaginative, bold.

Damascus, oasis in the vast desert plateau, cross-point for trade routes, prosperous since ancient times, was now capital of Nabatea. Caesar Tiberius allowed Nabatea to remain an independent kingdom under King Aretas, who permitted the large enclave of Jews in the city to worship as they pleased. Zadok wondered if somehow Saul knew that over the last year the senior rabbi of Damascus, Abijah, and the four synagogues there had sent letters to Caiaphas stating their mounting concern at the growth of the Jesus sect in the city. Could Saul have learned about those letters, or was this just another example of his instinct, his intuition?

"Yours is a worthy proposal," Zadok said at last, and mentioned the appeal from the Damascus synagogues. "However, acting alone, Caiaphas would not commission such a bold and unprecedented expedition. As it happens, his privy council will meet at the fourth hour tomorrow. Since I draft the agenda for these deliberations, I can add your initiative, but you must argue its merit. It will stand or fall on your reasoning and persuasiveness."

Saul hurried to his room. There he spent most of the night drafting a resolution and rehearsing the points he would make. This would be his first opportunity to stand at the podium and address the privy council of the court. If the mission were approved — and he had no doubt that it would be — he would hold power in his own right and in his own name. His arguments, he decided, would be logical and brief; the resolution should speak for itself.

The next day, when it came his turn to speak, he was ready. "Most esteemed High Priest, elders, brothers," he began, and cited the "historic action" by Caiaphas to make an example of the blasphemous Stephen as a strong step toward ridding Jerusalem of the Nazarene sect. Briefly, he recounted how, in searching the city at Caiaphas' direction, he and the Temple guards discovered that many in the sect had escaped — some to the Judean hills, more to Damascus.

Holding up the letters from the Damascus synagogues, he read from them, paused to fix the attention of his listeners, and asked: "Can we in good conscience refuse aid to our brothers in need? As our brothers in Damascus call, so, I submit, does the Lord himself summon us — for it is to this Sanhedrin that the ancients and the sages entrusted the Law. So clearly, and with such finality did Moses speak the word of God: Any Jew, man or woman, who serves another God must be seized and punished. If this high court does not enforce the Law —" Saul paused, "who will? No rabbi, no priest, no town court, bears such responsibility as this most supreme of courts. This Sanhedrin must speak and act for Jews in Israel — and not only here but in all lands.

"Therefore I propose that this privy council authorize me to lead an expedition to Damascus to arrest all of the Way, bind them, and bring them to trial before this court." His argument finished, Saul took his seat, so convinced of the rightness of his cause that he expected swift and full approval of his expedition by the privy council. It was not to be.

Aaron, treasurer of the Sanhedrin, insisted that no aid be sent until the synagogues of Damascus first agreed to pay for the expedition. Uriah, an ambitious young Pharisee, argued that Saul was too young and inexperienced to head such an important mission to another country. Nathan, the most articulate of the Sadducee majority on the council, asked: "Why go so far? As the traitors are in the hills around us, send the Temple guards there."

When Caiaphas cautioned that Pilate might object to provincial arrests as usurpation of his authority, Nathan replied: "Rome be damned."

"Yes, damnation to Rome!" said old Ahaziah. "That cruel Tiberius will levy another tax on us at harvesttime. When will we free ourselves of this yoke?" A chorus of voices joined in to vilify Roman taxes, the turncoat Jews who collected Rome's taxes, and the arrogance of Roman soldiers and officers. Joram, a frequent traveler to Damascus, questioned whether King Aretas would permit guards from the Temple in Jerusalem to make arrests in his dominion. Baladan dismissed the entire proposal, insisting that the security of the Temple itself would be in peril if a full company of guards should be absent for as long as two months. For two hours the dispute continued. To Saul it seemed that all was lost; not even Zadok spoke in support of the mission.

At the end, when Caiaphas began to look about with impatience, the Sadducee Nathan spoke again. "We must make no compromise with this pernicious sect. We have no choice but to destroy them wherever we can. This expedition to Damascus is imperative." He proposed a compromise: Saul to be appointed executor for the high court, to go with two armed men, bearing letters from High Priest Caiaphas to the four synagogues of Damascus. The letters would authorize Saul to act for the Sanhedrin in searching out members of the Jesus sect, men and women, and returning them to Jerusalem for trial.

Caiaphas ordered a vote. Saul held his breath. The Sadducee majority and one Pharisee raised their hands. He had won, with five votes in favor, and two against.

That very afternoon Saul met with the two guards assigned for the journey. Both were experienced in travel through mountain and desert, and both were eager to take part in the mission. Saul ordered them to be ready to leave at sunrise the next morning.

XI

THE ROAD TO DAMASCUS

The first day of Saul's journey into a new life began as towering shafts of light in the eastern sky cast deep shadows on the rude huts and barred doors lining the Street of the Prophets. Three men and a sturdy, two-year-old donkey laden with provisions and water made their way along the empty streets and out of Jerusalem by the Damascus Gate. The break of day foretold a glorious morning, a sign of God's favor.

Ambition, pride, and the excitement of a new challenge drove Saul forward as the road climbed through the hills to the north. This was the commencement of a momentous responsibility. The night before he had written in his journal that he was marching to Damascus not merely to bring justice against a handful of blasphemers in one city; it could be the beginning of a campaign to take arms against all who betrayed the Law. With Zadok as his advocate, he would go on as chief prosecutor to other cities, charged to bring down the wrath of God on any Jew who broke the Covenant. That was his destiny, his path to becoming Defender of the Law, a leader among the people of Israel. How proud his mother would be of him.

It was high summer, and so the travelers chose not to take the camel route to Jericho and then along the Jordan River through the withering heat of the Jordan Valley. With the moon in its last quarter, they could not move by night. The longer but more traveled route was the Roman road that wound its way northward through Judea and Samaria into Galilee, past Tiberias and Magdala and the other villages along the western shore of the Sea of Galilee. Thence, from Capernaum, they would make their way through the cool foothills in the lee of Mount Hermon to join the Silk Road into Damascus. Saul told his companions that each day they would count thirty stones marking the Roman miles, and so arrive on the eighth day.

Both of Saul's Temple guards were hardy travelers and easy companions. Hagri had the shepherd's way of long silences and keen observation; as a youth he had been a herdsman in the mountains of Decapolis. When the owner of his flock cheated him of his wages, Hagri wandered south; on the road he met pilgrims walking to Jerusalem and joined them. In the courtyard outside the portico of Herod's Temple, Hagri separated two quarreling street merchants, prompting a captain of the Temple guards to enlist him. Saul learned quickly to trust Hagri's even temper and discerning eye. From their first mile together, the pace was set less by the leader's impatience to reach Damascus than by Hagri's deliberate manner and measured step. Saul admired Hagri's serenity, and tried to copy it.

The older and far more voluble of the two was Mikbar, once an ironsmith in Damascus. He had some schooling, was fluent in Greek and Aramaic, and was relentlessly inquisitive. He asked about Saul's early life in Tarsus, about the Hebrew and Greek training of his youth, about the patriarchs of the tribes of Israel, about the countryside and villages they passed along the way, about the purpose of their journey. With the shoulders and arms that came from years of sweating at the forge, Mikbar towered above other men like a giant. This size, and his immense black beard, stirred awe among the strangers they met on the roads and in the hills.

Hagri and Mikbar were each armed with a spear, a club of thornwood, and a knife. Saul carried no weapon. The high roads would be safe; all were patrolled by Roman soldiers. Should they be attacked by bandits in the hills, Saul trusted the skill and strength of his trained and imposing guards.

On the first afternoon they reached Milestone XXX while the sun was still well above the horizon, so they walked three miles beyond to camp for the night outside a Roman fort. Hagri watered the donkey and tethered him in a patch of grass while Saul and Mikbar loosed the cord on their saddlebag of food and supped on bread, cheese, almonds, and cakes of dried figs. All was quiet. The journey had begun well. Saul was content. As he lay wrapped in a warm new cloak against the night chill, he looked up, searching the heavens for Ursa Major. He fell asleep trying to pick out the form of the great bear.

At first light the three set out again. Mile after mile they walked, up and down the brown hills, through the dry beds of winter streams, past forests of cedars on the mountainsides. On the third day they came across a lost lamb. After seeking Saul's permission, Hagri took the lamb into his arms and carried it until they came upon a shepherd who was pleased to add the lostling to his flock. On the fifth day, walking ahead through a gap between hills, Saul sighted Mount Tabor, blue in the distance on his left hand. Tabor was their marker, so they turned northeast to cross the ridge that led into Tiberias. When they reached the summit of that ridge, Saul caught his first, forever memorable view of the Sea of Galilee, a shimmering sapphire lake set like a jewel in a ring of forested hills.

From his studies with Gamaliel, Saul knew that the tetrarch Herod Antipas had founded Tiberias fifteen years earlier as the capital of the Roman provinces of Galilee and Perea. Hoping to gain favor with Caesar Tiberius, Antipas gave the city the emperor's name.

Upon arriving in Tiberias in midafternoon before the Sabbath, Saul found an inn where they could eat fresh meat and sleep in comfort before they rose to worship in the synagogue the next morning. Anxious though he was to continue his journey, Saul would not travel on the Sabbath. As it happened, a summer storm struck after noon; towers of clouds darkened the sky, flashes of lightning struck the surrounding hilltops, and thunder crashed and shook the walls of the inn. The shrieking winds of the tempest turned the placid Sea of Galilee into a hilly reach of angry waves.

By the next morning the skies were clear and the air refreshing. The three travelers walked on, following the shore of the sea past fishermen pulling their nets along the rocky beaches of Magdala, through the lush and fruitful plain of Gennesaret, and thence into Capernaum. There Saul did not tarry. He had read in the Sanhedrin agents' reports that this was the city that Jesus had called home; this was the city where he had inspired Peter and Andrew to become his first disciples.

Walking briskly, he looked about, surprised by the size of the throng in a busy market and the trading evidenced by stately processions of camel caravans arriving from the east. On a promontory overlooking the lake stood a Roman fort of granite blocks, and set back in a nearby courtyard was a fine stone synagogue. The people of Capernaum seemed not so bucolic and primitive as Saul had been taught. Still, he assured himself once again, this remote Galilean region of the world would not have been the site chosen by God to reveal the Messiah.

As Saul and his two guards continued their march through the villages around Galilee, he could not rid himself of the thought that he was walking the streets and shores where Jesus had walked, that he was passing the synagogues where Jesus had taught. These were the places where the disciples claimed that Jesus healed the sick and gave sight to the blind. If, as Barnabas claimed, these miracles were the work of God, if this man of Galilee were the Messiah, why had God not intervened and kept Jesus alive so that he might continue his teaching?

In his mind Saul began to form the plan to carry out his duty to find and punish the heretic Jews of Damascus. He would first deliver Caiaphas' letter to Abijah, senior rabbi of the synagogues. To make known his purpose to the community he would ask Abijah to bring together all the rabbis and elders of Damascus so that he could address them. They would be hungry for news of Jerusalem, so he would begin with a vivid account of how Caiaphas had dealt with the blasphemy of Stephen. He would tell them how, upon Caiaphas' orders, he and the Temple guards searched out and imprisoned all members of the Jesus sect in Jerusalem. He would conclude by reading Caiaphas' letter directing him to go to Damascus to conduct a pogrom against the dissidents.

Once he had the support of the Damascus hierarchy, Saul would ask for a list of all suspected of being of the Way. With the names, he would ask for additional guards, a prison, water, food, and chains to take the prisoners from Damascus to Jerusalem. He was sure he had planned well, and the thought of exacting justice quickened his walk.

When they reached the north end of the Sea of Galilee, the travelers followed the Roman road along the west bank of the Jordan River and crossed to the east at a shallow ford. As they walked upstream to fill their skins with fresh water, Mikbar noted that since ancient times this crossing had been known as the Ford of the Daughters of Jacob. Saul observed that Jacob had but one daughter. "Jacob," Mikbar replied, "was not always truthful."

From the Jordan the travelers turned to the northeast, climbing the rolling hills of green forest and making their way through the valleys of grasses watered by quick streams flowing from the crevices of snow that they could pick out near the three summits of Mount Hermon. In the afternoon, as the mountain disappeared in blue haze, they came to barren hills, and thence to a rocky steppe where the road was little more than a narrow trail. Here there were no milestones. On they walked, and by dusk they could see nothing ahead but an expanse of bleak desert stretching to the far horizon.

Night came quickly to the vast and lonely sweep of sand, and with it came the cold. After Hagri unburdened their donkey in the darkness, he stopped for a moment, looked about, picked up his spear, and quietly walked a short distance away. Against the starlight Saul and Mikbar could see him crouched on a hilltop, motionless. In time Hagri returned and said he had caught the scent of a pack of wolves. They built a fire of dry brush to warm themselves, staked their donkey close by, and set a watch for the night. Saul took the first watch; when it ended, he could not sleep. He was too impatient to journey on, too excited about reaching Damascus the next day.

At sunrise they marched on. The first hours of the new day passed swiftly, urgency silencing their voices and quickening their strides. Before the sun warmed the air they reached the old Silk Road leading from Sidon to the great oasis of Damascus. When they paused to slake their thirst, Mikbar studied the empty road ahead. "Here we turn east. We shall arrive in Damascus by late afternoon."

"We must hurry on," Saul said, not waiting for Hagri to finish watering the donkey.

An hour later a towering cloud rose overhead and the sky turned from light haze to somber gray. Unaccountably, the sun disappeared. The air became close, the heat oppressive. Saul resolved that if a summer storm should bring lightning and a deluge of rain, he would not try to find shelter but press on. Never in his entire life had he been more determined. His mission must come first; he would not delay, not for any reason.

The wind rose, first in gusts, to turn quickly into a shrieking gale. Then total silence, and an eerie, Stygian darkness enveloped the road. Mikbar shouted out a warning and pointed to the threatening storm. Saul, stern and resolutely striding well ahead of his companions, thrust his arm forward to signal: *Keep walking.*

Moments later a chilling sensation of doom swept over Saul, stopping him in his tracks. He felt his skin prickle like gooseflesh, his hair rise on the back of his neck, his knees quake with fear. At that instant the sky exploded into resplendent light, brighter than a thousand suns, dazzling, terrifying, a coruscating brilliance beyond the known world. Saul felt himself being taken out of his body, lifted, suspended in time and space, held aloft for long moments; then he began to fall — down, down, down, as in a nightmare, falling through mist and cloud in mysterious silence, plunging interminably, until at last his hands felt earth. Prostrate on the stones of the road, trembling with fear, his mind in a daze, Saul thought he heard someone calling: "Saul! Saul! Why do you persecute me?"

"Who are you, sir?" Saul asked, looking about, anxious to find the voice addressing him.

"I am Jesus whom you persecute."

The voice came from above, from the heavens, ominous and terrifying. Saul felt his blood turn cold. He was doomed. The voice had sentenced him to death.

"I know it is hard for you to kick against the prods." The voice again, this time with a tone of sympathy.

In awe and wonder, Saul managed to ask: "Lord, what will you have me to do?"

"Rise, and go into the city. There you shall be told what you are to do."

At that instant the radiant light disappeared, ending just as swiftly as it had burst from the firmament.

Struggling to rise from the earth, Saul heard his companions running to his side. "Master! Master!" Mikbar shouted. "You live! I saw you were felled as though struck by a stone."

"I was certain you were killed," said Hagri.

With the help of his two guards, Saul got to his feet. Bewildered, and in pain from the fall, he turned to look at them — but everything was dark. "I cannot see!" he cried out. "I cannot see!"

He felt Mikbar's huge hands grip his shoulders, smelled his hot breath, heard Mikbar exclaim: "Your eyes are covered with ugly crusts; they look like fish scales!"

Saul thrust his hands to his eyes, fingers pulling at the scales. "Blind!" he screamed. "Blind I am!" In despair he fell to the earth, weeping, striking the stones of the road with his fists, and lamenting: "Blind! Blind! Like a beggar I am blind."

"Here," Hagri said, splashing Saul's face from a waterskin. "Wash your eyes. They may be coated with sand."

The water felt cool and cleansing, and Saul eagerly dried his face with his sleeve. It was no use. Again and again he blinked, but nothing could he see. Weeping, beating his breast, he moaned: "I am blinded! Doomed to darkness."

Images flashed through his mind, images of all the blind men he had ever seen, and scorned, their wretched gropings, their pathetic helplessness. Better he were dead, he thought. What good is a blind man? One more beggar in the streets. He put his hands over his face to hide his anguish.

"Come," said Mikbar, helping Saul to his feet. "Damascus is not far. Let us go on."

Carefully, hesitantly, Saul began to walk, slipped on a loose stone, and almost lost his balance. "Take my hand," Hagri said with reassurance. "I will lead the way." It was slow and awkward, and demeaning to be guided by a subordinate, but with a strong arm leading, Saul could make his way along the road.

Sightless though he was, Saul's mind was racing, questioning. What had happened? Had he been struck by lightning? Had that blinded him? Had the voice deranged his mind? Had there in fact been a voice? Or was he hallucinating? It sounded so real — resonant, firm, authoritative, distinctive in timbre, delivered in scholarly Hebrew. What had his companions heard? And seen? He must find out.

"Hagri, was it lightning that struck me?" Saul asked.

"No, Master. There was no flash, no thunder, only a great light such as I have never seen. It covered the whole sky. And I heard a strange voice as though coming from the clouds, and you answered, but I could not understand any words being spoken."

"I, too, heard the foreign words," Mikbar broke in, "but no person could I see."

So he had not been hallucinating; both had heard the voice, but neither understood. In his mind Saul tried to construct a rational explanation for this mysterious incident. Could that voice from above have been the voice of God? It had happened in the old time. God spoke to Noah, Abraham, Moses, Daniel, among others. But those divine interventions took place a thousand and more years ago. He could think of no modern precedent.

Yet in this place and hour, there had been a voice, and it came from above. He had heard it, and so had Mikbar and Hagri.

God must have been there on the road, for only God could have taken his sight. But why would God do that to him?

Thinking back, he recalled that throughout history God used that power to protect the favored, as with Lot and his daughters, and to punish those who did wrong. Therefore, he must consider that God had blinded him as punishment. "But what have I done?" he asked himself. "This is unjust: I stand accused of persecutions when I was enforcing the Law."

Stumbling on a stone, Saul fell headlong. His hands cut and bleeding, he pushed up to his feet, muttering to himself. "Am I being told that I was wrong to hunt down and prosecute those of the Way in Jerusalem? Wrong to set out on this expedition to prosecute Jesus' followers in Damascus?

"I am not at fault. It is my assigned duty to enforce the Law. Are not all Jews instructed that the Law is the word of God, authoritative, supreme, to be followed to the letter? Not once at the Sanhedrin did I doubt that I was doing God's work. How could I not be certain — I was following the teachings of my childhood and at Gamaliel's House of Study, the writings and traditions handed down from the patriarchs and the Prophets. I believed my master Zadok. I trusted the chief priests of the highest court. Could Zadok be wrong? Could all seventy-one members of the Sanhedrin be wrong? If so, why was I singled out for punishment?"

Feeling his way over the stones, Saul continued to concentrate his thoughts, searching for a plausible explanation to the incomprehensible.

"Milestone three, Master." Saul recognized the Damascene accent of Mikbar. He could hear the footsteps of other travelers and the shrill cry of a camel driver. They were nearing the city, and the closer they came, the more Saul realized that he confronted a new situation and must think it through, calmly, deliberately. A long-ago lesson from Zagoreos came to mind: *Deliberate with reason, plan with logic, act with order.*

First, his circumstances: Blind, he was completely dependent on his guards; and they, left to themselves, would follow the plan and take him to the senior rabbi for Damascus. Fortunately, neither Mikbar nor Hagri knew that the voice from the sky claimed to be Jesus. If they did, they would report that to Abijah, and he, very likely, would suspect that Saul, the Sanhedrin's prosecutor, was a secret convert to the Way and charge him with heresy. Or worse, his two guards might turn on him now, here on the road, accuse him of being a turncoat, and see it as their duty to bind him in chains and take him back to the high court to be tried for blasphemy. Or they might just kill him, or simply abandon him, a blind man helpless in the desert to be devoured by wolves. Thus his very life rested in the hands of two Temple guards in the hire of Caiaphas, the very priest who had sentenced Jesus to be crucified. To save his life, Saul concluded, he must keep his secret from his two companions.

The far greater imperative was to carry out the instructions from the heavenly voice. He was not yet convinced that it was actually Jesus who had spoken to him, but the sudden burst of glorious light and his blinding proved that God was present at that moment. "Go into the city . . . ," he had been told. He must assume that this was a message from God, and no sensible Jew would ever risk disobeying a command from God. But where in the city should he go? Certainly not to Abijah. The most logical and prudent plan, he reasoned, would be to find a neutral place where he would be alone to await further instructions.

"Mikbar," he said, "since I am blind, there is no purpose in my going directly to the chief rabbi of the synagogues, as we had planned. Do you know of an innkeeper in Damascus who will harbor a blind man? I have money to pay him."

Mikbar took his time in answering. "I can take you to the house of Judas bar Elimelech, a good and kind man who keeps a small inn on Straight Street. At my forge years ago, I fashioned iron gates for his courtyard. I will ask him to find room for you." After a long pause Mikbar continued: "I am under orders from the captain of the Temple guards to report to the senior rabbi upon my arrival in Damascus. Therefore, I will deliver to him the documents signed by the high priest Caiaphas authorizing our mission."

Saul started to protest, but the loss of his sight had changed the equation of authority. He had no power to stop Mikbar from carrying out his orders. It seemed of little consequence, for the documents signed by Caiaphas would be of no use to the synagogues in Damascus without an officer of the court to enforce the decree of the Sanhedrin. Saul spoke with caution: "Tell the rabbi, Mikbar, that the one who came to prosecute those of the Way was blinded and so cannot execute his orders."

In late afternoon, or so Saul judged from the waning warmth of the sun on his back, Mikbar announced that he could see the walls of Damascus. Through the Western Gate the three travelers entered; and Saul heard the cries of the merchants hawking their clay pots and sensed the stir and commotion of a thriving city. Breathing deeply, he detected the cinnamon bark of a spice shop, the roasting of meat, the rank odor of a tannery. Soon they stopped on what sounded like a busy street. When Saul heard Mikbar walk away, he asked Hagri to find his money pouch in the saddlebags. The coins were all there.

Finally Mikbar returned with Judas the innkeeper. Yes, he would take a blind man. Relieved, Saul paid the innkeeper for two days — if the voice had been authentic, surely Jesus or another messenger from God would come by then. Speaking from the heart, Saul said farewell to Mikbar and Hagri, grasping their hands, expressing his gratitude for their companionship and kindness, and counting out fifty denarii to each as gifts.

While the innkeeper led him through a passage to a creaking door and into a room, Saul tried to fix in his mind the location of cot, chair, and table. Seated there, he tried to compose his thoughts, but he could not. Just as the blinding light had put out his eyes, so also had the mystifying exchange with the heavenly voice disordered his mind. One moment he found himself to be in a daze, bewildered, still wondering if he had imagined the incident; the next moment he remembered with absolute clarity all that happened.

Always in the past, Saul had turned to writing to order his thoughts. Now, unable to see, he must rely on memory. He would begin by explicating, in sequence, each element of the brief but momentous encounter. First there was the darkening sky, presumably an omen of the storm to come. Then the burst of resplendent light, which he and his companions agreed was brighter than the sun, unlike anything seen before. Certainly such a brilliant light could manifest God; had the Psalmist not said that God "covered himself with light as with a garment"?

Some force — and he could not be sure what it was — had struck him with such power that he fell to earth. To the ancients, falling was a metaphor for sin. Then came those first ominous words: "Saul! Saul! Why do you persecute me?" The speaker knew his name: of that there was no doubt. Technically, he had never persecuted Jesus, but he remembered reading an agent's report quoting Jesus: "Whoever harms my followers harms me." Therefore, he must assume that the speaker not only knew that he had persecuted Jesus' followers in Jerusalem but also that he was on this journey to persecute others of the Way in Damascus.

The next words had been spoken with some sympathy: "I know it is hard for you to kick against the prods." Why, Saul asked himself, would Jesus — assuming for the moment it was Jesus — have cited that ancient Greek proverb about the stupidity of the ox? First, the citation did lend authenticity to the speaker; it was well known that on earth Jesus often spoke in parables. But how could that proverb apply to him? Was he being ridiculed as a dumb ox under yoke, obeying no one but his master Zadok? Looking back, he had to admit that, like a harnessed animal, he had followed the traces of ambition, vanity, and pride. Could it be that the voice claiming to be Jesus was enjoining him to rebel, to kick against his master's prods, but warning that it would not be easy?

Next there had been silence, and somehow, though seized by fear and awe, he had found enough presence of mind to speak. "Lord," he had said, and in that fraction of time he had assumed that the voice from the heavens was indeed divine, "what will you have me to do?" Instinct had prompted that question. From all his studies he knew that when God spoke directly to a man, he had a mission for him.

Finally, the succinct command: "Rise, and go into the city. There you shall be told what you are to do." Why, he wondered, if the voice was a messenger from God, had that messenger not told him then and there what he was to do? Moreover, if he were to be given a new mission of any importance, why had he been blinded? That was illogical, self-defeating. Without sight, a man cannot lead, organize, or accomplish anything useful.

An hour passed. Then another. With care, feeling for obstacles, Saul walked back and forth across his room. *Be patient*, he admonished himself. The street noises lessened, so he assumed that darkness had fallen. Perhaps the one who called himself Jesus was waiting for night. But the room was silent except for the brush of his footsteps on earth. With a sigh he found the chair and put his head on the table.

At that moment Saul thought he heard footsteps. He held his breath. Had Jesus arrived? Silence. Then came a soft knock on the door. Saul leaped up, blundered his way across the room, knocked over a bench, and fell. In haste he clambered to his feet, felt along the wall until he found the latch, and opened the door.

"I brought food and drink, and water to bathe your feet." It was the cheerful voice of a young woman.

"Who are you?"

"I am Hannah, servant at the inn. Judas the innkeeper sends you the best of his food and drink, and told me to wash your feet after your long journey."

"No! No!" Saul replied. "Go away!" Dejected, and angry, he slammed the door. He had expected Jesus, but it was only a servant. In a fury of resentment Saul vowed that he would neither eat nor drink until he heard from Jesus again.

He found his way to his cot and there he lay, bewildered, despairing, head in hands. Why had Jesus forsaken him? Pitying himself, Saul wept, and the weeping made him all the wearier, causing him to fall more deeply into dole and wretchedness. In time the weariness of his body and the confusion of his thoughts conquered his weakened spirit, and he drifted past the threshold of consciousness into sleep.

Some hours later Saul awakened. All was silent, not even a cock-crow, so he concluded it was still deep night. He had been dreaming, and in the dream he was standing on his mother's pavilion, waiting for her, eagerly anticipating her appearance. At last she stepped from the shadow of a fluted column and stood apart, looking at him, her beautiful eyes awash with tears. Erect as always but immobile, she searched his face. Without a word, she bowed her head in sadness and placed her slender hands over her eyes as if grieving. Slowly she turned away and, not once looking back, moved into the shadows.

Saul sat up quickly, not yet fully alert but alarmed. Always before, when she came to him in a dream his mother had embraced him, spoken with warmth and affection, encouragement and love. But this time she was mute. This time a great distance separated mother and son. How should he interpret this dream? Was she, by turning away, rejecting him for something he had done, or was about to do? Somehow he could not escape the feeling that never again would she come to him.

Now wide awake, Saul rose from his cot and stepped carefully, hands out before him, groping for his chair. Lost in darkness, he fell over the bench again, striking an arm and knee on the hard earthen floor. The stinging pain, the confusion of blindness, the unsettling silence of his mother — all reduced him to despair as he lay bleeding. A day and a night had passed and Jesus had not come to him. Perhaps this Jesus did not exist, would never reappear, then he would be left in misery in this remote inn, blind, unable to walk unaided, consigned to beg from strangers. Failure loomed like a specter: All the years of study wasted; all the aspirations and prospects of his young life brought to a sudden and tragic end.

Head in hand, lamenting his plight, Saul let himself suffer in his misery and hopelessness. Hour after hour he dwelled on his misfortune, beating his breast, cursing his lot, wailing that he had been abandoned, rejected, punished unfairly. Finally, near the end of that second day, he wearied of indulging himself. "Enough!" he blurted in self-disgust. "Bad it is; I make it worse."

Rising to his feet he pounded a fist on the table and cried out: "Am I a weakling? Am I a coward? No! No! I have not journeyed this far to accept defeat." He had a choice: He could continue to wallow in self-pity, or he could find a way to go forward. How, he was not sure. But he knew he had reached a critical turning point in his life. He would either conquer his affliction and find a new life of purpose, or accept death.

Death might be easier, he thought; he could simply starve himself. But he wanted to live. He thought back to the dark hours of childhood asthma and how he had learned to persevere, knowing the struggle for breath would in time come to an end. He heard the words of the crippled Musonius, "There is no tragedy that courage cannot conquer." And Zagoreos, "Look inward, Paulos, look inward." There was Targon, calm and resolute in the storm, quickly marshaling his resources to save the *Pegasus*. He recalled the wisdom of Gamaliel: "God does not give us a greater burden than we can bear."

How often in the past he had been guided by their counsel; now, more than ever before, he must turn to them. But they were only guides through the darkness, his darkness of sight and spirit; to find a way ahead, he must rely on courage, fortitude, and strength of will. He must summon the resolve and indefatigable spirit that were part of his being, that lay deep in his soul. "Look inward, Paulos . . ." Zagoreos was right; he must reexamine his situation methodically, then proceed to a line of reasoning.

"God has intervened in my life." He spoke each word deliberately, straining his mind to comprehend the enormity of that fact. "To what end I cannot yet know. But his presence there on the road I cannot dispute. God was there." Drawing on his scholarly training, he decided to postulate the reality of God's intervention as the basic proposition for a line of analysis and reasoning. "As God was there, I must and do believe he was there for a purpose. God never acts without a reason. Next, it is fact that a voice spoke to me on that road, and that voice claimed to be Jesus. Was it?"

After considering all possible explanations, he asked: "How could that voice *not* be Jesus? It is inconceivable that God would permit any false speaker by his side. Therefore, I must assume that it was indeed Jesus who spoke to me. Moreover, the speaker was all-knowing: He addressed me by name and knew everything I am doing. God alone is all-knowing. Therefore, it is plausible that Jesus spoke to me as a messenger from, and for, God."

Weighing the import of that assumption, he concluded: "If Jesus is now, three years after his death, the chosen messenger of God, then I must at least consider that Jesus was, as his disciples contended, the anointed, the 'beloved son' of God. In that event, the evidence sustains the disciples' claim that Jesus was the Messiah."

Pacing about to contemplate the grave implications of his chain of reasoning, Saul wondered why the Messiah would have appeared as a humble provincial carpenter and not as the mighty warrior king that Jews had been expecting for a thousand years.

He stopped. What was that sound at the window? In silence and expectation he listened, but it was just a gust of night wind rattling a loose shutter. "Let us further assume," he continued, copying a tactic from Gamaliel, "that the earthly Jesus was in fact the Messiah, as reported at the time. Then Barnabas was right when he returned from Galilee that long-ago day. And Stephen spoke truly when he reminded the high court that in the olden time stubborn Jews disowned Moses and Joseph as we in the present time disowned Jesus. And the reports of Jesus' miracles, at which Zadok and I scoffed, were true."

Still, there were questions: "Why did God permit his son to be crucified? Our infiltrators of the movement brought evidence that God's intent was to show mankind that Jesus was man, mortal, one of us. Then it was said that God brought Jesus back from the dead, and there was strong evidence that he in fact did so. The reason, from the reports, was to show that Jesus was not only one with man but one with God — the chosen, the Messiah."

Saul grimly shook his head. "If my reasoning is correct — and both logic and evidence strongly support it — then I was wrong."

All was quiet in the streets outside. A new day would soon begin. Point by point, and hour after hour, Saul reviewed his argument from initial premise through logical assumption to stark conclusion. He challenged each particular. He reexamined every issue. At the end he found that the preponderance of evidence permitted but one conclusion: There was more proof that Jesus was the Messiah than that he was not.

"Two days ago I had eyes to see," he mused, "but I was blind to truth. Today I am blind of eye but I see the truth. Jesus, the one I persecuted, is the Messiah. I know that to be true."

He fell silent, at once awed and alarmed as he tried to comprehend that momentous reality. Nothing in his twenty-seven years of life had prepared him for this revelation. It was hard to believe, but he must accept the reality that a miracle had happened to him on the road to Damascus. God had stopped him in his headlong pursuit of misguided action, turned him, transformed him. God had sent Jesus to him for a purpose, yet to be disclosed. Logic permitted no other conclusion.

In his heart and soul Saul knew that God had changed his life for all time. But many things he could not understand. Blind, how could he carry out a mission; indeed, how could he serve any useful purpose? And yet, he could hope. The Lord God who punished him by taking his sight also had the power to forgive him and restore his sight. Isaiah had written of it, and Barnabas had witnessed the incident in Capernaum when Jesus had restored the sight of two blind men.

On that occasion Jesus had first required the two blind men to show their faith that he could in fact make them see again. On the issue of faith, Saul was not sure he could qualify. "Knowledge I have," he said to himself. "Faith I do not yet understand, much less have."

Perhaps faith was an emotional force that would come to him as it had to Barnabas and Stephen and all of the Way. At the moment he felt the need to thank God for delivering him from ignorance to truth. Falling to his knees, he shut away from his mind all fears and thoughts of his misfortune, and so in time he was moved to a peace of mind and spirit that he had never felt before. In calm and confidence he raised his hands to the heavens. "Lord

God, I know that you brought me here for a purpose. Show me the path you have chosen for me, and I will follow it."

As he continued to pray, Saul's thoughts moved upward to a higher level of consciousness, and in that liminal state of the senses he had a vision. He saw the face of a kind stranger coming the next day, a man called Ananias, who would lay his hand on Saul's forehead and restore his sight.

XII

STRANGER

In the old section of Damascus named for the Semitic storm god Hadad, a wool merchant respected for his honesty and industry knelt at the window of his stone house at the break of day, reciting a thanksgiving song of David, when he had a vision.

"Ananias!"

Instantly and without question the merchant recognized the voice, although he had not heard it for more than three years. He turned and replied: "Behold, I am here, Lord Jesus."

"Rise up, Ananias, pass along on the street being called Straight to the inn of Judas, and there seek a Tarsian named Saul. For behold, Saul is praying, and has seen in a vision a man by the name of Ananias coming in, and putting on him a hand so that he may see again."

"Lord," Ananias replied, "I have heard from many about this man, how he jailed and prosecuted your followers in Jerusalem. He is here in Damascus with a warrant from the chief priests of the Sanhedrin to arrest and bind in chains all who invoke your name."

"Go, for this man is my chosen instrument to bear my name before gentiles and kings and the people of Israel. I myself will show him how much he must suffer in my name."

The streets of Damascus were empty when Ananias rattled the iron gates of the inn of Judas. As he entered Saul's room, he saw a man smaller and younger and less formidable than he expected. Above the gaunt frame, sloping shoulders, and thin neck rose an unusually large head. A narrow forehead and prominent nose dominated the upper part of his face; the strong jaw was swathed in a well-trimmed beard appropriate to officials of the high court. Dense black curls covered the stranger's temples but thinned at the top of his head. Most striking were the bulging eyes, open, the pupils crusted over, the lids covered with scabs.

Ananias took a deep breath. "Brother Saul, the Lord Jesus has sent me so that you may see again and be filled with the Holy Spirit."

Saul turned his face and attention toward the direction of the voice. "I have been waiting."

Ananias touched the tips of his fingers to Saul's forehead. "Receive thy sight!"

Saul turned his face upward, and in an instant the scabs that covered his eyes fell away.

"I see," Saul said quietly, as he looked upon his deliverer. "I see!" His voice rose, and he turned right and left, observing the room with curiosity. When he faced Ananias, Saul saw that this was indeed the stranger he had seen in his vision the night before, an older man kind of face and confident of manner. With a shout of joy Saul seized Ananias' shoulder: "I see again!"

Ananias stepped back. "There is more," he said. "The Lord Jesus commanded me also to deliver this message: He appoints you as his chosen instrument to carry his name before gentiles and kings and the children of Israel, to open their eyes as he has opened your eyes, to turn them from darkness to light and from Satan to God, to teach them that they may be forgiven of their sins and made acceptable to God through faith in the Lord Jesus."

"God has given me that mission?" Saul asked in wonder.

"Jesus gives you that mission," Ananias said firmly. "Jesus and God are separate but as one."

"Why was I chosen for this purpose?"

"That I was not told," Ananias said. "The Lord Jesus commands; he does not explain." He paused. "It could be because of your uncommon zeal. But you were serving the wrong master."

Saul started to ask another question, but he hesitated, staggered, and reached for the table to keep from falling.

Ananias looked at Saul's pale face. "When did you last eat?"

"Three days ago I vowed I would neither eat nor drink until Jesus came to me again."

Ananias helped him to the chair. "Sit here. I will fetch food and drink." As soon as Hannah arrived, Saul took a deep draft of water, broke off a crust of bread, and, eyes bright with excitement, turned to Ananias. "How did you come to know Jesus?"

Ananias reflected for a moment before he began his story. "As a trader in wool, I journey from Antioch to Beersheba, through the hills and valleys of Judea and Syria. Ten years ago I chanced to be in the wilderness, buying wool, when I heard a compelling teacher by a village stream. He was a desert radical of priestly descent, and he spoke with fiery conviction against those Jews who take from the poor to clothe themselves in gold. His followers called him John the Baptist, for he immersed each believer, man and woman, in a stream and brought them up again to symbolize death of sin and rebirth in spirit. Some thought this John a prophet, but he said no, the true prophet was soon to come. That was the first time I heard of Jesus."

"Did you see Jesus when he was on earth?"

"Yes, many times," Ananias said. "I sought him out in Galilee and made it my purpose to hear him in the synagogues, on the shores of the sea, wherever he appeared. And I happened to be in Jerusalem — indeed, I was entering the portico of the Temple — when Jesus overturned the tables of the money changers. The riots that broke out that day provoked the Roman legionnaires and the Temple guards to round up everyone, the curious, the innocent, as well as those of us they recognized as followers of Jesus. By good fortune I escaped in the night and fled to Damascus. Here I have prospered and become a deacon in the Way."

"How many belong to the movement in Damascus?"

Ananias hesitated, then decided he would not reveal that he had suspected Saul. "At least eighty here in the city, and thirty more in the river villages nearby."

Saul lifted his eyebrows in surprise. "There are even more than we at court suspected."

"King Aretas tolerates any and all gods, so long as those who venerate their deities keep peace and order," Ananias said. "Yet we must guard our secret well, for it is the Jews, and particularly the senior rabbi, Abijah, who contrive to destroy us. We, too, are Jews of course. We go to the synagogues. We revere the Torah. We keep the Sabbath. But on the third day of the week we of the Way assemble — at times by the River Abana, or on a hillside outside the city walls, or in someone's house. We sing. We pray. And one of us who heard Jesus in life — usually Samantha — will recite one of Jesus' parables."

Saul pushed his plate away. "I would know more of my mission."

Ananias shook his head. "Only the Lord Jesus knows and can tell you what your mandate is to be. What do you intend to do next?"

Saul looked about in uncertainty.

"Rise," Ananias said. "Be baptized and wash away your past."

"I am ready," Saul replied.

When they reached the swift waters of the River Abana, the two men waded from the rocky bank until they were waist-deep. Ananias placed his right hand behind Saul's back and his left hand on his chest. "Do you repent of your sins?"

"I do repent and ask forgiveness for the many wrongs I have done," Saul replied.

"I baptize you in the name of the Father, the Son, and the Holy Spirit." Ananias plunged Saul beneath the clear swirling waters and slowly brought him up again. "Your sins are forgiven. In these waters you have been buried with Christ as in his death, and you are raised to new life in his resurrected glory. Thus you are born again. Your enter a new life. Use it as God intends."

Saul came up out of the stream charged with energy and resolution. Dripping and disheveled, he strode to the riverbank and turned to Ananias. "You say I am born anew, and so I am. Jesus commanded that I shall bear the truth to Jew and gentile alike. Therefore, I will begin my mission this hour. I will go first to the chief rabbi, Abijah, and ask to speak to the elders of the synagogue. To them I shall recount how Jesus came to me on the road, and that I now know that Jesus is the Messiah for whom we have so long waited."

Ananias raised his hands in caution. "They will not believe you. And may harm you."

"I have no fear of these rabbis," Saul replied. "They are misguided, as I was. As I am appointed a messenger from God, I must speak."

Ananias shook his head. "Bold you are, Brother Saul, perhaps too bold. It would be better if I gathered our members tonight at the house of Amon so you may tell them how Jesus came to you."

"I will do both," Saul said. "The Jews of Damascus must learn the truth, so I will go there first."

By the time Saul found the synagogue, the morning sun had dried his cloak and the brilliance of the day had lifted his spirits. He had escaped his prison of darkness. He could see again. He could walk unaided. He could observe the cheerful Damascene shopkeepers calling to each other in the busy streets. He could look up at the sky, see palm trees, flights of birds.

At the synagogue, a basilica of fine cut stone, he was led to the private room of the chief rabbi, Abijah.

"I am Saul. I come from Jerusalem."

Abijah leaped up, opening his arms in welcome. "We have been expecting you." The rabbi looked at Saul intently. "But you are not blind. Your companions told us you had been struck by lightning on the way and blinded."

"My sight was taken and restored by acts of God," Saul said. "Now I would speak in your synagogue on my mission."

"And so you shall," Abijah said. "Mikbar delivered the letters from Caiaphas directing us to aid you in rounding up the members of this pernicious fragment of our people who follow a false prophet. We are ready to help you." With that, he directed an attendant to go about in the neighborhood and bring in all he could find to hear the prosecutor sent by the Sanhedrin.

To the score of artisans, shopkeepers, and elders assembled, Abijah said: "Behold, this is Saul, sent by the high priest of the Sanhedrin to rid us of dissidents and apostates. Speak, Saul."

Saul stood and waited in silence to fix their attention. "It is true that I was dispatched by Caiaphas to arrest and bind all of the Way here in Damascus and return them to Jerusalem to be put on trial for heresy." He paused and studied the faces of the devout gathered before him.

"My brothers, I was mistaken. Caiaphas is mistaken. You and all who have believed we are dutiful Jews are mistaken. For Jesus was no false prophet. He is the son of God. He is the Chosen One." The room was silent. Saul continued. "How do I know? I know because three days ago Jesus spoke to me on the road outside this city."

There was muttering in the assembly, forcing Saul to raise his voice. "Hear me, O men, all of you! This was no dream. This was no hallucination. I heard the Lord Jesus. He spoke to me, in his own voice, out of his own mouth. Jesus lives. The prophet we nailed to the cross was the Messiah —"

The muttering rose to angry words. Rabbi Abijah paled, his jaw dropped, and he sat looking at Saul in astonishment. From the congregation an elder, white of beard and red of face, shouted: "Away with this blasphemer! He desecrates this holy place." Others took up the cry and shook their fists at Saul, provoking Abijah to stand and raise his hands for silence.

Turning to Saul, the chief rabbi pointed his finger at him and said: "You were sent to defend us. Now you have joined the heretics. You have become the enemy."

"I am not the enemy!" Saul shouted. "Do not be blind, as I was blind. See the light. I am witness to this truth: Jesus is the anointed one."

"Heresy! Heresy!" shouted the elder to Abijah. "Call the guards."

A cacophony of voices swept the assembly: "Begone!" "Blasphemy! Blasphemy!" "Stone this heretic."

"Listen to me!" shouted Saul. "Hear the truth." But the face of the assembly was turned against him. Some covered their ears; others ran up to Rabbi Abijah, shrieking in dismay and rending their cloaks. Raising his voice over the disturbance, Abijah called out to Saul: "Go! In the name of God, go. You have betrayed us. Go quickly, before blood is spilled."

Walking back to the inn, Saul began to grasp the Sisyphean dimension of his task. Ananias had warned him, but Saul, out of arrogance and new conviction, expected that at least some of his Jewish brothers would accept his account of finding the truth about Jesus. He should have known. Four hundred years it had been since Judaism had accepted a prophet — so long ago that when Jesus had appeared in their midst in Jerusalem, they could not accept the reality that God had sent to mankind the greatest of all prophets. He remembered something Gamaliel once said: "Few, not even the wise, recognize history as it happens."

At dusk Ananias knocked at Saul's door, and the two men made their way to the end of Straight Street and the house of Amon, a young potter, close by the western wall of the city. Their host met them at the door, hanging his head in shame. "I asked many of our people to come," Amon said, "but only four are here — Tobias the fuller, myself, my wife, and the ever-faithful Samantha."

"Why do the others stay away?" Ananias asked.

Amon drew Ananias aside. "They suspect that you have been deceived," he whispered. "They believe the prosecutor from the Sanhedrin only pretends to join us; that this Saul connives to find us out and put us in chains."

"So I believed initially," Ananias said, "but hear his story before you judge him."

Aware that he was being put on trial, Saul recounted in detail the circumstances of his journey, the darkening sky, the heavenly luminescence, the words Jesus spoke, the despair of blindness. "Ananias will confirm that Jesus appeared to him this morning in a vision and told him to remove the scales from my eyes so that I would see again, so that I could begin my mission to tell the world what I have witnessed."

No sooner had Saul finished than Tobias spoke up. "Even if I could accept your story, I cannot forget that you carried out the order to put Stephen to death by stoning." He jabbed his finger at Saul's chest. "I saw you there, exulting. I cannot forget that when you started arresting others of the Way in Jerusalem, my wife and I barely escaped. I cannot forget that you came here to put us in irons and march us to Jerusalem to be tried by a court as despotic and venal as Caesar himself." He turned to Ananias. "It is well known in the streets that the rabbis and elders of this city evicted this man from the synagogue today. Even now the chief rabbi Abijah petitions King Aretas to throw this Tarsian in prison for fomenting public disorder; we learned this from a servant in Abijah's household." Tobias shook his head in bitterness. "Go from this city, despised one, for here you will cause more harm to the Way than any good you can bring." He shook his fist in Saul's face and left.

After a moment Samantha came up to Saul and touched her slender fingers to his arm. She was slight and spare, a tiny woman with merry blue eyes, but there was something in her erect shoulders and raised chin that suggested nobility and courage. Once she had been wealthy; her husband was a banker and the elected ruler of the Jewish city-state of Tiberias. It was there that she first saw Jesus and began to follow him as he taught in Galilee. Her husband divorced her for joining the Way, but returned her dowry. Samantha then immigrated to Damascus, where she earned such respect within the movement that members chose her as the first woman to become a deacon. Now, as always, she spoke in a firm voice that encouraged obedience.

"I believe your story," Samantha said to Saul. "I believe it, strange as it is, for I trust Ananias. And certainly it is in character for Jesus to enlist to his cause one who had persecuted his followers. Well do I remember how he persuaded the despised tax collector Zacchaeus to give his wealth to the poor."

She looked at Saul and shook her head. "Brother Saul, every woman and every man who enters the door of the Way discovers that it is not easy to serve the cause. At the very beginning of your mission, you go into the synagogue as a stranger and embitter our fellow Jews, the very people we want most to persuade. And to us, who came to believe in Jesus long before you, the story of your conversion comes as a shock. The incident is too improbable for most of us to accept it. In time we may, yes; but for now, you must give our simple minds an interval to grasp the enormity of Jesus returning to earth for the first time since he ascended to the heavens three years ago."

Saul listened intently; from childhood he had been quick to recognize a well-informed instructor.

"Worst of all, Brother Saul," Samantha said, spreading her arms out wide, "worst of all is your message: It is vain, indistinct, and unconvincing. I perceive that in the afterglow of your revelation on the road you can think of nothing else. I understand that feeling. I saw Jesus, many times, and each time I came away bearing the glow of eternity. But it is not enough for you to say over and over, 'I had a vision! Jesus spoke to me!' Few will believe you; fewer still will care.

"If you are to accomplish your mission, you must tell people what Jesus means to them and what he can bring to them and why they should follow him. I heard him say we must love God and our fellow man — a clear and simple message, as far as it goes. It is a message so easy to mouth and so hard to follow. The lessons in Jesus' parables are not always obvious; indeed, he crafted his homely tales to intrigue us, knowing we would better remember a riddle than a speech."

Ananias opened his mouth to say something, but Samantha raised her hand to stay his words. "More I have to say," she said, and began to pace back and forth.

"Who is Jesus? And why should we follow him? That is the issue. There are other gods; indeed, as this civilized city is a crossroads for convictions as well as trade, the deities offered in this region present as many choices as a bountiful market at harvesttime. At one stall there is Apollo, at another Artemis, at another Zeus. Walk on and find the Sumerian triad — Anu of the sky, Enlil of the storm, and Ea of the water. Look to Anatolia for the mother goddess Cybele, to Persia for Mithras, to Babylon for Marduk. Turn to the south and discover Osiris, master of the Nile, and Ra, the glittering sun-god creating his pyramid. And there, at the end of this crowded market, what do we find? The humble Jesus, adorned not in gold and jewels but in the rough-woven cloak of the poor."

She stopped to confront Saul. "Who is this new god? And what does this Jesus offer to women, men, and children? It is up to us to answer. All too brief were the days of his teaching on earth. He spoke to provincials, and he wrote nothing. Who among us will examine Jesus' words and his life, define his message, and articulate it so clearly that the shepherd in the field and the housewife shaping her loaves for the oven will not only understand, but come gladly to the Way? The singular message of Jesus has yet to be fully grasped and spoken, much less written. The task awaits the right person. If you can do that, Brother Saul, you will light the world."

Saul stood entranced, engaged by the force and directness and logic of this tiny woman's words. "I am ready to begin," Saul said.

"You were baptized today?" Samantha asked.

"Yes. Ananias baptized me in the River Abana."

"This you would not know," Samantha said, "but immediately after Jesus was baptized, he walked alone into the desert. He went there to meditate, to search his own conscience and soul, to speak and listen to God. When he came out of the desert, Jesus knew not only his purpose, but could foresee the full course of his life."

"I, too, shall go alone into the desert," Saul said.

Except for the winds drifting and sculpting the restless sands, and a random scattering of oases where water unaccountably springs from the earth, the vast steppes surrounding Damascus are silent and empty. By day the sky is an upturned bowl of molten lead. From rising to setting the sun burns the eyes, the skin, the flesh itself. Darkness falls quickly, closing in like a shroud. Then the chill reaches the bones, and the rare creature of this wilderness, a jackal or a serpent, must find a den or die. Only the brave and the unwanted venture here; only the nomad with his camel, or the fugitive fleeing injustice, or those in search of themselves. It was into this immense expanse of loneliness that Saul ventured, and for three years wandered, searching for meaning in his past, waiting in vain for Jesus to reappear and tell him how he was to carry out his mission.

XIII

FUGITIVE

Looking far to the east, King Aretas' guards at the Babylon Gate could see the drifts of windblown sand that marked the coming of a long camel train from Mesopotamia. By afternoon the cameleers were within the walls of Damascus, unloading their cottons and silks, their bags of millet and spelt before watering and feeding their treasured beasts. Arriving with them was a desert wanderer, a man with long face and unkempt black beard, heavy bowed legs, and worn sandals. He had joined the caravan in Havilah.

Once he passed the scrutiny of the guards, Saul asked the way to the house of Ananias. There a servant replied that his master was on a journey to far Judea. So Saul walked about until he found the house of Amon the potter. At his knock the door opened, and the eyes of Amon's wife widened in astonishment.

"The king's soldiers are searching for you!" she cried out. "Enter, quickly!"

Saul hurried inside. "Why do soldiers seek me?"

"To arrest you," she whispered, as she bolted the door. "Amon set out to find you. Come! There is an empty cabinet behind the potter's wheel where you can hide."

An hour later Saul heard footsteps. He made no sound, holding his breath until he recognized the voice.

"It is I, Amon. Now that it is dark, you can come out."

Saul crawled from the cabinet. "What have I done to this king? I left Damascus three years ago."

"Yes, but the chief rabbi knows you are here," Amon said. "You were spotted by an elder of the synagogue as you came through the Babylon Gate. This old man sells salt there. He remembered your face, and ran to tell Abijah." Amon clasped Saul by the arm and looked him in the eye. "Whereupon Abijah told the king you come in secret to lead a rebellion.

Whereupon the king sent his soldiers into the streets to seize you. Then he will put you to the sword for treason."

Saul shook his head and opened his palms. "How can this be? I bear no threat to this king. After all this time, I thought my appearance in the synagogue would have been forgotten."

"Old Abijah never forgets, Brother Saul. Nor is he alone in this; he acts on orders directly from the Sanhedrin."

Saul felt the chill of raw fear. "Zadok," he muttered. "My mentor has become my enemy."

"The king ordered a watch on all gates, but we have a plan for your escape," Amon said with spirit. "Risky it is, but we have no choice. A boy of the Way will lead you across the city to the dwelling of Samantha, which was built with two others high in the south wall near the river gate. In one room she has a window that opens to the outside of the wall. We hope it is large enough for you."

"When do we start?"

"Now. There is no time to waste. The royal guards may search our houses."

"How old is this boy who will lead me?" Saul asked.

"Ten, maybe eleven."

"Can I trust him?"

"You have no choice." Leading Saul into the other room, Amon handed Saul a threadbare hooded cloak and a stick. "Cover your head, and hobble slowly as though you were an old man."

From the shadows appeared a sturdy boy with impudent bright eyes and even white teeth gleaming in his swarthy face. "This is Clement," Amon said.

"Sir, we shall have an adventure tonight," the boy said cheerfully. "I will scurry about pretending to be a young thief scheming to snatch fruit from a food stand or pick a pocket. This will divert attention to me. You are to plod along well behind me, keeping me in sight and affecting deafness if anyone stops you. When we get to the stone stair at the wall, move quickly up the steps to the third door. They are expecting you."

"God speed and protect you," said Amon.

The boy Clement played his role well, brushing against strangers and provoking them to clutch their purses, even taunting an armed guard to chase him up a dark alley. Saul hobbled on until his guide reappeared ahead. When they reached the wall, the boy tilted his head toward the stairs and drifted away into the shadows. Saul looked up to the top of the crenellated battlement, bounded up the steps, and opened the door.

"Welcome, Brother Saul," Samantha said softly. "You must speak in whispers. It is almost time for the guard to walk his post overhead."

Saul surveyed the room, lit only by a low candle. "Are you alone?"

"Yes," Samantha said. "I expected a man of the Way to help me, but he must have feared to come."

"You risk your life to save mine," Saul said.

"It is my choice," she said. "Indeed, it is my duty." In a stern voice she asked: "What did you learn in the desert?"

"I came to see what to expect from the Lord and what to expect from myself," Saul replied. "I went into the desert confident that Jesus would come at once and tell me where to go and what to say. When, after more than a year, I heard nothing, I was sorely disappointed. Then I realized that it was not up to Jesus to find me, but up to me to find Jesus. So I decided that I myself would create the message that would bring the multitudes from darkness to light. Day and night I questioned, examined, reasoned, trying to compose the argument that would convince Jew and gentile alike that the Messiah had come. I wrote. I postulated ideas. I spoke them aloud to empty sands. I felt mocked by the silence of the desert. Failure caused me to doubt; doubt provoked me to dismay, dismay to anger and despair."

"You were being tested," Samantha said.

"Yes, so I realized in my third year," Saul said. "I recognized that I must prove not only my patience but my steadfastness as well. If I did not believe, how could I persuade others to believe? By searching within myself, I came to see that all rests on faith."

"So the desert was a seminal experience," Samantha said.

"Yes," Saul said. "There I learned to trust in the Lord, but rely on myself. I went knowing only that I had been given a mission; now I know that it is my responsibility to discover how to accomplish that mission."

"What will you do now?" Samantha asked.

"I need to know more, so I will go to Jerusalem, to see those whom Jesus chose as his disciples and learn from them."

"Yes, and good," Samantha said. "But beware of the long knives of the Sanhedrin."

The tramp of boots overhead silenced both. When the sound faded, Samantha said: "Now we must act. We have half an hour until the guard returns, and soon the moon rises. Do you have money?"

"None," Saul said. "Nor do I know how to find the disciples in Jerusalem."

"I have been to the central house of the movement," Samantha said. "You enter by the Damascus Gate, turn left to the caverns that lie north of Fort Antonia, and find an old mud house with a broken corner that has been repaired with unfired brick. Ask for Peter, the one Jesus selected to be first among the disciples."

From a table she took a small purse of coins, handed it to Saul, and led him by the arm to the small window in the stone wall.

"It is fifty feet down," Samantha said. "I borrowed a grain basket and this rope of flax. I will put the basket out the window and hold the rope while you climb in. Then I will hand you a waterskin and three days' bread, and lower the basket. When you are safely on the ground, I will bring in the basket."

Saul looked at the tiny woman. "My weight in the basket will be more than your hands can hold."

"I must try," Samantha replied. "We have no time to seek help."

Saul looked around the room quickly, searching for something that would serve as a bollard. He seized a bench and stood on it to reach around a smooth, round roof beam overhead. "This will serve," he whispered, and looped the rope twice around the beam. "It is a device a sailor employs to multiply his strength." He showed her how to keep the loops in spiral to control his descent, doubled the knot on the basket, and put the free end of the rope in her hands. "I am ready. When I reach ground, I will signal with two quick pulls on the rope."

On his first attempt Saul could not get through the window, so he took off his cloak, covered his shoulders with lamp oil, and pulled his body through the opening and into the basket. It hung motionless for a few moments, until Saul signaled Samantha to feed the rope over the beam. It dropped, falling free for twenty feet, then halted so abruptly that the basket tilted precariously. Suspended in midair, Saul looked up but could see nothing. If he called out the guard would hear. So he waited. Above he heard footsteps on the parapet. When the sound faded the basket began to move, slowly, down one foot, then another, and another until at last he felt the earth beneath his feet. Looking up, he could make out against the starlight the silhouette of a guard standing motionless on the parapet high above. Saul waited until the guard moved away, then pulled the rope twice. The basket began to rise and disappeared in the darkness.

By the light of the stars Saul found the Roman road to the west. All through the night he walked, and on through the dawn and morning until the milestones confirmed that he had cleared the border of Nabatea and thus the reach of King Aretas' guards. In the afternoon he left the road to climb the forested side of Mount Hermon. Hagri, on the journey north, had mentioned that on the side of the mountain were three caves with springs of fresh water. Saul found one, drank his fill of the cool water, filled his waterskin, and slept.

Refreshed, and elated at his escape, the next morning he journeyed on, stopping only by day to buy food in the villages and by night to sleep by the road for a few hours. Five days later, as he entered the Damascus Gate, Saul wondered if he would be recognized and stopped. But the centurion on post ignored the stream of travelers entering and leaving, and Saul easily found the mud house behind a crumbling outer wall.

At his knock the door opened, but only by a narrow slit. "I seek Peter," Saul said.

"Who are you?"

"I am Saul of Tarsus. I have journeyed from afar to speak with Peter."

He heard murmuring inside. Suddenly the door opened wide and a craggy hulk of a man stood in the entrance. "You are Saul? Yes, I see you are." He seized Saul by the arm and roughly pulled him through the entrance. "You are Saul the prosecutor who sent Stephen to his death. I was there. I watched as you celebrated his stoning."

Six other young men — some with eyes wide in surprise, others with faces grim and menacing — surrounded Saul. To each threatening face he looked in defiance. "Yes, I am Saul who once prosecuted for the court. But God has opened my eyes. Now I, too, follow Jesus."

The big man struck Saul's chest. "You lie. I, Prochorus, say that you lie. You are the Sanhedrin agent who arrested, jailed, and murdered our brothers who followed Jesus. You have come to lure Peter to persecution and death." He struck Saul in the face and pushed him toward the door. "Begone, you murderer."

"Wait!" cried one of the young men. "Consider: This agent of the Sanhedrin knows where we meet. Is it therefore prudent to set him free?" Saul detected the accent of an Athenian scholar.

"You speak wisely, Brother Parmenas." said another, and then a cacophony of voices: "Let him go." "Bind him, as he bound women and children." "Put him out of the city."

At last Parmenas raised his hands for silence. "We must consult our leaders on what to do. Meantime, let us impound this Saul in the storeroom and bar the door."

Weary from his journey and realizing resistance was futile, Saul followed Prochorus to a dank, small room. With no window or lamp, Saul sat in the darkness and wondered: What must he do to be believed? After drifting into sleep, he was startled by a burst of light that fell over his face. "Someone is here to see you," Parmenas said.

Blinking his eyes to adjust to the lamplight, Saul saw the outline of a tall and somehow familiar shape, and then he blinked and looked again.

"Barnabas!"

"Yes, Saul, it is I, Barnabas, ever your friend." Clapping each other on the shoulders, they laughed like schoolboys. "Come," Barnabas said. "I will take you to Peter's house."

"Is that wise?" Parmenas asked Barnabas. "We fear this man. He killed our leader Stephen, and now he would destroy us."

"Stand. All of you," Barnabas said. "Yes, my Hellenist brothers, it is true that Saul of Tarsus took part in the brutal stoning of Stephen. So also is it true that he persecuted every follower of Jesus he could hunt down in this city, and scattered the others. I, Barnabas, was one of many who fled Jerusalem to avoid persecution by this man. Indeed, the evil then in the soul of this persecutor caused him to set out for Damascus to arrest the followers of Jesus in that city."

Barnabas stopped and brought his voice low. "Then, brothers, on the highway near Damascus a miracle happened. Jesus himself descended from heaven and spoke to Saul." He paused to let the silence build. "Hear what I say, brothers: In that remote place, out of a light from the heavens, Jesus appeared to confront this agent of the Sanhedrin, rebuke him for his persecutions, and blind him. Three days later the Lord Jesus restored his sight and set him forth on his mission to spread the truth near and far. I say to you, my brothers, that Jesus came to earth to make this man one of us."

There was a long silence until Parmenas spoke. "We respect your standing in our community, Brother Barnabas, but how do you know this to be true?"

"I am certain first because I came to know this man in the school of Gamaliel twelve years ago, and it is not in his character to claim that Jesus appeared to him unless it was so. I am certain also because on my last visit to Damascus, our brother Ananias told me that Jesus came to him in a vision and verified the miraculous conversion of Saul. So now, my brothers, he is not merely one of us — and ponder this — he is the only one of us in this room chosen by Jesus himself. Each of us came to Jesus, but Jesus came to Saul. Remember that."

Not one of the Hellenists spoke. At last Barnabas broke the silence. "Now I shall take Saul to Peter."

The familiar streets of Jerusalem seemed unchanged, teeming with soldiers, donkeys, shopkeepers, people dressed in rags, people dressed in fine linens and woolens. As the two walked together and reminisced about their school years with Gamaliel, Saul suddenly turned and said abruptly: "Tell me about Peter."

Barnabas thought for a moment. "Simon. *Petra. Cephas.* 'On this rock I will build my church.' So Jesus told Peter and the other disciples outside Caesarea Philippi. And sturdy as a rock Peter is. He is the one disciple with the patience and understanding to hold our quarrelsome factions together. But he lacks diligence, Saul. Indeed, he abandoned his duty as leader for a time and went back to fishing in Galilee. As a consequence we almost met disaster, for we are a house divided."

Barnabas put out his left hand. "The Hellenists — you saw them there — are good Jews, but would interpret the teachings freely. They believe the Way is inclusive, open to pagan and Jew alike. They teach in Greek."

He raised his right hand. "The opposing faction is conservative Hebrew, led by James, the half brother of Jesus and the self-appointed keeper of the flame. He holds that we remain first and foremost a sect of Jews, that we must continue to follow the Mosaic Law and all the statutes, and that we must speak and teach only in Aramaic. James would exclude all from the Way except those born Jews and those God fearers who undergo circumcision. So bitter have been the arguments between Hellenists and Hebrews that at times I feared our cause would founder. Consequently, some of us convinced Peter he must come back from Galilee, as he alone is respected by both factions."

For a time they walked in silence. "Our movement needs a strong leader, Saul. Our numbers are few; our enemies many. We are condemned by the high priests of the Sanhedrin as apostates, and we are cursed by Pilate, that puppet of the Romans, as troublemakers. We are searching, struggling." He turned to Saul. "What will you say to Peter?"

"That I, like Peter, was chosen by Jesus; that I, too, am searching. Three years ago Jesus commanded me to be his witness to the world, but I have not yet found the words that persuade people to follow him. So I journeyed here to learn from the disciples whom Jesus chose while he lived, perhaps to join them."

Barnabas turned to enter a courtyard, and they climbed the steps to an upper room. It was bare, the walls scabrous. A broken shutter hung askew at the one window. "Wait here, and I will tell Peter you have come." The wait was long. Voices were raised inside. When Saul heard the words *plot* and *conspiracy*, he felt sure that Peter would refuse to see him.

Suddenly the door opened and a solid block of a man strode forward. He wore a faded fisherman's smock, presented a broad and open face, graying beard, wide shoulders, and muscular arms. His thick fingers and hands bore calluses and scars.

"So you are Saul," Peter said, surveying his visitor with curiosity and undisguised suspicion. He had expected a pale scholar. Instead Peter saw a man of the road, browned by desert wind and sun, robust of chest and leg, and younger than he had expected. Peter thought him homely — the head oddly large, the piercing black eyes bulging from their sockets.

"Why do you wish to see me?" Peter asked.

"Jesus appointed me to bear his name before gentiles and kings and the children of Israel," Saul replied. "I came here to tell you and the other disciples of my mission so that we may work together, toward a common purpose."

Peter raised his great gnarled hands, palms open toward Saul, and pulled himself up to his full height. "Hold, stranger. Hold there. I am in charge here. Jesus appointed me to be first among his disciples and to lead the entire community of his followers."

"I know that Jesus in life so commissioned you," Saul said, "but that was long ago. More recently, Jesus appeared to me and directed me to witness to the world that he is the Messiah."

Peter spat. "Hah! You are late to know. Many years ago, soon after I became his disciple, I recognized that Jesus was the Messiah and told him so." Peter paused and glared at the stranger. "Now you say Jesus returned to earth and spoke to you. When did this occur?"

"Three years ago."

"So long ago?" Peter laughed with scorn. "And why have you waited until now to tell us?"

"I went into the desert to meditate, to comprehend what it meant for Jesus to reveal himself to me, and to await his instructions on his message and my mission."

Peter raised his eyebrows and smiled. "And did Jesus reappear to give your further instructions?"

"No, he did not."

Peter shrugged and looked at Saul with disdain. "Now tell me, Saul of Tarsus, why would Jesus appear in a far country to you, a lackey of the Sanhedrin that put him to death, and not here in Jerusalem to those of us who follow him and his teachings?"

"There are two answers," Saul responded quickly. "First, I have been told that Jesus called not only the righteous but also sinners to repentance. Second, Jesus gave me a mission extending beyond that of the disciples he chose on earth."

"So you say." A faint smile came upon Peter's face. "Are there witnesses?" he asked.

"No," Saul replied, "but I would tell you of this happening, and you may judge the truth of what I say."

Peter studied his visitor for a few moments, concluded that he might be demented, but doubted that he carried a dagger in his sleeve. "Very well. Let us go into the other room. I will listen to your story."

The private chamber of the first disciple was sparsely furnished with a table of wide-sawn boards and twelve crude benches. Peter sat in the middle and motioned Saul to a bench opposite. Barnabas found a place at the end.

"Begin," Peter said.

Saul told his story in precise detail, at some points even embellishing his account. Chin in hand, Peter listened, intent, ready to seize on any weakness or falsehood. At the end he said, "Tell me again about the sound of his voice."

"The voice was at once tender and compelling, a voice that could not be denied."

Peter looked away for a time in thought, and then fixed his eyes on Saul. "Either in truth you heard Jesus, or you are an accomplished liar sent by Satan to destroy us."

"I must speak," Barnabas interrupted. "Saul has both talents and faults, but lying is not one of them. Who better than I, who has been both his friend and his victim, can testify to this?"

Peter turned to Barnabas. "But there were no witnesses to this revelation. Saul admits that neither of his companions heard Jesus."

"You, but not all, saw Jesus after he rose from the tomb," Barnabas replied quickly. "The revelation to Saul is indeed confirmed by our brother Ananias. Do you not believe Ananias?"

"Ananias is a good man," Peter said, "but how do we know he was not deluded?"

"Ananias deluded?" Barnabas said. "Put aside your suspicion, Peter. It is confirmed that Saul was blinded by the great light from the heavens. His two companions so reported to the captain of the Temple guards when they returned to Jerusalem. They told that Saul had been blinded by a light such as they had never seen before, and described how they led him into Damascus by the hand. And Saul was made to see again by a miracle performed by Ananias, who found him and restored his sight on instructions given him by Jesus in a vision. Who better than you, Peter, knows that only God and Jesus can give another the power to perform a miracle?"

Peter threw up his heavy hands in dismay. "The presence of this man in Jerusalem can only bring trouble, Brother Barnabas. If I accept Saul into the Way, how do I explain my action to our Hellenists, who will never forget that this man openly took part in the murder of the saintly Stephen? And when I stand before our next assembly, how do I answer to the charge that this was the very man appointed by the chief priests to jail and prosecute and terrorize all our poor but loyal followers in Jerusalem?"

"Let me reply," Saul said. "Those things I did, yes. But I do not now blame myself for stoning Stephen, or for carrying out my orders from the high court to arrest and put to death other followers of Jesus here in Jerusalem. Then I was a slave to the Law. Then I did not know the truth about Jesus. Then I acted in ignorance."

Saul struck his fist on the table. "You know the truth, Peter. You know in your heart that it was Jesus who came to me on the road to change the course of my life. Your reproach is nothing to me, for I was rebuked by Jesus in person for the harm I did to those who believed in him. That rebuke burns like a flame in my mind and in my heart and in my soul." He rose to go.

"Wait!" Peter said. "Wait. Haste not. I intended no offense. Let us continue to talk. Compromise is always possible. What do you wish of me?"

"I came here to learn from you," Saul said. "I came here to find out about the life of Jesus on earth. I came here to ask you, the first disciple, to tell me everything, all that you saw and heard and know about the man Jesus."

Peter sat back and closed his eyes in thought. "I was there at the beginning. I remember the first time I saw Jesus. My brother Andrew and I had beached our boat on the sands of Galilee and brought our catch ashore to take to the market. There stood this man, looking at us. 'Come after me,' he said to Andrew and me, 'Come after me and I will make you fishers of men.' There was a strange power in his voice, a force we could not deny, so we went with him. We gave away our catch of fish that day and went with Jesus. Farther along the beach we came upon our fellow fishers James and John, the sons of Zebedee, as they repaired their nets. Jesus called them also to come with him, and they did. So we all walked into Capernaum, and Jesus stayed at my house that night."

Peter put his hands on the table and leaned forward toward Saul. "My wife wept when I told her I had quit fishing to go with Jesus. 'How will we eat?' she asked. 'We will have no money and my mother is sick of a fever.' Jesus heard, and walked into the room where my mother-in-law lay ill. He took her by the hand, bade her rise, and the fever left her. Thereafter my wife never again complained about my devotion to Jesus.

"So on the next Sabbath day Jesus went into the synagogue and began to speak. Immediately he was interrupted by a man who shouted: 'You, Jesus of Nazareth, have come to destroy us!' Well, Jesus saw that the man was beset by a demon, so he said, 'Be quiet. Come out, unclean spirit!' And the man convulsed and fell to earth as the demon left him. When that happened, everyone in the synagogue looked upon Jesus in wonder, for they realized that here was a teacher with such authority that he could command a demon and be obeyed. So they listened."

"Do I hear aright?" Saul asked. "That someone dared to shout down Jesus as he spoke? That is what happened to me in Damascus in the synagogue."

"O yes," Peter replied. "Not all who heard Jesus accepted him. But the poor did, and the hungry, and the lonely, and the despairing, and the defeated."

"What moved them?" Saul asked.

Peter pondered the question. "Well, they saw the power of Jesus to heal. In those first days a leper, ugly and grotesque with scabs and holes in his flesh, knelt before Jesus and begged to be made clean. Jesus held out his hand and touched this man, and said, 'Be thou clean.' In an instant the leprosy disappeared. The man was whole."

Peter raised his thick hands and shook his head. "A crowd gathered of course, and they spread the news that Jesus could heal. The more he healed, the more people came to be healed. The sick, the lame, the blind, one by one they came to beseech Jesus: a man with palsy, a paralytic, a laborer with a shriveled hand, a bleeding woman, a lunatic, a mute, a deaf man, the servant of a centurion, and many who could not see. He even raised from dead the son of a widow." He paused to reflect, then added: "He said he could heal only the sick and lame who believed that he could heal them."

"The miracle of healing," Saul said slowly, "is a visible act of thaumaturgy that can persuade anyone, from the pagan at his plow to the prince in his palace. But what did Jesus say to crowds drawn by his healing? What was his message?"

"He taught that God had given him the power not only to heal the body, but also to forgive sins," Peter said. "'Repent your sins,' he would say, 'for the kingdom of God is at hand.'"

"What did Jesus mean by that?" Saul asked.

Peter grimaced and scratched his head. "My head is burdened with so many questions." He pointed to his window. "Evening comes and I am weary. Tomorrow we can talk further. I will ask James the brother of Jesus to join us. He is not only the leader of our community here in Jerusalem, but also the scholar of our movement."

He pushed back his bench and stood. "Stay in my house. It is not safe for you to go about the city, Brother Saul. Among others, our own Hellenists have sworn vengeance against you, but no harm will come to you under this roof."

XIV

OUTCAST

Light was just beginning to silhouette the peaks to the east of Jerusalem when Saul woke the next morning. Eager to learn more, he rose and hurried to Peter's private chamber, but found it empty. Impatiently he waited.

When James walked in with Peter, Saul studied him. This half brother of Jesus was small of stature, his face pale and insipid, framed by a thin and neatly trimmed dark beard. His hands were soft, white as bone; there were no signs of toil, nothing to suggest he was a carpenter's son. As he sat at Peter's right hand, James arranged his fine white linen robe with care before he looked up at Saul and spoke. "The eleven disciples and I last saw my brother at the time of his ascension," he said. His voice was precise, the words deliberate. "Since and betimes, in Galilee and elsewhere, pretenders have claimed that Jesus appeared to them. As first brother and the one appointed to safeguard my brother's legacy, I have taken the responsibility to inquire into each report. None has been valid. Not one. So you will understand my skepticism that Jesus came from above and spoke to you."

Saul said nothing. He turned to Peter, who looked away.

"You admit your encounter was brief," James said. "What proof can you show that my brother appeared to you at all?"

"The evidence is here," Saul said, touching his head and heart. He scowled at James. "Skeptics you are, all of you, save Barnabas. Where is he today?"

"We decided to talk to you by ourselves," Peter said. "Perhaps if James hears your story —"

James interrupted. "Yes, I will listen."

Again Saul recounted his transcendent hour on the Damascus road, describing in vivid detail the storm-filled sky, the great light, the voice of Jesus, the rebuke, the instructions, the stumbling to the inn, the anxiety of blindness, the coming of the stranger Ananias, and the scabs falling from his eyes.

At the end James sat in silence for long moments. At last he looked up and spoke. "Your story is more convincing than I expected . . ."

"But you suspect me, all of you," Saul said. His voice was curt, angry. "Why was that towerhouse of a guard stationed outside my door last night? I came not to murder you in the night but to join my mission with yours."

Peter leaned forward and looked Saul in the eye. "My fear was not of you, Brother Saul, but for you. Zadok, upon learning you are in the city, ordered your assassination. I posted Nekoda, my most trusted servant, to stand watch over you."

"God watches over me," Saul said. "I fear no man."

Peter rested his chin on his hand, studied the younger man for a moment, and said quietly: "Not yet have you been flogged and chained and imprisoned for your belief in Jesus, as I have. But to the matter: What do you wish of us?"

"If I am to bear Jesus' message to the world as he commanded, I must know what he taught and did during his time on earth," Saul replied. "As I have answered all your questions, so do I expect that you shall answer mine. I ask you, James, what did Jesus mean when he said, 'The kingdom of God is at hand'?"

"My brother wanted to illuminate the profound difference between a tyrant man-king, Tiberius for example, and the benevolent God-king, who will come soon from the heavens to rule over all the earth. He was also trying to convince his listeners that God is in spirit already here on earth; that is, we can find God within us, bid him live within each of us — if we so choose."

"And did his listeners understand this concept?" Saul asked.

"Few did, and they the handful of the schooled," James replied. "I told my brother that this theory of God's kingdom and God within us was difficult for people to understand, that he should explain it more clearly."

"What did he say?" Saul asked.

James shrugged. "He just looked at me."

"You say that Jesus promised that God will come soon to reign over the earth," Saul said. "Did he say when this will happen?"

"'Soon' was all he would say," James replied. "And then he would repeat, 'Soon.'"

"I ask this of you, James: By what words did Jesus persuade people to follow him?"

"The most complete exposition of my brother's message is a sermon he delivered in the second year of his teaching," James said. "I was not there. Peter was."

"I well remember," Peter said. "A great multitude had gathered outside Capernaum — from the villages, from Syria and beyond the Jordan, and many from Jerusalem. One morning Jesus led this great throng away, westward to a mountain. So many were the people that Jesus instructed me to bring the Twelve close so that we would hear. Then he stood on the crest of the mountain so that all the multitude might see him, though some were too far away to hear his words."

In a voice intense and certain in memory, Peter recited all two thousand, three hundred and eight words that Jesus had spoken that day. He began with Jesus' blessings — for the poor, those who mourn, the meek, the hungry, the pure in heart, the peacemakers, all those persecuted for following him. Jesus encouraged them not to hide their commitment to him but to raise his light before the world. Peter told how Jesus not only affirmed the sanctity of the Law that God handed down to Moses, but went beyond to enlarge on mankind's duty to keep the Ten Commandments. Peter spoke well, demonstrating authority and confidence as he recounted, word by word, the most comprehensive sermon that Jesus had ever preached.

Saul was so moved that long moments passed before he could speak. At last he asked: "Ananias told me that Jesus restated our obligation to follow the Commandments handed down to Moses."

"Yes," Peter said. "He simplified our duty to this: 'Thou shalt love the Lord thy God with all thy heart and all thy soul and all thy mind; and thou shall love thy fellow soul as thyself. On these two Commandments hang all the Law and the Prophets.'"

"Another question," Saul said. "That parable at the end about the one house built on rock and the other house built on sand — it is akin to Aristotelian rhetoric. Where was Jesus schooled in speaking?"

"It came naturally to my brother," James said. "His only schooling was the synagogue in Nazareth. We were fortunate, he and I. The village rabbi was learned, and this small synagogue had not only the five books of the Law of Moses but also the historical books, the Prophets, and the poets. My brother read everything, and his mnemonic gift was such that he could instantly recall anything he had ever read."

"Yes," Peter said, "but Jesus recognized that a good story is remembered longer than a passage from Scripture. One day after he had spoken to a crowd — it was one of his first appearances — he brought the Twelve together in private and said, 'To you it has been given to know the mystery of the kingdom of God. But to those outside, all things are being given in parables.'"

"Both my mother and father were storytellers," James said. "It was part of our growing up. When my brother began his public teaching, he favored the parable because of its brevity and simplicity. He could relate each story to the everyday life of a particular audience, reveal a truth to them at the same time, and give them a moral to take back to their humble lives."

Eager to say more, Peter asked: "Do you want to hear the twenty-four parables, Brother Saul?"

"If you would know my brother's teachings, it is essential that you remember the parables," James said. Turning to Peter, he added: "Let us instruct Saul in an orderly way. If you will describe the time and circumstances for each parable, and relate each story, I will explicate its meaning."

Peter began with the story of the sower who cast his seeds, some falling by the wayside to be eaten by birds, some on stony ground, others among thorns, and still others on good soil. James interpreted. Seed was a metaphor for words from God. Satan intervened to take away words that fell by the wayside. Rocky soil referred to people without moral roots; they might welcome God's words but could not sustain growth in difficult times. Thorns were lust and greed that choke out God's truth. Finally there is the fertile soil of good men and women who hear God's word, nourish it, sustain it, and harvest by a hundredfold the seed that was planted in their hearts.

Saul asked: "Did Jesus compose each parable as part of a grand design for his divine message, that is, is each story a single tile in a comprehensive mosaic?"

"I don't believe so," James said slowly. "Each is a fragment of an incomplete whole. My brother did not have time to build an entire structure. And he knew his days on earth would be brief."

Next Peter recited the parable of the pearl of great price, and then the three systematically discussed each of Jesus' stories — the leavened wheat, the lost coin, the good Samaritan, the barren fig bush, the prodigal son, the tenants of the vineyard who murdered the son of the owner, and the others. For days the tutorials continued. Meeting from morning to sunset, the three men covered not only all the parables and teachings of Jesus but also the temptation, the transfiguration, the travels, the final journey to Jerusalem, the last supper, the betrayal by Judas, the arrest on the Mount of Olives, the trial before Caiaphas and the chief priests, the second and final trial before Pontius Pilate. Rubbing at tears streaming down his weathered countenance, Peter went on to describe Jesus' struggle as he bore his cross to Golgotha, his wincing in agony as the iron nails pierced his palms and feet, and his anguish in appealing to God as death neared.

After a long silence Peter said quietly. "I did not believe Mary Magdalene when she ran to tell us that the tomb was empty and that an angel had told her Jesus had risen, but others reported that Jesus was indeed alive. So I called together the Eleven — Judas had killed himself and Matthias had not yet been elected to replace him — to the place of our last supper to consider these reports. Not one of us believed that Jesus had risen from the tomb."

Peter lifted his hands, his eyes wide with wonder. "And then! Suddenly Jesus appeared in our midst, more angry than I had ever seen him before. We hung our heads in silence as he rebuked us for not believing Mary Magdalene and the others he sent to tell us of his resurrection. Then he gave us a simple command: 'Go ye into all the world, and preach the good news to all creation.' With final words of encouragement to us, Jesus ascended into heaven. It was the last time we saw him, and that was more than five years ago."

"In those five years," Saul asked, "what have you done to take the good news to all the world?"

"We are so few, and so hindered," Peter said. He raised his scarred right hand, and pointed directly at Saul. "You yourself hurt our cause here in Jerusalem. After the killing of Stephen, when you arrested and prosecuted our members here in the city, it was as though a wolf had scattered the sheepfold." He shrugged and opened his left palm. "On the other hand, your vicious actions helped our cause outside Jerusalem. When our best fled, they carried the seeds of Jesus' teaching abroad — to Ptolemais, Sidon, Alexandria, Antioch, Damascus, and beyond. In each place they made new converts." He shook his head. "In fact, we may have more followers of Jesus in the other nations than we now have here in Jerusalem."

"Here we have been forced to accommodate," James said. "We have an understanding with the Sanhedrin, where at least two members are secret followers of my brother. Caiaphas will not arrest our present members so long as we do not openly solicit new members in the city."

"What is your accommodation with Pilate?" Saul asked.

"Pilate and Torquatus, the present chiliarch of the cohort stationed here, know that we assemble in small numbers for worship," James replied. "They tolerate us, just as they tolerate Temple worship, so long as we create no disturbance."

"How closely do you follow our traditional worship in the Temple or synagogue?" Saul asked.

"We have no priests, and sacrifice no animals," James said. "We assemble mornings, usually, sometimes at night. After greeting each other and giving thanks, we sing a hymn and recite together the special prayer to the Lord God that my brother taught at his sermon on the mountain. The deacon may read a Psalm or some other lesson from the Torah. He, or some member, may repeat one of my brother's parables and explain its meaning. We sing another hymn, pray, then return to our work and homes."

"When we eat together," Peter said, "we follow the special ritual of our last supper with Jesus. When he broke the loaf that night, he gave each of us a morsel, and said, 'Take. Eat. This is my body which is given for you. Do this in remembrance of me.' And then Jesus took the cup of wine and said, 'Drink of this cup, each of you. This is my blood of the new covenant.'"

"Do you assemble on the Sabbath?" Saul asked.

"All our members are faithful Jews," James replied, "so of course we continue to observe the Sabbath day. Then, on the first day of the week, the day that my brother was resurrected, we of the Way gather to worship as he taught us."

"Do you tax your followers to pay costs, as the Temple priests do?" Saul asked.

"Tax we do not," Peter replied. "Indeed, we have no authority to impose a tax, even if our poor could pay it. Some of the Way bring tithes of grain, oil, and wine. And those few among us who have property are generous; we can always count on Barnabas and his aunt."

"Are there no gentiles in the Way?" Paul asked.

"Of course not," James said. "For any gentile to join us, he would first have to become a Jew and make the blood sacrifice of circumcision. That is the rule we have laid down."

"How many followers of Jesus can you count in Jerusalem?" Saul asked.

There was a long pause before anyone spoke. At last Peter said: "I count five hundred at present."

"Or fewer," James said.

Saul could not resist a reproach. "So few? Five years and more to enlighten and convert, and you have fewer than five hundred out of a census of more than one hundred thousand Jews in the city?"

James' face turned red with anger. "The fault is yours! We have never recovered from the havoc you created among us."

"I was not to blame!" Saul replied, striking his hand on the table. "Before I was redeemed and released by Jesus himself, I was a prisoner of the Law."

Peter raised his hands in conciliation. "Calm yourselves, my brothers. I have forgiven your blows against us, Brother Saul. But you must understand that we have no choice but to go slowly with our work in Jerusalem. We dare not risk offending the chief priests or Caesar. Yes, we are few, but we are firm in purpose. In good time we will grow. Remember the parable of the mustard seed. This smallest of seeds, the word of Jesus, has been planted in the earth."

"Yes, and every seed and every vine must be cultivated if the harvest is to be abundant," Saul said. "Is each disciple given a field to tend?"

Peter hesitated. "Well, no," he said. "I believe one is teaching in Syria, another in Sidon, another in Joppa. Some of the Twelve had no bread in their houses, so they returned to their wives and children." Peter waved to the window. "Evening has come. Let us resume at noon on the morrow."

In his room that night Saul reflected on his fortnight with Peter and James. He was disappointed in both. He thought Peter earnest and loyal but indolent, and wondered why Jesus would have entrusted to this unschooled fisherman two momentous tasks: articulating his profound and unprecedented philosophy, and constructing the organization to sustain and advance this new concept of God and man. Peter was woefully unprepared for such responsibility, neither educated nor experienced. He had overseen nothing larger than a fishing boat, and he was illiterate. Barnabas had arranged for his nephew John Mark to teach Peter to read and write. But at least Peter was honest, without guile. As for James, Saul considered him pretentious, affecting scholarship, and defensive about his shortcomings. James' sole merit was kinship.

Neither Peter nor James seemed to be dismayed that there were no more than five hundred followers of Jesus in Jerusalem. How strange it was that the movement of a supremely activist leader had fallen into such a passive state — and all because the appointed leaders feared Caiaphas and Pilate. Fear bound Peter and James like iron shackles. Yet by their own accounts, Jesus had never hesitated to disturb the public peace; in Galilee, in Samaria, in Jerusalem, he had always marched forth with courage and spoken out for his convictions.

Saul was sure he was right to come to Jerusalem after his solitary years in the desert. The two weeks of instruction had been time well spent; Saul was more intrigued than ever about Jesus. The tutorials had not satisfied but increased his curiosity.

He was beginning to see the many facets of Jesus: miracle worker, messenger, teacher, leader, a man of mystery by his own design or by God's. Like the best of leaders, he set himself apart from his followers, always above them, speaking actually and metaphorically from a mountaintop, and yet by his words and actions he made himself one with them. He told stories that the peasant and the housewife could understand. He healed their bodies. He lifted their souls. It was the mark, the very essence of one born to command — to be above the people and yet be of the people.

Listening to Peter and James, Saul had learned that not only did Jesus possess extraordinary power to perform miracles, but he was also uniquely charismatic. There was no question in Saul's mind: Jesus was a philosopher greater in mind and spirit than any who had ever come before. But why did he not define the whole of his momentous concept? He left fragments, not a complete book of his teachings. And why he chose these particular disciples was incomprehensible. Among the whole lot there was not one with the competence or boldness of spirit to lead. After fifteen days with Peter and James he could now better understand why Jesus had come to him on the road. The Twelve were ineffective. "This movement will founder," Saul surmised, "unless one person steps forward to raise the Messianic banner and proclaim to all that he will carry forward the enterprise that Jesus began."

He folded his arms and closed his eyes the better to concentrate his thoughts. "Who better than I to lead this cause?" he said aloud. "Who better than I to compose and articulate the message of Jesus? Who better than I to take his good news to the world? If not I, who?"

This visit had confirmed his mission. He must not, and he would not fail.

When Saul awoke the next morning, he bounded from his cot and slipped out the back door of Peter's house. Making his way through the narrow streets toward the Temple Mount, Saul passed the door of the school of Gamaliel, and then the door of the court of the Sanhedrin where once he had served Zadok and Caiaphas. Would they believe what had happened to him on the road to Damascus? Gamaliel, yes; he was ever curious and open of mind. But Zadok and Caiaphas were hard of heart. Could he someday find a way to convince those two of the truth about Jesus? Suppose, after his meditations in the Temple, he should simply walk to the House of Hewn Stone, enter, find Zadok and Caiaphas, and persuade them to give him the opportunity to go before the seventy-one priests and elders of the Sanhedrin and tell his story. There he could deliver a detailed account of how Jesus revealed himself, and ask the court to consider that evidence and formally decide whether to accept Jesus as the Messiah. The court had reversed itself before; why not on this critical issue?

As he started up the steps of Solomon's Porch, Saul chanced to look back. There, fifty yards behind him, waiting at a corner, was Prochorus, huddled in the midst of five ruffians armed with clubs. Saul stopped, waited until he caught Prochorus' eye, and raised the sole of his sandal in contempt.

His anger melted away after he entered the inner court of the priests and looked up at the Ark and scrolls. "Blessed are you Lord God king of the universe, who has sustained me and enabled me to live to see this season." The quiet, the beauty, the serenity of the nave soothed his thoughts and lifted his spirits, and he closed his mind from all but beautiful things, the sound of the sea, a glorious sunrise in the desert, the whisper of wind in the cedars of Mount Hermon. So calm and content was he that time and solitude carried him across the liminal threshold of consciousness and into a trance; and in the trance he heard the voice of Jesus, speaking now with urgency: "Make haste, Saul, and get thee quickly out of Jerusalem, for they will not believe thy testimony concerning me."

"Lord, they know that once I imprisoned and beat those who believed in thee. And when the blood of thy martyr Stephen was shed, I stood by and held the coats of those who killed him."

"Depart at once," Jesus commanded, "and I will send thee far hence unto the gentiles."

The trance ended. Saul leaped to his feet, elated, excited, exalted. Jesus had not forgotten him. After an absence of three years Jesus had appeared once more to reaffirm Saul's standing with God and to redirect the course of his mission. The thrill of seeing and hearing Jesus in the great Temple itself caused Saul's hand to tremble and his skin to shiver. Commanded to go, he would leave Jerusalem at this very hour. But where? "Far hence," Jesus had said, "unto the gentiles." He would stop at Peter's house to retrieve his cloak and journal; Jesus would then direct his path.

With a brisk and resolute step, Saul walked from the inner court and out the Beautiful Gate. There to his surprise stood Barnabas, his big feet planted wide as he leaned against a column, his amiable face turned grim. Saul took his old friend by the arm as they walked along. "My brother Barnabas, I must leave Jerusalem at once."

"Yes, but how did you know?" Barnabas asked. "Peter sent me with the order for your departure."

"Peter is ordering me out of Jerusalem?"

"Yes, for your life is in great danger. Last night, at midnight, an informer told Peter that Prochorus and four other Hellenists took a blood oath to kill you to avenge the death of Stephen. For your sake, and the sake of the movement, Peter decided that you must be sent beyond the reach of the Hellenist assassins — and Zadok's. James concurs. Thus, my brother, you are to leave this hour. Nekoda will escort you to Caesarea. There you are to board the next outbound ship. It is the *Karnak*, an Egyptian grain ship that sails tomorrow on the evening tide, for Tarsus."

"Exile, again," Saul said. Twelve years had passed since his banishment from Tarsus, and now the Way he had joined would deport him back toward a home that no longer existed. Saul turned to his old friend. "How did you know to find me at the Temple?"

"Peter had you followed."

Saul elected not to mention the new revelation from Jesus. If Peter and James learned that Jesus had appeared to him again, and in the Temple itself, they would become even more jealous. "I go, Barnabas, not in flight, not in fear, but because there is no more to be learned from Peter and James."

Slowly the two resumed their walk, choosing a path between the paired columns of the vast porch. Saul took his friend by the arm. "I came here, Barnabas, to learn from those who knew Jesus on earth. I have been disappointed, for neither Peter nor James nor any other disciple can tell me what I want most to know: the clear and simple message Jesus intends that we should deliver to mankind. The miracles, the parables, the sermons — all are meaningful, yet no one of us has yet set forth that one clear and brilliant sentence that says to every man and every woman, 'This is why you must follow Jesus.' Thus I leave Jerusalem knowing more, but not enough. And now I see more clearly that it is up to me to divine Jesus' message and take his good news afar. So I go, Barnabas, to press on with the mission that God assigned me."

In silence the two walked down the steps leading downward toward the West Gate of the Temple Mount, where three men waited. "Nekoda has your journal and cloak," Barnabas said. "He and two other trusted guards will escort you to Caesarea."

"I need no guard," Saul said. "More than once I have escaped assassins."

"It is not only your life that we defend, Saul, but also the cause that we serve."

Saul hesitated, then nodded. "Since it is you who ask, Barnabas, my answer must be yes."

At the gatehouse Saul and Barnabas faced each other. Suddenly, impulsively, the two clasped hands. "Fare thee well, Brother Saul," Barnabas said.

"God be with you," Saul replied, wondering if ever again he would see his one and only friend.

Nekoda interrupted. "Come quickly, Master. You are in danger in this city. Hasten we must to Caesarea."

XV

HOMECOMING

On the fifth day, plodding northward despite her leaky planking, patched sails, and inexperienced captain, the *Karnak* moved past Cyprus and changed course for Tarsus. Saul, earning his passage as a deckhand, was first to point out the Taurus Mountains, dimly visible through the haze off the port quarter.

The sight of the enduring and majestic peaks prompted Saul to go to the captain and volunteer to climb the mast and stand watch as the ship approached the Cydnus estuary.

Aloft, Saul stood on a yardarm, one arm wrapped around the mast, and searched. He could not see the entrance to the harbor, but he knew it was close, for the color of the sea was changing with river mud. Then he sniffed a rank and familiar odor, and breathed deeply. To himself he smiled: O yes, it was tannin, the faint but unmistakable acrid smell of tanneries that lay along the river to the south of Tarsus.

Like the breaking of a dam, the smell of tannin released in Saul a flood of memory: wealth, elegance, a family divided. But all that was past, long past, his mother poisoned, his father robbed and destitute before he, too, died.

Still, Saul told himself, there was much to look forward to. Tarsus was home. He was eager to see Rachel. She would be nineteen now, and he hoped his sister had inherited their mother's beauty and calm grace. And Uncle Enoch, his sole remaining elder kinsman by blood, was probably the chief rabbi of a synagogue by now. They would share their observations about Rabban Gamaliel, about life in Jerusalem.

He would see Zagoreos: Tomorrow he would go early to the academy and surprise him. Favorite tutor and favorite pupil would again engage in a spirited dialogue. And Phoebe: What would it be like to see her after twelve years?

Shifting his bare feet on the yardarm, Saul formed a plan: First day, home with Rachel and Enoch; second, visits with Zagoreos and Musonius and his other teachers, a run on the long stadium course, a bath at the gymnasium, and a discourse with young students. On the third day he would see Phoebe, and Pan, find out about his friends and classmates, and learn all that was happening in Tarsus.

"Then I shall resume my mission," Saul said to himself. "First, I must create the message I am to deliver to the world. Second, I will find any and all in Tarsus who follow Jesus, organize them, and bring others to the Way."

At the same time he must earn his bread; the custom of the movement was that no leader would receive money from the common contributions. Perhaps he would teach. Certainly he was qualified to tutor logic and rhetoric at the Academy or the Stoa; he could ask Zagoreos to arrange a position. It would be complementary — teaching young Greeks for shelter and bread, teaching the gospel to carry out his orders from God. Thus by enterprise and diligence he could accomplish in Cilicia what had been denied him in Judea.

Saul stood his post at lookout as the *Karnak* tacked past the headland, entered the Cydnus, and rode the swelling tide upriver toward the main docks. Scene by scene, as he studied the city in the long shadows on that late afternoon of early summer, he recognized the once familiar: busy streets where he ran as a youth, the Jews' quarter where he had lived. Beyond, to the northwest, stood the Academy, and the gymnasium, and the stadium. The sights warmed and pleased him; it would be good to be home.

The tide turned as the sun was setting, so Saul climbed into the longboat with five other crew to tow the *Karnak* to a new stone dock in a row constructed since he had left. When he and the crew finished unloading the jute bags of barley, Saul accepted his two denarii from Captain Rodinak, bundled his cloak and journal under his arm, and crossed the wharf. The city streets, the shops, the huts of mud brick, and the houses of stone — in the dusk all looked smaller than he remembered. Something was different, strange, disorienting. He felt himself an alien in his own land, his apprehension mounting as he headed across the city.

The house where Enoch lived was no longer there; an abattoir stood in its place. Questioning a passerby, Saul learned of a new synagogue in the

Jews' quarter. Once he found the building in the dark, he knocked on the door of the connecting house. He heard movement inside, and could see lamplight through the shutters of a window, but there was no answer. Again he knocked, and again.

At last a woman's voice called to him from an upper window. "Why do you disturb this peaceful house in the night?" Saul thought the voice familiar.

"I seek the rabbi Enoch," Saul replied.

"Tomorrow he will be at the synagogue," the woman replied and closed the shutter.

"I am Saul, nephew of Enoch. I ask that you open the door that I may see him."

Saul could hear voices inside as he waited. At last he heard the bar lift. The door opened, and Enoch stood on the threshold, holding before him a lamp that guttered in the night breeze.

Enoch had changed: He had shrunk, his back was bent, his dark cheeks wrinkled, peppered with scabrous, irregular spots of darker skin. But the eyes were intense, instantly reminding Saul of his mother.

For a long moment Enoch peered from the doorway in silence, looking at the face and clothing of Saul. "Yes, you are Saul," Enoch said at last. "But why do you come to this house of God?"

Saul opened his hands in surprise. "I returned to Tarsus to see you, my kinsman, and to see Rachel, my sister. May I enter? Is my sister here with you?"

Enoch stood aside, slowly. Saul stepped in from the street and closed the door. "Rachel is not here," Enoch said. "In your absence I arranged a marriage for her, to a cotton merchant in Jerusalem. She sailed to Caesarea three months ago."

Saul grimaced and shook his head. "How I would like to see her once more. Tell me, is she wise and beautiful, like Mother?"

"Rachel is a credit to this family," Enoch said. "She will be a commendable wife and bring children into the world." His voice was cool, his manner distant. There was an awkward silence as the two stood just inside the door. "I must tell you this, Saul," Enoch continued. "Your presence here in this house is painful for me. For I received a letter from your former patron Zadok relating how you turned your back on the Law and all the teachings of our fathers —" He shook his head and lifted his arms in dismay, "— to follow this imposter of Nazareth. How can this be? You were well schooled in Tarsus. You learned Torah. An intelligent youth you were when you left this city. What beguiled you? What demon possessed you?"

"Enoch, I can answer. Hear my story."

Enoch hesitated, then beckoned Saul into his study and motioned him to a chair by the lamplight. "First," Saul said, "I must ask: Who poisoned my mother, Enoch?"

After a mournful sigh Enoch said: "The Roman prosecutor could not be certain whether it was Malech or some vengeful servant in the kitchen. Since your father was lost in madness, there was nothing I could do to punish the deed."

Saul put his face in his hands to regain his composure, then began his story. He had excelled above all others in his studies in Jerusalem, earned appointment to the Sanhedrin as a clerk of the Law, relished the life but was dismissed for mistaken loyalty.

"For six years I suffered in exile — poor, hungry, lonely — before Zadok readmitted me to the court," Saul said. "I resolved to make up for lost time. I committed to the Law, Enoch. I exceeded all other clerks and scribes at the Sanhedrin in knowledge of the Law. I influenced court decisions. I tasted power, and that sweet taste stirred higher ambitions. I foresaw that I could rise to greater power by enforcing the Law. I would stamp out all Jews disloyal to Torah." He stopped. "Did word of the trial of Stephen reach Tarsus?"

"No," Enoch replied. "Who is Stephen?"

"Stephen led the young Hellenist Jews who followed Jesus; he was brought to trial by Zadok for blasphemy, and executed. It was I who planned the trial and prepared the arguments for Zadok. When Caiaphas handed down the sentence he ordered me to oversee the stoning of Stephen."

Enoch drew back and his eyes widened. "You took a life?"

"Execution was the order of the court, and I was the officer designated to carry it out. There is more: I contrived a scheme, and won Caiaphas' approval, to arrest and imprison all of the Jesus sect in Jerusalem and take guards to Damascus to hunt down the dissidents there."

"You, a mere youth, were entrusted with such authority?" Enoch lifted his eyebrows in surprise.

"I had resolved to surpass all others, even Zadok, in my zeal to persecute the enemies of the Law. So I set out on my mission. And then, Enoch, on that road to Damascus, I was felled by a great light and from the heavens Jesus spoke to me —"

"Stop! Stop!" Enoch cried, clamping his palms over his ears. "I will not listen to this . . . this . . . this abomination, this heresy."

There was a long pause. "You do not believe me," Saul said quietly.

"The devil possessed you," Enoch said, shaking his head. "Or you were hallucinating from some potion."

Saul waited for silence, then spoke in a low and soft voice. "Enoch, the risen Jesus was on that road. He spoke to me, rebuked me, then blinded me, and three days later sent a man named Ananias to restore my sight. This was no dream, no fantasy; Jesus revealed himself to me, and I have followed him since. I follow him, Enoch, because I know he is the Messiah."

Enoch raised his hands as if fending off an enemy. "That Nazarene was not the Messiah," Enoch said firmly. "He was a sorcerer who pretended to be one chosen by God, nothing more."

"You are mistaken, Enoch. From David's line God sent his son to free us, not from the yoke of Rome but from the captivity of sin. It was God's plan that Jesus be crucified to atone for the sins of mankind; three days later, God brought Jesus back to life."

Enoch ground his teeth and shook his head. "Resurrection?" He spat out the word. "In all our gloried history, Saul, God returned no mortal to earth after death."

"Until Jesus," Saul said, quickly leaning forward. "That singular event, resurrection, proves that Jesus was the Messiah."

Again Enoch shook his head and waved his hand in dismissal. "A delusion, Saul, nothing more. For more than two thousand years our people have lived, labored, sinned, strayed from God's order, and suffered the punishments of slavery and flood and famine. We atoned. We sacrificed. We repented and found our way back to God.

"Is all this nothing, this history? Is Torah nothing? Are all the statutes that order our lives nothing — simply because one obscure demagogue is executed by the Romans for declaring himself a king? I believe not. I speak to God in my prayers and God speaks to me. He has made no mention of Jesus to me."

"Because, my kinsman, both your head and your heart shut Jesus out."

Enoch closed his eyes. Back and forth he shook his head and pursed his mouth to speak. "Your mother did so hope that you would in some way become a leader of our people. Never would she have thought that her son would betray his heritage as a Jew . . ."

"That is unjust," Saul broke in. "I am in every way as loyal a Jew as you. You are not so wise as my mother. She kept her mind open to truth. And I will pay tribute to her memory by bringing the truth to Jew and gentile alike — as God has commanded me to do." He stood and picked up his cloak. "I go now."

"No," Enoch said. "Do not go, Saul. It is near midnight, and you have no place to sleep. The streets of Tarsus hold many dangers in the dark. My congregation will understand that I shelter my sister's son for one night, despite his apostasy."

Zagoreos was not present in his chamber at the Academy the next morning. Saul had risen before dawn, hurried through the dark streets to the school, and found his way to the room where he had so often met the tutor he admired above all others. In time a young teacher came by, inspected Saul's rough garments, and asked why he was there.

"I seek Zagoreos," Saul replied. "Is this still his chamber?"

"Zagoreos left more than five years ago." The young teacher frowned as he stared at Saul's face. "Are you a Jew?"

"Yes, I am a Jew of this city. Why do you ask?"

"Jews are not allowed in this Academy," the teacher replied. "This is a school for Greek and Roman."

At the Stoa, Saul learned that the crippled Musonius was dead, taken down by a fever. Well, he thought, there was still Pan. Of all who had brought zest and laughter to his youth, only Pan remained. Or had he also left the city? With a mounting sense of dread Saul hurried through the crowded streets and out the western hills to the Scipio estate. He gave his name at the gate and was told to wait outside. After a long time the gatekeeper returned and began to tell Saul how to reach the main pavilion.

Saul brushed him aside. "I know the way," he said.

Pan did not rise to greet Saul. He reclined on a long and pillowed lounge set on a platform of red-veined marble, his once slender body now obese. Attending him were five young boys with painted cheeks and lips.

As Saul stood waiting, Pan surveyed his face and dress. The youthful face of his classmate was wider, heavier, and scored with fine wrinkles. The mop of black curls was receding above the forehead. But the eyes were the same, the dark eyes that pierced like a lance. "You face is worn, Paulos. Your robe tells me you are poor." Pan laughed. "Or is this some role you play?"

Saul glanced toward the array of slender boys, and Pan waved them away. "Go! I tire of you." When the two were alone, Pan studied the sagging posture of his visitor with a measure of concern. "Are you ill, Paulos? Shall I send for my physician?"

"Not ill of body, but low in spirit. My mother and father dead. My home gone. My sister gone. My uncle my enemy. My mission suspended. I come to you, Panaeus, my friend of old, because you offered me a place here before I left for Jerusalem. Now I must ask for shelter for a brief time."

"Granted."

Saul hesitated for a moment before he blurted out: "Pan, who killed my mother?"

Pan's face took on a rare seriousness as he observed the anguish on Saul's face. "Malech, without a doubt," he replied. "He tricked a servant into poisoning her food. Then he paid the magistrate's clerk eight hundred denarii to escape punishment." Pan waved a hand toward Saul. "You, Paulos, were away, and your father was demented, so I arranged Malech's ruin."

Saul looked up in surprise. "You did? How?"

"It was not difficult," Pan said, reclining again. "I bribed the Roman commander at the time to buy no more tents and saddles from Malech. So he sank into debt, and when his lenders took your father's shops and house, Malech was left penniless. He went away, with a caravan to Syria, and has not been seen again."

It was a long time before Saul could speak. Pan lounged in silence, toying with a silver goblet of wine.

"Why did Zagoreos leave the Academy?" Saul asked.

"He learned that scholars in Alexandria had collected four hundred thousand books in one great museum, and he must see them," Pan said. "But he never returned." Pan laughed. "I stopped attending the Academy. The tutors told me I was too old. In truth, I was."

"Where is Phoebe?" Saul asked.

"O the lovely Phoebe," Pan said. "After you left, she, too, sailed away. I know not where. Soon after, Tiberius summoned her father Epicrates to be chief magistrate in Rome. Phoebe's brother, our classmate Alcmaeon, went also to Rome, and plays the lyre at court." He paused and looked intently at Saul. "You have said nothing of yourself, Paulos. My spies tell me that you worship a new god."

"Yes," Saul said. "I found one who changed my life, Pan. Changed it forever. His name is Jesus. He is the Messiah for whom we Jews have waited."

"Good," Pan said lightly. "Your new god has not yet appeared among the Jews in Tarsus. I inquired." In his smile there were still traces of his boyishness. "You know, Paulos, that all gods are the same to me, except for the one I most often worship — Priapus."

Saul remembered the last party he had attended at this estate, when for two days Pan entertained twelve of his classmates with footraces in his private gymnasium, jugglers, musicians, dancers, banquets heaped with haunches of meat and mounds of bread and fruit, and a comely *hetaira* for each guest. On the second afternoon Pan had unveiled a marble statue of Priapus, a grotesque head on the naked body of a dwarf, with an enormous erect phallus and testicles as big as melons. Saul, with the others, had joined in the merriment celebrating the idol.

Pan clapped his hands to summon a slave. "Escort my treasured friend Paulos to the Selene cottage. Take him food and drink when he asks. At all other times, let no one disturb him." To Saul he said: "Your words and your manner tell me that you do not wish to be near the debauchery in this pavilion, so I will put you in the guest house most distant." Again he turned to the slave. "Bring pens, ink, and ample papyrus to my honored guest. He writes."

Alone in the remote cottage, Saul felt the burden of weariness weighing on his flesh and bones. The journey, and even more the disappointments, called for rest and sleep. But he would not rest. He immediately found his pen case, went to the desk, and drew forth a crisp and unmarked sheet of papyrus. At the top of the page he wrote one question:

Why should people follow Jesus?

He must find a simple and succinct answer. He could not go forward with his mission until he could answer that question. In Damascus, Jesus had told him what to do; recently, in the Temple, he had told him where to go. But in neither vision had Jesus told him what to say.

> The message is up to me. Absent instructions, I must act on my own: first, conceive and compose the message; second, take that message afar. A daunting challenge, but who better to accomplish this mission than I?

That day, and the next, and for seven weeks thereafter, Saul sat at his desk, paced the floor, stared at a blank page, and tried to order his thoughts. He looked to the distant mountains, pondered and meditated from first light until his lamp burned low at night, concentrating, applying logic and reason, composing, discarding. He stopped only to observe the Sabbath.

On those days of rest and abstention he walked into the city to an older synagogue in the Harran community where he was not known. There he said his prayers, listened to the reading of the Torah, and meditated. He reflected on how God intervened to aid the patriarchs in their times of trouble, and traced the pattern of God's actions to preserve Israel. How, he wondered, did the coming of Jesus fit into God's plan to affirm his covenant with Jews and reach out to gentiles? Reasoning, applying logic, reaching a conclusion — these had always come so easily to him. But now his mind could not find a path through the maze.

Late one night Saul began to write, not with his usual swift pen but with a hand that often halted, suspending thumb and forefinger over the page as he threaded his way through a dialogue with himself.

> Why follow Jesus? I follow him because he came to me on the road and commanded me not only to follow him but also to bear his message to the world. I must obey; I can do nothing else. But no other man or woman will experience the revelation of Jesus as I did. Therefore, I must answer to Jew and gentile alike this question: What will Jesus do for you, for your life on earth, and for your soul beyond this life on earth?
>
> Before I can answer, I must first account for why God sent his son to live among us. Probably, God saw a need. He saw that he must

intervene because we, his chosen people, had strayed, even forsaken him. We had broken the Commandment to put God first in our hearts and souls and minds. We were wandering like lost sheep. I know this to be true because I myself, staunchest of Jews, had gone astray. I had come to worship not God but the Law. And not only I, but the highest priests of Israel also erred. They revered the statutes of man more than the power and glory of God. They who sacrificed in the Temple, they of the Sanhedrin who governed our people as Abraham and Moses once did, they made of the Law an idol.

Seeing this, God sent Jesus to lead us back into the fold, to show us the way to the shelter of his grace. To revive our faith, God armed Jesus with the most powerful weapon ever created: truth. God commissioned Jesus to deliver a message at once old and new, ever momentous, ever compelling: It is faith, not the Law, that binds us to God.

We should have known this. We should have remembered Abraham, Moses, David; all were appointed leaders because of their faith, and all led by faith. But what is faith?

He put down his pen and walked out into the darkness. The night was still, the sky clear, the stars glittered across the vast dome of the firmament. All the heavens seemed to be watching over mankind that night, and so they would to the end of time.

Back at his desk, he drew the lamp close.

Faith is the star that guides us through the unknown. Faith is constant; it is what I know to be true without proof. It is believing what I cannot confirm by reason. Faith reaches beyond reason; it is superior to reason. Faith is like the air. I know it is there. I can feel air move as wind, see it bend grain in the field and lift the wave at sea. But I cannot hold air in my hand, just as I cannot hold faith in my hand. Faith is trusting. At night I yield up my conscious thoughts to sleep, trusting that I shall wake at morning. Faith is believing. I set out on a great journey believing I will arrive safely. Faith is accepting. All that once I had, now I have lost; this loss I accept for I know that Jesus promises a gift far greater than comfort and gold — the gift of life that has no end.

Faith was the message that Jesus brought from God to the world. In Galilee, Jesus healed by faith; indeed, he healed only those who had faith that he could heal them. By his deeds Jesus personified faith. He died in faith to God's plan and purpose, that his earthly son was to be a sacrifice for all the sinners, all the lost, all the outcasts, all the forgotten of all the world.

Thus the Crucifixion: This was God's way of showing that he cared so much about the people of earth that he would offer the life of Jesus to atone for and cast away the error and sin of each of us. So, by God's plan, Jesus died for all, from the humblest to the highest. Why, then, did God resurrect Jesus on earth?

His purpose was clear, manifest: The Crucifixion was humanity's action to try to stop God's work through Christ. The resurrection was God's countervailing action to demonstrate that the divine will can never be thwarted by human design.

The whole of Jesus' life was essential to God's plan. When, three days after he was killed, Jesus left the tomb and walked in Jerusalem, first among the women, and then among the disciples, and then among more than five hundred others, these many witnesses saw for themselves the extent of God's power. By this miracle, by the triumph of Jesus over death, God proved that the soul of every mortal may also be resurrected after death. Jesus' death and resurrection burst open the gates to everlasting life for all who have faith.

Saul paused and lifted his pen, suddenly caught up in memory. He was a small child, being taken by his mother and servants through the Doric colonnades into the great public square of Tarsus to celebrate the accession of the new Caesar, Tiberius. To the eyes of a child it was a marvelous spectacle: Trumpets pealed. Cymbals clashed. Tambourines clattered. Costumed acrobats tumbled on the dais. A lion roared in its cage. A poet sang the virtues of the new emperor.

Years later, at the Academy, Saul learned that the Greeks had invented a particular word to be used only to celebrate the good news of the coming of a new king or a great victory: *evangelion*. After reflecting for a few moments, he leaned forward and resumed writing.

> The good news of Jesus warrants a celebration far greater than any royal event that any race or people have ever known. By his coming, earth is changed forever. Jesus is the new king — not of palaces and provinces but of souls. He governs within us. By his power he conquers sin and wrongdoing. He brings peace to our mortal souls. By his victory over death, he promises that each of us may also overcome death if only we have faith.
>
> What will Jesus do for you on earth? He will bring joy to your countenance, love to your heart, purpose to your hand, and hope to your soul. With Jesus at your side, you will have no fear, not of hunger, not of danger, not even of death. For it is he who will liberate your soul from your body when you die, he who admits your soul into God's heavenly kingdom.
>
> Jesus appeared to me on that Damascus road because I was foremost among sinners, first among those who persecuted him and his followers. If God can forgive me, the chief of sinners, he can forgive any sinner. That is why Jesus commanded me to take the good news to the world and in time give me the faith to carry out his mission.
>
> Though I have faith, and though I persevere through faith, how am I to persuade my hearers in the synagogue and in the marketplace that Jesus also offers each of them the gift of faith? How will they know to believe in Jesus?
>
> Open your heart and your mind in prayer and meditation, I will tell them. Jesus will come. Be patient. Be receptive. Believe. He will come. Reach into the innermost recesses of your soul to discover that precious core of assurance and confidence that is faith. Begin your journey. Treasure awaits at the end, but you must find the path yourself. If you will believe in Jesus, if you will have faith in him, he will bring peace to your mind and soul, and grant you life everlasting.
>
> This is the good news I shall take to the world.

With these words Saul put aside his pen and stood at his desk. He carefully arranged the sheets of papyrus side by side, arranged left to right in the Greek style, and read aloud the passages he had written. It was a beginning. The message was not as simple and moving as he had hoped, but it was a start.

The Sabbath was the next day. He would go to the Harran synagogue where he was not known and ask to be heard.

XVI

HERALD

"They say you killed a man." The old rabbi's voice was shaking, and his hands trembled as he stood inside the doorway of the Harran synagogue with a young rabbi at his side. "I have seen you here, lo these many weeks, and watched in fear. Your uncle warned me, yes, warned even every rabbi in the city, that you might bring here your disease of heresy. Go! A leper you are. You will not pollute this house of God."

So surprised was Saul that he raised his hand to protest. The young rabbi, fearing Saul would strike the older man, stepped between them and escorted Saul to the outer gate. "The old resent the new," he said. "I, Japheth, know of Jesus; but the rabbis of Tarsus, led by your uncle, persuaded Rome to outlaw the sect in the city." He lowered his voice. "You might go to Mersin."

"Where is Mersin?" Saul asked.

"To the south, on the sea, two days across the mountains. Mersin is an independent community of woodcutters, so small and remote as to be outside Rome's interest, or taxes."

"Are there followers of Jesus in Mersin?"

"So I have heard," Japheth said. "The one who will know is Salathiel, the rabbi and village ironsmith. But tell no one that I sent you."

Walking away, Saul debated what to do: If he defied the local authorities and spoke in the marketplaces of Tarsus, he would surely be jailed and silenced. That would accomplish nothing. Or he could take his message to the Cilician villages along the Roman road east of Tarsus, but Enoch, out of malice, may have warned the synagogues there. Or he could follow the advice of young Japheth and go to remote Mersin. But go he must, somewhere, and at once. The time had come to act, to begin his mission, to find an audience willing to listen. He knew what to say. Three years it had taken to synthesize the message; he would delay no longer, not another hour. If Japheth spoke truly, Mersin could be the exemplar of a community open to the Way. Saul's instincts told him the young rabbi could be trusted. "Then it is resolved," he said aloud. "I shall go to Mersin."

Southward, through tangles of brush, under a canopy of pine and oak, Saul made his way, climbing over rugged crag and circling plunging gorge. Two days later he crossed a ridgeline and there below him, at the edge of the forest, was a half-moon bay, with one small boat riding at anchor. At the shore a knot of men wrestled timbers onto a barge.

From the water's edge the land rose steeply, and on this escarpment were scattered rude huts of mud and logs. There was no street; the paths between the houses — thirty-six he counted — were suited more to goats than men. At the far edge of the settlement a stream of white water tumbled down from the mountain above. From one shelter near the water rose thin smoke; surely that was the place of the ironsmith. Upon reaching the hut, Saul said: "I seek Salathiel."

The gaunt youth standing at the forge looked up, his hammer poised over the reddened clump of iron. "I am Salathiel. Who are you, stranger?"

"I am Saul of Tarsus, a man of God, called to enlighten men and women. You are the rabbi of Mersin?"

"I am," Salathiel said, brushing the soot from his brow with a sleeve. "Six days of the week I labor at this forge; on the seventh I offer the teachings to the twenty-one Jews who work and live here, and to seven gentiles who fear God but are not circumcised. Why are you here?"

Saul had resolved never to hide his mission. "I follow Jesus, wherever he may lead me, and I seek the community of others who follow Jesus."

Salathiel put down his hammer and looked down at the scratches on Saul's bare legs. "The journey by land is so hard that surely your coming has a purpose." He glanced at the fire in his forge, added charcoal, and turned back to Saul. "Two men and three women who read the Torah with me here also belong to the Jesus sect. I do not. But my synagogue, though it is but a small hut at the summit of the hill, is open to all. We will hear you, Saul of Tarsus, on the Sabbath. I will tell my people that a stranger has come into our midst, a stranger who may be a herald of God."

Pointing with his hammer, Salathiel said: "Go now to the hut of Ophelia."

Never had Saul received such an open welcome, nor found such easy generosity. The cheerful, talkative, and self-assured matriarch of the community, Ophelia, led him to a clean and vacant log hut, handed him herbs to heal the cuts on his legs, and shared her meager table. On her cool porch her seven-year-old twins imitated his urban Greek accent and climbed on his knees.

Isolation made Mersin independent; necessity put all to work. The loggers, mostly Cretan and Cyrenian, loaded the boats that took away the lumber and brought back the grain stored in the warehouse, open to all in the community. Now only seven bags of barley remained, for the spring grain boat had been lost, along with six men of Mersin, and it would be another month before wheat arrived from Alexandria. Yet Mersin survived. Young boys netted fish and trapped game. Older youths took their bows into the dense wood and with their flint-tipped arrows brought home deer and boar. Young girls spun wool and milked goats. The old men drove sheep to high pasture in the clearings opened by the loggers. All meat, nuts, tubers, and mushrooms gathered from the forest were shared. No one had money; no one needed it. When any dispute arose in the community, Ophelia settled it by decree, backed up by all other women in the community.

By the day of the Sabbath, all Mersin had heard of the stranger from Tarsus, and curiosity brought them up the hill. With his synagogue overflowing, Salathiel read from the Law and the Prophets, then beckoned Saul to his side.

"Saul, a man of God, has come to Mersin with a message. Hear him. Judge for yourselves his words and his beliefs."

Saul stepped forward, surveying the assembly. "I have seen the meager stores in your granary," he said. "One day soon, a mother of Mersin will rise in the morning, search the sea, and find on the horizon the sail bringing the wheat for your bread. Instantly she will know that her children will not hunger in the long winter ahead, so she will shout forth the good news; and all Mersin will rejoice."

He paused, touched his hands to his chest, and said, "I, too, bring you good news. I come from afar not with bread, but with a greater gift, a treasure from the Lord God. I bring you the promise of a better life on this earth, and the greatest gift of all — the promise of life eternal." He could see interest in their eyes, and doubt.

"How can this be?" Saul asked. "How can anyone live after death?" Lifting his arms and raising his voice, he proclaimed: "Because all things are possible by the mighty hand of the Lord God, the one true God who created the world and who rules the world. Such is the power of the Lord God that he can cause the earth to tremble and the sea to rage and fire to erupt from the mountaintop, but he protects those who follow him."

They were listening. Their faces were grave, their eyes intent. So he told them about Jesus, how he healed the sick, made the blind to see and the lame to walk and sought to bring God's chosen people back to faith, but was executed because people did not believe who he was or understand why he had come. "Three days later God brought Jesus back to life. Yes, God used his mighty power to resurrect his son from the tomb, a happening that no man or woman had ever seen before — or since. Why? It was part of God's plan. He sacrificed his son for us, for all people. Who among us would sacrifice his beloved child for the sake of others? God did. He gave his son's life to atone for our sins, and resurrected him to show that we, too, can live after death. Thus the Lord God, out of love for you, offers you the promise of eternal life."

Except for the waves breaking on a sandbar and the song of a bird, there was no sound.

After a time Ophelia stood and looked at Saul. "I know no god. What must I do to accept the promise of your God?"

"Have faith," Saul replied. "Believe in the Lord Jesus Christ."

Ophelia shook her head. "How can anyone have faith in a god in a far land we will never see?"

Saul pointed to the swift stream rushing along at the southern end of the hillside. "You trust the winter snows to bring the spring flood that carries your logs down the mountainside." He raised his hand toward the horizon. "Your sailors trust the wind to bear your boats across the sea." He turned to Ophelia. "To trust what you cannot see is faith." He paused, slowly turning from right to left. "You must discover faith within. I can teach you about Jesus and his wondrous works, but you must search within your mind and heart and soul if you are to find faith."

Saul walked from the mound. He would say no more. It was his plan on this first Sabbath to get attention, take the first step toward establishing himself as a teacher worthy of respect, and engage the interest of the community leaders. If he could win the leaders of Mersin to the Way, others would follow.

Over the next weeks Saul continued to speak to the people of Mersin on the Sabbath. On other days he worked where he was needed, hefting logs, mending a sail, collecting tanbark to turn boarhide and deerskin into leather. By his energy and teachings he felt his standing growing within the community. And then the conversions began. The first to come to him to be baptized were the widows Sarah and Miriam, Jews of Alexandria. Next came three more Jews, then Viganus and his wife, Livius, then one gentile family of nine.

With a congregation of twenty-one, and more expected, Saul arranged with Ophelia that the followers of Jesus could be free to meet on their own, at sundown on the first day of the week. He appointed Josiah and Deborah as deacons, and instructed them in the order of service — hymns, readings from the Torah, reciting Psalms, discussing parables and sayings of Jesus, sharing barley bread and water, and praying.

The grain ship *Thutmose* arrived from Alexandria, and all Mersin joined in rejoicing. The entire community feasted on young lamb roasted over a pit and leavened bread, complemented with an amphora of new wine. As summer waned two other boats arrived, the *Paneas* from Antioch, loaded with more wheat to exchange for oak timbers, the other an ungainly barge from Issus. This was the *Linter*, a slow platform for rough logs owned and commanded by Perez, a portly and bearded Syrian known in Mersin for the quality of his iron and bronze ingots and the generosity of his nature. On this visit he brought ashore a gift of two young oxen to assist loggers in moving timber.

When his boat was almost loaded, Perez came to Saul's hut. "Come with me to Issus," he said. "I have listened to you. I believe in your Jesus. Many in my synagogue would follow you."

Saul sat back in surprise. He was flattered, and delighted. Issus was a city in western Syria, neither as populous nor as cosmopolitan as Tarsus, yet a growing, thriving center for trade by sea and land. This was opportunity. And what more could he accomplish in Mersin? In eleven weeks he had baptized twenty-eight new followers of Jesus, one in four of the entire community. The deacons Deborah and Josiah had demonstrated their teaching skills and devotion; they could carry forward what he had begun. He had come to this small community to test his message, and the test had succeeded. Now it was time to cast the seed of the gospel in broader fields. He would go to Issus.

"We sail in two days," Perez said.

Two days would give Saul time to instruct his deacons and followers, and to express his gratitude to Salathiel and Ophelia.

Issus, at the head of the Gulf of Alexander, was confined by steep mountains to a narrow strip of land reaching into the sea. Here Alexander, marching eastward in conquest, defeated the Persian army of Darius III so swiftly and decisively that Darius abandoned his harem and barely escaped with his life. The cadre of warriors Alexander left behind created a new city and prospered, opening markets for trade and importing workers for their shops and shipyards.

The main synagogue of Issus was constructed of whitewashed stone, the greater part of it a new addition to accommodate the growing community of Jews in the city. In a garden at the eastern side stood the house of the rabbi, Nehemiah, who greeted Perez warmly and invited Saul to speak on the next Sabbath.

Within a day word spread through the city that a herald of God was in their midst, bringing a throng to hear Saul speak. As the audience was predominantly Hebrew, he decided to begin with a proclamation: "I bring you good news: The ancient prophecies are fulfilled. A savior has come and with him a new age for mankind."

He told the congregation the story of Jesus' life and death, drawing from the message he had written out in Tarsus and used in part in Mersin, concluding with God's promise of eternal life. He found himself caught up in his own fervor, so convinced of his own beliefs, so dedicated to his mission that his voice and his words captured and inspired the people of Issus. Sabbath after Sabbath, old and young, Jew and gentile, crowded the synagogue to hear the stranger from the east challenge the old order. So many gentiles crowded the synagogue on each Sabbath that a young physician, Democedes, invited Saul to assemble them separately at his house. Thus it came about that Saul spoke on the Sabbath at the synagogue and on the first day of the week to an even larger number of gentiles. Within four months Saul had baptized thirty-two Jews and fifty-six gentiles. As he had in Mersin, he trained and appointed deacons, Annia, wife of Democedes, and Sosibius, a shipowner, to assist him.

In time the excitement that Saul brought to Issus spread to nearby villages, so he began to cover a wider territory. On the days he was not preaching in Issus he would go to Erzin, or Aegae, or Alexandretta. In each community he would baptize new members, train the best as deacons, establish the order of service, and instruct leaders on how to keep the assembly active and united until he could return. His plan succeeded except in the coastal city of Payas. There the rabbi had Saul arrested as a troublemaker and persuaded the Roman magistrate to sentence him to be flogged. Bleeding and in pain, Saul escaped to Issus to heal his wounds.

Recovering in the house of Democedes, Saul continued his teaching in Issus. One morning he saw in the congregation a round and merry face he instantly recognized from his distant past.

Aram of Miletus had been a struggling third-former in the school of Gamaliel when Saul was keeper of the scrolls. Jolly, gregarious, and talkative, Aram was inept as a scholar. When he failed in his studies, his father, owner of forges that made iron and brass tools for stone carving, put him to work. Six years later here he was in Issus. After the service Aram came up to Saul with a warm smile and a deferential lowering of his head.

"Greetings, Rabbi Saul," Aram said. "I heard you were in Syria."

"Aram!" Saul said. "What brings you to Issus?"

"I travel in search of tin and zinc for my father's smiths in Pergamum and Miletus," Aram said. "There is a tin mine north of Erzin, and I go there today to buy for my father. But how came you to Issus?"

"I serve the Lord Jesus," Saul said, "and it was he who sent me here to deliver the good news to the people."

"I know that you follow Jesus, and so do I," Aram said with enthusiasm. "They talk about you all over Judea."

Saul frowned. "They do? But nobody knows me except in the city of Jerusalem."

"Not by face, I suppose, but certainly by reputation," Aram said. "They marvel that the man who once persecuted the followers of Jesus is now the one bearing the good news to this region."

Saul was taken aback. "Who is saying these things?"

Aram thought for a moment. "In Gaza, Philip called you 'the messenger of Jesus to the nations beyond Judea.' In Joppa, Peter told me that you work more diligently than any of the apostles." Aram paused. "Do you know, Rabbi Saul, that Peter was almost executed?"

"No!" Saul said. "Is he alive? What happened?"

Aram scratched his head. "Well, after they killed James —"

"They killed James?" Saul said. "The half brother of Jesus?"

"No, not that one," Aram said, shaking his head. "James the fisherman, son of Zebedee, brother of John."

"Why?" Saul asked.

"After the old Caesar, Caligula, was assassinated, Claudius, the new emperor, appointed Herod Agrippa to be his procurator over Judea. Anxious to please the high priest and elders of the Sanhedrin, Agrippa decided to execute one of the most popular disciples of Jesus. He had James seized and ordered a soldier to cut off his head."

Saul shuddered, wondering if Zadok had instigated the killing.

Aram continued: "When Agrippa saw how much the execution of James pleased the high priest and his court, he had Peter arrested and chained to the prison walls, with four squads of soldiers guarding him day and night."

"How did Peter escape?" Saul asked.

"On the night before he was to be killed, an angel came to Peter in prison and tapped him on the arm, saying, 'Get up quickly, and follow me.' When Peter looked around, the chains had fallen away. He was no longer bound. The guards were sleeping and the jail door was unlocked. Peter followed the angel past the guards, out the door, and into the street."

"Where did Peter go?" Saul asked.

"To Samaria."

"Is he in Samaria now?" Saul asked.

"I don't know," Aram said with a shrug. "But maybe he can go back to Jerusalem now."

"Go back?" Saul asked. "Agrippa will seize him and execute him."

"Agrippa is dead," Aram said. "After Peter escaped, Agrippa was so filled with rage that he executed all four squads of prison guards and left Jerusalem to go to his palace in Caesarea. He was seated on his throne, acting like a god in front of a delegation from Tyre and Sidon pleading for bread, when suddenly he dropped dead. When the royal embalmer opened Agrippa up, he said that his insides were eaten by worms."

"Did another Herod succeed Agrippa?" Saul asked.

"No," Aram said, "Rome reduced Judea from a kingdom to a prefectural province, and appointed Cuspius Fadus the prefect. He's Roman, concerned with trade and taxes, not the Sanhedrin."

Saul smiled at the former student of Gamaliel. Aram could never recall half of the six hundred and thirteen commandments, but he excelled as courier. "Where will you journey next, Aram?"

Aram scratched his head. "Antioch. A good market for my father's tools, and my favorite teacher, Barnabas, is there. He baptized me. Do you know Barnabas?"

"Indeed I do," Saul said. "He is in Antioch?"

"For three years now," Aram said. "We have many followers of Jesus in Antioch, and all because the Way was ravaged in Jerusalem six years ago."

"What do you mean?" Saul asked.

"The persecutions after the murder of Stephen drove the people of Jesus out of Jerusalem. They fled all over but especially to Antioch — so many came that Peter sent Barnabas as overseer. Now, under Barnabas, the movement is even more successful." Aram looked up at the sun. "Time for me to leave, Rabbi Saul."

After the two clasped their right hands in farewell, Saul left the city and walked, head down, to a remote part of the rocky shore to ponder the valuable news brought by Aram.

Barnabas overseer in Antioch: How had he attained such authority? He was neither philosopher nor orator. Probably Peter had come to rely on Barnabas for his kind nature and his early faith in Jesus. Antioch was important, the cosmopolis of the east, third largest city of the Roman Empire, after Rome and Alexandria. It was far greater than Jerusalem, or Tarsus. And here he was consigned to the backwater of Issus. Where was just reward for merit? He had surpassed Barnabas in every way in school, and now Barnabas had surpassed him. Jealousy provoked him to anger, but then he thought again and rebuked himself. Envy was sinful; he should be joyful that Barnabas, his only true friend, had succeeded.

There must be good reason for that success. Barnabas must also have developed an effective message. He wondered what it was, how it compared with his. Surely they could learn from each other. And should. He looked to the south. There, across the open sea, lay the port of Seleucia, and Antioch. It was no more than two days by ship, or three by foot. Annia and Sosibius could conduct services until Saul returned. He clapped his hands together. "I shall go to Antioch."

XVII

ENDURANCE

Early the next morning, while fastening the thongs on his sandals, Saul heard a soft knock on his door. Minyas, chief slave to Democedes, whispered, "A Roman soldier stands at the door. He seeks you."

Saul picked up the cloak and waterskin he would take on his journey to Antioch. At the front of the house a hoplite brought his spear forward.

"You are Saul?"

"I am."

"My orders are to arrest you and deliver you to the magistrate. Come with me."

"What is the charge?" Saul asked.

"My orders are to bring you in."

The magistrate Polemon was not Roman but a local Greek, a corpulent and black-bearded money changer who had bought his office and profited from it. He wasted no time. "You are charged with plotting rebellion against Caesar," Polemon said, pointing a fat finger at Saul.

"Who brings this charge?" Saul asked

"My agents report that you incite Jews against Caesar," Polemon said.

Saul looked to right and left. "Where are my accusers? Is it not Roman law that the accuser make the charge in court?"

Polemon thrust out his chin and narrowed his eyes. "I, *praetor urbanus* appointed by Caesar Claudius, make the law in Issus," he said. "I find you guilty of seditious tendencies and sentence you to forty lashes minus one. I decree also that you are banished from Syria. Once you are flogged, to Tarsus you will go." He pointed to the soldier who had brought Saul in: "Take the prisoner to the whipping post."

Stumbling from the prodding of the spear as he was marched through the streets, dreading the second flogging in a month, Saul stripped his body naked to the waist and leaned his shoulder against the heavy pole, stretching out his hands to be tied. Praying for strength, he held his breath and waited for the lash.

He heard the soldier setting his feet behind him, heard the crack of the whip before he felt the coarse bullhide thongs strike his bare back and bring a stinging streak of pain racing through his muscles and nerves. One. "Endure," he whispered. Two. "Endure." Three. He found himself exhaling after each stroke, inhaling and holding his breath for the next one. Eight. Anticipating the pain hurt as much as the blow itself. Ten. He was sweating, gritting his teeth to keep from crying out in pain. Fifteen. Sixteen. The sequence, over and over: crack of leather, the heavy grunt of the soldier as he brought down the whip, the thump of lash cutting naked flesh, the excruciating pain. He could feel blood running down his back; the fresh wounds from Payas were being opened. Twenty-one. He wanted to cry out, to beg for mercy, to do anything to stop the pain, but he would not. Twenty-nine. He could last. He knew he could. He would defeat this pain, prove his courage, show his resolution. Thirty-four. The pain racked his body, causing his knees to buckle. He was hanging by his arms. At thirty-six he was close to losing consciousness. "Endure. Do not give in." Thirty-eight. Thirty-nine. At last it was over. Helpless, he hung against the whipping post until the soldier loosed the ropes tying his hands. His legs crumpled, and he fell to earth.

In moments someone was kneeling beside him: Perez, with an earthen jar of water. Draping a clean cotton cloth over Saul's bloody wounds, Perez led Saul to the house of Democedes. Annia was waiting, grinding cloves with mortar and pestle. "This will hurt," she said, sprinkling the clove dust on his wounds, "but it may stop the flesh cuts from putrefying." Her eyes filled with tears as she finished binding his body with the cloths she had soaked in aloe and marjoram oil. "You must go now, Saul," she said. "Democedes has been told by the magistrate that we can no longer shelter you."

Saul turned to Perez. "Will you help me to the road to Antioch?"

"Antioch?' Perez said. "That is unwise, Saul. It is the magistrate's order that you return to Tarsus."

Saul nodded gravely, and got to his feet. "Annia," he said, "I appoint you and Sosibius to celebrate the good news of Jesus in this community. As deacons, you are to conduct the services on the first day of the week as we have done, and baptize those who wish to come to the Way of Jesus."

"I promise," Annia said, "and may God give us the wisdom and the courage to keep our congregation in the faith."

Bleeding from shoulder to waist, hurting with every step, Saul set out for Tarsus in a cool rain. After an hour he collapsed; facedown on the earth, he let raindrops ease the pain that racked his body. Struggling to his feet, he found a heavy stick to steady his balance and walked on. As the pain worsened with every mile, his anger mounted at the injustice he suffered. Why, after years of being welcomed and respected in Issus, had a petty Roman functionary turned against him? Why had he been denied reunion with Barnabas in Antioch? Why was he was still being punished? Would it never end? Jesus had told Ananias in Damascus: "Saul will suffer for me." But why did it continue? Had he not transformed his life? Had he not committed body and soul, all his being, to Jesus? Had he not worked with more zeal and initiative than any other? Would he always be relegated to the outer fringes of the movement? Was he doomed to controversy — or, even worse, insignificance? Why was he being sent to Tarsus, of all places? What could he accomplish in the city where his own uncle had mobilized the authorities to prevent him from speaking?

For six days Saul struggled, dropping by the roadside in exhaustion, surviving on scraps of bread Annia had given him, scorned by other travelers, who held their noses as he passed. At last he hobbled through Tarsus and out to the gate of the Scipio estate; the guard recognized him and waved him toward the central pavilion. Halfway up the marble steps Saul collapsed. Pan, reading a scroll, looked up, then leaped from his couch in alarm. "Paulos! Is that you? What happened to you?"

"A flogging in Issus," Saul said. "The second in a month." A slave helped Saul to his feet. "Once more, Panaeus, I come to you for help. I have no other place to go."

"Welcome you are, Paulos, and welcome you will always be," Pan said. With a look of concern he came closer to examine the haggard face and bent frame of the friend of his youth.

"Take off your cloak," Pan said bluntly.

As Saul bared his back, the two *hetairai* attending Pan shrieked in alarm at the long bloody scabs crusted with dirt from the road and the open sores infested with maggots. "Fetch my physician," Pan ordered the older *hetaira*. "At once."

After one look at the wounds, Pelagios the physician immediately took Saul to the Aesclepius cottage, where he kept his knives and medicines. For the next hours Pelagios and his nurse cut out Saul's festering sores and dressed them with ointments and boiled linen. The surgery over, Pelagios said to Saul: "Your body rages with fever. You must stay here in this hospice to be treated, or you will die of the poison in your blood."

After two weeks under Pelagios' care, Saul walked to the pavilion to thank his benefactor. "You rescued me," Saul said. "I owe you my life."

Pan beamed with satisfaction. "Pelagios tells me that today you can leave our hospice, Paulos, so I shall put you in the Undine cottage. It has a pool fed by a warm spring. Aspasia will attend you there." Saul saw the glint of mischief in Pan's eye. Fifteen years earlier, during their school years, the svelte and bright-eyed girl Aspasia had been Saul's assigned *hetaira* at the frequent revelries Pan staged at the Scipio estate. Now she would be a mature woman.

Within another week the warm waters and benevolent sun of summer restored Saul's body and spirit. He asked Aspasia to bring his journal from the library, where Pan had secured it for safekeeping. But he wrote nothing, realizing that if he recorded the bitterness that consumed his thoughts, it would be a screed of envy, anger, and self-pity.

Afternoons he swam in the pool, all serious thought giving way to the bubbling and healing waters. There immersed, he would bask in the sun as Aspasia softly played the lyre, or read to him from Sappho and Ovid. One afternoon she put down her lyre, walked to the edge of the pool, loosed the ribbon that fastened her chiton, let it fall to the tiles, and entered the pool. Saul looked at her. He had not seen a woman naked since he was a student in Jerusalem, and the sight of his voluptuous companion obliterated, in an instant, all restraint. His desire for her was sudden, intense, and over-whelming. She moved close to him and said softly, "Paulos, let me heal your other wounds." Gently she took Saul by the hand, and led him out of the pool and into the cottage.

He awakened slowly, from the depth of a long and tranquil sleep, one moment drifting through a pleasant dream of childhood, the next dimly conscious of an almost forgotten contentment of body and mind. The quiet breathing of the woman beside him, the scent of myrrh that perfumed her body, the soft couch on which they slept, the stillness of the night; all suffused his thoughts. Such ease, such pleasure, such repose he had not known since youth. And this could continue to be his. Pan, ever generous, had invited him to remain on the estate as philosopher in residence, and even offered to endow a new academy in Tarsus where Saul could teach. The offer pleased Saul, tempted him. But he knew he must not accept. His mission, indeed his commanding purpose in life, lay elsewhere.

The first crow of a cock sounded on a distant hill. A new day would come soon. Was it time to move on? The respite, the time of healing, had been a gift; and Saul felt no remorse for accepting it. It was a measure of recompense for the pain to his body and the humiliation of spirit he suffered by being uprooted from his work and his followers in Syria. Nor did he feel remorse for sleeping with a woman. Yes, he had broken a covenant by succumbing to lust, and he must ask forgiveness for that act. But Aspasia belonged to no other man; he belonged to no other woman. They were bonded by a long and warm friendship, mutual respect for the well-spoken word, and respectful love. Why was it wrong for such a man and woman to share their passion? Their pleasant days together had been essential to his healing, and their night of rapture came as the culmination and proof of his recovery.

And recovered he was. Strength had returned to his legs; he could walk again without a crutch. He could flex his arms and lift his shoulders without pain to his back. With his healing complete, the conclusion was self-evident: He must end his isolation in this haven of wealth and again take the gospel to a waiting world. Far too long had he been idle.

But where should he go? His own uncle had barred him from every synagogue in the region. Rome, after outlawing the Way in all Cilicia, would arrest him if he spoke in the Tarsus agora. Go east? Join Barnabas in Antioch? The magistrate Polemon had banished him from Syria; if he returned there, he doubted he would survive another beating. Probably the vengeful Polemon would simply order his execution for treason. Jerusalem? No one there wanted him.

Yet, somehow he must proceed toward his mission. He must devise a way to bring people to Jesus in a manner that would not provoke rabbi or Roman. He must go again among the people, as Jesus had done, work among the poor, the hungry, the afflicted, the burdened, the oppressed, the lowly, the forgotten. It was they who needed to hear the good news that he could bring; it was they who awaited the promise of a better life.

That was his mission, and he must find a way to continue it. In the meantime he must earn his bread. On that very day Saul left the Scipio estate for the last time. For two years he worked with his hands for Mahlon, a kind old tentmaker who had once been an overseer for Saul's father. From first light to evening Saul pounded coarse strands of Cilician wool into felt, shaped the heavy fabric into tents, sewed the leather grommets that held the ropes, and took his turn sweating over the tanner's vats to convert raw hide into strong leather. He lived in one small room he rented in a mud house nearby, furnished only with a rope cot, a broken chair, and a scrap of plank for a writing table. He ate little, surviving on the thick gruel that Martha, the plump and motherly wife of Mahlon, brought at noon each day to the workers in the shop.

On the Sabbath, Saul slipped into the rear of the nearby synagogue to listen to the readings and prayers. He never spoke there. On the first day of the week he went to the house of Ephoros, a fellow worker whom Saul had converted to the Way. By lamplight, in an upper room, Saul addressed the three or four who gathered together, led them in hymns and readings, and consecrated the bread and wine they shared as the body and blood of Jesus.

It was a time when Saul wandered in a wilderness of doubt, waiting day after day for a heavenly message that did not come. Every morning and every night he prayed to the Lord God for direction. Silence. He put himself in trances hoping to hear again the voice of the Lord Jesus. Nothing. The oak tree by Mahlon's shop turned from green to brown to bare branch, and the north wind chilled the bones of Tarsians and dusted the streets with snow. Saul waited. In time fear crept into his mind, fear that he had somehow failed in his mission and would never again be called to duty, never again be summoned to stand before a rapt audience and deliver the message of faith in Jesus.

In his hovel one night he sat by the low flame of a lamp and probed for an answer.

> Is the Lord God testing my faith? Perhaps so, therefore I
> must not waver. He has made me a prisoner, a captive of cir-

cumstance, kept apart from the mainstream of the great
movement that the Lord Jesus brought to humanity. I long
to return from exile. I am in the prime of life — three and
thirty years have I lived — and I cannot fathom why God
decrees that my best years should be wasted toiling at a
bench and serving a mere handful of converts. I am ready to
march in the cause of the Lord Jesus. I am eager to raise
before all people the banner of faith in God. Seven years ago
I was chosen by the Lord Jesus to take the good news of his
beneficent grace to all men and all women of the world, to
bring them into the kingdom of heaven. Instead I anguish in
idleness. Be patient, I tell myself. But how can I be patient
when there is so much to be done for the world and so little
time? Still, I know that the Lord God has a purpose for me.
Jesus himself told me that he has a plan for me. Faith I
teach; faith I must practice. I know that it is not up to Jesus
to follow my desires; rather, it is up to me to follow his will.

By such meditation Saul often gave himself good advice. But it was more
easily stated than followed. Seasons passed, and then another year, and
another. Saul's disappointment turned to dismay, dismay to resentment,
resentment to anger. He could not conquer his own impatience. Days and
nights he struggled with despair, wondering if his useful life was over.

Then, one warm afternoon in early spring, he moved his bench into the
sun on the busy street outside the shop. Head down, bent over his task, concentrating on forcing a heavy brass needle through thick leather and felt,
only subconsciously did he become aware that someone was standing close
by his bench. Someone was watching him work, probably an indolent
passerby. Glancing down, he saw that the sandals were the best of leather,
dusty from a journey. The feet were large, very broad and unusually long.
In an instant Saul knew who it was, for only one person in the world had
such long feet.

Saul looked up. There stood Barnabas.

XVIII

SUMMONS

"At last! I've found you at last." Barnabas shouted with joy, clapping his hands. "I knew I could find you." Impulsively he seized Saul by the shoulders. "All my messengers returned in defeat, but I was certain I could track you down."

Eyes wide in astonishment, Saul was too surprised to speak. For the first time in months, perhaps years, his face broke out in a smile. "Barnabas." His was not a shout but a whisper. "My brother Barnabas."

"Put down your tools," Barnabas said, elated. "Come with me to Antioch. We need you, Saul."

Seated on the marble steps of a nearby monument, Barnabas looked at his once and ever friend. The long and solemn face seemed even longer, more solemn. The black curls over Saul's brow had receded, heightening the forehead; the black beard reached to his chest. And Saul's eyes, always penetrating and luminous, seemed to burn with even greater intensity. More and more, Barnabas thought, Saul looked the prophet.

"Barnabas, how can I go to Antioch?" Saul asked. "I am anathema in Syria. The Roman magistrate in Issus barred me from entering the country."

Barnabas shook his head with vigor. "That local magistrate's order means nothing in Antioch," he said. "We have members there who can influence the governor."

Saul rocked back and forth on the bench, studying his classmate of old. Barnabas had never been one to boast. "Barnabas," he said slowly, "Aram of Miletus told me of your success in Antioch."

"Antioch was fertile soil that had never been plowed. We are simply sowing the seeds, and the movement is taking root and growing. Three good leaders have I, Saul, but I need a fourth, and that is you."

"But how will you overcome objections from the Hellenists, and from Peter and James? They doubt my *bona fides*, and I mistrust them."

"Philip is now the leader of the Hellenists, and he has become your advocate," Barnabas said. "In time he will influence the other Hellenists. As for Peter and James, I will deal with them. They will put aside their opposition when they see how many people you will bring to Jesus. Furthermore, Peter and James oversee Judea. I preside in Antioch." Barnabas grinned. "Anyway, you never cowered from opposition."

Saul shook his head. "In many places where I have gone, Barnabas, I have provoked my fellow Jews or the Romans and caused trouble. I will not do that to you."

"Antioch is different, Saul. The people and the authorities are open and tolerant as well as industrious. Many are well schooled, either by rabbis or in the three Greek academies for gentiles. It is also a beautiful place, the most modern of cities, the most diverse and engaging urban community. The public baths are sumptuous, with mosaics of spirit and imagination. There are museums, and a fine library. I live in a cut-stone house off the Nymphaeum, where the statuary was fashioned by the finest sculptors in the east." He placed a hand on Saul's arm. "Come with me, Saul. As we shared a house as students, let us share a house as apostles for Jesus. And share my responsibility for the churches of Antioch. I need you."

Saul weighed Barnabas' summons. It was a great challenge, and opportunity. Antioch: a crossroads of trade and ideas, a center of energy and consequence. He could test his message in a city that was both a thriving metropolis and prestigious political capital. He had no reason to remain in Tarsus: He was barred from teaching, and he had lost family, status, means, everything he had known as a youth. But there were risks: A prominent role in Rome's third city might provoke the Hellenists, or Zadok and the other zealots of the Sanhedrin. Still, these were risks he must take; the cause must come first. Antioch could be the beginning of the great mission that the Lord Jesus himself envisioned when he revealed himself on the road to Damascus, and again in the Temple in Jerusalem. Not by coincidence, and not by perseverance alone had Barnabas found him; it was destiny.

Saul looked up at the sun, then turned to Barnabas. "I will go with you to Antioch. If we leave now, we can walk twenty miles yet today."

"Better than that, Saul. An ore ship is waiting. We will be there in two days."

Saul blinked and gazed at his friend in wonder. Was this Barnabas, the stammering and hesitant youth he had first met seventeen years earlier, now transformed into a leader of assurance and command?

"Barnabas, I must first tell Mahlon, and offer my thanks," Saul said. "I was poor, and he took me in."

They stood at the bow of the *Evagoras*. Breathing deeply of air with the tang of salt, listening to the hiss of the prow breaking its path through sun-streaked wave, feeling the gentle breeze off the stern quarter, Saul relished life again. The sea always lifted his spirits; every voyage was adventure. Suddenly he turned to his deliverer: "Barnabas, how did you find me?"

"By a process of inquiry and reasoning, some of which I learned from you," Barnabas replied, beaming. "When travelers told us that you were no longer teaching and organizing in northern Syria, I was certain that someone had intervened to silence you. That caused me alarm, for every one of us knew of your diligence and commitment. So I sent a messenger to Issus with instructions to find you and bring you to Antioch. On his return he reported that you had been put on trial for inciting rebellion against Caesar, flogged, and deported to your native country. So I sent another messenger to Tarsus. He, too, failed to find you. Nor could he discover any follower of Jesus in the city, search though he did. By his account, the rabbis of Tarsus had persuaded the Roman governor there to imprison anyone even talking about Jesus."

"True," Saul said. "It is the doing of my uncle."

"I didn't know that," Barnabas said, shaking his head. "At any rate, that report led me to believe that you could be in prison in Tarsus. As soon as I arrived on my uncle's ore boat three days ago, I went to the imperial prison, prepared to buy your freedom; but you weren't there. Since you were prohibited from teaching the gospel, I thought you might be teaching philosophy. I went to the Academy, then to the Stoa — nothing. Since your family fortune was lost long ago, I asked myself: What could Saul do with his hands? The most likely answer: Make tents, as your father did. I searched from one shop to the next until I found you today."

For a long time Saul looked out at the sea in silence. At last he turned and said quietly: "Barnabas, the Lord Jesus sent you to deliver me from exile; of that, I have no doubt. Now, tell me of all that you are accomplishing in Antioch."

"When I arrived in Antioch five years ago," Barnabas began, "there was no order in the Way. Cypriots were teaching one doctrine, Cyrenians another, and Syrians still another. Each professed to know the truth, though not one had ever seen or heard Jesus. Exercising the authority conferred on me by Peter and James, I summoned all followers to a conclave. I told them we must follow the teaching of Peter — that the Lord God conferred on Jesus of Nazareth the power to do good and heal, and that anyone who believes in Jesus shall have his sins forgiven. My effort succeeded only in part. We continued to speak with conflicting voices. Something had to be done. A year ago Peter decreed at my request that none may minister for Jesus in Antioch except those I ordain as apostles. I then identified the most promising of all our members, selected three, and —"

He picked up a lump of pitch dislodged from the deck planking and motioned for Saul to walk with him to the forward hatch cover. "This is Antioch," he said, sketching an irregular pentagon on the boards. "After Alexander of Macedonia conquered Syria, he awarded the country to Seleucus Nicator, one of his generals. Seleucus chose this site as his capital for three reasons: fertile plains nearby, abundant fresh water, proximity to trade routes by land and sea. Seleucus laid out the city with straight streets and square blocks and named it for his father, Antiochus. Today no other city of the Roman Empire enjoys such civic well-being. No city can claim wider prosperity. Of every ten men in Antioch, one is rich, eight earn good wages, and only one is poor. This according to last year's census."

Pointing to his map, he continued: "The western wall of the city stands on the banks of the River Orontes. The eastern wall courses along the range dominated by Mount Silpius, and includes here the Iron Gate, the dam the Roman engineers built to keep the spring torrents from flooding the city. On the north is the Tiberius Wall, with the gate opening to wheat and barley fields, vineyards and orchards. There begins the road to Beroea and silver mines beyond. At the southeast corner is the aqueduct and the main reservoir. The south wall has two openings. First is the Daphne Gate, which leads to fields of rice, cotton, and flax. Second is the Bridge Gate. It is here that Rome profits, by taxing all goods carried on the roads leading north twenty-five miles to Alexandretta and south eighteen miles to Seleucia Pieria. Seleucia is the deepwater port on the Orontes estuary that serves and supplies the largest ships. We will land there."

With his pitch marker Barnabas drew a long line from north to south on his city map. "This is the colonnaded Street of Herod and Tiberias." He drew another line from east to west. "This is the main market street that runs from New City Island eastward to the Acropolis and the Citadel."

Saul studied Barnabas' sketch, his sense of anticipation mounting.

"To bring order to our work, I divided the city into quadrants and appointed a minister for each," Barnabas said, pointing out the four areas on his map. "Each is about one square mile in area, and each has a different character. The northwest, which contains the royal palace, the mint and principal administrative offices, the museum of art, and the excellent library given by Augustus, I assigned to Manaen. He is a scholar who grew up in the royal household of the Herods, as a foster brother to Herod Antipas. He was educated as a prince, has a courtly manner, and stands in favor with the governor, Laurentus Justinius. Laurentus is new, sent out from Rome by Claudius six months ago. He is a young equestrian, charismatic, and pop-ular in the city. Laurentus worships the Roman gods, of course. However, he believes tolerance benefits trade, so his policy is to welcome all tribes and beliefs and gods to Antioch. It is good for us to have one so committed to the Way, as Manaen is, so acceptable to the Roman currently in political power."

"How did a foster child of the ruthless Herods come to Jesus?" Saul asked.

"A good question," Barnabas said. "A year or so after I arrived in Antioch, Manaen sought me out to confess the conflict in his soul — gratitude to the Herods for his rearing and schooling as a Jew, hatred of the family cruelty. I persuaded him that no man is accountable for his brother's sin, and encour-aged him to dedicate his life to the Lord Jesus. And he has. Manaen lives on palace grounds. His converts — Roman scribes and clerks and their families, and Jewish attendants in the palace and imperial houses — assemble in his house for worship."

Barnabas pointed out another part of his crude map on the hatch cover. "Here in this northeast quadrant are the artisans and craftsmen who make the wares and ornaments that Antioch sells to the world. Here are the pot-ters, the coppersmiths and silversmiths, the goldsmiths and gem polishers, the spinners and weavers of cotton and linen, the glassmakers and rug-makers. My minister for this busy quarter is Lucius of Cyrene, a sailor lamed by a falling mast in a storm at sea. Lucius is no orator. He can neither read nor write. But he is a storyteller. Every day he can be found sitting on a bench by a public fountain, recounting tales of adventure to a rapt gathering of women and children, always concluding with a story about Jesus. At sunset, when the workers put down their tools to savor their beer, Lucius sits with them in dialogue about the Way."

"How did Lucius find Jesus?" Saul asked.

Barnabas stepped back and contemplated Saul with bemusement. "Do you remember Phineas of Tyre, at the school of Gamaliel?"

"Why, yes," Saul said. "We thought he looked like a young Moses."

"Exactly," Barnabas said. "Phineas — though we kept it secret at the time — was one of the seven in school who went to Galilee to see and hear Jesus, and returned committed. Then he, like the rest of us, had to flee Judea after the death of Stephen. When you carried out your pogrom against us in Jerusalem, we scattered. Phineas ended up in Cyrenaica, where he has brought many, including Lucius, to Jesus."

"How many people live in Lucius' quadrant?" Saul asked.

"Fifty-two thousand, by the census of the tax collector last year," Barnabas replied. "It is the second most populous of the four." He tapped the pitch on another part of his map.

"This southeast quadrant is where the rich live. Their estates sprawl over the verdant hills rising to Mount Silpius. Their mansions are walled with the purest marble and the finest cedar and sandalwood. The courtyards of their villas are paved with mosaics of splendor and originality. The pagan rich are mostly Roman. Some are Greek. A few are Persian and Egyptian. All are idle, having long ago made or inherited their wealth. By day the men ride in their silver-studded chariots to the amphitheater to bet on the gladiators and vie for the best seats at the Theater of Caesar. At night they pleasure themselves with mistresses. Their wives show off their silken gowns and jeweled sandals, their chalices of filigreed gold, and amuse themselves with youthful lovers. They, both men and women, like to be entertained, so I assigned them my best orator, Symeon, who is also called Niger."

"And these pagans listen to him?" Saul asked.

"O yes, they come for Symeon's performances, as they go to plays," Barnabas said. He smiled. "In further display of their wealth, they compete in showing off their retinues of servants and slaves."

"Do many join the Way?" Saul asked.

"A handful of the rich, yes; and they give handsomely for our poor," Barnabas said. "But many, many more of the servants and slaves have been baptized."

"Did you convert Symeon?" Saul asked.

"One day, when I was speaking to an assembly, an imposing black man stood and asked a question. There was something about his bearing, something about the penetrating timbre of his deep voice, that suggested he could be a teacher and leader. So the next morning I sought him out, and we talked the full day. I learned he had been taken as a child from the black tribes south of the headwaters of the Blue Nile and sold at a slave market in Thebes. A grain merchant bought Symeon there, took him to Alexandria, and trained him to keep accounts. In time Symeon earned his freedom and immigrated to Antioch, where he loaded cargo to pay for his bread. During our talk that day he asked me if Jesus cared about black people. I told him how Jesus had brought to his side all manner of men and women, and particularly the lowly and the persecuted, and how Jesus had thought of himself as a slave to all humanity. And I explained that Jesus did not just care for all people, but gave his life for all people."

"So he was persuaded?" Saul said.

"Not immediately," Barnabas replied. "Weeks went by. Then early one morning he knocked at my door in great excitement. 'I heard a voice,' he said, almost shouting. 'In my prayer last night I heard a voice, saying, "Symeon, slave to man you are no more. Now, this day, accept Jesus to be your master."'"

Saul grasped Barnabas' arm in admiration. "Good work, Barnabas."

"Not my good work, but God's," Barnabas said. "I believe that the Lord Jesus looks with favor on us as his instruments. Indeed, I am certain that he led me to Antioch and opened the door to opportunity." He reflected for a moment, then raised his hand. "Symeon and I worked out his basic sermon, which he delivers with such imagination and variety and oratorical skill that the amphitheater is crowded on the first day of every week. And the plate on the stage is always filled with coins of silver and gold, which go to the poor. Symeon takes nothing for his teaching, for now he earns good wages by keeping accounts for the owner of the largest granary in Antioch."

Barnabas turned again to his map. "The southwest quadrant holds the most people, the busiest markets, the widest diversity — indeed, all the races of the earth are there. It teems with life and bustles with activity. Dockworkers, wagon masters, shipwrights, sailmakers, sailors, prostitutes, seers, sorcerers, rogues, ragged urchins, innkeepers, wine sellers — all are there. Mingling among them are tax collectors, bankers, rabble. The craftiest of traders, the meanest of ruffians, the boldest of thieves are there, along with Roman troops keeping order. It is the quadrant where we should have accomplished most but have done least. It presents us with the most difficult challenge; therefore, it is our greatest opportunity. This quadrant, Saul, is yours to conquer."

Saul looked at the map for a long time, gravely nodding. "You would appoint me as minister for this part of Antioch?"

Barnabas shook his head. "No, Saul, the Lord Jesus himself appointed you as his apostle. I am his messenger, sent to bring you where now you are most needed."

"It is true that Jesus called me," Saul said softly, looking away. "Then he exiled me for long years to test my faith. Now I must regain that time lost." He turned abruptly. "Tell me, Barnabas, in all Antioch, how many have you brought to the Way?"

"Three hundred forty-seven," Barnabas replied. "Lucius baptized one hundred forty, Symeon ninety-two, Manaen eighty-one. I baptized thirty-four in your quadrant."

Saul narrowed his eyes and said with quiet intensity: "In twelve Sabbaths, Barnabas, I will have brought more to the Way than all of you together."

Saul did not quite reach his mark. By the eleventh day of Elul, three months after he landed in Antioch, he had baptized three hundred and twenty-one persons. By any measure but his own, Saul had succeeded. But he had resolved before arriving in Antioch to exceed all expectations; when he fell short, he vowed to redouble his efforts.

And redouble he did. In Antioch, as before, Saul presumed that his first obligation was to bring his fellow Jews to Jesus. Every Sabbath he delivered his message to the congregation in at least one and sometimes two synagogues. But he was more cautious in Antioch than he had been in Damascus, where his zeal had brought down the wrath of rabbis and elders.

On other days Saul went among the people, cajoling them in the marketplaces, entreating the women filling their jars at the brimming public fountains. In speaking to gentiles he was far more bold. He had, in exile, come to know pagan men and women. They were simple folk, existing in a brutal world, usually hungry and cold, ill clothed and meanly sheltered, cowering in fear of Roman spear and sword. But in Antioch they were different. Most Antioch families lived in warm houses and ate good bread, fish, and meat. Yet their souls were hungry. The pagan gods offered them were for the most part cruel, vengeful, given to conniving against each other and slaying mortals without cause or conscience. Saul calculated that he must address his message to their deepest concerns — hope on earth, and comfort against the yawning void of death.

In childhood he had mastered the Greek vernacular of the street, and in this common tongue he appealed to his gentile listeners: "Many are the gods and goddesses given to Greek and Roman. But I ask you: Does Zeus, or Apollo, or Athena, or any other, bring you a better life? No. They are myths, false gods.

"I come to you with word of one true God, a generous and wondrous God, the one who made the sky and earth and sea, who sends you rain from heaven. As he brings fruit and grain to satisfy your hunger, so also can this God can bring joy to your life on earth and show you the path to eternal life."

Since his audiences were primarily Greek, Saul added the Greek nomen *Christos* to the Jewish name of Jesus. So he would proclaim: "This God of all sent his son, Jesus Christ, 'the anointed one,' to earth to offer hope to your spirit and peace to your soul. He asks only that you repent of the evil you have done, and he will forgive you." He would tell them the story of Jesus' miracles — healing the sick, making the blind to see and the lame to walk, defying the authorities to help the poor — and how he had sacrificed his life so that all men and all women would have a better life. "Put your faith in Jesus Christ, and he in turn will keep faith with each of you. This is Christ's promise: If you believe in him, then he will take you, at the end of your time on earth, into the Lord God's everlasting kingdom."

So many filled the streets to hear Saul that shopkeepers complained the crowds were blocking their stalls, costing them money. Barnabas and Saul were summoned to the palace to appear before the throne of the governor.

"We note with interest the growing numbers of your cult in the city," Laurentus Justinius said. "Your message escapes us," he continued with a shrug, "but it does not concern us. Your claques lauding Christ so fill the marketplaces that you impede the exchange of goods and money. That we forbid."

He raised his jeweled right hand toward the two. "This is our command: You 'Christians' — as our oracle calls you — may gather in the streets in numbers no greater than ten. On the days you celebrate your gods, you may congregate in the designated places of plebeian assembly, that is, the circus, the forum, the amphitheater, and inside private buildings of your followers. But you will not assemble in streets, markets, or other public places where goods are bought and sold." He pointed a long forefinger at Barnabas: "We hold you responsible as leader of your cult."

Barnabas bowed his head in deference to the governor. "I understand, Your Excellency, and I accept your conditions as necessary to good order," he said. "I regret that in our enthusiasm for our cause we have disturbed the peace that your wise governance brings to Antioch."

With an imperious wave of hand, Laurentus dismissed the two.

Chastened, Barnabas was silent as he and Saul walked toward the house they shared off the Nymphaeum. Suddenly Saul stopped. "Barnabas! This is a portent, a boon to our churches."

Barnabas frowned at Saul in wonder.

"Laurentus' decree instructs us to act as we should have long ago," Saul said. "As we cannot assemble in the marketplace, we must erect our own buildings for teaching and worship. Every Jew knows his synagogue; but where does a gentile go to revere Christ? To the house of a follower, or into the street where he may be scorned and spit on. Our movement requires more than a room in a follower's house; indeed, our Christians deserve an entire house of our own making, a building of beauty and dignity where we feel the presence of the Lord Jesus Christ."

Barnabas stood in the street, shaking his head. "How you dream, Saul. We are not so wealthy as the old Jewish families who came here three hundred years ago, prospered, and built Antioch's synagogues."

"There is nothing we can't do, Barnabas," Saul said, shaking his fist. "I will go today to Nearchus, the dealer of wheat and millet who came to Jesus three months ago and who gives freely to our cause. Nearchus owns an empty granary at dockside. I will today ask him to set up an altar in this granary so that our followers may meet to worship in private as Laurentus directed. Nearchus also owns bare land along the riverfront, and I will ask him to build a basilica for us there."

Saul took a stone and traced in the dirt the outline of a structure. "We need a building large enough for three hundred of our followers to assemble and perform the ritual of breaking bread and drinking wine in communion with the Lord Jesus Christ." He paused. "Barnabas, we shall build for four hundred. This will be the first of many basilicas where gentiles may assemble to honor the glory of the Lord Jesus Christ."

Barnabas frowned and pondered for a moment. "Will Nearchus do this?" he asked.

"With God's help, we can persuade him," Saul said.

XIX

ADVANCE

One evening soon after the end of his first year in Antioch, Saul brought his journal to his desk and dipped a new pen into the greenglass vial that a convert had fashioned for his inkstand. The pen in hand brought back memories of his treasured olive wood pen case, lost after the flogging in Issus. The thought of that gift from his mother stirred a deep longing for her. He closed his eyes and tried to re-create the image of her face, but her features were unclear, as if seen through dark glass. He had vowed never to forget her; now, fifteen years after her death, he rarely thought of her. Yet he felt no guilt. He had convinced himself that busy days, endless challenges, and the call of duty left no time for remorse or grief.

Were she alive, she would be proud of him; of that he was certain. She would see, as he had, that destiny had brought him to Antioch. Here he had not only proved himself, but excelled above all others. In a year he had brought one thousand, eight hundred and twenty-two souls to Jesus Christ. He had built a churchhouse where five hundred men and women assembled at one time to hear him deliver his message, to attest their faith and share the sacred bread and wine that symbolized Jesus' body and blood. He had created a school to train deacons in the rituals and responsibilities of worship. The ministers who had preceded him had adopted his message. They had followed his example and built churchhouses. He, with Barnabas, could boast that more men and women followed Jesus in Antioch city than in Jerusalem, indeed more than in all Israel.

Antioch he had conquered. Now he must march forward, take the offensive in a new campaign to liberate people in other lands from ignorance and sin, from despair and fear of death. That was his mission: to advance the good news of the coming of Jesus Christ into far nations of the world.

"Tomorrow," he said to himself, "I will tell Barnabas of my plan."

The next morning, as their servant cleared the table after their customary robust breakfast, Saul could delay no longer. "Barnabas, Antioch we have won to Christ. But Antioch is but a beginning."

Barnabas looked at Saul, saw the face aglow, the dark eyes flashing, and waited.

"I propose, Barnabas" —" Saul spoke slowly and deliberately —"that what you and I have accomplished in Antioch, we replicate in other great cities of the world."

Barnabas sat back and raised his hands in dismay. "Leave Antioch? Abandon our responsibilities here?" He shook his head vigorously. "We cannot do that!"

"We would not abandon Antioch, Barnabas, but take the logical next step. Jesus spoke in villages. We are winning for him a city. Antioch is the model, the exemplar of what we can do in other urban communities. Where, Barnabas, is the future of the movement for Christ? It is in the cities, the capitals of political power, the centers where goods are made and exchanged, where traders come and go, where people work and live."

Barnabas shook his head. "Our work is here, Saul. Antioch depends on us."

"Our work has neither bounds nor borders, Barnabas. Consider: Augustus not only built the roads of the empire but also posted his solders on his roads to keep them safe for trade and travel. His triremes swept the seas of pirates. As Augustus made the world safe for trade, so also did he make the world safe for you and me to travel afar and spread the gospel of Jesus Christ." He seized Barnabas by the arm. "We can market our faith in other lands just as Nearchus sells his wheat in Rome, and just as Nathan sells his amphorae of good wine in Ephesus."

Barnabas raised a hand. "But Saul, there is still so much to be done here."

"And what remains to be done here can be accomplished by the ministers and teachers and deacons we have trained," Saul said. "Our followers — their numbers, their faith, and their fervor — have reached a critical mass that will not only sustain itself but thrive and grow. We have so established the Way of Jesus Christ here in Antioch that collectively our churches form an institution that will perpetuate itself, a corporate body that will live through generations yet unborn."

Barnabas rocked back and forth in his chair, pondering. At last he spoke:

"Well, I would agree that the churches here can probably carry on for a brief time without us."

"Not just carry on, Barnabas, but prosper and expand. Indeed, our success here has inspired me to envision a grand design of what we can do. Consider: Since times of old, kings have ruled by spear and sword. Philip, Alexander, Julius Caesar, Augustus — each created an empire by invading a country, setting up a center of strength and power in an existing or new city, and ruling with a handful of loyal and high-ranking officers. From fortress or palace these officers brought order and benefits. The Caesars, for example, recruited cadres of native peoples, trained them to manage the day-to-day business of the provinces, and compensated them with money and status. The indigenous they made Romans. And thereby they made it possible for the conqueror to march on and capture new nations."

Saul raised his arms and exclaimed: "We — you and I, Barnabas — shall also conquer. Under the banner of Christ we shall invade nations near and far. Our weapons are faith, hope, the promise of eternal life. We will march forward with word and cross. Wherever we go, we will bring men and women to Christ, baptize them, organize them, train them to teach and recruit and expand their numbers and influence. All that we have accomplished here augurs for success. We have infused a profound belief and new ethic into a significant constituency of Antiochenes. We can do this elsewhere. We can overcome wickedness and despair in civilized communities across the Roman Empire, and beyond, yes, to the ends of earth. Together, in time, we and our apostles and followers will bring about the worldly kingdom of God that Jesus promised."

Barnabas exhaled noisily and rubbed his eyes. "Bold you are, Saul," he said, then shook his head. "But we are so few. Let us build here for another year or two, marshal our resources, and then consider your plan."

"The time is now, Barnabas. The world is waiting for the good news of Jesus Christ, for the faith and hope that we can bring, for deliverance from sin and darkness. The world is waiting for you and me to bear the gift of salvation to all the peoples of earth. This is our vision; let us make it come to pass." He stopped and raised his hands in appeal. "Tell me now, Barnabas, is there anyone better than you and me to undertake this mission to the world?"

"That I cannot deny," Barnabas said. "But I fear leaving the church in Antioch. I cannot forget how divided and ineffective we were in my first years here. Suppose something happened to prevent our return if the others needed us."

"We will never be many days away, Barnabas. We are fortunate to live in a new time when journeys are swift and safe. Wherever we go, we will use young converts as couriers to report to and from Antioch. If our followers here need us, we will return."

After a long silence Barnabas asked: "Where would we go, Saul?"

"We should test our message in a small bowl, as the baker first proofs his yeast," Saul said. "Thus I would begin in a province nearby. I suggest Cyprus — the port of Salamis. If all goes well there, we go on to the capital, Paphos. You have often told me that Cypriots, like Antiochenes, are industrious and open of mind. Cyprus also has the advantage of being only a day's sail from Seleucia. Once in your country, we will experiment. We will speak to both Jew and gentile, and judge our success by how many we bring to Jesus."

Barnabas looked Saul in the eye. "Such a mission," he said slowly, "would require the approval of Peter and James."

"Why?" Saul exclaimed. "They contributed nothing to our accomplishments here."

"Because Jesus himself appointed Peter to oversee the church," Barnabas said. "Because Peter and James sent me to Antioch. Consequently, before I could leave my responsibilities here, I must have their consent."

"They will reject any initiative I offer, Barnabas." Saul threw down his hands in despair. "They are set against me."

"Not true, Saul. They acknowledge and respect all that you have accomplished here. Before we address Jerusalem, however, we must — in fairness to our three fellow ministers — present your proposal to them."

And so the five leaders of the Way in Antioch met to hear and discuss Saul's plan, after which Lucius the Cyrenian proposed they fast for a day and then meet again to pray. At sunset on the next day they convened in Barnabas' house to ask for guidance. All spoke. All listened. At last Symeon pronounced, "I believe God would have us separate Barnabas and Saul for the work to which he has called them." He rose, as did Lucius, and then Manaen. Together the three placed hands on the foreheads of Barnabas and Saul and blessed their mission.

At noon on the next day Barnabas was reading in his courtyard when he noticed his servant opening the gate. Looking up, he recognized his visitor, a man he had last seen on a back bench in Peter's meeting room for the Twelve. It was Agabus, a wizened hunchback and prophet of the Way.

His cloak, hood, and sandals were streaked with the gray dust of the road. He crept forward, in small but resolute steps, to confront Barnabas. When another servant brought a jar of water for the traveler to wash hands and feet, Agabus impatiently brushed it aside. In a voice that was an astonishingly deep rumble for so small a body, he began to speak.

"Lament for our people, O fortunate one. Lament, for hunger lies ahead. In the year to come rain will fall no more in Judea. The sun will burn the fields of grain. Grape and olive will shrivel. Lamb and ox will stumble from thirst. Bird of the air and animal of the forest will sicken and die. The wind will raise great clouds of dust that will bring gloom and darkness to morning."

Barnabas dismissed his servant and listened, all through the afternoon, to the prophet. In solemn tones Agabus told not only of drought and misfortune to come but also of the work of the Twelve, of mounting resistance among Jews to Roman occupation, of other happenings in Jerusalem. At nightfall, when Saul returned, Barnabas said: "This is Agabus, seer and counselor to Peter and James. From Jerusalem he brings bad news. He foresees in the years ahead drought and famine in all Judea. The Twelve, knowing that Antioch is as wealthy as Jerusalem is poor, sent him to me. He appeals to us to help the church of Jerusalem by donating money that he will deliver to feed our poor brothers and sisters of the Way in Jerusalem."

Saul was intrigued by the strange little man with the crooked back. He was beardless, hairless, with a skull of ridges and depressions and a wrinkled face with pale hazel eyes that glittered in the lamplight. There was sonorous conviction in the voice. There was a curious but unmistakable presence to the man despite his bent frame, and an odd but powerful charisma.

After a servant had led Agabus to a cot set up in a downstairs pantry for the night, Barnabas whispered. "Famine will cost us followers in Jerusalem, Saul."

"Is Agabus to be believed about the famine?" Saul asked.

"Yes, unfortunately. As a prophet, he is unequaled." Barnabas shook his head. "Saul, we must stay here and collect aid for Jerusalem. We must put off your mission."

"Not at all," Saul said. "Consider, instead, that Jerusalem's plight presents opportunity. We will help, certainly. We will appeal to all our followers here to give for the poor of Jerusalem. We will collect all they hope for, and more, to demonstrate our commitment to the community of Jesus Christ. And then we will not send these contributions by a messenger. Instead, you and I will take this money to Peter and James. If we, the ministers of Antioch, demonstrate such charity, how can Peter and James not sanction the mission that we have found to be God's will?"

Barnabas scratched his head, pondering. "Well then, shall we send Agabus back with our pledge of assistance?"

"We should keep him here," Saul said. "Let Agabus speak to each of our churches of Jerusalem's need. By his words and appearance he will stir their sympathies, as he has ours. As our assemblies see him and hear his appeal, Agabus, in turn, will witness the spirit and vigor of our followers. Once he returns to Jerusalem, he will be witness to how Antioch serves Christ. Let us, Barnabas, make Agabus an ally, our advocate before the Twelve."

On a crisp and sunny morning of early autumn, a small and odd caravan arrived at the Joppa Gate of Jerusalem. The Roman guard posted there observed a hooded hunchback on a donkey, a tall redhead with wide shoulders and a genial manner, a balding and bearded man bright of eye with a determined thrust of jaw, a second donkey bent with waterskins and saddlebags, and a stalwart Roman centurion marching briskly on either side. The gate guard, assuming the three dusty travelers were prisoners, pointed out the street leading to the jail. No, the senior centurion said, he and his armed comrade were appointed by Governor Laurentus Justinius as escort for valuable cargo.

The escort was necessary. So many Antiochenes had contributed silver and gold for the poor of Jerusalem that the route and time for transport became common gossip, and palace agents learned that a band of thieves plotted to ambush the travelers on the road to Laodicea, kill them, and take their money. Manaen spoke to Justinius; Justinius acted.

Once the caravan reached the house of Peter, Agabus dismounted and proposed that he go in first to inform the apostles of the delegation's arrival. Only Peter and James were present that morning, and they opened their arms to welcome Barnabas and Saul into the meeting room of the Twelve.

Barnabas, as leader, upended their three pouches on the rough-sawn table. The first contained fifty-two shekels of gold, the second a greater sum, eighty talents of silver, and the third even more, six hundred and twenty Roman denarii.

So astonished was Peter that he could not speak. Back and forth, back and forth, he turned his head, gaping at the coins on the table. At last he found his voice. "Such a gift! Such a gift!" He laughed aloud. "Never before have I seen so much money." He turned to James. "Our poor will eat." He turned to the visitors. "How grateful we are, to you, Barnabas, and to you as well, Saul."

"And to Agabus," Saul broke in, "for it was he who eloquently persuaded our churches of Jerusalem's need."

"Agabus, too," Peter said. "Surely you are weary after such a long journey. Come, each of you, a maidservant will bathe your feet and bring you food and drink. We welcome you to this house."

Neither Barnabas nor Saul moved, and there was a long silence. It had been agreed that Barnabas would propose the mission to Cyprus. But just as he started to speak, Peter raised his hand. "But before we break bread, perhaps you could tell us your work in Antioch. How many follow Jesus there?"

"We have now baptized three thousand, one hundred and seventy-seven in Antioch and nearby cities and communities," Barnabas said. "Every week we bring more to the Way."

"So many!" Peter exclaimed. "How do you attend them all?"

"By diligence and organization," Barnabas said. "Each of our four ministers has elders, deacons, and teachers to assist him. Each conducts a school to train leaders, both young and old.

"We have built five churchhouses within the city walls, another in Daphne, and two more in Seleucia. On the first day of every week all are filled."

Peter sat back, smiling in admiration, as James lifted a hand to speak. "Tell us, Barnabas, of your three thousand, one hundred and seventy-seven, how many are gentiles?"

"Almost half," Barnabas said.

"And are these gentiles circumcised before they are baptized?" James asked.

"No, they are not," Saul said, interrupting. "When Jesus instructed me to bring all to him, Jew and gentile, he said nothing about circumcision. Nor did he say that anyone must first become a Jew if he is to be saved."

"Nevertheless," James replied calmly, "from the beginning we have assumed that all who wish to follow Jesus should first become Jews, and no man can become a Jew unless and until he is circumcised."

Barnabas raised his hand and said: "But wait. Peter, did you not convert a centurion who was not circumcised?"

After a long silence Peter replied: "An angel of the Lord commanded me to baptize Cornelius, for the Holy Spirit had come upon him." He shrugged, brushed his hand aside, and smiled. "But we can discuss all this later," he said cheerfully. "Come, let us dine together."

When all had eaten, Barnabas presented the plan for the mission to Cyprus. Peter and James listened in silence, at times frowning and raising their eyebrows. "We are here," Barnabas concluded, "to inform you of our plan and to assure you that Antioch will remain in good hands during our absence."

In a voice of concern Peter asked: "How long would you be away from Antioch?"

"Two or three months in Cyprus, depending on how well we are received," Barnabas replied. "Then we may visit Pamphylia on our route of return."

Peter pulled at his beard. "You then seek our approval?"

Saul broke in: "We will go whether you approve or not, for this mission is the will of the Lord God." Barnabas seized Saul's arm, trying to silence him.

"Six weeks ago," Barnabas said quietly, "we who lead the Antioch churches — Manaen, Lucius, Symeon Niger, Saul, and I — fasted and prayed for guidance. As we were together in prayer the Lord God spoke to Symeon, saying, 'Separate both Barnabas and Saul to me, for the work to which I have called them.'"

"Well then," Peter said, "as the Lord God has spoken to you, you must —"

James interrupted. "Peter, perhaps you and I should also pray, and ask God to guide us as we consider the wisdom and consequences of an undertaking that is without precedent."

For a moment Peter pondered James' intervention. "Yes, we too should seek guidance." He turned to Barnabas. "When would you go?"

"As the season for sailing will end within a month, we must move quickly," Barnabas said. "We intend to leave Jerusalem tomorrow on horseback, reach Antioch in eight or nine days, and sail on the first boat from Seleucia to Salamis."

"Let us rest tonight," Peter said, "and meet tomorrow morning."

That night, tossing on the cot in the spare room of Peter's house, Saul tried to contain his anger. The sound of Barnabas' calm and quiet breathing across the room vexed him even more. Why had Barnabas not joined him in declaring that the mission to Cyprus would go forward whether Peter and James approved or not? Saul was not sure what he thought of Peter — was it contempt, resentment, pity, or the sum of the three? Neither in ability nor zeal had he ever matched his commission from Jesus. If Peter was a rock, he was buried in the stagnant waters of Jerusalem, while in the world beyond, the Christian movement was a clear and quickening stream bearing hope to humanity. And James — Saul scorned his pomposity, his pretentiousness. Here was one who had not even followed his half brother in life but who had, after Jesus' death, arrogated the right to speak for him. And now it was James who was contriving to thwart the mission. He was sure that James would trick Peter into delaying their journey, or rejecting it outright.

"It is not Barnabas they oppose; it is I," Saul told himself. "They oppose me because Jesus spoke to me not once but twice, but not to them since he ascended. It is jealousy that has turned them against me. They would destroy me if they could. If Antioch were not four hundred miles away, I could not have accomplished all that I have. Had they been nearby, Peter and James would have interfered, questioned my initiatives. Now that I have made Antioch the beating heart of the body of Christ, I will begin my campaign to bear the message and cross of Jesus to every corner of the world. Nothing will stop me. I will go despite any orders that may come from Peter. Jesus himself told me to go to the far countries and bear his message to Jew and gentile alike. I will go, even if I must go alone."

The next morning Barnabas and Saul waited in Peter's meeting room for an hour, and then another. Barnabas was calm, confident. "They will confirm this mission; I am sure of it," he said. Saul was grim, silent. He felt as though he were on trial, standing on the prisoner's stone before the Sanhedrin, waiting for a verdict.

In the third hour they heard footsteps outside. Peter came in, followed not by James but by a young man, in his twenties, scholarly, gowned in fine linen. At first Saul did not recognize him. But Barnabas leaped up and exclaimed with joy: "John Mark! My favorite cousin — how tall you have grown! How handsome you are with your trimmed beard. How is Aunt Mary?"

John Mark remembered Saul from the visits to his mother's house, and greeted him warmly. "You taught me how to improve my writing," John Mark said.

"And now," Peter said, "John Mark is our best scribe and interpreter." He paused. "And to affirm our support for you, we have assigned him to accompany you on your mission to Cyprus."

"Splendid!" Barnabas said. He stepped to John Mark's side and put his long arm around his cousin's shoulder. "What good fortune to have you with us." He stopped. "But has Aunt Mary consented?"

"Yes, yes," Peter said. "We saw her this morning. She hesitated at first, but she was reassured when I told her that you were sailing to her homeland. And I promised her that both of you will look out for John Mark as though he were your own son."

Saul felt caught in a trap. Given Barnabas' enthusiasm for the company of his cousin on the journey, he could not protest. But he was certain that Peter and James had contrived to plant a spy within his mission.

XX

EXPEDITION

In the last days of autumn the journey from the eastward sea to Salamis is spirited and swift. The wind streams out of the north, strong and constant, raising choppy waves and long swells. In the ancient time the Phoenicians learned to craft hulls and sails that took advantage of these elements, building tradeships that seemed to spring like antelope from wavetop to wavetop. All who sail benefit from the legacy of those masters of the sea.

The *Adora*, broad, sturdy, and small, was more cockleshell than longship. Only half filled with jute bags of barley from the last of the harvest, she rode high in the water, tossing, plunging, yawing, hurrying along her course. Her cheerful captain and helmsman, Nokos, had made the journey from Seleucia to Salamis and back so often — at least once a week except in winter — that he boasted his beloved *Adora* could find her own way. "The course is a straight line," Nokos explained to Saul, who sat beside him at the tiller. "Hold Mount Atchana directly astern in the morning. From noon, follow the sun until it sets. When the stars appear, keep bright Cygnus abeam. And at dawn, lo, there is Cape Andreas. Follow that finger of golden sand down to the knuckle, keeping well offshore to hold the wind, and there is Salamis."

All through the night Saul sat by Nokos, both wrapped in heavy cloaks to break the chill of the north wind. He breathed the good salt air, tasted the zesty spray on his lips, and listened to Nokos' tales of men and ships at sea. Barnabas huddled in the lee of the forward hatch, remaining close by John Mark: It was the younger man's first venture at sea, and no sooner had they cleared the harbor than he began vomiting. The three were the *Adora*'s only passengers.

The harbor of Salamis was a great arc of sea open to the east. Longships, outbound and riding low with copper ingots, competed with fishing boats bringing their catch to market. Nokos maneuvered nimbly among them and brought the *Adora* to her reserved wharf. With cheerful words and warm embraces he escorted his passengers ashore.

Saul, setting foot on the cobbled stones of Salamis, felt his spirits soaring. He was eager to meet the immediate challenge: to bring Cypriots to Jesus Christ. But deep in his soul he knew that this expedition was merely a start, the initial casting in his plan to sow the seeds of faith to the ends of earth. Beyond Saul's vision awaited a greater destiny: He was beginning a long and storied adventure, a journey of twenty years and tens of thousands of miles that would exalt and punish him, bring him triumph and tragedy, lift him to glory and inflict him with pain and suffering. The restlessness of his spirit and the zeal in his nature would make of him a man without home or country. Duty would come first; all else would be cast aside.

On the brisk and sunny afternoon of their arrival, Salamis mingled the scents of sea and spice and smoke. Food sellers, tinkling little brass bells, hawked their crisping meats and yeasty breads in the narrow crowded streets. Hammers rang on metal. A donkey brayed. Through the throngs the three visitors made their way, Barnabas taking John Mark, still weak of knee, to the best inn as Saul set out to find the synagogue. He and Barnabas were as one in believing their first obligation was to deliver the good news of Jesus Christ to Jews.

The main synagogue of Salamis was an imposing structure, a rectangle of pristine cut stone of an unblemished ivory in color, set back in a court bounded by low walls that framed an entire block of city land. Rabbi Barak lifted his arms in welcome once he learned this fellow teacher had been so recently in Jerusalem. Barak had heard stories of the Nazarene rabbi, and was curious to know more. He offered to gather a few of his faithful in the synagogue to hear Saul the next morning. And on the Sabbath, he would invite Saul and his companions to speak to the entire congregation. With a deferential tilt of his head Barak added: "Use the common tongue of Greek, for Aramaic is not readily understood by all here."

At the impromptu assembly, with only eleven present, Saul recounted the latest events in Jerusalem and spoke at length of mounting opposition to Roman taxes and the cruelty of Claudius' rule. He closed by mentioning just enough about Jesus to provoke his listeners. His intent was to stir their curiosity, get them talking so that community gossip would fill the synagogue the next day.

On the Sabbath, after Barak had read from the Law and the Prophets, he invited the visitors to come forward. Barnabas, as leader of the delegation from Antioch, spoke briefly before he presented Saul as the visitor appointed to teach that morning.

Saul had invested time and thought toward what he would say in this first major address in a new country. He must impress but not startle; engage but not offend. Every audience was different, and he was learning to sense their mood and estimate their level of knowledge. Still, it was mostly instinct that enabled him to select the words that would connect to their hopes and fears. Here in Salamis he would try to appeal to the mind of diaspora Jews, most of whom longed for, but would never see, Jerusalem. These merchants and artisans were exiles conflicted daily by holding to Mosaic ethic while dealing with pagans unburdened by conscience or standards. To reach these Jews with his good news, he must lean heavily on Jewish tradition and teaching, then lure them to follow his reasoning that a new era had come in their long and great history.

And so he did, retelling the legends of Abraham, Isaac, Jacob, and Moses, citing Isaiah's prophecy that God would send a new leader of David's line, proclaiming the good news that Jesus Christ had come to deliver all from sin, and then, as scripture foretold, be crucified and resurrected. "All this was God's plan: to bring us back the faith of our fathers, to renew his message to mankind — *Atone, trust in God, and your sins will be forgiven.*"

Saul stopped. He had said enough. He had learned that he could not in one day overcome any good Jew's commitment to tradition and rituals. If any Jew or gentile wanted to hear more, he or she would come to him. He closed with a prayer and resumed his seat among the congregation.

As the synagogue emptied, Barak rushed to Saul, grasped his hand, and commended him. "Will you meet tomorrow with our elders? Will you speak again on the next Sabbath?"

On the third day of the week, two gentiles, a butcher and his wife, came to the Alashia Inn to speak to Barnabas and Saul. "We are God fearers, but not Jews," Monica said. "Can we follow Jesus if my husband, Kronos, does not suffer the pain of the cutting to become a Jew?"

"The Way of Jesus Christ is open to all," Saul replied. "If you believe in him, if you repent of your sins, then you can be baptized and be one with us."

On the following Sabbath, Saul spoke again in the main synagogue, to an even larger assembly; on his third Sabbath in Salamis, the congregation was larger still. Word of his teaching spread. From the nearby village of Temis came Rabbi Beeri, who invited Saul to speak in the Temis synagogue.

Barnabas was highly pleased at their reception in Salamis, and said so to Saul. But Saul was dismayed. The crowds and the enthusiasm had brought twenty-one gentiles into the Way, but after a month only seven Jews had come to the Alashia Inn to find out more about Jesus, and only three of those had asked to be baptized. "We must be patient," Barnabas said as he and Saul walked about in a public square near the inn.

Saul shook his head. "Why do our brother Jews not come to us? Why do they not see the truth?"

As they talked, they saw John Mark coming toward them with Carchem the innkeeper and an imposing stranger. He was trim, held his head of well-coiffed curls high, and strode with authority in the white toga of a Roman official.

"He comes to arrest us," Saul whispered.

"I think not," Barnabas said. "Look at the happy face of the innkeeper."

Carchem, chest swelling with pride, announced the visitor. "The esteemed proconsul who rules this great senatorial province of Rome, Sergius Paulus, has sent his notable representative in this city, Horus Apollonius, as emissary to deliver a message to the important guests of my inn. I now present to you the emissary of the proconsul."

Horus Apollonius acknowledged the introduction with a slight bow of his head and turned to Barnabas. "Word has reached the capital city of Paphos of your teachings in Salamis. On this day I received a messenger from his eminence Sergius Paulus, the proconsul of the great Caesar Claudius for this province. The esteemed Sergius Paulus extends his greetings to you, and would have you come forthwith to Paphos, where you will be welcomed to his palace, for he desires to hear the word of God."

The three Wayfarers left early the next morning. Horus Apollonius had directed them to follow the coastal route, shorter than the valley road, but more difficult. Sections of the mountain road — not yet completed by

Roman engineers — were narrow trails winding along sheer bluffs dropping to the sea. Saul plotted the journey: thirty-six miles to the old Roman fort at Citium the first day; forty miles to Episcopi the second day. They could sleep at an inn frequented by pilgrims who came by boat to ascend Mount Olympus. From Episcopi it was only thirty-two miles to Paphos, so they would arrive in the capital by midafternoon. Each carried bread, dried figs, and a waterskin.

Saul set the pace with the soldier's stride he had learned in his youth. Barnabas, with his long legs and loping gait, kept up easily, but John Mark fell behind again and again. Every stop to wait for the youth made Saul more impatient. By the time they reached Episcopi on the second day, John Mark's feet were blistered and bleeding. The next morning Barnabas looked at his cousin's swollen feet and bought a donkey for John Mark to ride on to Paphos.

They passed through the gate of the city in early afternoon and found an inn. As soon as they washed and purified themselves, Saul insisted that they go immediately to the palace. The doorkeeper inspected them, up and down, and consulted with a palace functionary who, after excited whisperings with other functionaries, led the travelers to carved double doors adorned with heavy brass. As they stood outside the doors, functionaries in more elegant robes whispered among themselves, apparently in spirited debate. At last a guard opened the doors, and the three entered the throne room.

The proconsul Sergius Paulus bore the marks of an old soldier. The sleeve of his white linen toga lay limp where his left arm had been severed in an obscure battle at the Rhine. Thereafter his talent for logistics led to victories that won him appointment to the Senate. Now, except for a fringe of grizzled gray at his temples, he was bald. His face was fissured with the bronze wrinkles often seen in field soldiers; his eyes were deep blue, steady, direct. He sat with princely authority, stiff and erect in a great chair of carved oak. Pages lounged at his feet. Courtiers stood respectfully waiting for his bidding. A dark-haired woman, evidently his wife, sat in a smaller but distinctive chair at his left. She was attended by one woman of her age, and four maidens.

"Come forward." It was a voice accustomed to command, spoken by one knowing it would be obeyed. A courtier whispered in the proconsul's ear as the three came forward. There was a long silence as Sergius Paulus studied each in turn before he looked Barnabas in the eye and spoke. "You are a Cypriot, of a wealthy family of Soli. Yet you stand before me in the plain robe of a peasant. Is such display of dress required by your god?"

"Not required, Your Eminence," Barnabas said respectfully. "The Way of Jesus Christ is open to all, to the great and the humble, to general and hoplite, to rich and poor. But most of our followers are the less fortunate, the hungry, the poor. Thus we dress as they, as outward evidence of an inner truth, that all are equal in the sight of Jesus Christ, whose word and spirit we have brought to your most excellent province."

Sergius Paulus lifted his eyebrows and rested his chin on his hand as he pondered Barnabas' response.

An older courtier suddenly stepped to the proconsul's side, pointed to the visitors, and blurted: "Do not listen to these imposters, Your Eminence. Their gods are false."

Without a moment's hesitation Saul stepped forward, fixed his eyes on the courtier, raised his hand toward the man, and spoke in a firm and loud voice: "O you, Elymas the sorcerer, full of all guile and of all cunning. You child of the devil. You enemy of all righteousness. Will you not stop perverting the right ways of the Lord?" He stopped abruptly, took two paces toward Elymas, and proclaimed: "And now, behold! The hand of the Lord is upon you. You shall be blind, not seeing the sun for a season."

The mouth of Sergius Paulus fell open in astonishment. He drew back to look at the court seer, for Elymas was staggering, as if struck by a heavy club. Helpless, he stumbled and stretched out a hand, crying out for someone to lead him.

Murmurs of dismay passed among the courtiers, as all present looked in awe at Saul. With a quick movement of hand the proconsul signaled a page to take Elymas by the hand and lead him from the throne room. With the return of the dignity of the court, Sergius Paulus spoke to Saul. "I am an old soldier," he said quietly. "I have campaigned in many lands, seen strange happenings and odd events of all kinds. But never before have my old eyes witnessed such a miracle. What I have seen here is so astonishing that it proves that you are men of a God whose power is supreme. Speak to me now, briefly, of your doctrine. Then I shall ask questions. For now I do believe in your God, and I would know more about him and what tribute he requires of his subjects."

For the balance of the afternoon Sergius Paulus and Saul engaged in a spirited dialogue, with the proconsul constantly probing: Why did God choose Jesus to be his son, rather than someone else? Who schooled Jesus to lead? How did he heal the sick? Did he and his courtiers forage for food as he journeyed about? Who supplied the money to support his campaign? What, he asked each of the three, did Jesus look like? Did he ever take a wife? Enjoy women? Why had the Jews betrayed one of their own? Did he carry no sword to defend himself? Why did his followers not take up arms and protect him? Had the three seen him crucified? Had they seen him after God raised him from the dead? Would Jesus come to earth again? What would it be like for a mortal to live in God's heavenly kingdom?

As evening came Sergius Paulus called for a banquet to honor his visitors and assigned them rooms in his palace. By his command, they were to go about Paphos, teaching, answering questions, and reporting to him each day on how many Cypriots they had brought to Jesus Christ.

In his room that night Saul sat at a great window, scanning the dark city, contemplating the stars in the glowing bowl of the firmament. Barnabas opened the door quietly and came in, bearing an oil lamp. "I would talk with you," Barnabas said.

"And I would talk with you, my brother," Saul said. "But we need no lamp to light what we say."

After they sat in the darkness for a time, Barnabas was first to break the silence. "Saul, how did you perform that miracle?"

"The first part was simple," Saul said. "As we waited outside the throne room, I heard the courtiers arguing, in Latin. The older was saying that Elymas the court sorcerer, evidently a favorite of the proconsul's wife, had contrived to bar us from speaking. The younger insisted that Sergius Paulus had commanded our appearance and we should be brought in. The older replied that if we went into the throne room, Elymas would use magic to make us disappear. So I knew his name and anticipated his intervention."

Saul was silent for a long time. "However, I must confess that striking Elymas blind was not a forethought. Nor was it my plan." He paused. "Barnabas, you must tell no one of what I am about to say: The truth is that I do not know how I performed that miracle. The words were put on my tongue by some compelling force, by some cosmic element that came upon me in quickness of necessity." He fell silent. "In that moment of urgent need I felt the power of God. There is no other explanation."

Below them they heard the tramp of boots and shouted commands sig-naling the changing of the palace guard at midnight.

"What struck me after the miracle," Barnabas said, "was the energy and gusto of your dialogue with Sergius Paulus. Instead of being awed by what you had done, your manner indicated it was commonplace. How did you manage that?"

"The intervention came and went in a moment," Saul said. "And instantly I knew it was up to me to elevate the discourse to the level of the miracu-lous event that all in the throne had witnessed. Sergius Paulus helped. He questioned like a tutor. He was far more learned than I expected."

"You were at your most persuasive," Barnabas said. "You must have inher-ited your father's talent for selling what you craft, for here — as in Antioch and Salamis — you show all of us how to market faith in God."

Saul turned in surprise. "You did not know my father."

"Not in person," Barnabas replied, "but through you I came to know both Isaac and Abigail. I concluded that both were remarkable, that your mother in her wisdom articulated excellence while your father in his trade demon-strated it."

Saul looked up to the sky in silence. Barnabas was right: He had gained far more from his father than he had ever acknowledged. The bent old man was inventive, resolute, and remarkably successful in the profession he had chosen. Isaac saw that travelers needed portable and reliable shelter, so he fashioned superior products to meet that need. In his mind Saul found a par-allel. He, too, saw a need among men and women, and resolved to fill that need. He, too, fashioned his wares to suit the listener. But selling an idea was far more difficult than selling something you can see, touch, hold in your hand, or use as shelter from a storm.

Barnabas' mention of Isaac transported him to his youth, and a wave of guilt swept over him for the way he had treated his father, disdaining his busi-ness even as he delighted in the benefits it brought. He could not remember ever expressing his gratitude for his father's gifts. Except for his father's inge-nuity and industry he would never have enjoyed the best schools, the grandest mansion, the loyal servants, the good life. From the perspective of fifteen years since his father's death, Saul could see himself and lament the truth: Youth is too absorbed in itself to express gratitude. Why had he never told his father that he loved him, except in that last letter, when it was too late?

As the two sat in darkness, Saul sensed that more was on Barnabas' mind. At last Barnabas said: "My brother Saul, there is something else I must say. Very simply, by your words and your actions you have demonstrated that you are the true leader of this expedition. Peter directed me to command, but Peter does not see what I see: that it is you who leads this bold campaign for Jesus Christ. You created this enterprise. You won its sanction, in Antioch and in Jerusalem. You are first among us in teaching the gospel in Cyprus; that has been self-evident from the day we landed in Salamis. I have prayed long and hard, erased all doubt, and decided this: You are to lead this mission. I will follow."

Saul was quick to respond: "What will Peter say?"

Expecting that reaction, Barnabas replied: "It is the Lord God's decision, not Peter's. When I see Peter, I will tell him the truth that I recognize and he must accept: God chose you to be first among us to take the good news to the far nations."

Saul was silent. Barnabas had not merely borrowed his thoughts, but spoken them aloud. Long had he hungered for command. Nine years it had been since Jesus came to him on that Damascus road. Nine years of waiting. Now at last he was being offered the responsibility he thought due.

"Very well, Barnabas," he said. "I accept command. I will lead this mission. Once we have completed our mission in Paphos, I will travel on to Asia."

"And I will go with you," Barnabas said, and stood to leave.

"Wait," Saul said. "Be with me longer, for there is more I would say." He waited for Barnabas to sit again. "For some time this has been on my mind, Barnabas, and tonight I made my decision: I will no longer use my birth name of Saul; from now on I will be called Paul."

"You are giving up your Jewish name?" Barnabas' voice was filled with surprise. "Why?"

"First, we minister to a Greek and Roman world. We speak in Greek. We think in Greek. Most who hear us know no language but the common tongue of Greek. Reason tells me, therefore, that as leader of this expedition to Greek and Roman, I should be known by a name that is Greek and Roman. Second, Jesus transformed me from the one I was into the one I am, so I should take a new name."

"But surely you will continue to go to the synagogues and speak to Jews," Barnabas said.

"Of course. That remains our first priority. To win Jews, I speak as a Jew. Our brothers will always recognize that I am a Jew. To win gentiles, I must speak as a gentile and be known by a gentile name. So I shall be Paul."

"Well, it is Paul you are," Barnabas said cheerfully. "And from this day forward it is Paul you will be."

For three months Paul, Barnabas, and John Mark remained in Paphos, teaching, baptizing, and organizing. And so the winter passed, and the first warm days brought the promise of the spring breezes that would open the sea-lanes. Eager to resume his travels, Paul asked the proconsul for permission to leave on the next boat bound for Asia.

"Give me an accounting of your work here," Sergius Paulus commanded.

"Your Eminence, we have instructed and baptized the seventy-two members of your court who joined the Way at your bidding," Paul replied. "In addition we have brought one hundred and eighty men and women to Jesus Christ through our teachings and exhortation in your capital city. In the barracks that you in your generosity gave us for a school, we have trained a score of deacons and elders to continue teaching and conducting the rituals that affirm our faith and bring us closer to God. You gave your consent to the appointment of the centurion Lepidus Faustus as first among deacons, and we observe that he continues to demonstrate the depth of his faith and his ability as a leader. Thus, Your Eminence, the church here is in good hands. With your consent, I would travel on to the Roman cities of Asia, where I propose to found other churches."

"The report of a good soldier," Sergius Paulus said, looking about to courtiers nodding their approval. Rubbing his meaty hands together, he continued: "I grant you and your companions leave to go to Asia. As no tradeship is ready to sail, I will send you to Perga on the proconsul's barge. I am sending there a cargo of fifty horses for my old comrade, Junius Sabinus. He commands the Fulminata Legion now stationed in Pamphylia. In return, Junius Sabinus is lending me a cohort of his engineers for a year to lay out and construct the new road to Polis. I need these troops. You need a ship to Asia. So be it."

Two days later the *Boreas* was loaded and ready to sail on the morning tide. She was a big ship, heavy, slow, built with spaces for troops between the ribs and tight stalls lining her deck to protect horses in a rough sea. The entire vessel smelled strongly of stables.

Sergius Paulus arrived on the dock to bid godspeed to the three who had brought him to the Way and been his guests. On the hillside overlooking the harbor every Christian in Paphos had assembled. After a spirited admonition to keep the faith, Paul lifted his hands toward the crowd, delivered a final blessing, and stepped aboard.

That night the *Boreas* was swept off course by a late-winter gale that struck in the darkness, forcing the crew to take in all but a storm sail for steerage. For the next day and another night the storm continued. On the third day the sun rose in a brilliantly clear sky, and Crantus Quintus, captain of the *Boreas*, confessed to Paul that he was lost. So he sailed northward until he saw land, and recognized the coastal range of Lycia, far to the west of their destination. By beating back and forth against the wind, the *Boreas* reached the mouth of the Kestros River estuary eight days later.

Paul used the time to plan his land journey into the Galatian territory: From Perga they would take the Roman military road north, up into the mountains to a vast plateau, and past the great lake fed by the River Anthios, to Pisidian Antioch. It was an ancient city, hellenized by Seleucus I, romanized by Caesar Augustus. The latter had made it the hub of troop and trade movement in his provinces of Pisidia and Phrygia, building fortresses and roads linking it with other areas he colonized to control and profit from the mines, quarries, and artisans of the region. There had long been substantial numbers of Jews in the major Galatian cities; this Paul knew from his library years with Gamaliel.

Once ashore at the landing on the Kestros River, the three Wayfarers walked five miles west to Perga and entered through the River Gate. It was a small but elegant and inviting Roman city, a walled rectangle with wide streets bordered by Ionic colonnades.

"We should find a comfortable inn here," John Mark observed.

It was a warm afternoon, and he was sweating from the walking. Paul stopped and leaned over to tighten the thongs on his sandals. He looked up at the sun, still high in the sky, and shouldered his pack. "It is ninety-three miles to Pisidian Antioch," he said. "We will fill our waterskins at the city well and set out. We can make fifteen miles before darkness falls."

John Mark slumped in despair. "Can we not rest for a day?" he pleaded.

Barnabas raised his hands in appeal to Paul. "He is weak from five days' sickness at sea. He needs meat and bread and sleep."

"No," Paul replied. "The storm delayed us. We must press on. Our mission must come first." He turned to John Mark. "Summon up your strength. You can rest in Antioch."

Suddenly John Mark burst into tears. "I want to go home to my mother."

Paul looked at John Mark not with sympathy but with disdain. The youth was simply not suited for the hard life of the road. "Then go." Paul's voice was cold and angry. "Go to your mother. Our mission cannot wait."

XXI

EMBATTLED

Once they passed through the north gate of the city wall, the road leading Paul and Barnabas toward Pisidian Antioch seemed to promise a swift and easy journey on that warm spring afternoon. It was a new imperial way, of granite blocks quarried nearby and well fitted by Roman military engineers. For the first three miles it ran straight and true, as though a plumb line had been laid down across the fertile plain, through orchards, vineyards, and fields of cotton. Then the road began to climb, winding like a glistening ribbon up the foothills, through groves of olive and pomegranate, oak and walnut.

Higher, higher, they walked, past a shepherd tending his fat sheep in a greening meadow, past patches of wild crocus and anemone. Except for a woodcutter and his oxcart of logs coming down the mountain, the road was empty. Sweating from the climb, they reached a low pass between two peaks and stopped at a spring. The water was bracing cold, sparkling with light as it ran from the hillside. Looking south, they could glimpse the sea in the distance, at least two thousand feet below them.

As the road continued to rise the oaks gave way to a forest thick with towering masts of pine. On they trudged, until at Milestone X the paving abruptly ended. Ahead was little more than a narrow footpath that followed the shoulder of a long canyon, crossed a mountain stream to the opposing shoulder, recrossed, lost itself in the forest, and appeared again on a ridge that towered high above them.

At dusk, with the wind rising, Barnabas saw a low rock shelf shielding a patch of moss. Paul gathered fallen branches and deadwood while Barnabas brought flint and dry tinder from his pouch and started a fire. They ate, wrapped themselves in their cloaks, and slept.

At daybreak a dense mist lay over the canyon, and it began to rain. They walked on. By midmorning the mountain brook they had crossed and recrossed had risen, becoming a roaring torrent fifty feet wide. At a ford Paul did not hesitate. "I will go first," he said, wading into the stream. Twenty feet from shore he lost his footing on slippery rock and disappeared below the turbulent waters. Barnabas threw off his pack, ran downstream along the bank, and dove into the water. By good fortune he caught the end of Paul's cloak and dragged him to shore. Once Paul got his breath, Barnabas broke into a smile. "I always said I was the better swimmer."

"Today you proved it," Paul said quietly. "You saved my life." Shivering from the cold, he said: "Let us try the ford again. We must go on."

"Very well," Barnabas said, "but we will cross together."

This time they succeeded, and moved on. At midday, climbing to the top of what they thought was another ridge, they stopped and looked in amazement. They had come to the edge of a high plateau that stretched before them like an endless table of grassland, empty and silent. Paul pointed the way ahead. "Lepidus Faustus told me to walk north until we reach a great shallow lake. There we will find the Roman road from Colossae into Antioch." Two more days of walking brought them through the arch of the Western Gate of Pisidian Antioch. At Barnabas' insistence, they went to the best inn, bathed and purified themselves, ate meat and bread, and slept.

The synagogue in the city was old, well tended, and even larger than Paul expected. Rabbi Ithamar and his assistant, Bildad, greeted Paul and Barnabas warmly. Paul had decided to state their mission clearly. "We are Jews who follow the teachings of Jesus, a rabbi of Nazareth, and we would speak of his teachings to your congregation."

"We have heard of this mythical Nazarene," Ithamar replied. "We are curious to know more, and so will hear you on the Sabbath two days hence."

In new robes and prayer scarves, purchased in the city by Barnabas, the Wayfarers went into the synagogue on the day of the Sabbath and sat down. The benches filled rapidly, and Paul could hear the footsteps of women behind the screen in the adjoining chamber. On the platform the five rulers of the synagogue took their places in the chief seats, followed by the rabbi and his assistant.

At his pulpit Rabbi Ithamar opened the scroll and read, in Hebrew, the

Law. Bildad followed by reading, in Greek, from the Prophets. With a sweeping gesture toward the visitors, Ithamar declaimed: "Men, brothers: If there is a word of exhortation to the people, speak."

Paul stood, walked to the pulpit, and raised his hand for silence. "Men of Israel and you who fear God, listen: The God of our people of Israel chose our fathers and raised high his chosen people when they dwelled as strangers in the land of Egypt. And with a mighty arm God parted the waters and led them out to freedom. For forty years he made them wander in the wilderness so as to put their faith to the test. Their faith proved, God then brought these chosen Israelites, our ancestors, to the land of Canaan. Seven other nations then occupied this land, so God put them out so that his people might hold this blessed land as their inheritance forever.

"For the next four hundred and fifty years God gave his people judges, prophets, and kings, promising that he would raise up for Israel one of King David's descendants, Jesus, a savior. My brothers, sons of Abraham, this message of salvation is meant for you. What the people of Jerusalem and their high priests did, though they did not realize it, was to fulfill the prophecies read on every Sabbath: They condemned Jesus and provoked Pilate to put their savior to death. I have come here to bring you the good news: God fulfilled his promise of old by raising Jesus from the dead. My brothers, it is through Jesus that forgiveness of sins is proclaimed to you, and to every believer."

Many heads were shaking, too many to ignore. Paul felt it his duty to warn them. "Beware, unbelievers! Remember the warning God delivered to his people through the prophet Habbakuk: 'Behold, you despisers, and marvel, and perish, for I will perform a work in your own days that you would never believe if you were told of it.'"

Paul stepped from the pulpit and took his seat. Barnabas was beaming with pride. The assembly was silent as Ithamar closed with a crisp benediction.

Outside the synagogue a number of Jews and even more gentiles, women as well as men, approached Paul and Barnabas. "Come to us at the inn," Paul said. "All your questions will be answered."

In the weeks that followed Paul and Barnabas were besieged — by young and old, Greek, Roman, Jew. Some had been at the synagogue; more had heard street conversation about the eastern strangers' promise of salvation and eternal life. Paul, in the courtyard, instructed and explained; Barnabas, in the public square, held his listeners spellbound with accounts of seeing and hearing Jesus in Galilee.

On the morning of the fourth Sabbath, it seemed the whole city had crowded into the synagogue to hear about the gifts promised by the outsiders. When Paul and Barnabas reached the steps leading to the door, they were stopped by Pashur, chief ruler of the synagogue. "You blasphemers will speak here no more."

His head high, Paul replied to Pashur in a firm and even voice, "As Jews it was our duty to proclaim the word of God to you first; but since you have rejected it, since you do not think yourselves worthy of eternal life, behold, we turn to the gentiles."

Turning to the crowd, Paul proclaimed: "For so the Lord has commanded us: 'I have made you a light to the nations, so that my salvation may reach the ends of the earth.'"

With that, he and Barnabas led the throng to the main square of the city and up the twelve steps to the Rostrorum Augustalis, where for an hour Paul spoke of the coming of Jesus Christ and his promise of forgiveness and salvation for all.

Returning to the inn, Paul sat down with Barnabas to form a plan. So many Pisidians had come to them that they must immediately arrange baptisms in the river outside the city. They must also appoint and train deacons. They would need a house where they could teach and conduct the rituals of worship.

"Marius the coppersmith offered us a meeting place," Barnabas said.

"Good," Paul said. "We open there tomorrow."

Barnabas was silent for a moment. "I have a question, Paul. When did God command you and me to be a light to the gentiles?"

"The command to 'us' is a command to all Jews," Paul replied. "So God spoke through Isaiah. The good news of deliverance by Jesus Christ was to go first to Jews, and we Jews would in turn take it to gentiles. When priests and rulers of synagogues refuse to let Jews listen, as here, it is our duty as apostles to become this light to the gentiles. Ever since Jesus revealed himself to me near Damascus, I have known that Isaiah's prophecy is a command of God that I must carry out."

Barnabas thought for a moment. "Should we then avoid the synagogues in our travels and go immediately to gentiles?"

"No," Paul replied. "It is still our duty to speak first to our brother Jews. If their ears are closed to the truth, it is then that we turn to the gentiles."

"Why, Paul, do some rabbis and elders welcome us, as in Salamis, and others bar us at the door, as here?"

"Here it is jealousy," Paul said. "Our message brings more people into the congregation than their reading of the Law. But there are many other reasons, some deep in our blood. We were chosen; the corollary is that we exclude. Typically, the more devout the Jew, the more he thinks of the gentile as a lesser being. We are, moreover, a stubborn race — to survive, we have had to be. Our minds are not merely strong, but also filled with tradition, rules, convictions that are taught in childhood and confirmed in our habits and beliefs as adults. Gentiles, at least most who hear us, are unschooled; they are not afflicted by dogma. It is easier to enter an empty mind than one that is full."

The next morning a maidservant knocked on Paul's door. "An official comes for you," she said anxiously. Paul rose from his desk, called Barnabas, and together they went to the gate of the inn.

Drawing himself up, the stranger said: "I am clerk to Cragus Corunus, magistrate of this Roman colony of Antioch. He sends me to bring you before his court."

The clerk led Paul and Barnabas to the courtroom and ordered them to stand before the magistrate. On a row of benches to the right sat Pashur and the other rulers of the synagogue, all in white togas; on their left were four women gowned in silk and adorned with jewels.

"You are charged with disturbing the peace on the holy day of the Jews," Cragus Corunus said in a loud voice. "By proclaiming yourselves as oracles, you led a rabble through the streets of the city to the Rostrorum Augustalis. There, by crafty hints that you hold unseen power from an unknown god, you incited citizen and slave alike to disturb the peace. Your accusers have testified to these facts and are in this court."

Paul raised his hand to speak. "Is this not a Roman city where all people are free to worship the god of their choice?"

"Free we are," the magistrate replied, "but not to create a public disturbance. Therefore, I order you to leave this city. This day."

The clerk escorted them to the inn to collect their belongings. "We will travel east to Iconium," Paul said, as they shouldered their packs and water-skins. Outside in the courtyard, a delegation waited. Marius the copper-smith spoke for them: "As the archons of the city exile you, how are we to learn more about Jesus Christ?"

Paul looked at the faces, hopeful but concerned. "Choose some among you and send them to us in Iconium. We will teach your leaders there, and they will return and teach you. In the meantime, remember this: Love God and love your neighbor, and the grace of God will abide with you."

To their delight, the elders of the synagogue in Iconium opened their doors and arms to Paul and Barnabas the first Sabbath — then, to their dismay, turned against them the second. The proud old rabbi, Benaih, invited them to his study and said, with tears in his eyes, "If you remain here, the rulers will bring you to trial for blasphemy and stone you to death."

"You give us no choice," Paul said. To Barnabas he added: "We will travel to the east. Surely, somewhere, someone will listen to good news."

As they set out for Lystra, capital of Lycaonia and the nearest city, Barnabas persuaded Paul to join a camel caravan. "We are marked men," Barnabas said. "It would not be wise to travel alone." They found the cameleers good companions, taciturn and tireless; the milestones passed quickly.

Inside the Western Gate of Lystra they found a small inn where they could wash away the dust of the road and purify themselves. The proprietor was an older widow, Lois, who managed the inn with her daughter, Eunice, and Eunice's son, Timothy. The women were spare, energetic, and bright of eye; the son, a shy and slender youth. As all dined together, Paul said: "Tell us about Lystra."

The older woman was quick to reply. "My ancestors fled Babylon many generations ago and followed the Silk Road to this valley between the two rivers. Weavers, farmers, herders, they were, handing down the skill from father to son. As a small girl I remember that at harvesttime fierce men would ride down from Black Mountain on their fast horses and seize our grain. In time the armies of Caesar Augustus came from the west — columns and columns of soldiers in brass armor with swords, spears, pikes, horses, char-iots, a terrifying sight. But we were not harmed. Not a lamb did the soldiers take without paying."

Lois clapped her hands with delight. "We had never seen coins before. And then one day the tribune of the cohort brought the people together in the market square and told us the great Augustus had conquered this region and proclaimed Lystra a military colony. Soldiers built a fort, built the Via Sebaste that runs from the Cilician Gates to far Ephesus. And when the fort and the road were finished, many soldiers remained. They took wives, opened shops, planted cotton and grain, plums and vineyards. Like the Greeks before them, they worshiped Zeus, and they built the great temple to their god that stands outside the North Gate. But they never made us worship their gods. They let us live as we had lived. They let us prosper. They protected our fields and harvests. Ever since Augustus, we have known peace and order in this valley."

"How many people live in Lystra?" Paul asked.

"Seven thousand by the last census of the tax collector," Lois replied.

"How many are Jews?"

"Three hundred twenty of us, I would say," Eunice replied. The grandmother nodded.

"Is there a synagogue?" Paul asked.

"Yes," Lois said. "It is old but adequate. The rabbi, Obed, earns his bread as a potter."

At breakfast the next morning Paul said to Barnabas: "Here I will not risk teaching in the synagogue, but speak openly in the marketplace." Barnabas agreed, and they asked Timothy to take them to Lystra's busiest square.

The autumn sun was bright and strong, the air crisp, the stalls filled with brass pots and the brimming harvest of grain and fruits. A row of steps led to a wellsweep overlooking the square; Paul decided to use the top step as a podium. Barnabas and Timothy would stand beside him to observe the crowd.

"Come!" Paul shouted, beckoning with his arms. "Come and hear what good news I bring to Lystra. I am a messenger of the God of earth and sky, the one who brings you the full harvest that we see before us in this market." Three men, and then five, and then five more stopped to listen. Paul motioned for them to move closer. "Hear me! From the east have I journeyed to tell you of one who will better your life on earth and take you into his heavenly kingdom. He will comfort you. He will heal you in body and spirit. And he asks only that you believe in him."

Stretching his hand toward others who might swell the gathering, Paul glanced to his right. There sat a cripple, and something prompted Paul to look again — the whole countenance of the cripple was alight. Seeing the twisted hands raised in prayerful appeal, Paul thought: *He believes. He believes.*

"Stand upright on your feet!" Paul commanded in a loud voice.

Instantly the man stood, hesitated for one moment, then boldly walked down the steps and toward the onlookers.

"Behold!" Timothy exclaimed. "It is Thestor the Lame. Behold! He walks."

From all the stalls of the market, men and women came running to see. Thestor was the cripple who begged in the market square; he had been born with crooked legs. Now he was walking about as any man.

A babble of voices; men began running, shouting, pointing to Paul and Barnabas, all speaking in the Lycaonian dialect. "What are they saying?" Paul shouted to Timothy over the din.

"They believe you are gods come down from Olympus, appearing in the form of men — that Barnabas the taller is Zeus and that you are Hermes the messenger." Pointing across the square in alarm, Timothy cried out: "Look! They are going to sacrifice to you as gods."

Into the square, to the beating of drums, marched a procession led by a priest robed in white, carrying knife and spear, followed a retinue prodding forward two white oxen adorned with garlands of flowers.

"Stop them!" Paul shouted to Timothy. "Barnabas! If they sacrifice to us, it is blasphemy against God." Paul rushed into the crowd, beseeching: "Stop! We are not gods but men, mortals like yourselves. We come to bring you good news of the one true God, to turn you from your vain idols to the living God who made the heavens and the earth and the sea and all things in them."

With his hand on the hilt of his knife, the priest of the temple to Zeus carefully approached Paul and Barnabas, peered at them closely, and pricked the arm of Paul with the point of his blade. When blood began to flow, the priest nodded. "You are men, not gods," he said, and turned to walk away and counsel with his followers.

The crowd surrounded Paul and Barnabas, muttering and cursing, the language strange and the tone menacing. Suddenly one of the shopkeepers struck Paul across the face and shouted: "You tricked us. You profaned our gods." Others took up the cry, and the excited crowd quickly became a mob. Men with hard faces and bulging eyes struck with sticks and leather, separating the two and knocking Paul to the ground. As soon as he fell, a frenzy seized the rabble, and the first stone flew, then another, and a rain of blows, one to the head that caused Paul to lose consciousness. Thinking him dead, the mob dragged the limp body through the streets and dumped it outside the gate, leaving it for the jackals that prowled in the night.

There he lay.

Barnabas had been pushed to the other side of the square, where he knocked one assailant sprawling and then a second and a third. The crowd, fearing his strength, let him go. Running to the gate to rescue Paul, Barnabas met Lois, Eunice, and Timothy, who had gone for help. They found Paul there, his body crumpled, bloody, and unmoving, his eyes closed.

Swiftly Lois knelt, put her fingers to Paul's throat, and then touched his chest. "He lives," she said. "Bring water from the well at the gate. Quickly!" She bathed his face, his arms, his shoulders. When she touched a bleeding cut with the cloth, Paul winced and opened his eyes. He tried to whisper something but could not speak. As an infant raises his arms to be lifted, so did Paul. Barnabas and Timothy helped him to his feet, and he stood, unsteadily at first, then seemed to recover his senses. He took one careful step, then another, and walked, his jaw set against the pain. Back at the inn Paul was bathed and fed broth; then he slept.

In the night he awoke and looked across the room, where Barnabas lay sleepless. "We must persevere in our mission," Paul said. "Ill fortune has come to us here, but we must press on. Tomorrow we leave for Derbe."

"But Paul, your body was broken. Derbe is two days' east. You cannot walk that far."

"I can walk to Derbe," Paul said. "I have walked in pain before. We leave at sunrise."

Derbe was too poor, and too small, for a synagogue. It was a primitive town with few Greeks, fewer Romans, and only ten soldiers to keep order. The first to settle the town had been mountain tribes who found it easier to grow grain near the flowing river and keep flocks of sheep on the grassy hillsides than to hunt food with clubs in the forest. Paul and Barnabas taught without challenge in the narrow streets and crude marketplace. The pagans of Derbe listened, believed, and committed to live by the teachings of Jesus Christ. The olive merchant Gelon opened his pressing shed for their assemblies, and welcomed them to his table.

Two months after they arrived, Paul fell ill of a strange miasma. His body burned with fever, yet he shivered constantly. Delphine, the wife of Gelon, brought him into her house, fed him herbs, and with her daughter watched over him. Despite their care, Paul's skin turned yellow, his eyes swelled almost shut, and the eyelids formed a sticky and loathsome coating. He could not rise or speak. He lay on a cot and suffered.

Determined to carry on their mission, Barnabas continued to teach. One day five strangers came to him. They were from Lystra, had heard of Jesus from Lois and Eunice, and wanted to know more. Barnabas told them of traveling to see and hear Jesus in Galilee, of witnessing miracles of healing, of finding faith himself, and of pledging his life to instill faith in others. For weeks the five received instruction; then they returned to Lystra as baptized Christians, promising to send others to Barnabas.

And others came, not only from Lystra but also from Iconium, Antioch, and small villages in the region. As the winter passed the fever left Paul, and he began to recover. With Barnabas, he instructed their Christian visitors, teaching them hymns and prayers, and training aspiring deacons in the rituals and services.

One morning, when Barnabas was sure that Paul was fit and strong for the road, he said to him: "My brother, I judge it to be time to return to Syria, to the people and churches we founded in Antioch. Three years it has been since we left. We promised our deacons and followers there that we would return."

"I agree, Barnabas. It is time."

Barnabas smiled; he had not expected such quick consent. "Then let us go swiftly. Gaius, one of our converts, will give us horses. Now that spring has come, we can ride the Via Sebaste to the Cilician Gates and be in Antioch in nine days."

Paul shook his head. "No, we must retrace our journey, visit our followers in the cities, and judge if they hold to the faith."

"But we may be attacked and imprisoned," Barnabas said.

"We will not speak in any synagogue, or in an public place, but only where our believers assemble in private," Paul said. "Christians must see that we live, that we endure, and that we persevere in our mission."

So Paul and Barnabas left Derbe and returned to Lystra, thence to Iconium, thence to Pisidian Antioch, remaining in each city only as many days as it took for them to greet every man and every woman who had been baptized to Jesus Christ, and to exhort them all to continue in the faith. In no place were they set upon, but Paul warned his fellow Christians: "It is only through many afflictions and hardships that we can enter the kingdom of God."

At last it was the day to leave Galatia. To speed their journey Barnabas persuaded Paul that they should take horses to Perga. Roman engineers had completed the road; a bridge now vaulted the stream where Paul had almost drowned. Not in Perga, but in nearby Attalia, they found a new ore transport, the *Krios*, that would sail in five days directly to Seleucia. So Paul and Barnabas used the time to proclaim the good news in the forums of Perga and Attalia.

As they boarded the trim new vessel, Barnabas said, "Paul, I commend you on the end of a successful mission."

"This is not the end of our mission," Paul said. "It is the beginning."

XXII

CHALLENGE

In the courtyard of Barnabas' comfortable stone house in Antioch, a late-afternoon sun cast long shadows across the fountain. Summer was near, the air warm and fragrant with blossoms of apricot and orange. After three weeks back home, Paul and Barnabas were rested, and deeply gratified to find that the movement had not only grown during their absence but exceeded their highest expectations.

"Our lives seem too peaceful, too comfortable, Barnabas," Paul said. "Such good fortune cannot last."

Barnabas laughed. "Ever the pessimist," he said. "All goes well. Or did until this morning."

"What happened?"

"Lucius reported that three strangers were in his church telling his gentile members that they must be circumcised."

"What!" Paul exclaimed. "Who were they? Where did they come from?"

"From Jerusalem," Barnabas replied. "They told Lucius they represent the authority of the Twelve."

"The Twelve sent them? I cannot believe that."

"Nor did I," Barnabas said. "But that was their claim. Yesterday Lucius saw them accosting his members after the worship service. So he sought them out today. They informed him that authorities of the church in Jerusalem had decreed that only the circumcised could be admitted to the company of Jesus."

Paul raised his fist. "Damn them! They are spies sent by James. He is a troublemaker, devious and treacherous. You and I settled that issue in Jerusalem before we left for Cyprus." Paul ground his teeth. "What did Lucius tell them?"

"He sent for me. I confronted the three, reminded them that I oversee

244

Antioch by the authority of Peter, and ordered them to leave the city. Two of Lucius' deacons escorted them to the gate and saw them go."

"We have not heard the last of these Judaizers," Paul said. "We are still contesting over what God intends — to include or exclude. On this, Barnabas, we must never yield."

The stranger standing on Barnabas' threshold a month later was fresh of face, polite in manner, and stalwart of arm and leg. "I am Elam, sent by Peter and James to extend greetings to you, Barnabas of Cyprus, and to bring you to a high council of disciples, apostles, and elders."

With a sweep of his arm, Barnabas invited the visitor into his house. "A high council?" he asked. "For what purpose?"

"To consider certain questions of doctrine; so I was instructed to say."

Barnabas was not surprised. He had been expecting repercussions from his expulsion of James' agents. There had never been a high council before; surely Peter and James had called it for one purpose: to resolve the issue of circumcision. He would welcome clarification. After the three Judaizers had insisted that all Christians must be circumcised, a tide of anxiety had swept through the congregations. Churchmen young and old talked constantly of balancing earthly pain against heavenly salvation.

"Who is to come?" Barnabas asked Elam.

"You, as overseer of Antioch. Paul of Tarsus, as one who has brought most gentiles to the Way."

"When does this high council convene?"

"As soon as you arrive," Elam said. "Peter instructed me also to tell you that the Twelve would welcome a report on your mission to Cyprus and Galatia."

"Gladly," Barnabas said. "Elam, rest here from your journey. The maidservant will bring you water and food."

Barnabas left his house immediately and found Paul on the main dock, talking to a circle of seamen. "A messenger has come!" Barnabas said, his voice rising in excitement. "From Jerusalem! He brings a summons from Peter and James. You and I are to attend a high council of disciples and elders to discuss doctrine — probably circumcision."

Paul listened, his face grave. "I know."

"How?" Barnabas asked. "Did the messenger find you first?"

"No," Paul replied, and led Barnabas aside. "Two nights ago I had a vision. An angel of God appeared to me and commanded: 'Go to Jerusalem and bring together the church of Christ Jesus.'"

"So you already planned to go to Jerusalem," Barnabas said.

"At first I resisted," Paul said, "for I do not accept the authority of Jerusalem. I was appointed independently, by Jesus Christ himself, therefore I am subject only to Jesus Christ, and not to Peter, nor to James. Yet reason dictates that the division over circumcision could be fatal to our cause. I hold one view, James another; Peter alone can decide what is right and best for the church. Where, I asked myself, lies my responsibility? I concluded it is to persuade Peter to open the Way of Jesus to all. So I shall go to Jerusalem, not in submission to authority but as an equal. I go in obedience to God's command to bring unity to the church."

"I had no vision," Barnabas said, "but I expected my banishment of the Judaizers would provoke James to act."

Paul nodded in agreement. "The alacrity with which they responded means that James believes he has the support to win."

"The messenger told me that Peter also asks that we report on our mission," Barnabas said.

"Excellent!" Paul said. "As you were chosen by Peter to lead our mission, Barnabas, you should make that report. Jerusalem trusts you. Tell this council how we proclaimed the gospel, bringing Jews and gentiles together in the rituals honoring Jesus without violating the Law or statutes. There stands the proof that our message and our methods work."

"And you will lead the debate against circumcision?"

"I will. And it will be rigorous, before the hostile audience that James is sure to assemble. But words will not be enough, Barnabas. I will force the issue in a way that all present will remember."

Barnabas raised a questioning eyebrow. "What do you mean?"

"I will take an uncircumcised Christian into the midst of these Judaizers and defy the so-called pillars of the church to cast him out." Paul stopped and lifted his hands toward Barnabas. "Could Peter, who has himself baptized gentiles without requiring circumcision, dare expel him?"

"Not and be consistent," Barnabas said.

"Exactly," Paul said. "It will be far more difficult for the council to reject a gentile Christian face to face than in absentia. By staging this confrontation, I force Peter's hand — before James and his Judaizers."

"Who will you take?"

"Titus the ironsmith's apprentice," Paul said. "He is one of the best students in my school for deacons. His mother is Greek, his father Roman. He looks the gentile; with his yellow hair and pale skin, he will stand out before the council assembly. Titus is articulate and courageous. In school debates he holds his ground against opposition."

"A good choice," Barnabas said. "But suppose that Peter orders Titus to be circumcised."

"If he should — and he may — then we lose," Paul said. "The church is sundered. Our mission ends, Barnabas, and our time and energies have been wasted."

Barnabas winced. "So it is Peter who will determine the future of the church."

"No, Barnabas, it is you and I. It is we who must win this battle against circumcision, for that is key to the far greater issue: Does God save by faith, or by the Law?"

"When do we leave?" Barnabas asked.

"Tomorrow at first light," Paul said. "We must win, Barnabas. We must keep the movement open to all. You and I have seen that outside Jerusalem there are simply not enough Jewish converts to form the critical mass necessary to sustain a living and growing church. If Christianity cannot grow, it cannot live."

By the time he sighted the walls of Jerusalem, Paul was filled with the resolve that comes on the eve of battle. Twelve days on the road had given him time to marshal his arguments, and warm receptions by fellow Christians in Sidon and Tyre, Tirzah and Shechem, had lifted the spirits of the three travelers.

Once inside the Damascus Gate they pushed through the crowded streets to Peter's old mud house.

"Welcome! Welcome!" With warmth and ebullience, Peter greeted the visitors at the door of the chamber with the rough-sawn table and twelve benches. "A messenger ran ahead of you from the north hills to tell us you were near."

At the door with Peter stood James. The faces had aged. Peter's was more crevassed, his head more gray, but his hand was still strong and his arm robust, as if he had spent that very day pulling nets. James was the surprise. Instead of the scholarly mien and trim appearance, his beard was long and unkempt, his feet were bare, and he wore a cloak of camel's hair belted with leather.

Entering the room, Paul saw another man, a stranger. The man looked up from his writing and said: "I am John, son of Zebedee." His voice was quiet, his manner contemplative, detached. This was the disciple Jesus had called beloved, the once thunderous, now most somber, of the Twelve.

As Peter and James looked with curiosity at the stranger with yellow hair, Paul said: "Before you I bring Titus, a gentile and deacon of the church in Antioch."

Peter nodded, looked at Titus briefly, and said: "We welcome you to the mother church for this important gathering. We who were given authority by Jesus decided that we must come together as a council to discuss and resolve issues of doctrine. Now that you are here, we will meet tomorrow, at the sixth hour. We have our own church building now."

"What are the issues to be resolved?" Paul asked.

James raised a hand and spoke. "Surely you know that many of our followers here in Jerusalem insist that gentiles desiring admission to the church must meet three conditions: They must be circumcised. They must obey our laws on eating. They must forswear fornication. We decided, therefore, to listen in open assembly to their views, and to your views, as you are foremost among us in converting the uncircumcised. Then we shall decide what is to be."

"Who will decide?" Paul asked.

"The three of us," Peter said, putting one hand out toward James and the other toward John.

"We were informed that the Twelve would be present," Barnabas said.

"Except for John and me, all are away on missions or toiling for bread," Peter said. "We will judge on their behalf."

"I am eager to debate this openly," Paul said. "But I condemn those who sent false brothers stealing into Antioch to confuse and frighten our gentile followers. I have come to Jerusalem to tell the pillars of the church that I teach the gospel that Christ Jesus himself gave to me: It is faith in Jesus and not the Law that frees a soul from sin and brings salvation. I am here to make certain that my work is not in vain."

Peter opened his arms. "We hear you, Paul. We know what you have accomplished. God has graced you and your mission. Let it be known that we are partners in the service of the Lord God."

"Then why," Paul asked, "did Jerusalem send lackeys to spy on us, and spread doubt among our people?"

Peter shook his head in dismay. "Who sent them I cannot say; it was not I. This I do know, Paul: God needs us both. As Jesus entrusted me to take the gospel to the Jews, so also did he entrust you to take the gospel to the gentiles. Let us make this a covenant between us." He stood, and with his big right hand reached across the table. "Give me your hand in fellowship." At those words he took Paul's right hand. James, after hesitating a moment, placed his right hand over the outstretched hands. John then joined hands with the others. "This," Peter said, "is the seal of our covenant in the service of Jesus."

The solemnity of the occasion silenced all at the table. At last Peter sat back on his bench and said to Paul: "We ask only that you remember our poor."

"That, always, I am more than ready to do," Paul replied.

They rose to go, and Peter drew Paul and Barnabas aside. "Do not be alarmed," he said, "but I have instructed Nekoda to accompany you to your inn and remain outside your door tonight."

"Why?" Paul asked in vexation.

"Because," Peter said firmly, "we know that Zadok, upon learning of our council debate, devised a plot to seize you, keep you from speaking, and bring you to trial before the Sanhedrin."

Paul started to protest, but Barnabas raised his hand. "The council must come first," he said. "We accept your protection."

As Paul, Barnabas, and Titus walked with Nekoda to their inn, Paul said: "Barnabas, can you discern from this encounter today what these nominal leaders will decide tomorrow? Does Peter have the stomach to stand against James?"

"Exactly what I was wondering," Barnabas said. "Peter vacillates. More precisely, he accommodates, for it is his nature to bend with circumstance, to agree with the last person to talk with him. But his intuition about what is best for the church is usually right, so I believe that on circumcision, Peter will be for us. James? He is against us. John, wisest of the three, can sway either or both." Barnabas shook his head and opened his hands. "I do not know John's mind. He rarely speaks, and no one has yet seen what he writes."

XXIII

RESOLUTION

The church in Jerusalem had originally been built by Joseph of Arimathea to store amphorae of wine, abandoned, then given to Peter as the assembly place for the Way. Over time volunteers had whitewashed the walls, inside and out, erected a new roof, and installed twenty-four rows of rough benches on either side of a center aisle. Altar and pulpit stood on a platform facing the assembly; a cross of rough wood hung against the stark alabaster of the rear wall. An iron nail had been driven into the foot and each arm of the cross.

Just before the sixth hour Paul, Barnabas, and Titus entered the church and seated themselves at the table reserved for them near the front, on the left. The room filled rapidly, with Pharisees occupying all benches except for the small faction of Hellenists. Around the walls and behind the benches crowded men and women, old and young, while a throng of others waited outside the entrance. A hush fell as a door opened at the side of the altar and seven elders, none known to Paul, entered and seated themselves on the platform. One of them, Barnabas whispered, was Obadiah, a militant Pharisee and chief among James' growing number of staff assistants. After a long pause, the door opened again: First Peter, then James, then John entered in solemn procession and took their places in armchairs in the center of the platform.

Peter raised his hand to silence the low murmur of voices. "John, will you open with a prayer and blessing on this council." That accomplished, Peter again lifted his right palm and said: "I proclaim this council in session. The first order on the agenda is the report by our brother Barnabas on the mission of the Antioch apostles to Cyprus and Galatia."

Barnabas began by describing their arrival at the synagogue in Salamis, the warm reception by Rabbi Barak, the crowds they attracted. "Some were

Jews; more were gentiles. As they found faith and committed to Jesus, we baptized them, and taught them the rituals —"

"Question!" sounded a loud voice. Heads turned to look toward a man in a long brown cloak, standing at the front on the right and raising a hand toward Peter.

"Tell your name," Peter said,

"I am Itzak, a Jew of this city, a Pharisee, and a follower of Jesus known to you," he said, gesturing toward the platform.

"You may speak," Peter said.

Itzak turned to Barnabas. "Before you baptized gentiles in Salamis, did you inform them that they must be circumcised? Has this gentile at your table" — he pointed to Titus — "been circumcised?"

Paul stood immediately and addressed Peter: "I ask to speak to this issue."

"Granted," Peter said.

Paul turned toward the questioner: "By what authority do you say that a follower of Jesus must be circumcised?"

"From the teachings," Itzak replied. "In the Torah, God said to Abraham, 'You shall keep my Covenant, you and your seed after you in their generations. Every man-child among you shall be circumcised. And it shall be a token of the Covenant between me and you.' Surely you, a Jew and Pharisee, do not advocate breaking the Covenant."

"A Jew and Pharisee I am," Paul said, "and as such I keep the Covenant, which, I remind this council, was based on faith. 'Abraham believed the Lord,' the Torah records, and the faith that Abraham placed in God is the very essence of the Covenant between God and his chosen people. Yes, we children of Abraham are bound by this Covenant; but gentiles are not."

"So long as they remain gentiles, they are not bound," Itzak retorted, "but if a man is to join our Hebrew religion, he must accept the covenant of Abraham and follow the Law of Moses." He turned to face the platform. "I ask you, Peter: Did Jesus not say that he came not to abolish the Law but to fulfill it? Did he not say, 'In no way shall one jot or tittle pass away from the Law'?"

Peter nodded but said nothing.

Itzak pointed a finger at Peter. "Were you not there in Sidon when the woman of the abominable Canaanites pleaded with Jesus to cast out the devil from her daughter, and he refused, saying, 'I was not sent except to the lost sheep of the house of Israel'? And did Jesus not also tell her that he would not waste his time on 'gentile dogs'?"

"Well do I remember," Peter replied. "But there is more. The woman persisted and told Jesus, 'Even little dogs may eat of the crumbs falling from the table of their lords.' With that, Jesus looked at her and said, 'O woman, your faith is great. Let it be as you desire.' And from that hour the daughter was healed."

"Nevertheless," Itzak countered, "we know from Jesus' own words that he equated gentiles with contemptible tax collectors. And I ask you, Peter, when Jesus chose you to found his church, did he say, 'Admit the uncircumcised'?"

Paul wanted to intervene and reply that Jesus, through Ananias of Damascus, had commanded him to take the gospel to gentiles; but he checked that impulse. Not once had he been able to convince a public audience that Jesus had appeared to him on that Damascus road; certainly this hostile assembly would scoff and jeer if he spoke of it now.

To Paul's surprise, it was John who responded. "Let me put this issue in perspective," he said. "In the early days of his ministry, Jesus believed his primary mission was to bring salvation to his fellow Jews. When the high priests refused to listen, he came to see the broader purpose of his life, his teachings, and his foreordained death. It was to bring all the children of earth to God. Surely it is implicit in what Jesus said in this very city. 'I am the Good Shepherd, and I know the sheep of my fold, and they know me.' That was his affirmation that Jews were first and favored. Then Jesus went on to say, 'And I have other sheep which are not of this fold. I must also lead those, and they will hear my voice, and there will be one flock, one Shepherd.' Such was his belief that in time, and through his sacrifice, all people could be brought into the fold and into the glory of God's kingdom."

Itzak, unrelenting, made the gesture of washing his hands. "The issue is purity — the purity of the Jewish faith. This movement began among Jews, for Jews. How can you, Peter, James, and John, our leaders, allow this purity to be contaminated? How can you ask us to break the bread of communion with the unwashed, to eat with those who touch the meat of swine? A thousand and more years have passed since we were given a divine Law that isolated us from all heathen. Are we now to be told that the statutes and customs that bonded us as a people are to be abandoned? I say, no! The Law is the Law."

The benches on the right erupted with cries of support and the clapping of hands. Peter raised his hands to silence the assembly and gestured for Paul to respond.

"Great is the Law," Paul proclaimed, "but greater than the Law is faith. So it was with Abraham, Moses, David, the Prophets. So it was with Christ Jesus. 'Believe in God, believe in me.' Those are Jesus' words. Jesus taught faith, lived by faith, healed by faith, gave his life for us in faith. He died on that cross" — with his left hand Paul pointed to the wooden cross above the altar — "He died on that cross to demonstrate for all time and to all humanity his trust in God. Jesus gave his life to show each of us that faith will free us from sin, that trust in God will bring us into the everlasting kingdom." Paul turned to confront the leaders and elders. "Conversely, if it is the Law that saves, then Jesus died for no purpose."

Turning again to address the assembly, he said: "Some here would stand at the gate of heaven and turn away all but the chosen children of Abraham. But Jesus turned away no man, no woman, not the poor, not the leper, not even the tax collector or the prostitute. Instead he came to earth to open wide the gate to eternal life, and this is the promise made to each of you and to every other man, woman, and child on earth: 'Come. If you have faith in Jesus Christ, you shall enter.'"

A great quiet came over the assembly. At last Peter rose from his chair and said: "As is known, some ten years ago God chose me to take the gospel to the gentiles of Caesarea. God knew these gentiles believed in him, so he gave them the Holy Spirit, even as he has given it to us. God made no distinction between these gentiles and us, since he had already purified their hearts by faith." Peter opened his arms in entreatment before the assembly. "Now then, why do you test God, by putting a yoke on the neck of the disciples that neither our fathers nor we had strength to bear? It is through the grace of the Lord Jesus that they, as we, are saved."

Paul listened intently. Peter, in his declamation, was being Peter, dissembling, trying to please everyone. He had once more justified his own action in converting the centurion Cornelius, but again treated it as an isolated incident, not a precedent for admitting the uncircumcised into the Way. Indeed, Peter had not even mentioned the contentious word — *circumcision*. John's metaphor of the shepherd was encouraging, but James was silent. Perhaps he would speak now. But no. Instead Peter asked Barnabas to resume his report on their mission to Cyprus and Asia.

"The first miracle of our journey took place in Paphos," Barnabas began, and went on to describe how the proconsul Sergius Paulus and his court came to join the Way and help them found the church in the Cypriot capital. City by city — Pisidian Antioch, Iconium, Lystra, Derbe — Barnabas briskly recounted their adventures, speaking plainly of both their successes and their misfortunes. "We were welcomed by some, turned away by others. But in every place we found more gentiles than Jews eager to hear the good news about Jesus. We made no distinction, embracing in fellowship all who put their faith in Christ. We baptized them. We taught them the rites of worship and appointed deacons. We established churches that will sustain their faith and make them as one with those of us who early came to believe in Jesus Christ."

Once more Itzak rose to respond. "So these apostles whom you appointed in Cyprus and Galatia created churches not governed by Jews but ruled by gentiles, for gentiles. Thus these rogue churches are separate, unrelated to Judaism. If this movement spreads through the creation of gentile churches, then the Way of Jesus will move further and further from Judaism. In time our legacy from the patriarchs could metamorphose into a gentile religion. I ask you, Peter, and James, and John: Is that what you want? I say no! If you do admit gentiles into this select and holy order, let them be a small portion among us; let us not become a small portion among gentiles."

From the benches came a roar of shouting and clapping and stamping of feet. As the demonstration continued, Peter, James, and John conversed among themselves, their expressions showing concern and gravity. At last James rose, slowly, deliberately. In an instant a hush came over the assembly. All knew that James' verdict would carry the mother church, and thereby unify — or divide — Christianity.

"Men, brothers, hear me," he began. "Simon Peter recounted that God first took out from all the nations one people to bear his name; thus God made us his chosen. And as the prophets wrote, God said: 'I will return, and I will rebuild the fallen tabernacle of David, and I will set it up so that the rest of men may seek the Lord, even all people of all the nations, for I have invoked my name on all of them.' Thus says the Lord God. And God knows all things that were and are to be, from the beginning to eternity." He paused, surveyed the assembly, and weighed his hands before him as if balancing a scale. "For this reason I judge that we should not make it difficult for gentiles who turn to God, but impose on them only these restrictions: They must abstain from fornication. Further, as they may break bread with us, they are to maintain the purity of our sacred food laws, that is, they must not eat meat from strangled animals, nor victuals made with blood, nor food offered as heathen sacrifice."

Paul did not move. He had resolved that he would show no emotion at the verdict — no joy if he won, no despair if he lost. He had determined that none in Jerusalem could ever say that Paul flinched in defeat or gloated in victory.

And victory it was. Faith had triumphed over the Law. Gentiles were free from circumcision. James had simply omitted the requirement. Paul was intrigued by the deft circumlocution in James' verdict. It was not Paul's way of speaking; he would have been direct, emphatic: No gentile need be circumcised to enter the Way. But James, in ruling against his own followers, against the most conservative of Judaizers, had to soften the blow. This he had done by indirection on the primary issue of circumcision, and by confirmation of the lesser issue, food statutes. For a precedent James had turned to the Mosaic Law; it permitted Jews to allow gentiles to live among them in certain circumstances, but only if they abstained from eating food denied to Jews.

From experience Paul knew it was unrealistic to expect gentiles everywhere to eat as Jews, but he understood that James had to appease his constituents, most of whom lived here in Jerusalem. The important thing was that James had judged in Paul's favor on the central and critical issue of circumcision, and no judgment could carry such weight and force with the Judaizers as a decree by James. So it had been settled by this high council: The Way was open to all.

Wholly engrossed in examining James' reasoning and judgment, Paul did not at first respond to the gentle nudge from Barnabas, who was trying to bring him back to focus on the platform. There the three leaders were consulting with the seven elders; Obadiah was angry, gesticulating and shaking his head. The discussions continued, vigorously, with darting looks here and there toward the assembly, now becoming more and more curious and restive. Finally the three leaders nodded in unison, and James rose again. He raised his hand for silence and began to speak. "I shall write in my hand what I have said before this council today, and my letter will be carried by two leaders among our brothers to be read in the churches of Antioch, Syria, and Cilicia. From among us we have chosen Judas Barsabbas and Silas, and delegated them for this mission."

"A balance of right and left," Barnabas whispered to Paul. "All in the Barsabbas family are strong Judaizers, and Silas is an ardent Hellenist."

Then Peter raised his hand, called for a benediction by John, and the council ended.

As the assembly dispersed, Paul waited, staring at his folded hands in silence until the room was almost empty. He was rising from his seat to go when he noticed a stranger standing nearby, evidently waiting to speak to him. Suspecting a vengeful Judaizer, Paul almost turned away, then observed that the manner and appearance of the stranger marked him as alien to Jerusalem. He was rotund of girth, and his face, round and pleasant as a rising sun, beamed with the ruddy comfort that comes from ample food and much wine. Surely he was Greek, for none but a Greek could stand with such pride of carriage or wear a peplum of such fine linen trimmed in purple. With a bemused glint in his eye the stranger asked: "Do you yet grasp the magnitude of your victory?"

Concerned that this stranger might be luring him to boast, Paul said only: "The council has spoken."

"And with great courage," the stranger said. His voice was warm, assured, emanating the aura of the elite. "It is never easy for a leader to rule against the hearts of his followers. To my surprise, this council has just opened the way for the unitary God of the Hebrews to become the one God of all mankind."

Paul was intrigued. The man had spoken not in the common Greek of the street, but with the polish and accent of a scholar. "And who are you?"

"I am Luke, of Thessalonica."

"How does a Greek scholar come to be in Jerusalem, and at a gathering of Jews?" Paul asked.

"Curiosity, in a word," Luke replied. "I was on my way home from Alexandria, where for six months I studied ancient medicines, when the grain boat stopped in Joppa for repairs. There at the inn I heard stories of the mystic Jesus. His followers recounted incidents of how he restored the sick to health, making the lame to walk and the blind to see, so I decided to learn more about the methods by which this Jesus healed."

"You are a physician?" Paul asked.

"By vocation, yes. By avocation, a student of great events and the uncommon men who shape history."

Paul invited the stranger to sit, and asked: "What have you learned about Jesus?"

Luke thought for a moment. "That we should not be skeptics about singular events that happen before our eyes," he said. "I scoffed when a devout young Christian in Joppa told me that Jesus was born of a virgin. I am a physician; female anatomy does not permit conception unless the hymen is breached. So, to explore this myth, I traveled to Nazareth and found Mary, the mother of Jesus." The timbre of Luke's voice changed to subdued tones of solemnity and awe. "I must tell you that it was a memorable experience, talking with this woman of such purity, such innocence, and such transcendent beauty, in that rude and rustic village. There is about her a radiance and luminous quality that I had never seen before, not in my own land nor elsewhere, and with that, a wondrous humility. To this day her eyes widen with astonishment as she tells how the angel Gabriel came to her and proclaimed, 'Hail, Mary, you are filled with grace. The Lord is with you! You are blessed among women!'"

"You talked with the mother of Jesus!" Paul was astonished.

"O yes," Luke said. "I arrived a skeptic; I left a believer. To listen to Mary is to be transformed; it is to know in the soul that this exemplar of virtue is telling the truth, that indeed God did confer on this humble virgin the honor of bringing into the world the promised son who would deliver his people."

"I did not know that Mary still lived," Paul said.

"Mary lives," Luke said, "and she is surprisingly vigorous and youthful for a woman in her seventies. She has the small house her husband, Joseph the carpenter, built for her before he died, and she earns her bread nursing the ill. While in Nazareth I also talked with Mary's neighbors who knew the boy Jesus, and with others who followed Jesus as he taught in Capernaum and the other villages of Galilee. Suddenly it came to me there one day: I should find as many eyewitnesses to the events in Jesus' life as I can, trace all things accurately from the first, and set down the full story so that generations to come may know of him."

"A splendid undertaking," Paul said. He wondered for a moment why none of the Twelve had written a full account of Jesus' life — but the answer was obvious: Except for John, most could neither read nor write. "Have you talked with the Twelve first chosen by Jesus?"

"I have just begun," Luke said. "I hurried here from Capernaum when I learned that the major leaders of Christianity were assembling, for it offered the opportunity to solicit their versions of the Jesus story. Not until I arrived three days ago did I begin to realize the significance of this first council of the church. Now I know it was far more momentous than I anticipated."

"What do you mean?" Paul asked.

"Today," Luke said, "Christianity stood at the crossroads: To the right, the narrow road of Judaism; to the left, the dead end of secession; ahead, the path that leads to accord between Jew and gentile. In truth, this council decision means that Christianity may in time reach to the ends of earth."

Paul slowly nodded his assent. "It is my mission to make it so," he said.

"Yours is the victory, Paul of Tarsus, and a mighty victory it is, but it was not only your own convictions and reasoning, but also the bravery and foresight of Peter and John, and particularly James, that brought you this triumph."

Paul closed his eyes in reflection. Not since boyhood had he heard the well-formed phrasing of a Greek scholar. He could learn from this man. He said quietly: "Yes, and a higher hand intervened as well."

Luke leaned back on the bench and for a moment studied the face of Paul. "In Capernaum," he said brightly, "I heard accounts of your extraordinary conversion, and of your success in Antioch. Will you tell me exactly and in detail what happened to you on the road to Damascus? And how you plan to lead this revolution of the spirit?"

Paul did not hesitate. "I will," he said, "but not at this time and place. Barnabas and I must resume our mission. We leave at once for Antioch, press on from there to attend to the churches we founded in Galatia, and then introduce Christianity into the regions of Phrygia and Mysia."

"Very well," Luke replied with warmth. "Let us meet in Troas next year. You will find me there at the house of my patron, Theophilus."

XXIV

SEPARATION

By the time the small caravan reached Byblos, Paul was seething with ill-concealed anger: Nine days they had been on the road, and they were only halfway to Antioch. Silas of Aswan was a strong and experienced traveler, but Judas Barsabbas, an older man who had never ventured far from Jerusalem, could walk only during the cool of the day. At dusk, as they tarried at the caravanserai in Byblos, Paul drew Barnabas aside. "Tomorrow: Let us rise at cock-crow and go ahead of the others. This dawdling pace I cannot tolerate."

Barnabas studied his companion. "You should go ahead, Paul. Take Titus and Silas with you. Barsabbas is weak of leg, and cannot travel alone. I will go with him." He put his hand on Paul's shoulder. "Is more on your mind, my brother?"

"Yes," Paul said. "I am anxious to resume our mission to far lands. Three years it has been since we first set foot in Cyprus. We need to visit the churches we founded there and in Galatia, reaffirm their faith, inspire them, renew their zeal. Then I propose we journey westward and take the gospel to Phrygia and Mysia. The world awaits us, Barnabas."

"So it does, Paul, and I, too, am eager to go, as soon as James' letter is read to our churches in Antioch."

"The letter of James changes nothing," Paul said curtly.

"Not for you," Barnabas replied, "but it will bring great assurance to every male gentile we have converted in Antioch."

All through the city of Antioch, great crowds gathered to hear the decree of the mother church in Jerusalem. By order of James, Barsabbas went first to Paul's churchhouse in the teeming southwest quadrant of the city:

The apostles and elders, your brothers in Jerusalem, send greetings to the brothers of gentile birth in Antioch, Syria, and Cilicia: Since we heard that some have gone out from here without authority to trouble you by saying, 'Be circumcised and keep the Law,' it seemed good to us, having become of one mind, to send chosen representatives to you along with our beloved Barnabas and Paul, who have given up their souls on behalf of the Lord of all of us, Jesus Christ. Therefore, we have sent Judas Barsabbas and Silas, who will confirm in person what we have written. For it seemed good to the Holy Spirit and to us to put on you not one greater burden than these necessary things: Do not eat food sacrificed to idols, food made from blood, or the meat of strangled animals, and abstain from fornication. Continuously keep yourselves from these, and you will do well. Be prospered.

With Paul and Barnabas in attendance, Barsabbas read the letter at special assemblies in every church in Antioch and surrounding towns, and Silas followed each reading with reassurances and explications. Once the edict was proclaimed to all congregations, Paul and Barnabas set the date to begin their second journey.

On the day before they were to depart, Barnabas was reading in his courtyard when he heard the gate open, looked up, and saw the broad countenance of Peter — and not only Peter but also an entourage, which included his wife, Anna; acolytes Phicol and Gomer; Hellenists Philip and Parmenas; and John Mark.

Planting his stocky legs at Barnabas' gate, Peter announced with good cheer: "So much have we heard about your good work here, Barnabas, we came to witness for ourselves."

Barnabas leaped to his feet, surprised and delighted. "Welcome to Antioch! Welcome! We will show you everything that the Lord Jesus has enabled us to accomplish here."

Since his house was too small to accommodate the full delegation, Barnabas escorted them to the nearby inn of Binnui, a Levite, and arranged for comfortable rooms and the best of meat and wine. When Paul returned home in the evening, Barnabas told him that Peter was in the city. Grinding his teeth in anger, Paul reluctantly agreed to postpone their departure, yet again.

With Barnabas as host and guide, Peter spoke in every church in Antioch, in Seleucia and Daphne, and in the smaller towns nearby, telling the congregations his stories of Jesus, confirming their faith, and joining them in the region's abundance of good food and wine at Christian feasts of celebration. As the visit ran on, from a fortnight to a month, summer waned, provoking Paul to fret and fume. At last he took Barnabas aside. "If we do not leave soon, winter will come and the northern gales will make it impossible for us to sail to Cyprus."

Barnabas shook his head in resignation. "What would you have me do — ask Peter to leave? He is my superior; he appointed me to oversee Antioch. I owe him not only my hospitality, but also my respect."

Hoping to ease the tension, Barnabas invited Paul, Peter, and his entourage to dine at Binnui's inn one evening with Lucius and seven of Lucius' gentile artisans. Peter was at his best, genial, spirited, loquacious, holding his audience in thrall as he recounted his first meeting with Jesus and their experiences of the early days in Galilee. Suddenly he stopped talking. The others looked up and saw that Obadiah, chief of staff to James, and two fellow Judaizers had just arrived from Jerusalem and seated themselves at a table across the room. Obadiah was staring at Peter, shaking his head with disdain at the gentiles with whom Peter was eating.

After an instant of awkward silence, Peter rose, left the gentiles, and walked over to sit down at Obadiah's table. With a scraping of benches, Peter's six traveling companions also got up and went over to the table of Obadiah. Barnabas followed.

Paul jumped up, clenched his fists, and marched over to Obadiah's table. Pointing his finger at Peter, Paul said loudly: "For seven weeks you have lived in Antioch as a gentile, eaten in the houses of gentiles, and shared communion bread and wine with gentiles in our churches. Now, out of fear of these stiff-necked Judaizers, you turn your back on gentiles. You are embarrassed that the faction of James sees you eating with the uncircumcised. You hypocrite! Your actions contradict the very essence of Jesus' message, that each of us is justified not by the Law but by faith. Where, Peter, is the apostle who was given the vision at Caesarea that God does not distinguish between Jew and gentile? Would you now, as first apostle, create a higher caste of Christians who were born Jews, and a lower caste of Christians who were born gentiles? Look at how you mock yourself. If you, being a Jew, live not as a Jew here in Antioch but as a gentile, why would you expect gentiles here to live as Jews?"

Peter sat in silence, his big hands clasped, his eyes looking down at the table. After a few moments Paul shook his head in disgust and stormed from the inn into the night. For hours he meandered through the broad streets and dark alleys; finally he found his way to the back room of his church. Brooding there, he told himself that he should not have been surprised at Peter's action; sudden and inexplicable change was part of Peter's nature. After all, this was the man who, in the hours before Jesus' death, had denied Jesus and thereby revealed a deep flaw in character, a lack of courage in crisis. But Paul could not understand, or accept, the disloyalty of Barnabas. He was angry at Peter, disdainful of his weakness; he was hurt, deeply hurt, by Barnabas. Curled up in his cloak in his lonely room, Paul fell asleep in anguish, bitter that he had been betrayed by his only friend.

Two mornings later Barnabas quietly opened the door into Paul's room at the church. Contrition marked his long face; there was sadness in the bowed head and slumped shoulders. "I was wrong," Barnabas said firmly. "I acted before I thought. I know how Peter fears James — fears deliberately provoked by James' followers. So I wanted to show my support for Peter. I did not think how it would appear to you, and to the gentiles at our table. I ask your forgiveness."

After a long silence, Paul looked away, raised and shook his hands in dismay. "What does it mean for our movement that the leader appointed by Jesus turns out to be a man of such duplicity?" he asked.

Now Barnabas waited, gritting his teeth before he replied. "Surely you understand," he said evenly, "that Peter is caught in the middle. His first duty is to prevent the factions of right and left from pulling the church apart. One day he favors the liberal and free-thinking Hellenists, the next the conservative Judaizers so rooted in statute and tradition. Give Peter credit, Paul. We have no one in the church who could better bridge the gulf dividing us."

Paul nodded, but said nothing.

"You see Peter as rival," Barnabas continued. "I see him as peacemaker."

Again Paul nodded in silence.

"I come to make amends," Barnabas said, "and to tell you that Peter leaves tomorrow morning to return to Jerusalem. Let us meet at noon, after he has gone, to begin our new journey."

Paul sighed with relief, looked Barnabas in the eye, and extended his right hand. "I will be there."

Within the hour Paul left his church, walked quickly to the main wharf, and found the sailing ship *Adora*. In two days Captain Nokos would be making his last journey of the season to Salamis. From his purse Paul drew two denarii and handed them to Nokos. "Passage for Barnabas and me."

Too excited to sleep that night, Paul rose in his room at his church, felt his way to his chair, and reflected. Tomorrow he and Barnabas would begin a new journey. "We resume the battle for truth that must never end," he said aloud. "Too long have we been delayed; too painful have been our differences. The past we cannot forget, but overcome it we shall.

"The far countries beckon. And I am free of the constraints of Jerusalem. More, much more, I have conquered my enemies within the movement. The action of the council accepts the dogma of my creation, that we are delivered from sin not by the Law but by faith in Jesus Christ. We are blessed, Barnabas and I, to have been chosen for this glorious mission: To bear the message of salvation and eternal life, to bring the world out of darkness into light."

He sat back to plan their itinerary. First, Salamis. Three days hence they would land there, remain two Sabbaths, no longer, then walk on to Paphos and pay their respects to Sergius Paulus. Perhaps they should winter in the capital, teaching, training deacons and elders in the school Sergius Paulus had donated, and spreading the good news into nearby communities. With spring, and favorable winds, they would sail to Attalia, spend two Sabbaths there, one in nearby Perga, then push north on the new Roman road to Pisidian Antioch.

Would the synagogue in Pisidian Antioch accept them this time, or would chief ruler Pashur again turn them away? If so, they would defy him. The Way was established there: This he knew from a letter from Timothy, who also reported progress in the churches of Iconium, Lystra, and Derbe.

From these cities he and Barnabas would press on into new territory. Northern Galatia held great promise. Zagoreos had once instructed his class in how barbarians from Gaul invaded, conquered, and transformed the land

and the people. Beyond lay Bithynia and Phrygia — pagan provinces of Rome he would convert into provinces of Jesus Christ. Then on to Mysia and Troas, where he would find Luke. He would make an ally of this scholar, show him how he and Barnabas went about their mission of expanding Christianity. Happy with his plan, dreaming of conquest, Paul returned to his cot and slept soundly.

Exactly at noon the next day, Paul opened the gate of Barnabas' compound. He had awakened at dawn, and all through the morning his sense of anticipation and excitement had mounted. Now that he saw Barnabas waiting for him in the courtyard, he tossed aside his cloak and waterskin and eagerly took his friend by the arm. "We board the *Adora* today, Barnabas. Tomorrow, at daybreak, we sail for Cyprus. At last! At last! Here is my plan, Barnabas: winter in Cyprus; spring, to the mainland to revisit our churches there; summer, on to new cities, new lands, new challenges."

"I knew you would have a bold plan for us," Barnabas replied. "There is one thing —"

At that moment a moving shadow caught Paul's eye; a figure was crossing a porch under the arches across the courtyard. "Is that John Mark?" he asked. "I thought you said that Peter and his entourage were to leave at dawn."

"They did leave," Barnabas said slowly, "except for John Mark." He paused. "Paul, John Mark asks to go with us on this mission."

"Go with us?" Paul replied in disbelief. "Go with us? John Mark withdrew from the mission in Pamphylia. He left us just as our work was beginning."

"He was young then, and had never before endured a hard journey," Barnabas said. "Three years have brought him to manhood. He is no longer soft of foot or weak of will."

Paul shook his head, firmly. "Barnabas, we are taking the gospel into a hostile world. In doing this, you and I know the risks we face. But it would not be prudent to subject your beloved cousin, and your Aunt Mary's only son, to the perils we may confront."

"You underestimate John Mark, Paul. I have warned him that the journey will be both difficult and dangerous. He wants to go."

"He hindered our mission in Cyprus, Barnabas, and he would hinder this far riskier and more ambitious campaign. It is our purpose to spread the gospel. That must come first."

"John Mark is eager to become an apostle," Barnabas said. "He has committed his life to it. He worked with Peter in Judea and Samaria, and he believes he will learn even more from being with us on this journey." He paused. "Do we not have an obligation, Paul, to train the next generation of leaders?"

"Of course we do," Paul said curtly. "But no responsible general takes an untrained soldier into a crucial battle."

"John Mark is stronger, more resolute, and more courageous than you saw before, Paul. He will not hinder us, but will work diligently, prove his merit and his endurance. You will see." Barnabas took Paul by the arm and said earnestly: "I want John Mark to go with us, Paul."

"No," Paul replied, setting his jaw. "He is not to go with us."

Barnabas stepped back and spoke with feelings long suppressed: "Paul, I have defended you against those who say you are arrogant, egotistical, and overbearing, disdainful of your presumed inferiors — which is all of us — scornful of any opinion you did not reach on your own, and contemptuous of any belief you did not create. Once more you are unbending."

"I know what others say of me," Paul said heatedly, "but experience has led me to ignore criticism." He looked at Barnabas with jaw set and eyes narrowed. "I listen only to Jesus Christ, for he, and he alone, is my guide."

Barnabas ground his teeth, his face turning red with anger. "Your obstinacy, this time, I will not accept." He looked directly at Paul and said slowly, measuring each word: "John Mark will go with us."

"No, he will not," Paul replied.

"Then," Barnabas said calmly, "he and I will sail tomorrow for Cyprus. If you are unwilling to mentor John Mark, I must do it alone." With a long, sad face he wiped the sweat from his brow, his voice quavering. "I ask once more, Paul: Will you go with us?"

"No," Paul said. "I will journey to other lands."

"So be it," Barnabas said.

"So be it," Paul said. With that, he picked up his cloak and waterskin and left Barnabas' house.

And so, after being as brothers for twenty-two years, Paul and Barnabas quarreled and separated. Brought together by chance as schoolmates, they had over time become a whole that was greater than their sum as individuals. Men of complementary abilities and skills, they had proved themselves the most enterprising and effective of all the apostles. Paul's intellect and zeal had been matched by Barnabas' common sense and restraint. By his unshakable convictions and overbearing nature, Paul invited controversy, created enemies; Barnabas was no less committed, but he listened and brought divided parties together. Paul was sensitive, suspicious, tinged with paranoia; Barnabas trusted everyone and found good in all.

Each was profoundly indebted to the other. Barnabas had shielded Paul from avenging Hellenists, intervened with Peter and James to validate the Damascus revelation, and rescued Paul from obscurity to give him the opportunity in Antioch that established his standing and reputation. More than once Barnabas had saved Paul's life. Yet Paul had also made to Barnabas lasting gifts: self-esteem, confidence, resolution. He trained his once hesitant classmate and partner to become an enterprising and forceful leader.

In Antioch the news of their quarrel spread quickly through the churches. Shocked ministers and deacons asked how such a long and effective partnership could be broken in a moment by such an unworthy dispute. The answer: Paul and Barnabas were men, not saints. They disagreed not over issues of doctrine or principle or faith; their difference was personal. Each had convinced himself that his position was logical and prudent, therefore justified. In that one encounter, being right was to each more important than serving their common cause to advance Christianity. Thus they parted. After their quarrel that autumn afternoon, the two friends never spoke, nor wrote, nor saw each other again.

From Barnabas' gate, Paul walked swiftly toward his church, his thoughts bounding from dismay at what had happened to speculation about how he should proceed with his mission. He might take Titus; he was staunch and loyal. But it would be better to have a Jew, someone older, with a wider range of experience.

Immediately he had the answer: Silas of Aswan had proved his merit, first by demonstrating his stamina on the journey from Jerusalem, then by speaking to the churches in Antioch and counseling the ministers about their work. Of his schooling Paul knew nothing, but in writing Silas' Hebrew was adequate, his Greek far better. Silas had once mentioned that he had served for a time in an Egyptian legion of the Roman army. Disciplined, trained to endure hardship — this was a man for the next mission.

Without losing a step, Paul changed direction, to the mansion of Manaen, where Judas Barsabbas and Silas resided. A maidservant took Paul to the garden where Manaen and Silas were conducting a seminar with aspiring deacons. Paul stood at the back, shifting his feet impatiently until he caught Silas' eye and drew him aside to a quiet corner.

"Silas, Barnabas and I concluded today that we should go separately on our missions," Paul said. "He will go to Cyprus, with his cousin John Mark as his companion; I travel elsewhere, to strengthen the churches in Galatia and then take the gospel to the farther provinces of Asia. Will you, Silas, go with me on this mission?"

Silas rocked back in surprise and studied Paul's face. "Did you and Barnabas have differences?"

"Yes, Silas, we quarreled and separated," Paul replied. "But our work will continue, he on his island, I on the continent. I need you to go with me, for I have seen that you are not only a capable teacher but a dependable companion on the road as well." Paul paused and raised his hand as though in warning. "I must tell you, however, that the journey will be hard and perilous."

"That is the way of our work," Silas said cheerfully. "The Lord Jesus never offered his disciples an easy life." He frowned. "What, exactly, would be my responsibility?"

"To be my fellow worker, to teach with me, to affirm the beliefs of our fellow Christians, to bring great numbers of gentiles to the Way, to baptize and instruct them, to train ministers and deacons, to show them how to create and maintain churches so that they, like the movement, will grow and prosper."

At once a deeply serious look came over Silas' face. "No good Christian could refuse such a challenge," he said. "Yes, Paul, I will go with you."

XXV

AFAR

Climbing through the foothills, they finally reached the high pass below Mount Ida and stopped to look down in wonder at the sprawling seaport of Troas. Never had Paul or his two companions seen so many ships — white sails moving on the shimmering blue water, the oars of triremes flashing rhythmically in the sunlight, the fishing boats pulling their heavy nets. From that height the entire city lay in miniature before them — the hippodrome, the amphitheater, the baths, the miles of city walls, the piers of the aqueduct that carried fresh water from mountain lakes.

Silas, who had studied Augustus' rebuilding of Troas at the Roman military institute in Alexandria, pointed out each fortification and its strategic purpose. Timothy, who had joined Paul's mission in Lystra, had never seen the sea before; now he stood gaping in awe at his first glimpse of a great harbor and city. The scape of land, sea, and sky was entrancing, but after a time Paul said quietly, "We walk on. Silas, if you have enough money for an inn, we will purify ourselves and go to the synagogue."

Troas had sheltered Jews for five hundred years. The Greeks, the Macedonians, the Romans, all in turn had welcomed immigrant Jews for their skills as traders and artisans; in turn, however, each conqueror had relegated Jews to the meanest quarter of the city. There they lived, worked, schooled their children, and prospered. Their synagogue, an imposing rectangle of gray stone, stood on a low hill rising directly from the sea. Its fine cedar doors stood open, inviting God's chosen into safe harbor.

It was late afternoon when Paul, Silas, and Timothy entered the quiet sanctum. For an hour Paul prayed and meditated, contemplating his mission thus far and yet to be. How pleased he was that Christianity was now deeply rooted in Galatia. He could look back on the work he and Barnabas had accomplished and be proud. Their churches had grown threefold or more. On this second journey he had come to realize that it was Barnabas, more than he, who put down such a solid foundation. He missed Barnabas, had thought about him almost every day of the eight months since he had left Antioch. But Silas had turned out to be a reliable partner. He learned quickly, spoke well, and never tired. And Timothy — an unexpected find. Paul had resisted having anyone so young on this arduous expedition, but Timothy's earnestness, accomplishments, and dependability made it impossible to say no.

How right his instincts had been: Timothy and Silas had proved their conviction and their courage in taking the gospel to Ancyra while he lay near death with the pox in nearby Pessinus. Though arrested, flogged, and imprisoned for their teachings, their faith never wavered; indeed, so dedicated were they that they began converting their fellow prisoners, and one new Christian contrived their escape. Paul thought of the fever that had dulled his mind and the pustules that had covered his body, of lying helpless, drifting in and out of delirium, wondering whether he would live and — if he did — whether he would be too broken in mind and body ever to preach again. He remembered his prayer as he lingered near death: "Lord God, heal this suffering servant that he may bear your name and your grace before multitudes afar." Fervently had he prayed; tenaciously had he believed. And God answered his prayer. For that, on this and every day, he would give thanks, thanks that he could press on with his mission, thanks that he could bring Jesus' message to mankind and bring mankind to Jesus Christ. "O most mighty God," he concluded, "give me the strength for the task ahead, give me the wisdom to know what to do and the courage to do it, and at the end take me into your heavenly kingdom."

Their prayers finished, the three were met at the door by a stocky man with well-combed black curls and trim beard. "I am Rabbi Tobias," he said.

"I am Paul, with Silas and Timothy."

Tobias studied the pockmarked face. "I know who you are and I know your teachings. I have a message for you. Luke awaits you at the villa of Theophilus." He pointed to a distant hill to the north. "He abides there, among the wealthy of Troas."

As they walked back to the inn in the dusk, Paul told the others of encountering Luke at the council, and of their appointment in Troas. "Timothy," he said, "go tomorrow to the villa of Theophilus and bring Luke to the inn. It is important that he and I continue our dialogue."

That evening the innkeeper's wife fed the guests great bowls of soup thick with lentils and fresh-caught fish, loaves of warm bread, and brimming cups of strong wine. With full stomachs, Silas and Timothy stumbled off to their beds of thick straw and slept soundly.

Long after midnight Paul, asleep in another room, was suddenly brought awake by a vision: A man dressed in the distinctive Macedonian style was standing at the edge of a shore, holding out his arms in entreatment, and speaking in the rounded vowels characterizing the Macedonian accent: "Cross over into Macedonia. Help us!" As the words echoed across the water, the man faded from view.

In an instant Paul leaped from his bed. The man in the vision was Jesus; of this there could be no doubt. Bursting with excitement, Paul raced to the door of Silas and Timothy. "Rise quickly! God has called me to take the good news to Macedonia. We go forth at once. Silas, come with me to find the first ship. Timothy, go immediately to Luke. Tell him we sail for Europe, and he is to go with us. Run. We must lose no time."

Entry from the Journal of Luke

Departing Troas on the morning ebb tide, we moved smartly from wharfside into open sea, where Phorbas, master of this good ship *Halcyone*, ordered the great main to be raised. At once a brisk south wind, common in early summer in these northern waters, filled the snow-white canvas, spurring the *Halcyone* to bound over the waves like a spirited stallion eager for battle. Sailing alone under an azure sky untouched by cloud, we course through islands that stand like sentinels in this "wine-dark sea," passing well east of Tenedos, breasting the current that flows southward from the Hellespont, and running due north past the peak of Imbros. Now, on a reach, the helmsman steers directly for the towering table mountain of Samothrace. Anchoring in the lee of the rugged coastline, we will await the barge that will deliver half our cargo of fine Trojan wine to the thirsty revelers who celebrate the Cabiri, the pair of deities, one young, one old, who protect the Phoenician sailors.

On the morrow, Macedonia. There Paul opens his campaign

for Christ in Europe. He will be the first apostle to plant the banner of Christianity on the great continent that holds such promise for the next civilization. He invades with that most formidable of all weapons, an idea.

How quickly he is transformed by the sea. In Jerusalem I saw a man exceedingly restless, impatient, driven by some inner fire and spirit. On this ship the morose countenance becomes cheerful. He smiles, even laughs. Clearly the sea is for Paul a haven, respite from his labors.

Illness has left its mark. His frame is small, spare, the legs curved as a bow, the quadriceps more sinew than muscle. The face is gaunt, marked with atrophic scars from the pox that is most often fatal. The eyes appear to bulge from their sockets. The kinesis of energy that I observed before we boarded may come from adrenal glands stimulated by coming near death; the experience can provoke even greater zeal in men of gravitas.

For his companions Paul has chosen brawn and brain. Silas carries himself with the muscular confidence of a centurion. He is in every way the good officer, self-assured, loyal, quick to follow orders, capable of giving them. Like every trained soldier, he misses no opportunity to sleep, for he knows there will come a day and a battle when the only rest will be death itself.

When young Timothy roused me at the villa early this morning, I thought him a servant at first. His shy manner masks a fine mind, a talent for diplomacy, and an engaging enthusiasm for all new experiences. It is difficult to believe that this is Timothy's first time at sea. He walks the deck with confidence, pulls at the windlass with the crew, and climbs the mast with the lookout.

Traveling as we are on this ship, the four of us are passen-gers into the future. Paul will make history. I will chronicle that history.

Written on the fifth day of the seventh month by the Julian calendar, in the ninth year of the reign of Claudius.

As the *Halcyone* entered the channel between the jagged peaks of the island of Thasos and the low coastline of Macedonia, Paul, Silas, and Timothy surrounded Luke at the port rail.

"Tell us of Macedonia," Paul said.

Luke looked about and pointed to a landing on the steep shore of the island. "There, ninety-two years ago, Brutus secretly sent the body of Cassius to be hidden so that his soldiers, retreating before the army of Antony after the first battle of Philippi, would not be demoralized by the death of their captain. The next day, in the second battle of Philippi, Brutus too was defeated and fell on his sword. It was this victory by Antony that ensured the wily Octavian would become, in time, the expansionist and long-reigning emperor Augustus."

Seeing such a rapt audience, Luke continued: "Caesar Augustus made Philippi both a Roman city and a Roman stronghold. He populated it with veterans of his armies and posted fresh foot soldiers and cavalry in the hills to defend against the barbarians to the north. It remains a frontier capital, a well-armed outpost of empire, and the principal city of eastern Macedonia."

"Philippi is capital of the province?" Paul asked.

"Yes," Luke said, "although in political status, Philippi is not a province but an imperial colony of two hundred thousand with all the privileges of Rome itself."

"What are the principal religions practiced by Philippians?" Paul asked.

"Worship of Jupiter and Mars, the usual Roman gods," Luke replied. "The old Thracians revere their goddess Bendis, and there is a sanctuary to Cybele."

"Is there a synagogue?" Paul asked.

"No," Luke said. "I should say there was no synagogue two years ago, when I was last there. There are few Jews, Paul, and they are often harassed by the functionaries of the praetor Aelius Haterius, but there are many, many intelligent gentiles."

"Then let us go first to Philippi," Paul said.

With the wind holding well into the bay of Neapolis, Phorbas first shortened, then dropped, his mainsail to ease the *Halcyone* gently to a dock on the eastern side of the long promontory on which Neapolis stood. Paul and his fellow travelers made their way through a throng of carts, pack animals, and shouting drovers to the center of the city and the road to Philippi.

From Neapolis, the Via Egnatia climbs steeply, twists through the Pangaeus canyons to a summit, and there at the high pass the travelers stopped to drink from a mountain spring.

"Behold," said Timothy, opening both arms toward the vast panorama of Philippi. A broad valley of green fields and brown marshland was ringed on three sides by mountains coursed with veins of iron, copper, and lead ores: in the foreground they could see an orderly grid of boulevards and streets, an immense mosaic of rooftops, a triumphal arch leading to the walled stronghold of the Acropolis, a stadium, and villas half hidden by tall cedars in the hills.

"A lovely city it is," Luke said.

"A better place it will be after we make it a center of Christianity," Paul said.

In less than an hour the four walked through the eastern gate of the city. Paul, on the premise that he would find fellow Jews in the busiest section of the marketplace, moved from stall to stall, speaking in Hebrew. At the open door of a weaver, a woman called out to him. "I, Eglah, am of the tribe of Ephraim," she said. "Why do you seek Jews?"

"I am a man of God," Paul said, "and I would worship with my people."

"Then come on the Sabbath, three days hence, to the bank of the River Gaggitas," Eglah said. "It is there that we chose our place of prayer, for outside the gate the waters are pure and the soldiers do not harass us."

"Is there a rabbi?" Paul asked.

"No, the proconsul sent him away," Eglah said. "With no rabbi, our congregation is small. Most who assemble on the Sabbath are women."

"I will come and speak," Paul said.

Thirteen women and three young men gathered by the river and stood about, looking with curiosity at Paul and his fellow travelers. With his back to the stream, Paul raised his right hand. "Seat yourselves on the riverbank, for I have much to say."

He opened with spirit: "I bring you good news, of the coming of a great prophet sent by God to bring us back to trust and faith." He was about to recount his usual stories of Abraham, Moses, and David when he observed the bright and engaged eyes of the women, as many gentile as Jew, and changed his mind. He would dramatize the power of faith by telling the story of Naomi, the Jewish mother who lost her husband and two sons in the foreign land of Moab. "Bereft and despairing, Naomi set out to return to her homeland of Judah and instructed her Moabite daughters-in-law to return to their homes. One did. But Ruth, the widow of her older son, Mahlon, refused, saying to Naomi, 'Whither thou goest, I will go. Where thou livest, I will live. Thy people shall be my people, and thy God my God. Naught but death shall part thee and me.' So Ruth, the foreigner from Moab, returned with Naomi to Bethlehem and there found favor with Boaz, a wealthy landowner and kinsman of her dead husband. So pleased was Boaz with Ruth that he married her, and she gave him a son, Obed, the grandfather of King David."

Heads were nodding; the little gathering of women liked Ruth's story. "As the prophets foretold, of David's line would come the greatest leader of all, not a warrior, not a conquering king, but the humble man Jesus, one who would heal the sick, feed the hungry, rescue the lost, exalt the poor — and sacrifice his life so that your sins will be forgiven." He paused and opened his arms. "What does Jesus ask in return? That you atone, that you have faith in God, that you love the Lord God with all your heart and soul, and that you love your neighbor. Believe in the Lord Jesus, for he offers life everlasting."

With that exhortation Paul moved aside, and a handsome woman in a fine cloak of purple linen stood up.

"I, Lydia, am not a Jew, but a God-fearing woman from Thyatira across the sea. Do you say that this Jesus offers salvation for gentiles as well as Jews?"

"Yes," Paul said. "To Christ Jesus, there is no difference — not between Jew and gentile, not between man and woman, not between rich and poor."

"You have opened my mind and heart," Lydia said. "I seek the grace of God." She turned to four other women with her, who began nodding vigorously. "All in my household are ready to accept the promise of Jesus Christ."

"Come forward, all among you who have faith," Paul said. "Follow me into this stream, and I will baptize you now."

Seven women came forward. When the ritual was complete and Paul had placed his hand on the head of each in blessing, Lydia said to Paul: "Now that you have brought me to believe, will you and your companions walk with me to my house in the city? There live others of my guild of dyers. I would have you speak to them as you have to us. Dine at my house. Remain there as you carry out your mission in Philippi."

Paul hesitated. They were living in a hovel of an inn, on the coins remaining from the purse given him in Pessinus. He was eager to speak to Lydia's guild, but he intended to earn bread and shelter with the labor of his hands. "Once I have spoken to your fellow workers," he said, "I must return to our inn."

Lydia shook her head and spoke with vehemence: "If you have judged me to be believing in the Lord, abide a while in my house. Trust me, as I trust you."

Luke put his hand on Paul's arm "Yield," he said in a low voice. "The woman's hospitality is a mark of her gratitude. There is no virtue in our present discomfort, and through her you may bring others to the faith."

So the four went to the house of Lydia, a spacious building of fired brick. On the ground floor, open to the street, rich dyes were sold and common weaving transmuted into noble raiment; on the upper floors were many rooms for Lydia's workers and guests.

This house of Lydia was to be more than a comfortable residence for Paul and his companions; it became the fountainhead of Christianity in Macedonia.

Many in the Philippian community of artisans and craftsmen came every day to Lydia's shop to trade, and so many heard Paul as he taught in her atrium that it quickly became necessary to find a larger place for assembly. By good fortune a wealthy customer, Minerva Mindarus, came down from her villa one morning to select linens and, at Lydia's urging, listened to Paul. Within the hour Minerva asked to be baptized and offered her in-town mansion to Paul as a place of worship. Silas and Timothy built an altar and benches for the great hall; there, thrice weekly, Paul delivered his message to the assembled Christians and others who came out of curiosity or hope.

When the numbers of new Christians reached fifty, Paul assigned Timothy to conduct a school for deacons and acolytes. As word of a new and foreign god spread through the community, loiterers in the market squares gossiped and mocked Paul and his companions as they walked to their churchhouse every morning.

It happened that a wild-haired girl began waiting for them, taunting and sarcastically crying out: "These men are slaves of the Most High God, who are announcing a way of salvation!" At first Paul ignored her, but he was told that she was a slave girl possessed by the demon spirit Python. Her two owners exploited her by collecting coins for interpreting her utterances as soothsaying. Paul remembered his Greek myths: Python, the dragon guarding the oracle at Delphi, was killed by Apollo, whereupon Python's evil spirit entered Apollo and gave him the power to divine the future. Paul pitied the girl, but he became more and more vexed as she accosted him day after day.

One morning, when she began ranting at him, Paul turned on her and declaimed: "In the name of Jesus Christ I command you, evil spirit of Python, come out of this girl!"

Instantly the slave girl fell silent. Her face became calm, and she looked about as if wondering how she came to be there. Her two owners rushed up and seized her. "Speak! Speak!" commanded Torgus, the older of her owners. But she merely looked at her masters as if they were strangers.

At that, the two slave masters turned on Paul. "You!" Torgus shouted. "You have destroyed our property. For this you will suffer." Paul tried to reason with them, but they struck Paul and Silas and dragged them through the marketplace to the open-air court of Mortinax, the chief magistrate.

He was an old centurion with one leg, a lip curled in cruelty, and an ugly sword scar across his prognathous jaw. Mortinax looked at the two bloody and disheveled strangers. "What is the charge?" he grumbled.

"Being Jews to begin with," Torgus said. "They are bringing great troubles to our city, Magistrate. They would impose their Jewish religion on us. As Romans we cannot even recognize, much less worship, their false god."

By that time a crowd had gathered before the judgment seat of the magistrate, and they heard Torgus' accusations with mounting excitement, nodding their heads and shaking their fists. Paul attempted to speak in defense, to ask for the full trial due a Roman citizen, but someone in the mob called out: "Beat them! Beat them!" Others took up the cry for vengeance. Mortinax folded his hands and looked on, allowing the mob to demonstrate, to feed on its own frenzy. At last he raised his hand for silence.

"Go, lictors," he ordered. "Strip off the garments of these Jews. Beat them with rods. Lay on them. When you have done with beating them, throw them into the inner prison."

The mob tore the coats from Paul and Silas, stripping them to the waist as lictors selected thick rods from the bundles it was their duty to carry. With the magistrate looking on, and the crowd howling with glee at every stroke, the lictors bloodied the bare backs of the victims with thirty lashes for each. Bleeding, gasping for breath, wincing with pain at every step, they were prodded through the street to the nearby prison.

"Put these two criminals where they cannot escape," the chief lictor told Maduros the jailer. Drawing his sword and proudly jangling his brass ring of iron keys, the jailer forced Paul and Silas into the darkest cell, and there he locked their feet in wooden stocks.

And there they remained, their legs cramped in the stocks, their bare backs dark crimson from congealed blood, their mouths parched from thirst, their bellies empty and groaning. After a time, Paul said quietly, "They can never stop us from praying." All through the afternoon and into the night he and Silas took turns praying aloud: "The Lord is my rock and my fortress, and my deliverer . . . the Lord looseth men out of prison: the Lord helpeth them that are fallen . . . They that sit in darkness and in the shadow of death; being fast bound in misery and iron; when they cried out the Lord delivereth them out of their distress, out of the shadow of death, and broke their bonds in sunder."

"Silence!" came a voice from another cell. "Let us sleep." The commotion brought the jailer from his house, and he ordered Paul to cease. Paul refused, continuing to pray and sing hymns and boldly confirming their faith in Jesus Christ. Over and over he and Silas intoned: "As Jesus endured, so can we endure."

Hours later, near midnight, a low and unmistakable rumble sounded in the distance, then quickly came closer and closer. "Earthquake!" someone shouted in the darkness as the earthen floor of the prison trembled, shook, and seemed to lift and fall away. Prison walls swayed, tilting at bizarre angles, sending great stones tumbling down, filling the air with choking dust. Above the noise came the cry of a prisoner shrieking in pain: "My leg! My leg! I cannot move!"

The earthquake had shattered the wooden beams of the stocks; Paul and Silas were free. From the moonlight streaming through a hole in the roof they could see that the prison doors had fallen from their hinges, and iron chains had snapped like twine. But all was silent; nothing moved.

At that moment Paul heard the voice of Maduros at the jail door: "Woe!

Woe! My prisoners have escaped." Drawing his sword, believing suicide would be better than the death by torture he would suffer for losing prisoners, Maduros raised the blade above his chest. Paul shouted: "Stop! Do no harm to yourself! All your prisoners are here."

"Light! Bring light!" Maduros called out to his servant, and when a candle was brought, he looked into every cell and saw that all his prisoners were present. When the jailer reached the innermost cell, he fell to his knees before Paul and Silas. "The power of your God has set you free. What must I do to be saved?"

Paul placed his hand on the head of the jailer. "Believe in the Lord Jesus Christ, and you will be saved — you and your entire household."

Weeping, the jailer rose and, bearing the candle before him, led Paul and Silas into his house. With hands become gentle, Maduros washed the ugly wounds on the prisoners' backs and poured soothing aloe on the welts raised by the rods.

Cleansed, clothed in a clean chiton brought by the jailer's wife, Paul delivered the briefest version of his message to the jailer, his wife, their three wide-eyed children, and the four slaves of the household. All asked to be baptized immediately. When all had been touched with water from the kitchen cistern, Maduros told his servants to set the table with bread and meat, water and wine, so that all of the household, free and slave, might celebrate with Paul and Silas.

Well before dawn the news reached praetor Aelius Haterius and his chief magistrate that the earthquake had miraculously opened the doors of the prison, but that neither Paul nor Silas had made any attempt to escape. Haterius, warned by the palace soothsayer that the two strangers might inflict another earthquake on Philippi, instructed Mortinax to release the Christians and order them to leave the city immediately. At first light, the chief lictor knocked on the door of the jailer.

When Paul and Silas appeared, the chief lictor announced: "Mortinax and the other magistrates have decided to set you free. Now go out from the city at once, and proceed in peace."

"No!' Paul replied hotly. "You beat us in public, despite our being Roman citizens and never legally condemned. And now you want us to leave secretly. No, indeed! Let your officials come here and admit their mistake. Let them escort us from the city in the custom due to Roman citizens."

"You are Roman citizens?" the chief lictor replied in astonishment. "Why did you not tell the magistrate?"

"We did, in loud voices, but your magistrate heard the mob and not us," Paul said.

Fearful that he and his superiors could all be punished for dishonoring a Roman citizen, the lictor left hurriedly. In a very short time an official cloaked in purple arrived, accompanied by four soldiers.

"I am Epitadeus, deputy to Praetor Aelius Haterius, who has just learned that a mistake was made and Roman citizens unjustly treated," he said. "The praetor regrets this incident, and begs your understanding. He is also concerned that some in the city may blame you for the earthquake. For your own safety, therefore, the praetor urgently requests that you leave the city at once."

"Tell the praetor," Paul said, "that Silas and I will leave Philippi by noon today on two conditions: First, all prisoners in this jail are to be released at once. Second, you and your retainers will escort us to our churchhouse so that we may assemble our followers, confirm and exhort them in the faith, and bid them farewell."

The deputy deliberated for a moment, then curtly nodded. "I, Epitadeus, exercise my authority as deputy and grant these two conditions."

After addressing, exhorting, and blessing the assembly of Christians, Paul brought together his companions and Lydia in a private room. "The hour of my departure is at hand," he said. "Luke, where should I go next in Macedonia?"

"Thessalonica," Luke replied. "It meets your first desideratum — great numbers of people. It is a cosmopolis of Roman, Thracian, Achaian, Illyrian, Gaul, Jew, Samaritan, Phoenician, Egyptian, Cyrenian — more than three hundred thousand by the last census. In all your travels, Paul, you have seen no city the equal of Thessalonica. It is not only the political capital of Macedonia, but by far the most important city of this entire region."

"Does the governor tolerate new religions?" Paul asked.

"Worship is by choice," Luke said. "Thessalonica is unique in the empire in that it is a free city governed by seven politarchs — citizens chosen by their fellow citizens to manage the affairs of state."

Paul nodded. "This is my decision. Silas and I will go to Thessalonica.

Timothy, I judge your deacons and acolytes here to need two more weeks of training. Accomplish that, then join us in Thessalonica. Once we have established a church there, we will take the gospel to Achaia. I have long believed we should establish a church in Athens, the very epicenter of learning, then go on to Corinth."

He turned to face his hostess. "Lydia, I ask that you oversee the work of Timothy and also select elders who will see to the growth of the church and to the preservation of the faith of its members. We would have no church in Philippi but for you. Its future will rest in your hands." He looked to each in turn. "Press on."

XXVI

FAILING

Athens: Poetry in marble. So Zagoreos had spoken in reverence of his native city. Paul had been thirteen then, listening to his tutor tell of a city of such beauty as to break the heart, a city where philosophy was more treasured than gold, where wisdom ruled. Now, standing on the Acropolis almost thirty years later, Paul looked on a scene of grandeur, a composition by the hand of the artist on a magnificent canvas of nature.

From this eminence he could see the well-planned open spaces, the parks where the wise and the foolish gossiped under the plane trees, exchanging new ideas and new philosophies, debating endlessly but concluding nothing. He could pick out the temples dedicated to a multiplicity of gods and religions, the groves of statues honoring myth and patron and hero. For five days he had walked among temples and statues, driven by curiosity, seeing in his imagination the glory of Athens five centuries earlier, seeing in reality an intellectual capital long in decline.

He had explored every part of the city, and the more he saw, the more he was revolted by the ubiquitousness of idols and by the sight of Athenians worshiping false gods. Greeks had dreamed up these mythical beings to explain events they could not otherwise understand; why else would people so well educated so delude themselves and pray to an image in inanimate bronze or stone — however well formed?

Undaunted by the impossibility of the task, Paul resolved to convince Athenians of the absurdity of their gods. Since they liked nothing better than to orate, theorize, and debate in public, he would confront them in public. Consequently, every morning Paul went out alone, having left Timothy to assist the new church in Thessalonica and Silas to establish a church in Beroea. Striding into the forums and marketplaces, he would find a platform to speak of the one true God and proclaim the good news of the coming of Jesus Christ, but Athenians either ignored or scorned him. "What can this beggar mean?" a student said, pointing to Paul's worn cloak. For all his assiduity, which to some Athenians seemed comic, Paul attracted not one convert.

In his third week, however, he aroused the curiosity of at least one patrician. Paul had just finished a spirited debate on the existence or nonexistence of afterlife when an Athenian in fine white linen approached. The stranger's peplum was bordered with a Greek key design in gold that indicated he held some rank in the city. "I am Dionysius, one of the hundred councilmen in the Areopagus," he said to Paul. "You bring startling things to our ears. We are minded, then, to know more of this philosophy which you teach. Will you speak to the council?"

Paul immediately recognized the importance of the invitation. The Areopagus was the ancient name given both to a freestanding eminence of rock close by the Acropolis, and to the royal court of judges that had met there five centuries earlier to decree a man's freedom or death. Now the Areopagus no longer held legal power, yet it was accepted as the peerless forum for Athenian debate on politics, philosophy, ethics, and religion. None but a recognized intellect was allowed to speak there. So Paul replied: "Excellency, I will be honored to speak in the Areopagus."

Never before had Paul addressed such a distinguished audience of intellectuals, philosophers, and thinkers. He knew he must forgo his usual opening appeal to emotion, and instead move them by logic and reasoning.

At noon the next day Dionysius met Paul at the foot of the hill, and together they walked up the sixteen stone steps to the rim of the court. From the top step Paul walked alone to the center of an open and level quadrangle, perhaps sixty feet on the long sides, around which a hundred of Athens' best sat on benches cut into the limestone outcropping.

Stretching out his hand, Paul began his speech in a strong and firm voice: "Athenians, I behold how in every way you exhibit your devotion to religion and fear your gods. As I have passed through your city and looked up at your objects of worship, I also found an altar inscribed: TO AN UNKNOWN GOD.

"As you do not know, then, whom you worship, I make him known to you. The God who made the world and all things in it, this one God being Lord of heaven and of earth, does not dwell in temples fashioned by the art of man" — Paul gestured toward the Parthenon to his left and above — "nor is he served by the hands of men, as though he had need of anything, for it is he who gives life and breath and all things to all."

Now he touched on the Greeks' notion that they originated from a higher order than other races. "And he made mankind of every nation of one blood, caused them to dwell on the face of the whole earth, appointing to each the season of their prominence, ordaining to each the boundaries of their dwelling places." To affirm his point of universality, he quoted from a Greek poet, Aratus. "As one of your poets has written, 'We are all his offspring.'"

Surveying his audience, Paul detected some interest, more disdain, but attention from all. "Being earthly offspring of God, we ought not to suppose that the Godhead is made of gold or silver or stone, engraved by the art and imagination of man." Now he saw frowns and heads shaking. "In past times the God of all has overlooked the ignorance of the less enlightened, but now he strictly charges all men to repent, for the Lord has appointed a day when he will judge the habited world in righteousness. This judgment is to be made by a man whom God ordained, and the proof of his appointment to judge each of us and all of us is that God resurrected this man from the dead —"

Upon hearing the word *resurrected*, the audience burst into laughter. Shocked, then furious at the ridicule, Paul began to walk away. Dionysius came quickly to his side, apologizing: "We will ask you to return at another time."

Paul shook his head. He had endured, all too often, the vehement opposition of his fellow Jews, and he had learned to deal with the parochial ignorance of pagans, but he would not subject his certainty of faith to self-appointed intellectuals who questioned everything and believed nothing.

Trying to comfort Paul, Dionysius said, "Though some of us do believe in one God, there are scholars among us who have proved by their study of the physical sciences that a body cannot come back to life."

Paul raised his hand to protest. "What your egoists do not open their minds to see is that the God who created the laws of nature can overcome the laws of nature."

Turning away, Paul left the Areopagus in deep disappointment. Head down, walking back to his inn, he remembered how in his youth he dreamed of going to Athens to study, and how, after his success in Antioch, he had put Athens high on his list of cities where he would take his mission. With great enthusiasm he had come here to deliver the good news of Jesus to a city renowned for, as Demosthenes said, "interest in the new." But Athens had mocked him. He would leave that day, that very hour.

With his last coin, Paul boarded the daily ferry from Piraeus to the far busier port of Cenchreae. Once ashore, he set out on the five-mile walk westward to Corinth, threading his way along a broad and well-paved Roman road among oxcarts loaded with fresh fish, fresh fruit, pottery, iron plow points, wine, bags of wool, bags of grain, and scores of other products shipped across the isthmus or made in Corinth for sale abroad. Once inside the city walls, wherever he turned, Corinth swarmed with people, in the dress of Egyptian, Asian, Roman, Cyrenian, Greek, Phoenician — and everyone shouting, buying, selling, bursting into raucous laughter, stumbling out of taverns. Never had he seen such crowds, or heard such street noise, or smelled so much spilled wine.

The road from Cenchreae became the main street leading Paul directly into the grand and glittering agora, the market square of Corinth. Raised sidewalks of limestone on either side were lined with colonnades and shops displaying gilded fronts and silk banners, giving the great square a gaudy and festive splendor. The shops were organized by wares — a fish market here, a meat market there, beyond an olive market, and farther on a grain market. A copious spring, the Fountain of Peirene, piped water to the shops and to the many taverns nearby, each proudly boasting an identity — the Tavern of Zeus, the Tavern of Dionysus, the Tavern of Health, the Tavern of Desire. Looking about, Paul could see to the west the theater, now being rebuilt and expanded, and to the south the *bema*, the raised platform for the high seat of the reigning proconsul. Far beyond to the south lay the Acrocorinth, erect pillars of rock rising almost half a mile high. Once an impregnable military fortress, it was now the site of the Temple of Aphrodite, where a thousand priestess-prostitutes worshiped the goddess of love and waited in luxurious palaces for tourists, and Corinthians, to climb the mountain and take their pleasure.

Walking to the north on the Lechaion Road, Paul passed a long basilica, the serene Temple of Apollo, and the amphitheater cut from the rock of a hillside.

Farther on he found the Lerna Asclepium, the healing springs littered with pottery arms and feet left as votive offerings by the injured and afflicted. Beyond, he found the Jewish quarter; soon he came upon a monumental gateway inscribed, in Hebrew and in Greek, SYNAGOGUE OF THE HEBREWS.

He stopped in wonder. This synagogue was the grandest Paul had ever seen. Erected on a freestanding hill in the wealthiest part of the Jewish quarter, it stood as a citadel, holding within its marble walls the feeling, the very essence, of the long history and enduring unity of the people of Israel. Sitting inside in the quiet, Paul looked about. The space for the congregation was a long rectangle, one hundred and sixty feet on the long sides, with polished marble columns spacing the carved benches of Bashan oak and a screen of filigreed marble separating the women's gallery. The shrine for the Torah, also of Bashan oak, suggested elegance and eternity. Not since Antioch had he seen walls with such intricate mosaics and delicate reliefs. He resolved to speak in this fine synagogue if the rabbi would permit. Then, looking at the raveled sleeve of his cloak, he knew it would be unseemly to stand in this holy place looking like a beggar. So he walked next door to find the rabbi.

"I am Paul, a messenger of God from the east," he said, "I have just arrived after a long journey, and have no money. Where may I find work?"

The rabbi was a thin man, lean of frame and long of face, with kind brown eyes and random streaks of gray in his black hair and beard. For a moment he tilted his head and looked inquisitively at the stranger on his doorstep. "We who are God's chosen people are all his messengers," he said pleasantly. The friendly eyes studied Paul's face, wrinkled and browned by sun and wind, and glanced at the worn leather of his sandals. "As surely you come from afar, do you have words of counsel that would be new to the congregation of Corinth?"

"Indeed I do," Paul said. "I bring good news that the words of our greatest prophets have been fulfilled."

Again the rabbi nodded pleasantly as he tapped together the tips of his fingers. "Does your message," he asked, "concern the *Chrestus* of whom we have heard?"

"*Chrestus* is the Roman way of saying the name," Paul said. "In proper Greek it is *Christus*, and to us Christ. I come in God's name and with God's blessing to celebrate the coming of the savior Jesus Christ to the world. I would speak to your congregation on the next Sabbath."

"You know that the emperor Claudius expelled all Jews from Rome last year because of this *Chrestus*," the rabbi said.

"I did not," Paul replied. Indeed, he was surprised. Who, he wondered, had taken the message of Jesus to the very heart of the empire? Surely it was not Peter, who lacked initiative; surely not John, who was too reclusive. "How did the name of Jesus cause this expulsion from Rome?" Paul asked.

The rabbi shrugged. "Accounts are murky," he said. "From the beginning of his reign, Claudius suspected all Jews and persecuted some. When the sect of *Chrestus* contested openly with the older generations of Hebrews and provoked disturbances in the streets, Claudius found a plausible excuse to issue his edict forcing all Jews to leave the city."

"Another exile for our people, another woeful misfortune," Paul said, shaking his head.

"Not for Corinth," the rabbi said with a smile and a sweeping wave of his hand. "Many forced from Rome immigrated to this city. They brought their skills, their gold, their energy; and they prosper here. And they share their wealth. Look at this magnificent synagogue. They care for our poor, though few are poor in Corinth, and they swell our congregation every Sabbath." He paused in thought for a moment. "Is this *Chrestus* a new prophet?"

"He is prophet and teacher, and miracle worker," Paul said. "I was appointed to bring his message to Corinth."

"I must first talk to Crispus, president of our synagogue," the rabbi said. "What is your trade?"

"My father was a tentmaker, so I know how to make felt and fashion it into tents, and I can weave cloth and sew leather."

"Then you must go to the house of Aquila, who is among the exiles from Rome," the rabbi said. "He is the finest tentmaker in Corinth, and works and lives near the haul-across." After pointing the way to Aquila's house, the rabbi opened his purse. "Here is money for bread."

"No," Paul said, "I eat no bread I have not earned. But may I know your name?"

"I am Ariel. And I will speak to Crispus."

"One more question," Paul said. "Is there a festival being celebrated that brings so many visitors to the city?"

Ariel laughed. "For pagans," he said, "Corinth is one continuous festival."

Paul could smell the house of Aquila before he reached it; the familiar odors of steaming wool, rank hide, and boiling vat were unmistakable. Making his way closer through the wide yet crowded streets, he could hear the rhythmic pounding of the beaters as they shaped and pressed coarse fibers into the stiff fabric that withstood rain and snow and desert wind.

The smaller part of the compound was old, little more than a mud-brick shed used as the tannery. Opposite, across a court, sprawled a new building of white stone that occupied most of a block. Through the side open to the court Paul could see rows of felters at their benches, and seamsters, many of them women, assembling tents. The upper story of the building appeared to be living quarters, but on the roof were seven more workers. From the shape of their low benches they seemed to be tooling and sewing leather.

Aquila came out from an inner room after Paul waited for a time. He was swarthy, sweating, and disheveled. He had a large head covered with a mat of long, unkempt hair, a wide forehead, a prominent nose, and brisk manner. He seemed hurried and harried.

"I seek work," Paul said. "I am a tentmaker."

"Let me see your hands," Aquila said.

Paul opened his palms, still callused from the weaving that earned his bread in Thessalonica.

"We need workers," Aquila said, "but you must first talk with Prisca. Wait here."

As Paul stood by in the courtyard, he witnessed something he had never seen before — a ship's mast moving across dry land. Stepping out into the street to look, he remembered his schoolboy lessons. Six hundred years earlier the tyrant Periander had devised a way to speed the shipment of goods across the isthmus: He had slaves cut a track, twelve feet wide, in the rock across the three-mile land bridge between the Gulf of Corinth on the west and the Saronic Gulf on the east. Gangs of slaves pulled ships from the water onto wide-wheeled transporter-wagons, and mules then towed the ships through the rock cut from sea to sea.

His attention drawn to the curious spectacle, Paul did not hear the woman coming up behind him. When he turned, she smiled. In a cheerful voice she said, "Lo, stranger, have you not before seen ships sail on land?"

Paul stepped back. It was not just that the woman was so comely, but her easy grace, her serenity of manner, her nobility of carriage, her flowing silks — all these things reminded him of his mother.

"You are a tentmaker?" she asked.

"I am first and foremost a messenger of God, an apostle of Jesus Christ," Paul said, and opened his palms. "My hands I use to earn my bread."

Prisca backed away. "You say you teach *Chrestus*? It was because of *Chrestus* that we left Rome."

"Are you a follower of the Christ?" Paul asked.

"No," she replied, "but we heard a stranger speak of him in the synagogue in Rome."

"Do you remember his name?" Paul asked.

Prisca grimaced with vexation. "Of course I remember his name — Merari. How could we forget? He caused such discord among the congregation that the elders put him out of the synagogue. So he took to the streets and markets, and created so many disturbances that Claudius expelled all Jews from Rome."

"Was this Merari from Gaza?" Paul asked.

"We assumed he came from Jerusalem," Prisca replied, "for he claimed he was sent to Rome by the leaders of your sect."

"Did you lose everything?" Paul asked.

She brushed the idea away. "No, just vats and benches and an old house. We are nomads, like Jews of old. We have made tents and saddles in Sinope, Byzantium, Ephesus, Rome, and now Corinth. Our treasures always go with us."

"What are your treasures?" Paul asked.

After a moment's thought, she said: "First is the love that Aquila and I have for each other. Next is Aquila's energy and skill in this trade. Then my talent for finding good workers, and getting the most from them by fair treatment and good wages. Finally a store of gold, which we keep ready in case we must move quickly."

"I bring you a greater treasure," Paul said. "It is, through Jesus, the promise of eternal life."

Prisca narrowed her eyes and studied the face of the strange man. "You are a man of some learning. So this I offer: Work for three days at the benches. If you demonstrate skill, we will pay your worth. If you continue to work diligently, not only will Aquila and I hear what you have to say about this *Chrestus*, but so will our workers and household. But you are not to cause disturbances in the street, as Merari did in Rome. We, like many other Jews who came here, have profited handsomely — far more than we did in Rome. So do nothing to provoke Caesar's proconsul to banish us from this thriving city."

Paul raised his hand. "But I must keep the right to speak in the synagogue."

She shrugged. "If the elders permit, yes." She beckoned with her hand. "Now follow me. Join us as we break bread with our workers."

XXVII

BUILDING

For his first month in Corinth, Paul experienced a life uncommonly good. Every Sabbath he taught and debated in the synagogue. One by one converts asked to be baptized. Weekdays he found comfort in toil he had once rejected as beneath him; working with his hands to cut and shape well-tanned leather gave him time to think. On his second day of work, and after a spirited discussion of ethics at the common supper table, Aquila and Prisca invited Paul to lodge in an upper room of their large house. Quickly he discovered how much he liked their company, and they his.

Aquila and Prisca were an odd match, one primitive, the other refined, but they shared a canny sense of business and genuine warmth for their extended family of workers, vendors, and customers. Paul they treated as a favorite brother, and he lost no time in adapting to personal comfort. Not since his youth in Tarsus had he enjoyed such a combination of a good bed, a solid desk by a sunny window, maidservants to attend his needs, new clothes, bountiful food, and motherly attention. Out of gratitude, he applied his best skills to his daily tasks; out of conviction, he persuaded first Prisca, then Aquila, then the entire household of servants and workers to become Christians.

At his fifth Sabbath in the synagogue in Corinth, Paul confronted a division in the congregation. As before, he delivered his familiar message — the prophecies, the chronology of Jesus' life, the crucifixion and resurrection.

Younger members, particularly the immigrants from Rome, and God-fearing gentiles followed every word, as they had from the beginning. But a faction of conservatives demonstrated against Paul, covering their ears when he used the words *resurrection* and *Messiah*. Later Ariel took him aside. "It is the banker Sosthenes who opposes you. He and his allies would bar you from further speaking."

"What do you counsel?" Paul asked.

"Crispus is president," Ariel replied, "and he ruled that you may continue."

A week later, at the end of Paul's presentation, Sosthenes openly disputed Paul's interpretation of scripture, provoking a long and contentious debate. To end the confrontation Crispus rose from his seat on the platform and raised his hand to signal for silence.

"I, Crispus," he said quietly, "have come to believe that the Lord Jesus is the Messiah." Not a sound was to be heard, not a whisper. "Others will differ," Crispus continued. "This I understand. As I respect their holding to the Law and traditions, so also do I ask that they respect my findings. Hear me, brothers and sisters, for of this I am certain. The prophecies of old have been fulfilled. The Lord God did in fact raise the man Jesus from the dead. By that act the Lord God proved to all willing to see that Jesus is the anointed one." After a pause, he added: "Jesus is the Messiah. Therefore, I and my entire household will be baptized and join our names with the family of Christians."

A hush fell over the congregation. There was shock and disbelief that the respected Crispus had committed to the new faith. After the benediction, members filed from the synagogue in unaccustomed silence. The very next day Sosthenes brought together the elders and demanded action. After hours of bitter argument they dismissed Crispus from office and chose Sosthenes to be the new president. Forthwith, he instructed Ariel to prevent Paul from speaking again in the synagogue.

Undaunted, Paul resolved to test the edict. On the next Sabbath he rose to speak and was immediately challenged. "You are an imposter and heretic," Sosthenes charged. "The rulers of this synagogue find that your teachings are perversions against the Law and your very presence is offensive. You will not speak again in this holy place."

Still standing, Paul said: "You, my own people, hear not. Henceforth I will go to the gentiles with a clean conscience."

Outside, a score of Paul's followers huddled around him, fastening their cloaks against a cold autumn rain. Anticipating such a break, Paul had arranged with Prisca that they could meet in her courtyard, and he so announced.

"Why go so far?" someone called out to Paul. It was Titius Justus, a gruff old soldier who had bridged the Rhine for Germanicus and now built mansions for the wealthy in Corinth. Justus had been one of Paul's first converts in Corinth. "My house is right here, next door to the synagogue," Justus said. "Come. There is room for everyone. Let us go in from the rain and cold."

Ten days later, as Paul worked at his bench inside the tentmaking shop, a servant came to say that two strangers awaited him in the courtyard. Could it be Silas and Timothy? Racing downstairs, Paul greeted his companions of the road. After a warm clasp of hands Paul asked: "Brothers, what is the news from Macedon? Do our churches survive?"

"Not only do they survive, they prosper," Silas said. "All send their greetings to you."

"I would hear your report," Paul said.

Prisca interrupted. "Not until they are fed," she said, observing that both were thin and haggard from the journey.

As the four sat at Prisca's common table, Silas and Timothy fell upon their steaming bowls of lamb and barley soup, warm bread, and goat's milk. Sated, Timothy wiped his face with his sleeve and began his report. "First, in Thessalonica we had eighty members when the brothers Nabal and Eli forced you to leave. We now have one hundred and forty — all gentiles. Second, persecutions continue, not by Jews but by pagan worshipers of Dionysus and Cabiri. Third, the congregation asked me to present two questions for answers and guidance. When will Jesus return to earth? Will those who die in the next days, before Jesus returns, be overlooked when he opens the gates to the heavenly kingdom? Fourth, two issues of legitimacy. A small faction questions the apostolic authority of Jason and his deacons, and a group of seven new members doubt the authority of the unknown man Paul. To be blunt, they suspect that you are an itinerant sorcerer moving from city to city seeking money."

To Paul the last item was a stinging blow. He was deeply offended that any Christian would suggest that he, who had endured beatings and hardship and prison, who had made a point of earning his own bread, was trying to profit from his teachings. It was an unfair accusation, but he must answer it. He asked Timothy, "In what way are Christians being persecuted?"

"They are mocked and scorned on the street and at their workplaces," Timothy replied. "Some are tempted by prostitutes of heathen cults."

Paul shrugged. "That is as nothing compared with the persecutions the

Sanhedrin ordered against the Way in the early days. I know. I was chief among the persecutors then." He turned to Silas. "What would you add to Timothy's summary?"

"Only this: There are problems, yes, but the successes are far greater. The church in Thessalonica is thriving far beyond my expectations — and possibly yours. We can be proud of what Jason and his fellow workers are achieving, and of how much we accomplished in so short a time. After Antioch, Thessalonica is our most promising venture into the pagan world."

"Of that we can be proud," Paul replied. "I love my brothers and sisters there as a father loves his children, and I do long to see them again. However, as Rome's ruling politarchs bar me from returning to Thessalonica, I will put my counsel in writing. By writing to our brothers and sisters there, we will answer their questions, assure them in the faith, and guide them for the future. Words spoken may disappear into the air; words written abide."

"Of course!" Silas interrupted. "As Judas Barsabbas and I read the letter from James to the churches in Antioch —"

"I do not imitate James," Paul said with a scornful glance. "I write to the church in Thessalonica because Rome will not let me go there." He turned to Timothy. "With your report as a basis, draft a comprehensive letter. Be not bound by the Hebrew form of letter, or the Greek or Roman form. We will create our own form. The letter is to come not from me alone, but from the three of us." He turned to Silas. "As we are writing to gentiles, Silas, we should use your gentile name rather than your Hebrew name. Thus we begin: 'Paul and Silvanus and Timothy to the church of Thessalonica: Grace and peace to you from God our Father and the Lord Jesus Christ.

"'We give thanks to God always concerning you all, making mention of you at our prayers, remembering without ceasing your work of faith and labor of love, and steadfastness of hope in our Lord Jesus Christ. For we know, beloved brothers and sisters, that not we but the Lord God has chosen you . . .'"

Paul paused so that Timothy could catch up. "That is the tone and feeling I want in this letter — closeness, concern, reassurance. You have heard me speak often enough, Timothy. Follow my manner of expression. Use my words and phrases and concepts.

"After the address and thanksgiving, make these points and in this order:

Compliment them, handsomely, on how they set an example for all churches in Macedonia and Achaia. Remind them of what we endured to take the good news to them. Assert my authority, as one given the message I teach not by any man but by Jesus Christ himself. Woe to any who call us charlatans; they are tools of Satan. Then, one by one, reply to the questions you heard and the concerns you observed. In particular, deny, vigorously, any accusation that we were greedy, or profited from them in any way. Emphasize that Silvanus and I — in addition to teaching every morning — worked afternoons and into the night to earn our bread and burden none."

He paced in silence for a few moments. "As to when Jesus will return to earth, that is in God's hands, but surely it will be soon. Assure them that when Jesus does return, the dead will not be forgotten, but those who died in Christ will rise before those who live in Christ. In the penultimate paragraphs, use imperative sentences to instruct on ethics and church life. Close with a blessing and my command that the letter is to be read to all the brothers and sisters in Thessalonica."

Again Paul waited until Timothy finished writing. "When you have completed your best draft, Timothy, give it to Silvanus for his comments and suggestions. When you both can say, 'This is the best we can write,' bring it to me."

For all of the next day Timothy struggled at his desk, drafting, discarding, facing the blank page in despair. He had the opening; Paul had dictated that. But what should come next? Finally, at twilight, the first acceptable words flowed from his pen. "And so you became an inspiration to all believers in Macedonia and Achaia, for the word of the Lord rang out from you . . ."

Thus encouraged, Timothy kept writing through the night, shaping ideas into words and sentences, heeding the creative subconscious that came and went like a guiding hand. The lamp burned low. He found another. In the stillness the only sound was his pen, faintly brushing papyrus. At last it was done. He read it aloud, from Paul's beginning through the compliments and exposition and exhortations to the closing grace. He was sure he had done well.

Early the next morning he found Silvanus and showed him the draft. "First, read it aloud, Timothy. This letter is for the ear more than the eye." Through the afternoon the two worked together, correcting, excising, clarifying, testing it aloud. Finally they were satisfied and took the new draft to Paul.

"Is this your very best?" Paul asked.

"It is," they answered, almost in unison.

"Then I shall consider it," Paul said. Reading the first words in his room, he began to feel a warm glow, an uplift of spirit. It was an excellent draft: compassionate, logical, clear, and comprehensive. It flowed. It moved. It flattered. It complimented. It sympathized. It instructed. It was sure to appeal to the faithful in Thessalonica. He was delighted that Timothy had so accurately transformed his oratorical best into written word. "The boy has a gift for writing!" he said happily.

Yet Paul could not resist making changes. To embellish his feeling for the people of Thessalonica, he added, at the end of one fulsome paragraph, "You are my pride and joy." To validate his conviction at another point he inserted: "God is my witness." And for the peroration: "May the God of peace himself sanctify you, make you perfect and holy; and may your spirit and soul and body be made pure for the coming of our Lord Jesus Christ. It is he who calls you. He is faithful, and he will come."

Manuscript in hand, Paul went down the stairs and found Silvanus and Timothy waiting by the warm hearth in the common room. "Well done, Timothy. Well done, Silvanus. These are the words of authority the Thessalonians need to hear. Incorporate my additions and engross three copies of the letter — two to go with you, one to remain here." He pointed out the window. "Winter rains are sure to come, so ask Prisca to enclose each letter in tent felt and leather to keep it dry."

"I will leave tomorrow at first light," Timothy said.

Spring arrived early in Corinth. Alongside the haul-across, hammers pounded against iron, ringing in dissonant chorus as fitters readied their ships for the seasonal winds that would bear them to Brindisium and Syracuse and Ephesus and beyond. In the markets food sellers hawked fresh onions and quarters of pink-fleshed spring lamb. Women cried happily to each other as they met by the swift-flowing river to pound winter soot from their robes. The benevolent sun and inviting azure sky brought Paul and his fellow bench workers out of the dark workroom and up to the rooftop.

One day Paul and Silvanus were working side by side when Silvanus casually turned to Paul and said: "I would ask a personal question."

"I will answer," Paul said. "I have nothing to hide."

"In Philippi, were you aware that Lydia lusted for you?"

"How could I not be aware?" Paul said. "She was discreet, but intent. And I was tempted, for I lusted for her. Had you and I not been jailed, I might have given in to sin."

"What do you advise vigorous young deacons about priapism?" Silas asked.

"To discipline themselves," Paul said. "We teach, so we are figures of authority; as leaders, we attract some women. It is a burden we bear. So I instruct our young men: Commit your total energies to ministering. Overcome temptation. Pray that God will remove this thorn from your flesh. As I do."

"Has God granted you that prayer?" Silas asked.

"Not yet. But I keep praying that he will."

Timothy returned to report that Thessalonians had been comforted and instructed by Paul's letter and that he had appointed Aristarchus, a young and high-born scholar, to work with Jason and the elders for two months, then report to Corinth on progress.

"You proved to be a good emissary," Paul said. "Now to the task here. Take over the training of deacons and aspiring ministers. Attend, in particular, to Stephanas. He and his family were among my first converts here, and I believe Stephanas has the ability not only to become chief minister of the church in Corinth, but also to oversee the churches I envision throughout Achaia. Assist Silvanus in expanding the satellite churches he has already founded in Lechaion and Cenchreae. Both are growing. There is much to be done, Timothy; much that rests on you."

Over the winter the church in Corinth had grown far beyond Paul's most optimistic expectations. Silvanus had baptized so many new members that Justus' house, even though large, could not contain everyone. A new church was necessary, a building large enough to embrace all members at one and the same time. Paul, moreover, had known since Antioch that a common enterprise of such magnitude would bond a congregation and at the same time give visual certification that Christianity would endure.

Justus took the first step by donating a large open lot behind his house. The location was perfect, fronting on a broad new street, but the courtyard would be private. Justus had constructed a wall, high as a man's head, to screen the new church from the synagogue next door. To comply with Roman property law, Silvanus commissioned Quartus, the church lawyer, to survey the property and write a deed of gift.

In two weeks Crispus, Silvanus, and Justus collected and banked enough money with Erastus, the city treasurer and a new convert, to start the project. Spurred by the enthusiasm of the congregation, Paul and Silvanus began making sketches for the masons and carpenters. Stone walls, some as thick as nine feet, would rise to a series of arches patterned after Roman viaducts. The nave of the new church, long and unobstructed, would accommodate at least five hundred worshipers. A great wooden cross would hang above the altar. At Prisca's insistence, the screen for women had been eliminated; families would sit together. Behind the reredos would be a small library and a chamber for their chief minister. "We will build an edifice greater than my church in Antioch," Paul confided to Silvanus.

A fortnight later, Paul strode from Justus' house one fair summer morning to take part with elders and masons in laying the cornerstone of the new church. Volunteers had dug trenches for the new foundation and carted chiseled blocks of limestone to the site. It was a day for beginnings, a day to be treasured, and a festive spirit was in the air.

When the master mason signaled that he was ready, Paul stepped up to the platform and placed his left hand on a square-cut stone inscribed in Greek, CORINTH CHURCH OF CHRIST. All bowed their heads in silence as Paul lifted his right hand and began to speak. "O Lord God, heavenly Father, from whom all good things come, pour your blessings on this church and on all who enter here. May it comfort. May it shelter. May it teach. May it offer hope. May it inspire. May it grow and prosper. May it stand always as a proud symbol of our faith in Jesus Christ. Grant us grace, O Lord, this day and all our days to come. Amen."

With levers and skids the masons moved the cornerstone into precise position and squared it to a plumb line. Handed a trowel by the master mason, Paul touched it to the cement. "I dedicate this church to the Lord Jesus Christ."

After a feast of celebration, members returned to their work and homes. Paul was on the site, reviewing the sketches with the master mason, when he heard a loud voice calling his name. There, climbing on a ladder from the synagogue side of the wall, was Sosthenes, shaking his fist and shouting, "Stop! Your building will desecrate this synagogue."

Suppressing his wrath, Paul said evenly: "I, Paul, am second to none in my reverence for every synagogue. As I respect your house of God, so also do I expect you to respect my house of God." He turned away and walked inside.

At noon the next day, a sweating, worried Justus came to the Paul at the tentmaker's shop. "Sosthenes is trying to stop our building," he told Paul. "He filed a protest with the tribunal this morning. Quartus ran to tell me."

"What does Sosthenes protest?" Paul asked. "Our church does not infringe on synagogue property."

Justus read Sosthenes' accusation from a document: "If this building is allowed, the shadow of this apostate sect will fall on the holy ground of my synagogue, and thereby pollute the chosen earth of God. As Roman law gives Hebrews the freedom to worship, so also does it protect our sacred place of worship from any pagan act of contamination."

"The charge is false!" Paul said. "Let us go now to the court and refute it."

"Not yet," Justus said. "Quartus advises that other cases awaited the new proconsul, who arrived from Rome only last week, so it may be a month before he can judge this dispute." Justus hesitated. "Quartus proposes that we suspend construction until this dispute is resolved."

"Absolutely not!" Paul's face reddened with anger. "The work is to go on, and with all possible haste."

Justus raised his hands in assent. "I understand your orders. I am an old soldier. The work on the church will continue." Again he hesitated. "Quartus also recommends that you not speak in public until the case is settled. He believes we should not further antagonize the leaders of the synagogue, many of whom have friends at court."

Paul turned on Justus in fury. "I will not be silenced!"

Chastened, Justus left, and Paul returned to his bench, seized his hammer, and pounded the leather on the wooden form. Once his fury cooled, he began to wonder if he had acted prudently. He had never been one to doubt a decision once he made it, but this one could be different. A half-built church would be a monument to failure — failure on his part, failure of the Christian mission in Corinth. And he could very well lose before this new Roman proconsul; indeed, he had never won in a Roman court. In Pisidian Antioch, Iconium, Thessalonica, Beroea, it had been the same. A faction of conservative Jews would provoke trouble, blame him as the malefactor, and persuade the local magistrate that he was the guilty one. Why was he always punished for a disturbance fomented by others? Was it to happen again, here in Corinth, where he had worked in peace for a year?

Suddenly he stopped, realizing there was yet another problem. On his first day in Corinth he had promised Prisca he would not disturb the peace of the city. She and Aquila had taken him into their house as though he were family, sheltered him, comforted him, encouraged him, filled a void in his personal life. He must do nothing to hurt them or their thriving business, so he decided to compromise: He would not speak in public until after the trial, but he would not stop the masons. The building must proceed.

That very night, as Paul slept, the Lord spoke to him in a vision. Out of the darkness came a light pure and dazzling, quickly followed by a clear and compelling voice: "Do not fear, but speak; and do not keep silence, because I am with you. I have far more people in this city than you know, so many that no one will set on you, or oppress you, or harm you."

Paul rose from his bed aglow. "Thy will be done," he said aloud. He had heard the voice of God, the same clear and commanding voice he had heard in the Temple in Jerusalem, in Galatia, in Troas, the voice to be obeyed. And obey he would.

Autumn had arrived by the time the court clerk brought the case of *Sosthenes versus the Church of Christ* before the proconsul of Achaia, Lucius Annaeus Novatus — also known as Gallio. Summoned before the high tribunal, Paul stood before the court in silence, on the stone of the accused. He had never before been in this impressive forum, paved and roofed in blue and white marble, with marble benches to the rear and along the sides. And he had never before seen Gallio.

The proconsul Gallio had the broad brow, wide nose, upturned nostrils, and heavy jowls common to one strain of Roman elite. His manner was reserved, his mien stern and appropriately judicious. Paul had learned that Gallio had been born to the equestrian family of the rhetorician Lucius Annaeus Seneca the elder, and adopted by the powerful senator and orator Junius Gallio. By blood, this proconsul was the older brother of Lucius Annaeus Seneca the younger, philosopher, tutor to royal heirs, and seducer of princesses. As a youth, the younger Seneca had briefly attended the Stoa in Tarsus with Paul. Unsure of whether the connection might help or hurt his case, Paul mentioned it to no one. Now, looking up toward the high judgment seat of the tribunal, he saw no resemblance between the fellow student he remembered and this graying proconsul.

Gallio gestured toward the accusers' bench, and Sosthenes rose to speak. "We accuse this man Paul of persuading people to worship God in a way that breaks the Law."

It was the same charge that Paul had faced in too many other cities; it was dangerous, for an exacting judge could twist the charge into treason. Instinctively he opened his mouth to respond, but Gallio instantly silenced him with a commanding look.

"Listen, you Jews," Gallio said, his voice a growl of drollery and scorn. "If there were some wrongdoing or crime, I would hear your complaint. But as it is a question about a word, and names, and about laws invented by you Jews, see to it yourselves. I will not judge these things. I dismiss this charge. Go."

Paul was astonished. The trial was over. Without speaking a word in his defense, he had won. As he walked down the broad steps from the open court, he saw that his followers were in the street celebrating the verdict. When Sosthenes came down the steps, the Christians seized him and began to beat him with fists and sticks — in full view of the proconsul. Gallio paused for a moment to watch the beating, shrugged, and turned to the next case.

As Sosthenes cried out in pain, Paul was torn. He, too, was angry, incensed at the insults from Sosthenes, and offended that he had been brought to stand before Gallio like a common thief. Jesus had said, "Turn the other cheek," but Paul had never been able to bring himself to do that. Conflicted, he turned to Silvanus. "Go and rescue Sosthenes from the beating. Remind our followers that Christians are men of peace."

In his room that night Paul sat at his desk, the flame of a lamp bright beside him, a new pen in hand, and a fresh page of his journal before him. He intended to record his victory in court. Yet he knew it was a victory not just for him and the church of Corinth, but for the cause of Jesus Christ as well. In times past and in other places, Rome had granted victory to the old order of Jews who vowed to stop his mission. Here, with the fair-minded Gallio, Rome left it for the people to choose between the old order and the new salvation that Paul taught. He must take advantage of Gallio's term as proconsul to establish the church so firmly that the next proconsul, and the next, would see Christians for what they were: a community for justice and civility; a force for peace and good order. He must not rest.

In the weeks that passed after Gallio's brusque deliverance of the Christian movement in Corinth, Paul redoubled his efforts.

Mornings he spoke — in the churchhouse, in the great agora of the city, in the meat market, in the fish market, at the docks in nearby Lechaion. At midday he hurried to Justus' house to inspire the masons and carpenters building his church, and to lecture the aspiring ministers and deacons in Timothy's classes. At Prisca's suggestion he opened a new school for women deacons and asked her to direct it. He went among the poor, offering them hope, and persuading the wealthy to give them work and bread and shelter. Afternoons and evenings he insisted on working at his tentmaker's bench to earn his keep. At night he wrote out instructions for the satellite churches that Silvanus founded in Megalopolis and Patrae and other towns that lay south of Corinth in the Peloponnesus. He ate little, and slept less.

"Why such zeal?" Prisca asked Paul one night as she and Aquila sat with Silvanus and Timothy at her common table.

"Don't you see?" he said. "For the first time the Christian movement can go forward in a city where none openly attack us — not Rome, not the Jews, not some cult driving itself into a frenzy over a Greek myth. In Corinth we are free, by order of the proconsul himself. How many times have I stood in the public squares of other cities and openly proclaimed the good news of Jesus Christ, only to have a Roman soldier point his spear and command, 'Desist! You disturb the peace!' Not here. Corinth is open to us. All Achaia is open to us. Gallio granted us freedom, and freedom gives us a chance to bring many to Christ. We must use it!"

Cold winds out of the north stripped the last leaves from the trees of Corinth. Winter was at hand. For Paul, this was a day long awaited: The church roof would be closed against the rains certain to come. From this time on, all Christians of Corinth could assemble in the church, even though carpenters had not yet completed the platform, benches, and altar. They had won the race against the weather.

To do so, Silvanus had organized teams of volunteer shipfitters to cover the stone arches of the church with thick cedar planks, splicing them with oak tenons much as they planked their ships. New teams of roofers then climbed up to lay squares of split shale that would protect the church from rain and storm for generations to come.

Paul rose early, for it was his welcome task to preside over the ceremony of cementing the last roof square that would mark the completion of outside work on the new building. This was a day to give thanks for a job well done, and to exhort all not to rest, ever. Walking briskly, he could smell the roofers' boiling pitch well before he reached the site. The chief mason, waiting for Paul, proudly handed him a trowel and asked him to offer a prayer of dedication.

"O Lord God, you have blessed all who built this magnificent tribute to your grace, and we thank you for the skill of their hands and the purpose in their hearts. Through these good and devoted men and women, you have created our church. Sustain us in our work, as you have sustained them in theirs. Keep this as a house of holiness, as you keep us in faith to the Lord Jesus Christ. Amen."

From that ceremony Paul looked in on a new class preparing for baptism, then returned to the workrooms of Prisca and Aquila, where he pounded leather until late afternoon. Silvanus came by to escort him to Cenchreae for an evensong service, to begin at dusk. It would be his first and long-delayed visit to the Cenchreae assembly. The thirty-three followers, all baptized by Silvanus, met in a tent set up the courtyard of Dexippus, a shipowner. Silvanus had trained Olen, a tutor in mathematics, to serve as deacon and to lead their worship services.

It was a magnificent afternoon as Paul and Silvanus set out on the five-mile walk. The winter sky was deep blue and cloudless, the breeze lively out the west, the sun warm on their cloaks. The tent-church of Cenchreae was full when they arrived, and all joined in the singing of hymns and reading of Psalms. The voices were clear and fervent, well accompanied by the lyre of an Athenian. The service of song required no sermon, but at the end Paul raised his right hand in blessing. "And may the peace of God that passes all understanding be with you now and evermore."

After the benediction, brothers and sisters lined up to speak to Paul, shake his hand, ask him a question, or plead with him to heal a sick child. It was almost dark when he reached the end of the line of followers. Silvanus had gone into Dexippus' house. Paul was alone — except for one figure who came out of the shadows at the rear of the tent and walked slowly toward him. It was a woman, covered in white linen, with a veil leaving visible only a pair of blue eyes. As she came closer, Paul caught the scent of jasmine.

Gracefully, delicately, she took a slim right hand and removed her veil. Paul started, so astonished that he could only whisper:

"Phoebe."

XXVIII

REMEMBERING

"Yes, Paulos, it is I, Phoebe, the girl who loved you when we were young, the woman who loves you still."

"Phoebe! Phoebe!" Paul kept repeating her name in wonder, his dark eyes wide and disbelieving. "I never expected to see you again, not in all my lifetime."

Phoebe smiled. "O but I knew. Never have I doubted that somewhere, sometime, we would meet again. The Three Fates were certain to honor a love such as ours."

"But . . . but," he stammered. "Why are you in Cenchreae?"

"I live here," she said simply. "This is my home. And this, Paulos, is my church. Silvanus and Olen are teaching me to become a deacon."

Paul looked at her, seeing not a woman of forty, with lines around her blue eyes and the full figure of middle age, but the svelte and passionate girl he had last set eyes on almost twenty-five years earlier in the flower garden of her father, Epicrates, Tiberius' chief magistrate in Tarsus. And Phoebe looked at Paul and saw not a bearded and balding man of forty-two, slightly stooped and bowed of leg, but the lithe youth of strong body, dark eyes, and black curls whom she had first glimpsed one day when he came to her house with her brother, Alcmaeon.

"When did you become a Christian?" Paul asked.

"When you did," she replied, reaching out to take his hand. "Do you not remember that I told you, 'Thy people shall be my people, and thy God my God?'"

"But how did you know that I became a Christian?"

"From Alcmaeon, who learned it from Pan and wrote me a letter. My brother is in Rome, a scribe at the court of Claudius, and aspires to be appointed a provincial magistrate."

Still shaking his head in surprise and delight, Paul asked, "How long have you lived in Cenchreae?"

"Many years," she said. "After the birth of my son, I . . ."

"A son? You have a son?"

She reached out to take both his hands. "*We* have a son, Paulos."

At that moment Silvanus walked into the tent. "Time to go, Paul."

Quickly she released his hands and whispered, "I have told him nothing of us."

"Go ahead," Paul said to Silvanus. "I shall stay for a time. Phoebe and I became friends in Tarsus long ago. We have much to discuss."

Silvanus looked at Phoebe, saw the enchantment in her eyes, looked at Paul, saw the gladness in his face, but said nothing.

As soon as Silvanus left, Paul asked, in a low voice: "Did you say we have a son?"

"Yes, yes," Phoebe replied cheerfully. "How could you not know? I told you, on our last hour in my father's garden in Tarsus, that I was with child, and I would bear a son, your son."

"Where is he, Phoebe? May I see him?"

"He is in Spain, or perhaps Britain. He is a soldier, Paul, a centurion in the Ninth *Hispana* Legion."

"You sent him away to be a soldier?" Paul asked.

"No, it was not my wish." She brushed a tear from her eye with a sleeve and took his arm. "Come. Let us walk to my little house. It is nearby."

After she regained her composure, she continued: "Paulos, my father summoned me about a month after you left for Jerusalem. I had thought I would be bold, but I was very frightened. He told me that he had learned of my condition from a servant, and asked if it was true. I confessed, and told him you were the father. I could see the hurt in his eyes, but he did not strike me. He told me that I must keep silent, for any public knowledge that his daughter was with child by a Jew would imperil his position as chief magistrate. So he sent me away to bear your child."

"Where?"

"To Pandateria, a small island off the western coast of Italy." Ruefully shaking her head, she added, "I was not the only high-born woman there to give birth in secret."

"And did you rear the boy there?" Paul asked.

"Until he was three. Then, against my will, a cousin to my father, General Lucretius Maximus Tercerius, sent soldiers to take our child from me. He was adopted and given the name Marcus Pleminius Tercerius."

"And you never saw him again?" Paul asked.

"Not once," she said sadly. "I tried. O I tried. First I went to the Tercerius mansion in Rome, but I was turned away by a servant. Later, the general sent a messenger to tell me that the boy would be tutored with his own sons, and at sixteen placed in the army. He warned that I must not try to find him or see him. But I did try. I found his training camp, but soldiers barred me at the gate. I journeyed to Spain. But it was a hopeless quest. So I returned here."

Walking slowly, they reached her house, and she led him into her small garden. Her maidservant brought bread, fruit, and wine. "This is my own," she said, looking about with pride, "'. . . a little space of land, with a garden, near the house a spring of living water, and a small wood besides . . .' Do you still like Horace, Paulos?"

Paul smiled. "Once, his *sermones* and *epistulae* I knew well, but now I recite scripture," he said. "Tell me, Phoebe, what name did you give our son?"

"Paulos, of course," she said. "'My darling little Paulos,' I would sing to him as he lay close to my breast."

"Did you come here from Rome?" Paul asked.

"No," she said, "My father granted me an estate, enough for me to live in comfort so long as I did not return to Tarsus. From Pandateria I moved to Naples, then to Rome, then Syracuse, then Corinth, then Cenchreae. I found my home in this busy but beautiful small city. Here I read, marvel at the sun as it rises from the ever-changing great sea to the east, and grow the flowers that make me young again." After a silence, she added: "But I am lonely, Paulos."

Impulsively he reached out with both arms to her. After a moment of hesitation she came to him, and they embraced, each remembering a carefree youth, each longing for a past that could never be recaptured. She sighed and whispered softly in his ear, "O how long have I waited for this moment, Paulos." Suddenly she leaned back and asked: "And did you think of me?"

"Just every day," he said.

Phoebe laughed. "I know your words are to beguile me, but I treasure them nevertheless." Taking his hand, she led him to the table the maidservant had prepared. "Now, come and sit beside me, Paulos. We will sup together, as you tell me all that has taken place in your life since you left me in Tarsus."

"On that last day in your father's garden," he said slowly, "I could not comprehend that you were with child. At eighteen I knew little of these things. I did not want to leave you, or any other part of my good life in Tarsus. My mother ruled me then. So I sailed away, believing I would return in a year." He sipped his wine, dreading what he must say next.

"It happened, Phoebe, that my leaving destroyed my family. My father disowned me, and turned his profitable business over to a malevolent worker, an infidel who robbed my father and bribed a house servant to poison my mother. For days I wept, blaming myself for her death. I lost everything.

"Anger and sorrow turned me into a zealot for the Law. I put women and children in prison. I plotted the execution of a classmate. I set out for Damascus to prosecute other followers of Jesus, and it was on that road that Jesus revealed himself to me, rebuked me for persecuting his people, and commanded me to take his message to the world."

For a long time they sat in silence. At last Phoebe murmured, "Such fools we are, Paulos, to think that we can direct our lives, when it is destiny that governs all."

"Yes," Paul said slowly. "I have come to believe that when I was in my mother's womb, the Lord God determined that I would become as I am."

Their talk turned to the happy times of youth. "Do you remember," she asked brightly, "when you won the laurel in the long stadium races? I was there to watch you." And so the two talked on and on, of footraces and tutors and classmates, of games and trysts, of poets and sunsets on the snowcapped Taurus Mountains. The crescent moon descended, and the night brought them close once more.

When Paul returned to Corinth the next morning, he went first to the churchhouse of Justus. There awaiting him were Silvanus, Timothy, and, to his surprise, Aristarchus. He had arrived from Thessalonica the night before to seek Paul's counsel.

"Firstly, and most importantly," Aristarchus said, "the congregation is confused and in fear about the coming of the Lord Jesus. They conclude from your letter that the day of judgment is at hand. Thus, many stopped working, saying, 'Why should we toil when so soon we shall die?' Secondly, the church is split. A faction is challenging the apostolic authority of Jason and the elders."

"On what grounds?" Paul asked.

"They oppose Jason's rules of diet and ethical conduct."

Paul brought his fist down on the table. "Those are not Jason's rules but precepts taken from Jesus' life and teachings," he said bluntly. "Christians should want to live by these high principles. Do you bring other problems, Aristarchus?"

Aristarchus shook his head. "It is the coming of Jesus that is striking such fear that it could split the church. That is why Jason sent me to you."

Paul raised his hands in vexation. "The return of Jesus to earth is to be celebrated, not feared. How can they not see this?" He turned to Timothy. "Write another letter. Tell our followers in Thessalonica to return to their work. Christ will come again, but it will not happen until after this premonitory sign: A man of Satan will appear in a holy place, effect miracles, and claim to be God. Some of the faithful he will delude, but then the Lord God will send his wrath to destroy this enemy. So instruct them to be on guard for the appearance of this antichrist.

"Conclude, Timothy, with a strong exhortation against idleness and disunity. Show your draft to Aristarchus for his suggestions. Then review it, as before, with Silvanus. When all agree you have done your best, bring the letter to me. I will close the letter by writing the peace in my own hand."

At his bench that afternoon Paul could not get Phoebe out of his thoughts. Her love for him was as ardent and generous as ever, and his love for her had been transformed by time and circumstance from the dalliance of youth into mature and respectful devotion. Now the thorn pricked his flesh. For twenty years he had avoided private encounters with widows and other lonely women who, he sensed, looked on him more as man than apostle. Phoebe was different. It was not just that he had known her in the happiest days of youth; their lives after parting had followed a curious similarity. Nomads, both had been. Wanderers: her mission to travel in search of her son; his, to travel in search of souls he could bring to Jesus. Once, long ago, their lives had been joined; now they were joined again. Their meeting was not by chance; it was destiny.

After his third visit to Cenchreae, Paul returned to Corinth the next morning to find Prisca. To her he revealed the full story of youthful love, the birth of a son, and now reunion. "I loved Phoebe as a youth, when love is such an inviting mystery," Paul said. "Now, in the afternoon of life, she still loves me and I love her more than ever. She answers to my spirit, and I believe I answer to hers."

"Then marry her, Paul," Prisca said.

"But how can I be a good husband and at the same time fulfill my mission?" Paul asked.

"Do any of the Twelve have wives?" Prisca asked.

"Peter has a wife," Paul said. "Certainly I have as much right to be married as Peter does."

"If Peter, why not you?" Prisca asked.

"But I am not as Peter," Paul replied. "As apostle to the Jews, he seldom needs to leave his Jerusalem home. As I was commanded to take the gospel to nations afar, I have no home. I must journey on and on."

"Did Jesus command you to deny yourself a wife?" Prisca asked.

"No, Jesus denied no man the right to have a wife," Paul said. "Indeed, Jesus reminded us that God created man and woman to be as one, and affirmed the indissolubility of marriage, saying, 'What God has joined together, let not man put asunder.' Thus Jesus blessed marriage. In fact, his first miracle, turning water into wine, occurred at the celebration after a wedding."

"Does Torah proscribe marriage for rabbis and priests?" Prisca asked.

"Just the opposite," Paul said. "Leaders were expected to marry and father children as an example to all Jews. Halakah says, 'He who has no wife cannot be called a man.' The only constraint against a priest was that he could not marry a divorced woman."

"Then you, too, should set an example for Christians: Marry Phoebe and have more children," Prisca said.

After a long silence, Paul said: "The end of loneliness; the love and devotion of the woman I desire; a child, perhaps a son, at my knee; the comfort of a home: All these things and more Phoebe would bring into my life." He shook his head in despair. "But if I marry, I must choose: Neglect the advance of Christianity, or neglect wife and children." He stood, paced back and forth, and raised his arms in appeal. "There is but one answer: My mission must come first. So it has been since Jesus first came to me on that road to Damascus; so must it be to the end of life."

"Then you must stop going to Cenchreae, Paul. It is wrong for you to practice what you forbid in your teaching."

Paul slumped in a chair. "I know that, Prisca. I must turn away from temptation. I shall give up that which is personal and pleasing and consecrate myself anew."

"Then go to Phoebe and tell her," Prisca said. "Your first obligation is to persuade the woman you love, and the one who loves you, that duty comes before all else."

Phoebe was reading in her garden when Paul arrived that afternoon. One look at his mournful face and she knew why he had come. Paul did not hesitate. "First and foremost," he said, "I love you as I love no other person on earth. Dear Phoebe, you lie closest to my heart and deepest in my soul. So it is and shall ever be. And were it my choice alone, I would come to you now and remain with you forever." He took both her hands. "But it is not for me to decide what I am to do with my life. The Lord Jesus chose me to lead a mission. From the beginning Jesus himself warned me that I would suffer in his cause, and suffer I have. I have been beaten, flogged, imprisoned, tortured, shipwrecked. But never have I suffered as I do now, for I come to say that I must leave Corinth, and leave you. It is the will of God, and I must obey his will."

Tears began to fill Phoebe's blue eyes as Paul spoke. When at last she regained her composure, she spoke in a voice both firm and measured. "Paulos, ours is a love that will never die, but it cannot — and it should not — stand in the way of the noble cause to which you are committed. This brief time we have had together is a precious gift to me. Were it in my power, I would bind you close and keep you by my side for all my days. But I have found the faith that you bring to many. As you believe, so do I. As you bow to destiny, so must I. You say you must journey on, and that I understand. But I hope and I pray that at some hour, on some day, in some glorious season, you will come again to my garden so that we may love again." Together they walked to the gate of the garden, and there they parted.

Striding briskly along the road to Corinth, Paul deliberated on where he should go next. Should he revisit the churches he had established, assay their progress? It had been almost three years since he had been seen in Antioch, and almost as long since he had traveled through Galatia. It was essential that apostles visit their churches often, or followers might weaken in faith and stray from doctrine.

Or should he plant the cross of Christianity in a new city? In Antioch he had concluded that Christianity was an urban movement, so his rule was to go to the center of action, to the political capital, to the place where trade routes crossed, where the harbor was deep, where the marketplace bustled with wares and people. Like those in trade, he was a purveyor, one who sold not bread or a tool to hold in the hand but hope to hold in the soul and belief to lift the spirit. The empire had many such centers, but the most promising was only four days' distant.

Ephesus was the largest and most prosperous Roman city in Asia. Indeed, it was the fourth largest metropolis of the empire. Moreover, the character and diversity of Ephesians — Ionian Greek, Roman veteran, Macedonian, Gaul, Phoenician, Carian, Lelegian, and a large Hebrew settlement — suggested the seaport would be fertile soil for Christianity. With hard work and good fortune, Ephesus could become as influential a Christian community as Corinth or Thessalonica.

By the time he reached Corinth, Paul had made a decision: He would do both. He would sail immediately for Antioch, remain there for a month or so, and then retrace his earlier journeys through Galatia. If he invested two or three weeks with each congregation, he could reach Ephesus in a year.

In the meantime he would send a mission to Ephesus to introduce the idea of Christianity and prepare the way for his coming. Certainly Silvanus was well qualified, but the churches of Achaia were too dependent on him. Timothy? No, he was invaluable as an assistant and instructor of deacons, but he had not yet matured to the point where he could lead a mission to a great city. Who else in Corinth was competent to plant the banner of Christianity in Ephesus? The answer, of course, was Prisca. She knew scripture. She had mastered the message Paul taught. She spoke with authority, and she could bring people together. But she would go nowhere without Aquila, and would the two of them give up their prosperous business for the cause?

Paul proceeded at once to the tentmaking shop, where he found Prisca in the common room. "Did you yield to temptation?" she asked.

"I did not," Paul said.

"Did you tell Phoebe the truth?" she asked.

"I did," Paul said, "and I believe she understands that my mission for Jesus Christ stands preeminent in my life." After a pause he added: "I leave Corinth at once."

"And go where?" Prisca asked.

"Before I answer, Prisca, did you once tell me that at some point you and Aquila would like to return to Ephesus?"

"True," Prisca said.

"That time has come," Paul said. "I now ask that you and Aquila sail at once to Ephesus and establish our movement there."

Prisca flung her hands up in astonishment. "Leave this good house? This pleasant life? This profitable business? Your affair, Paul, has touched your senses."

"No, brought me to my senses," Paul said. "I need your help, Prisca. Give up your easy lives here and take the cross to Ephesus."

Prisca folded her arms and sat back. "And where would you go?"

"First to Antioch and the churches Barnabas and I established there, then through Galatia to visit all my churches, and in one year I would join you in Ephesus."

She rose from the table. "Let me find Aquila," she said, "but I don't believe he will go."

When they returned, Paul repeated his proposal. Aquila scratched the top of his head and turned to Prisca. "Why not go as Paul proposes? It will be another adventure for us."

"But what would we do with our business here?" Prisca asked.

Aquila shrugged. "Why not hand it over to Justus and let him give the profits to the church? We have plenty for ourselves."

That same evening Paul walked to the churchhouse, found Silvanus and Timothy, and told them his plans. "The new church building will be complete in a month," Silvanus said. "Stay until then and consecrate it."

"No," Paul said. "It is you who built this church, Silvanus, and it is you who should consecrate it. Indeed, you must take my place to minister to Corinth and to oversee all churches we have established in Achaia."

"I will do my best," Silvanus replied.

Timothy spoke up: "Take me with you. It has been more than two years since I saw my mother and grandmother."

Paul shook his head. "It is essential that you stay here, Timothy, as first assistant to Silvanus. I will summon you when I reach Ephesus."

"Shall I gather the congregation for your farewell service?" Silvanus asked.

"No, I shall not say farewell to Corinth," Paul replied. "Though I will be away for a time, I shall return, for here I have given heart and soul to our church, and here I belong."

In two days Paul was ready for the new journey. The first ship east was the grain ship *Andromeda*, bound for Caesarea. Paul changed his plan: He would sail to Caesarea, reach Jerusalem in time to celebrate Pentecost, inform Peter and James of the progress of his mission to the gentiles, then walk on to Antioch to begin his campaign to revisit all his churches. But he missed Pentecost; the *Andromeda* was delayed by a storm. Vexed and impatient, Paul bounded ashore in Caesarea, hurried on to Jerusalem, and went immediately to the house of Peter to confer with him and James.

Opening the gate of the courtyard, Paul observed that the walls of the old building were still scabrous and unpainted, and the same broken window shutter still hung askew. An old servant answered the door and said that Peter had gone to Galilee and James to Gaza.

Dismayed that he had wasted weeks in coming to Jerusalem, it suddenly came to Paul that he could, and should, accomplish one purpose. More than once he had thought of it, but duty and circumstance had prevented. Now was the time, now the opportunity: He would find his sister.

Rachel had married a cotton merchant and moved to Jerusalem thirteen years ago, but Paul did not know the husband's name. So he set out for the market of spinners and weavers and began asking each shopkeeper if he knew of a cotton merchant married to a Rachel. He learned nothing and thought his search in vain, until he happened to glance down an alley off Herodian Street and see a small sign with one word, COTTON. The man in the shop was spare, balding, and preoccupied with counting skeins of yarn. "I seek a cotton merchant married to a woman of Tarsus named Rachel," Paul said. "Do you know of such a merchant?"

The man put down his work and looked at Paul with suspicion. "I am such a man," he said. "Why do you seek me?"

"I am Paul, brother to Rachel."

The man shook his head. "She had a brother, but his name was Saul."

"Saul was my birth name. Now I am known as Paul. I am Rachel's brother. May I see her?"

The man hesitated, then called out: "Jonathan, go upstairs and fetch your mother. A visitor awaits." A boy of eleven or so came out from the rear of the shop, ran out the door and up the steps to the upper rooms. As Paul waited, the man picked up a skein of yarn and said: "I am Asher. Be warned that Rachel holds bitter memories of her brother, if that is who you are."

Rachel entered the shop with a measure of poise and authority that instantly reminded him of his mother, but her quick and impulsive gestures were those of their father. She was taller than her husband. Her eyes, large and dark, widened at the instant of recognition. "Saul!"

"Your brother I am," Paul said.

Rachel frowned. "But why have you come now? It has been" — she quickly counted on her fingers — "twenty-five years since you —"

"— refused to work for Father," Paul broke in, "and thereby destroyed the family and caused us to lose everything."

The tense silence that followed was broken by Asher. "Bury the past," he said. "Rachel, the coming of your brother calls for feast and celebration. Tell the servants to prepare meat and bread and wine, and bring it to our rooftop. This is a day for rejoicing."

Rachel said little as they dined under the stars during the warm summer evening, but Jonathan was intrigued. "Tell me of your adventures in far lands," he pleaded. So Paul told the boy stories of great cities and strange customs, of nights in the desert, of sails taut in the wind and storms and shipwrecks.

With the fond eye of a mother, Rachel said, "In two years we hope that he will qualify for the school of Gamaliel. Venerable now, Gamaliel is; but still he teaches." After a moment she added, "Tell me, what happened to you at the school of Gamaliel that caused you to turn against the religion of our forebears?"

"I did not turn against our teachings, Rachel. Indeed, after I learned of the death of our mother, I became a zealot for the Law, appointed by the Sanhedrin to persecute those not observing the Law. I took the road to Damascus to persecute others — and it was on that road that the great truth was revealed to me. The Lord Jesus himself appeared to me on that road and commanded me to stop persecuting his followers and to take his message to the far countries. This I have done. This I shall continue to do."

"But why does the high priest of the Sanhedrin revile your name?" she asked. "More than once a high official named Zadok has come with Temple guards to search this house, believing he would find you here."

"I challenge the old order," Paul said. "I threaten their high offices and fine mansions, their power over lesser men. They are advocates and defenders of the Law, but Jesus brought us to see that faith is greater than the Law. This, in essence, is the message that Jesus gave me to take to the world."

The four were silent for a time. Jonathan had fallen asleep. Asher had listened with interest but said nothing. At last Rachel spoke: "Saul, stay with us for a time. Your adventures beguile our son."

"I cannot, Rachel. Tomorrow at daybreak I leave for Antioch, and Galatia, and beyond, to continue my mission."

XXIX

LOSS

On the Via Maris leading north into Antioch, the summer morning was alive with the shouts and cries of cameleers and carters vying for space on the road. Inside the city walls throngs filled the shops and markets along the Colonnade, jostling, bargaining, counting their coins. Pushing his way through the crowds, Paul stopped by a flowing fountain to look about. The raw energy of Antiochenes was infectious and invigorating. Paul loved this city for its bustle, atmosphere, vitality, self-confidence — all qualities that lifted his spirits.

From the Colonnade, Paul strode briskly to his church on the river. He had envisioned a fine basilica for his followers in this teeming southwest quadrant of Antioch, and it had been accomplished. Then and now he took pride in having built the first Christian church in Antioch; indeed, he had built the first church for Jesus' followers in any city. Now, six years later, his handsome church stood as an imposing tribute to faith.

Upon entering the nave, he stopped to admire his design and the work of the shipfitters and artisans who had crafted the arches, altar, and cross. It was what a church should be, a haven, quiet, restful, the stone walls cool, the oak benches warm and inviting. He had created a perfect place for man and woman to look inward to the soul, to think about the Lord God and his gifts.

At the rear of the church he found the door to the private chamber he had designed for himself. As he stepped inside, a young man rose from the desk, frowned in puzzlement, then exclaimed: "You are Paul! You are our leader, returned from afar."

"And you are?" Paul asked.

"Marius Marcenus, deacon of this church — of your church. I was a young student when you left. Now I serve Titus, our minister here."

"Where is Titus?" Paul asked.

"In the market square or on the docks," Marius replied. "Wait here, and I will bring him."

"We will go together," Paul said, remembering the challenge of exhorting crowds along the waterfront.

Titus, upon seeing Paul, leaped in joy. "A glorious day! Let us go at once to Manaen; he is now our overseer."

Manaen had built his own church on the palace grounds, in the Roman style, modest in size but elegant in architecture. When the three entered Manaen's private chamber, Paul complimented him on his enterprise. "A gift from the governor," Manaen said lightly. "He thought it appropriate that Christians of his household and civic offices have a suitable temple for worship."

"Titus tells me that the movement is going well in Antioch," Paul said.

Manaen turned to his desk and brought out a sheaf of papers. "Here is our census of Christians. My personal numbers are modest. I have added little more than a hundred to the followers I had when you left. But both Lucius and Symeon Niger have almost doubled their congregations. Each has built his own fine new church. In each quadrant we now have a school for children, and in Symeon's we established an academy for aspiring ministers and deacons. We prosper, Paul."

"Have you established satellite Christian communities in nearby towns and villages?" Paul asked.

"Only in the larger cities — Seleucia, Alexandretta, Harim," Manaen said. "In the small villages, collective superstitions have proved impossible to overcome."

"Has Barnabas returned from his mission to Cyprus?"

Manaen's face turned ashen. He looked anxiously at Titus and Marius. "Barnabas is dead," Manaen said. "We thought you knew."

The words struck Paul like a physical blow. Shocked, stunned, dazed, his mind could not encompass the reality. The ministers saw their strong leader sobbing, his face long and contorted in anguish, his head clasped in his hands, his voice ululating, his shoulders shaking with grief. For a long time no one spoke. Manaen summoned a servant, who brought strong wine. Paul sighed heavily, dried his eyes with a sleeve, and sipped from the cup.

"Good Barnabas died in his homeland in the cause of Jesus," Manaen said softly. "He was killed only four months after he left Antioch."

Sobbing once more, Paul said weakly, "How did it happen?"

"As you know," Manaen said, "Barnabas was a favorite at court in Paphos, bringing in new followers every week. One night he was lured into an alley by a man pretending to be lame. It was his nature to trust everyone. In the darkness he was ambushed by a band of thugs hired by an vengeful palace courtier. The villains stabbed Barnabas repeatedly and left him bleeding in the street. John Mark found him, still alive but barely. The proconsul's physician tried to save him, but could not. Sergius Paulus was enraged and ordered his soldiers to torture the thugs until they named the courtier who paid them. Then he executed them all, courtier and thugs."

"Was Barnabas buried a martyr?" Paul asked.

"Yes," Manaen said. "John Mark attended to that. And Sergius Paulus erected a grand and beautiful temple as a memorial to Barnabas."

"Where is John Mark now?" Paul asked.

"In Alexandria," Manaen said. "To console him, his mother sent him there to school for a year."

Paul looked away. He was trying to comprehend the enormity of the loss to the church, and to himself. He thought of their first meeting at Gamaliel's, their schooldays and good times, their different paths to the Way, how Barnabas found him and opened opportunity in Antioch, and their adventures together. Now his only friend, the man like a brother, was dead; never again would he see that freckled face or hear that earnest voice. He had secretly hoped, in coming to Antioch, that they might travel together again, to Asia and beyond, share again their leadership of their joint mission to deliver the gospel to new lands. Now that could never be. From now on he would be alone in his work, forever alone.

Paul lifted his head and turned to the others. "Though he gave his life for Jesus in Cyprus, Barnabas yet lives. Antioch is his greatest and most fitting monument. He was our leader in making Antioch the capital city of Christianity. So long as Christians abide here, so long will we be in this good man's debt."

He rose from his seat. "I will go now to my church," he said. "For a day and a night I will be alone with my grief."

At the insistence of the four ministers of Antioch, Paul invested three weeks with each of their churches. From morning until evening he taught, counseled, instructed in ritual, explicated doctrine, and exhorted congregations and leaders. At Symeon's request, he spent still another week teaching at the new academy. But he was eager to resume his journey, to reach the heart of Galatia before the deep snows and then walk on through Phrygia. He needed a traveling companion, someone strong and sturdy on the road yet articulate on the podium. He wanted a Jew, but none met his requirements. So he chose the yellow-haired Titus.

At first Titus was reluctant. His congregation was devoted and growing, and he was settled in a comfortable house where he continued his studies. But Paul persuaded him that the greater challenge in ministry was to go where pagans were mired in ignorance and superstition, to stir their souls to hope and lift them to faith. On the last day of the month of Augustus, Paul and Titus left Antioch at dawn by the Bridge Gate and turned to the north.

Eight hundred miles later, a weary and exasperated Paul arrived in Ephesus. "That was the worst of all my journeys," Paul said to Aquila and Prisca as he slumped into a chair at their house. "Ten months of opposition and disputation. Ten months, only to find that most of the good people Barnabas and I brought to Christ are lost."

"What do you mean?" Prisca asked. "What happened?"

"Treachery," Paul said. "Betrayal. By Peter and James. That band of evil Judaizers, the same three who struck fear into our gentile converts in Antioch five years ago, traveled from city to city, telling all our followers that they must be circumcised to be Christians. They created doubt and confusion, deliberately; and our local leaders — shallow of conviction, or incompetent, or both — failed to respond effectively. So the churches of Galatia are riven, sundered."

"All of them?" Prisca asked.

"Lystra, Iconium, Pisidian Antioch, the newer churches in northern Galatia, all save Derbe," Paul said.

"But did not Silvanus, on your last journey, read James' letter explicitly exempting gentiles from circumcision?" Aquila asked.

"He did indeed, confirming that the issue had been settled at the high council — by James. Or so I thought. But Asaph, the leader of the three Judaizers and claiming to speak for the mother church in Jerusalem, called the letter a forgery, a trick by me to make it easy for gentiles to become

Christians. He questioned my authority, insisting that because I was not one of the Twelve, I was not a legitimate apostle."

"Who sent them to Galatia?" Prisca asked.

"James," Paul said. "Of that I have no doubt. He sent them to Antioch and he sent them to Galatia. James is double-faced, a Janus of a man, never again to be trusted. And Peter, ever jealous of me, does his bidding."

Titus spoke for the first time. "They tried to kill us in Iconium. Fortunately one of the faithful warned us, and we could defend ourselves. A centurion guarded us as far as Colossae."

Paul ground his teeth. "A curse on James. And his Judaizers."

Prisca spoke up, trying to change the mood. "Let us brighten your day," she said cheerfully. "We can report progress in Ephesus. We have —"

"That I do want to hear," Paul interrupted, "but not yet. First I must try to rescue something from this disaster in Galatia. Though the churches are divided, I shall never surrender them to the perfidy of James' agents. Their leaders and the congregations must know the truth about me and how I received the gospel I brought to them, so I will put it in writing, in words that allow no misunderstanding, in words that reassure the faithful and rebuke the defectors. A strong letter may even bring back some who strayed."

"Do you want first to purify yourself and eat and rest from your journey?" Prisca asked.

"As soon as I am clean I will write. In my own hand."

From Paul, an apostle appointed not by human beings but by Jesus Christ and God the Father, and from all the brothers with me, to the churches of Galatia:

I am astonished that you so quickly turned away from the one who brought you to Christ, and have gone to a different gospel — not that it is truly a gospel. Instead, it is a perversion of the gospel, created by troublemakers who came among you to discredit me and disrupt you. Let God's curse be on them. I repeat what I declared to you in person: If any man preach any other gospel to you except that which you received from me, he is accursed.

I want to make it quite clear to you, brothers and sisters, that the gospel preached by me was given me by no man. It came to me through a revelation of Jesus Christ. You have heard of my past within Judaism, how I excelled above all others in my enthusiasm for the traditions of my ancestors and even persecuted the early Christians and wasted them. But when God called me through his grace and revealed his son to me, I accepted his command to take the good news of Jesus Christ to the gentiles of the world. But I did not seek out those apostles before me until three years later, when I spent fifteen days with Peter and James. In time they saw that the gospel for the gentiles had been entrusted to me, so Peter, James, and John offered their right hands in partnership — they to go to the Jews and I to go to the gentiles.

O foolish Galatians, who bewitched you? After you were given a clear picture of Jesus Christ crucified, right in front of your eyes, who put a spell on you? Before faith came, we were guided by the Law. Now you are all children of God by faith in Christ Jesus. Now there is neither Jew nor gentile, neither slave nor free, neither man nor woman, for you are all one in Christ Jesus. To him neither circumcision nor uncircumcision has any force, but faith working through love.

Did you find the spirit of Christ through the Law, or by the gospel I brought to you? Since you found Jesus through faith, can you be so stupid as to subject yourselves to circumcision? God forbid. I wish those who unsettled you with false doctrine might even go further than circumcision and castrate themselves.

With an angry flourish, Paul handed his draft to Prisca, who took it aside. After reading it, she handed it back. "Do you really want to say this?"

"I will say this and more," Paul said. "I will cite scripture and my experience to prove the Judaizers are wrong and evil. And I will write a conclusion against circumcision in big letters in my own hand. Then I shall put Galatia out of mind, and begin my task here."

The next morning, with the letter complete and dispatched to the Galatians, Paul asked Prisca and Aquila for a report. Much had been accomplished: They had converted forty-seven Ephesians and were holding weekly services in their house until they could complete a large tent to put up next door. For the future they had the promise of a lecture hall as a possible church building. They had found four promising deacons and started their training. They had heard a young Alexandrian named Apollos speak in the synagogue with eloquence and accuracy about Jesus, so they took it upon themselves to instruct him in Paul's message. He had moved on to Corinth, where Silvanus welcomed him as a new teacher; he was now stirring the congregation. And Timothy had arrived from Corinth — with Sosthenes.

"Sosthenes?" Paul said.

"Yes," Prisca said. "After your trial before Gallio he was touched by your intervention to stop those beating him and approached Silvanus, who taught him what it means to be a Christian. He came to Ephesus with Timothy to ask you to forgive him."

"Where is Timothy?" Paul asked.

"At the lecture hall we were offered, judging how we may best use it," Prisca said.

As they walked along, Prisca said: "It belongs to Tyrannus, heir to a mining fortune and one of our early converts. As a boy he was schooled in Athens, and here he thought to duplicate Plato's park and gymnasium of Academus. But no student enrolled, so he offered it to us for a church."

Timothy and Tyrannus met them at the door. After effusive greetings and warm clasping of hands, they inspected Tyrannus' empty academy. Paul saw immediately that it was too small for the church he envisioned for Ephesus, but it would be ideal for another and perhaps more important purpose.

On the road from Galatia he had remembered that in the desert he had learned he, and not the Lord, must judge how best to carry out his mission. Since parting with Barnabas he had tried to do everything himself. Henceforth, he decided, he would preach less; he could better invest his time and energies to training and supervising young ministers and deacons. The churches in Galatia had foundered, in great part, because he and Barnabas had not adequately instructed and developed deacons and elders. In Antioch, by contrast, they had trained apprentices with care and diligence, drilling them in doctrine and scripture, critiquing them as they practiced preaching in the marketplaces, overseeing them with diligence — with the result that the Antioch churches not only succeeded but flourished. In his mind Paul had formed a plan to qualify young ministers in Ephesus and send them out through the region; through subordinates he could reach more people with the gospel than he ever could alone. Moreover, a well-trained minister was the best protection against false doctrine from Judaizers or other outsiders bent on causing trouble.

"This is ideal," he said to Tyrannus, "but not for a churchhouse. Here, with your permission, we will create a *seminarium*, an academy to train ministers, deacons, acolytes, overseers, and all others who advance the faith and serve the church. From this school we will in time send apostles to take the message of Jesus Christ to all Asia."

"Excellent!" Prisca said happily. "When do we begin?"

"First, you and Aquila are to select the best candidates for the first class. Timothy, I ask you to design a curriculum that will include oratory, writing, scripture, the life of Jesus focusing on the crucifixion and resurrection, the nature of faith, hymns, rites, and rituals. Reserve the fourth day of the week for students to present their questions to me. This I learned from Gamaliel; it was his way to find out what we knew and what we did not know. Arrange every student's schedule so that he spends three afternoons weekly going among the people, learning how they live, listening to their woes and fears, discovering their hopes and dreams.

"Set high standards. Challenge them. Test them. Not until they are well prepared in this seminarium will we allow them to go into the marketplace to preach the gospel. Not until we are certain of their skills will we send them out to the cities of Asia."

Clasping Tyrannus by the arm he added: "Plato trained men to serve the state; thanks to you, we will train men to serve God."

XXX

CONCORD

The tent that served Ephesians as their temporary church was filled and overflowing on that splendid September morning. When Paul stepped from the next-door house of Prisca and Aquila, he looked up, pausing to admire the beauty of the cloudless Anatolian sky. The first touch of autumn filled the air, a season he always welcomed after the burning heat of summer. As he walked through the congregation, now a respectable one hundred and twenty Christians, a hush fell over the assembly, a sign of respect and reverence that always pleased him.

Standing on the podium, he observed new faces standing at the rear and sides of the tent. He would not disappoint them. For three hours he spoke with passion about the promise of salvation through Jesus, exhorted all to live in love, charity, and self-discipline, and led them in hymns, prayers, and the sharing of bread and wine. At the conclusion of the service he walked among them, blessing the children and exchanging with mothers and fathers the reassuring words of Jesus: "Peace be unto you."

On this feast day, he shared the bountiful table Aquila and Prisca served to their workers and friends. After a prayer of thanksgiving for their fellowship and good life, Paul, with Aristarchus and Onesimus as his companions, left to preach in the marketplace.

Ephesus was a new city in Paul's time, but it had an ancient history. Fought over often, conquered by Alexander, destroyed by earthquakes, it not only survived but prospered. Caesar Augustus surveyed the natural harbor and fertile plain of the Cayster River and commanded the city to be rebuilt as a trading center. Over time he and Tiberius gave the city an aqueduct, public baths, a gymnasium, a library, a temple to the fertility goddess Diana, and a magnificent theater seating twenty-four thousand spectators. From this theater to the harbor Roman engineers laid out and built a magnificent avenue, the Arkadiane. This wide mall was lined with colonnades sheltering banks, shops, inns, and jewelers catering to the wealthy, of which there were many in Ephesus. For plebeians, at a distance south of the elegant Arkadiane, there was the main agora, a rectangle three hundred by three hundred and sixty feet.

It was to this bustling marketplace that the humble farmer brought his onions, the butcher his bleating lamb, the fisher his catch, the ironworker his hammer and forge, and the baker his cartload of fresh loaves. It was to this agora that Paul came once weekly, sometimes twice, but always with two students from his academy. His purpose was twofold: to deliver Christ's message, and to hear his students preach and counsel them on their performances.

On this day, as on most days, most in the agora moved along, but some stopped to listen, or argue. A priest of the temple to Diana debated Paul, contending that the bountiful harvest was not the work of Paul's god but a gift from his fertility goddess. A housewife with a small boy listened for a time, then questioned Paul. After explaining redemption and salvation, he invited her to attend the next worship service in the tent. "Any person curious about Jesus represents opportunity," he said to Aristarchus and Onesimus. "Conversion, I discovered long ago, comes more easily in company than alone."

When he saw the mark on the horologium in the center of the agora nearing the ninth hour, Paul and his two students hurried to the lecture hall of Tyrannus. Seated at the front of the room as the students bent over their desks, he surveyed his accomplishment and was pleased. In six months he had created a successful institution. At least half of this first class of students would surely qualify as disciples; as he had planned, over time they and their successors would extend the reach of Christianity into new lands and generations yet unborn.

He was proud of them: Prisca, school overseer, surrogate mother of the class, wise counselor, was becoming an excellent speaker. If custom permitted a woman to preach, she would equal any man. Timothy was Paul's amanuensis, master of curriculum, close friend, best of traveling companions, and ever-reliable assistant in all things. Titus of Antioch, courageous but stolid, earnest in his studies. He was dull as a public speaker, but trusted

by everyone. Aristarchus, the well-schooled and high-born son of a poli-
tarch of Thessalonica. Aristarchus could be relied on to carry out a task if
given specific instructions, but lacked initiative. Secundus, also from
Thessalonica, a generous son of wealth, displayed a talent for persuading
others to contribute money, but he was inarticulate before a crowd or even
his classmates. Erastus, once treasurer of the city of Corinth, tried in vain
to grasp the essentials of philosophy; he could administer a large church
and congregation, but his words would never stir souls.

On the left, bent over his slate, sat the oldest of the class, Sosthenes. Before
his father made him a banker, his mother had sent him to be schooled in
Athens and then to a rabbinical academy in Jerusalem. His manner of
speaking was stiff, even pretentious; his gift was writing, which he did with
style and insight. Next to the oldest was the youngest, Onesimus, a volunteer from Colossae. Quick of mind and fluent of speech, he was not only
one of the most promising and engaging of students, but also the most
useful — fetching water from the well every morning, running errands for
Prisca, cleaning slates and rearranging benches at the end of the day. Gaius,
the horse trader from Derbe, was gregarious, loquacious, and a master of
persuasion. If he ever grasped the logic of Christ's message, Gaius could
become a formidable preacher. On the three benches next were the newest
students: Artemas, the broad-shouldered stonecutter from a nearby quarry;
Trophimus, a tall, golden-haired tutor of philosophy from Pergamum;
Tychicus, the stocky winemaker from Hierapolis; and Epaphras, the quiet,
sturdy carpenter from Laodicea. Each showed merit, though none had yet
proved himself on a podium. At the rear sat Sopater, the rustic of Beroea
who had risen to the challenge of urban life and become an eloquent and
confident speaker with a zest for public debate. Sopater, Paul judged, would
be the next to qualify to undertake a mission on his own.

At the end of the day Paul was reading in his private chamber at the
academy when Prisca knocked at his door.

"A delegation from Corinth representing Chloe just arrived and awaits
you," she said. "They seek your guidance on factional differences and doctrinal questions."

Chloe owned a weaving house in Corinth that employed twenty women at looms that produced cotton and woolen cloth sold throughout Achaia. A friend of Prisca, she had brought her household to hear Paul; all chose to be baptized. Chloe was by nature a leader. She possessed a good mind, great confidence in herself, and a strong will. Often she contrived to give women a greater role in church worship and activities. Paul resisted, holding to the Hebrew tradition that God intended man to be superior, and the two engaged in spirited debates on the issue. She lost the arguments but won Paul's respect. If Chloe had dispatched a delegation to him, it was important.

"Bring them in at once," Paul said.

When they entered, Paul immediately recognized the three — Megara and Annia worked as weavers for Chloe, and Iphigenia was the wife of a shipowner.

"Chloe sends you greetings," Iphigenia said. "She also asks that you continue to pray for her and her people, and hopes that you will come soon to the church of Corinth that holds you in such great esteem."

"That I pledge," Paul said. "What news do you bring from Corinth?"

"We need your help," Iphigenia said. "There are problems that only you can solve and questions that only you can answer."

Paul looked at the three, seeing serious faces and tense postures. "Does Silvanus know you are here?"

"Yes!" the three responded almost in unison. "Indeed, he encouraged Chloe to send us," Iphigenia said, and held up a scroll. "He approved our list."

"What is your first concern?" Paul asked.

"Our church is dividing into factions. Some say, 'I belong to Paul.' Others say, 'I belong to Apollos.' And still others say, 'I belong to Peter,' or 'I belong to Christ.'"

Paul frowned and shook his head. "We all belong to Christ Jesus. It was he, not Apollos, not I, who was crucified and who redeems us."

He began to read through their list. "Sisters," he said, "these issues deserve more than an impromptu discussion. Come tomorrow at the third hour. I will conduct a colloquy with the three of you on all points you raise. I will have a scribe present. He will record our colloquy and from it I will put in writing answers to your important questions: a letter that you may take back to Corinth."

As soon as the three Corinthians left, Paul summoned Sosthenes and told him that he was to record his meeting with Chloe's people the next day.

"But I have no experience in writing such a letter," Sosthenes said.

Paul dismissed the objection with a wave of his hand. "I will instruct you. Every good letter opens with the address and greetings. Take this down: 'I, Paul, called by the will of God to be an apostle of Jesus Christ, and Sosthenes, our brother, to the church of God existing in Corinth, to those who have been consecrated in Christ Jesus and called to be God's holy people, with all those in every place calling on the name of our Lord Jesus Christ. Grace to you and peace, from God our Father and the Lord Jesus Christ.'

"The next part of a good letter is the thanksgiving, actually a written prayer. It is our fervent appeal for God's grace, and, by indirection, it is a compliment to the recipients. Thus we say: 'I always give thanks to my God concerning you, for in everything you were enriched by the revelation of our Lord Jesus Christ, who also will confirm you to the end, blameless in the day of our Lord Jesus Christ.'

"Next we come to the body of the letter, the longest and most detailed part by far, and this of course you will write from our discussion tomorrow. Finally there is exhortation, commendation, benediction, and grace. I will write these in my own hand."

Paul stopped and lifted his palms. "You will do well, Sosthenes. Come at the third hour tomorrow. Prisca will be present also. She is wise, and has a sensitive ear and eye for the fitting word."

At the appointed hour, the six gathered in Paul's private chamber — the three Corinthian women sitting respectfully on the bench along one wall, Prisca intent and earnest on a chair near them, and Sosthenes at the writing table. Paul stood in the center.

"Iphigenia," Paul instructed, "from your scroll, read your first concern."

"As I told you yesterday, depending on who performed their baptisms, some follow you, others Apollos, still others Peter —"

Paul interrupted. "This is my answer: As we all belong to Jesus Christ, how can there be divisions? Was Christ divided? We were all baptized in the name of Jesus Christ. Where among you there is jealously and strife and divisions, are you not living by your baser inclinations, rather than what you have learned from God? We are fellow workers of God. According to God's grace given to me, I laid a foundation of the gospel; but another builds on it. Let no one glory in men, whether Paul, or Apollos, or Peter, or the world, or life, or death, or things present, or things to come — all are yours. You are Christ's and Christ is God's."

Paul paced the floor. "No one among you should be puffed up with his or her own importance, and make comparisons one over the other. I do not say these things to shame you, but to warn you as my beloved children. If the Lord wills, I shall come to you shortly; and I will concern myself not with what self-important people say, but whether they have power. For the kingdom of God is not in word but in power. What do you desire? Shall I come to you with a rod, or in love?"

All were silent after the long and discursive answer.

"Iphigenia," Paul said, "what is the next problem?"

"One of our brothers is sleeping with his stepmother," she replied. "And yet he continues to share in our worship."

"Purge him from your midst," Paul said. "Do you not know that a little leaven leavens the entire lump of dough? When we say, 'Christ our Passover is sacrificed for us; so let us keep the feast,' we are not eating the old bread of malice and evil, but the new unleavened bread of sincerity and truth. Never share bread with anyone who is a fornicator, or a covetous one, or an idolater, or a reviler, or a drunkard, or a plunderer."

Iphigenia read further from her scroll. "Some of our members who have complaints against each other are seeking compensation in Roman courts."

"Shame to them," Paul said. "How can the unjustified administer justice to those already justified? Brother against brother judged by unbelievers! Is there not a wise one among you who will render judgment fairly? It is failure to have lawsuits among yourselves. Why not instead be defrauded? Do you know that unjust ones will not inherit the kingdom of God? Do not be led astray — neither fornicators, nor idolaters, nor adulterers, nor abusers, nor homosexuals, nor thieves, nor covetous ones, nor drunkards, nor revilers, nor plunderers shall inherit the kingdom of God."

Annia spoke up. "As a Jew, I am concerned that some gentile members of our church say, 'Jewish laws do not apply to us. We can consort in any way that brings us pleasure.'"

"The body is not for fornication, but for the Lord," Paul replied. "Do you not remember that your bodies are members of the body of Christ? He who fornicates sins against his own body. Your body is a temple of the Holy Spirit, received from God."

Annia continued: "What, then, is the rule for conjugal relations?"

"Let each man have his own wife, and each woman her own husband," Paul replied. "Let the husband give due kindness to his wife, and likewise the wife to her husband. The wife does not have authority over her own body, but the husband. And likewise the husband does not have authority over his own body, but the wife. Do not deprive one another unless by agreement for a time that you be free to fast and pray. And come together again, or Satan may tempt you. But I give you this as permission, not by command. I desire that all men be as I am; but each person has his own gift from God, one this way, one that way."

"How do you advise widows?" Annia asked.

"To the widow, and to the unmarried man, I say that it is good for them if they also remain as I. But if they do not have self-control, let them marry. It is better for them to marry rather than to burn with desire."

"What is your counsel if there is such disagreement between husband and wife that they separate?" Annia asked.

"I enjoin the married — not I but the Lord — not to separate. But if the woman is separated, remain unmarried, or be reconciled to her husband. A husband is not to leave his wife."

Another question from Annia: "If a husband or wife becomes a Christian, and the other does not, should they remain married?"

"This is my ruling, not the Lord's," Paul said. "If any brother has an unbelieving wife, and she consents to live with him, let him not leave her. And a sister who has an unbelieving husband, and he consents to live with her, let her not leave him. For the unbelieving husband has been sanctified by the wife, and the unbelieving wife by the husband. Thus your children are holy."

Paul raised a hand in admonition. "If the unbelieving one separates, let them be separated. The brother or sister is not tied in bondage to the unbeliever. As God has called each, or not called one or the other, so let them walk."

Megara, the youngest of Chloe's people, had waited in silence. Now it was her opportunity. "You say, Paul, that all should remain as you are. Do you propose that virgins in the church should not marry?"

"On this I have no command from the Lord," Paul said. "But I give judgment, as one having received from the Lord the mercy to be faithful. If you are a man and you marry, you do not sin. If the virgin marries, she does not sin. But those who marry bring on to themselves worldly troubles, and I would spare you these. Like a ship in full sail, time moves swiftly now to the day when Jesus returns to earth. So it is good for people to stay as they are, for the world as we know it will soon pass away. The unmarried one cares for the things of the Lord, thinks how to please the Lord; but the married man cares for the things of the world, how to please his wife. The fitting thing is to wait for Jesus without distraction."

After a moment of reflection he added: "If a man strong with passion finds he is behaving indecently toward his betrothed, let him marry. He does not sin by doing so. But he who is firm of heart and holds enough command over his will to keep his virginity, he does right. So that they who marry do well; they who remain virgins do better."

Iphigenia read from the scroll again. "It is the custom of pagans in Corinth to sacrifice meat to their false gods, and their priests sell in the market the parts they do not eat. May Christians eat this meat?"

"We know that an idol is nothing in the world, and that there is no other God but one," Paul said. "He is all things to us and we are all things to him. Food does not commend us to God, so you have freedom to eat. But be careful of how you use that freedom. Rather than eat meat that offends your brother, better you should eat no meat at all."

He stopped his pacing, tilted his head to one side in thought, then to the other. "Eat everything being sold in a meat market, examining nothing because of conscience. For the earth is the Lord's. And if any unbeliever invites you to dine, and you desire to go, eat everything set before you, examining nothing because of conscience."

Prisca raised her hand. "But Paul, your first response to Iphigenia's question is inconsistent with the second."

Paul shrugged. "I know. I will clarify it in the writing. What is next, Iphigenia?"

"Some object to providing house and bread for those who minister to us in the church," she said.

Paul's face reddened with anger. "Am I not an apostle? Am I not free? Have I not seen our Lord Jesus Christ? Are you not my work in the Lord? My defense to those examining me is this: Have we not the right to eat and drink? Have we not the right to have a sister, a wife, as Peter, the other apostles, and Jesus' brothers? Who plants a vineyard and does not eat of its fruit?

If we have sowed spiritual faith in you, may we not reap of your worldly things? In the Temple, those attending the altar partake from the altar. So also the Lord ordained those preaching the gospel to live from the gospel.

"But I have not used this privilege. I offer the gospel without charge to you. I enslaved myself to bring as many as I could to Christ. That I might win Jews, to Jews I became a Jew. To gentiles I became as a gentile, that I might win them to Christ. To the weak I became weak, that I might win the weak. I became all things to all men, so that I might save some."

"Should women cover their heads and faces when worshiping in the church?" Megara continued.

"Know that God is head of Christ, Christ is head of man, and man is head of woman," Paul said. "A man ought not to have his head covered while praying to God, for he is the image of God. But woman is the glory of man; because of this, the woman ought to have authority over her head. Judge among yourselves. Is it fitting for a woman to pray to God uncovered? Or does nature itself not teach you that if a man indeed adorns his hair, it is a dishonor to him? But if a woman should adorn her hair, it is a glory to her. But if anyone thinks this to be contentious, we do not have such a custom in the church of God."

"This question concerns the ritual of the Lord's Supper," Iphigenia said. "Some bring bread and wine into the church for the ceremony, then eat and drink it before others arrive. Is this proper?"

"No," Paul said. "Coming together in this way will do more harm than good. Such an assembly is not the Lord's Supper. Remember that I received from the Lord this ritual that I delivered to you: On the night in which he was betrayed Jesus took bread, and giving thanks he broke it and said, 'Take, eat, this is my body which is broken on behalf of you; this do in remembrance of me.' After supping, he took the cup, saying, 'This cup is the new covenant in my blood; as often as you drink, do this for remembrance of me.'

"Therefore, as often as you may eat this bread and drink this cup, you solemnly proclaim the death of the Lord, until he shall come. Whoever should eat this bread or drink this cup unworthily, he is guilty of profaning the body and blood of the Lord."

Annia, taking her turn, said: "Often you have spoken of spiritual gifts. Do they come to all?"

"The same God is working all things in all. For each one is given some part of the spirit: to one, a word of wisdom, to another, a word of knowledge, and to another, faith, and to another, the gift of healing, and to another, the power of miracles, and to another, prophecy, to another, the gift of prayer, to another, the interpretation of languages.

"Even as the body is one, it is made up of many parts. So also is Christ. For we all were baptized by one spirit into one body, whether Jews or gentiles, whether slaves or free, all were given to be unified in spirit. You are the body of Christ, each a member, each a part of the whole. And God placed some in the church: firstly, apostles; secondly, prophets; thirdly, teachers; then miracle workers, then gifts of healing, help, governing, language. Zealously strive after the better gifts."

"When will women be permitted to speak in church?" Annia asked.

"The custom is for women to be silent in churches," Paul said. "It is not allowed for them to speak, but to be in subjection, as the Law says. If they desire to learn anything, let them question their husbands at home, for it is a shame for a woman to speak in a church."

The four women began shaking their heads vigorously, and Annia interrupted: "But you said earlier that women may prophesy in the church, so long as their heads are covered. And we have women deacons in Achaia who speak. Would you now impose the rule of the synagogue on our church of Christ?"

"Indeed it is my belief that we should observe the Law of Moses on this," Paul said, "but it is not the command of God."

Prisca interrupted: "Again you are inconsistent, Paul. Are you suggesting that your opinion is superior to God's permit?"

Paul did not answer.

After an awkward silence Iphigenia said: "Some wonder about the resurrection. They ask, 'How is a dead person brought back to life?' and 'What sort of body do people have when they return?'"

Paul spoke bluntly: "I taught you the gospel revealed to me. Christ died for our sins. He was buried, and raised the third day, according to the scriptures. You received it and accepted it. Now stand by it. It is the word by which you will be saved if you hold fast to it: otherwise, you believed in vain. In truth, Jesus was raised from the dead. If not, why are we baptized in the name of the risen Christ?"

He looked at Iphigenia, but she sat waiting. Again Prisca intervened. "The second part of the question, Paul. In what body do we return?"

"Foolish ones! The seed you sow is not made alive unless it dies and is buried. You sow a bare grain, of wheat or barley, and God gives it body according as he wills. So also the resurrection of the dead. It is sown a natural body; it is raised a spiritual body. We shall all be changed — in a moment, in a glance of the eye, at the last trumpet. For a trumpet will sound, and the dead will be raised incorruptible, and we shall all be changed."

Iphigenia raised her scroll. "One final question," she said. "When should we collect for the poor of Jerusalem?"

"On the first day of the week, that is, the Lord's day, let each of you put something by, storing up as you have prospered, so that there will be collections when I come to Corinth, possibly to spend the winter with you before I take the money to Jerusalem."

When the colloquy ended, Iphigenia rolled and tied her scroll. She and her sister delegates rose to go. "As you have come as delegates of the church to seek my authority," Paul said, "the three of you should carry this letter to the church of Corinth."

"When will the letter be completed?" Iphigenia asked.

"In two days," Sosthenes said.

Iphigenia looked to her sister delegates; all agreed to wait for the letter.

By carefully following Paul's directions and working through the night, Sosthenes completed the letter by the next morning and handed it to Paul. Taking the draft, Paul set to work, reviewing the letter sentence by sentence. Reading his own blunt words and imperatives, he was gratified that he had responded to the Corinthian women with such candor and energy. Some answers were confusing, yes, but he reminded himself that some questions have no clear answer. The more he read, the better he liked what Sosthenes had done. At the end, however, pondering the whole of the letter, he thought something was missing — some passage that would touch the better nature of all Christians. Taking out a fresh sheet, Paul wrote a hymn to love.

> If I speak with the tongues of men and of angels; but I do not have
> love, I have become as sounding brass or a clanging cymbal. And if
> I have prophecies, and know all mysteries and all knowledge, and

if I have faith so as to move mountains, but do not have love, I am nothing. And if I give out all my goods, and if I deliver my body that I may be burned, but I do not have love, I have profited nothing. Love has patience, is kind. Love is not envious. Love is not vain, is not puffed up; does not behave indecently, does not pursue its own things, is not easily provoked, thinks no evil, does not rejoice over wrong, but rejoices with the truth, quietly covers all things, believes all things, hopes all things, endures all things. Love never fails. If there are prophecies, they will pass away; if tongues, they shall fall silent; if knowledge, it will be forgotten. For we know in part, and we prophecy in part; but when perfection comes, that which is imperfect will end.

When I was a child, I spoke as a child, I thought as a child, I reasoned as a child. But when I became a man, I put away childish things. For now we see as in a dim mirror, but in time face to face. Now I know in part, but then I will fully know, even as I also was fully known. And now faith, hope, and love; these three things remain, but the greatest of these is love.

When Sosthenes made the changes and engrossed the complete letter, Paul summoned Prisca and asked Sosthenes to read it aloud to the two of them. At the end she said: "I commend you both for this epistle, except for your opinion that women should not speak in church."

"Do you suggest I should say what I do not believe?" Paul asked.

"No," Prisca said. "But I suggest you are stubbornly refusing to admit your inconsistencies. Further, by diminishing the women of Corinth you fail to recognize the part we have in bringing men, as well as other women, to Jesus Christ."

Paul made no change, but summoned the three delegates to attend him as he inscribed the conclusion in his own hand:

The churches of Asia greet you. Aquila and Prisca greet you in the Lord, together with the church that meets in their house. The brothers and sisters all greet you. Greet one another with a holy kiss.

This greeting with my hand. Paul.

If anyone does not love the Lord Jesus Christ, let him be anathema.
Our Lord, come.

The grace of the Lord Jesus Christ be with you. My love be with
you all in Jesus Christ. Amen.

After fanning the page until the ink was dry, Paul handed the engrossed
parchment to Iphigenia. "Tell Silvanus that this letter is to be read for six
weeks to all services in all churches of Achaia. May God bless you and keep
you and speed you on your journey."

XXXI

ADVERSITY

All was going well in Ephesus until one summer afternoon when Paul, striding from the market square to the schoolroom, saw Prisca running toward him. Her face was pale, anguished. "I have bad news," she said. "Onesimus is a runaway slave."

"Onesimus a slave? A fugitive slave? Who says he is?"

"He confessed it to me just now," Prisca said. "He saw soldiers arresting a runaway in the marketplace, and feared he might be caught and cause you to be flogged for harboring him."

"Did he say who owns him?"

"Philemon of Colossae," Prisca said. "Onesimus told me that he heard you speak in Colossae, and was inspired to be a Christian. He did not believe this possible as a slave, so he ran away from Philemon's estate, hoping to find you in Ephesus. And of course he did."

Paul shook his head. "A most promising student, and a favorite of all in our academy," he said, "but we must return him to Philemon. I abhor slavery. Neither my father nor mother ever owned a slave. I have never understood how Jews, whose ancestors were in bondage, could make a slave of another human being. But it is the way of life accepted by gentile and Jew, emperor and housewife."

"Onesimus is waiting in your chamber at the academy," Prisca said. "He is pleading for you to let him stay. Timothy is trying to comfort him."

When Paul entered, Onesimus fell on his knees and wept. "Don't send me back. I may be killed for running away."

Paul put his hand on the youth's shoulder. "Rise, Onesimus. You know that Jewish statute and Roman law make it a crime to harbor a fugitive slave, so I have no choice but to return you to your owner. But I know Philemon to be a devoted Christian, kind and just. By returning on your own initiative, you will make it much easier for him to forgive you."

Onesimus' sobs continued. "Do not despair," Paul said. "You have given your life to Christ, and he will see you safely out of this predicament. I will give you a letter to carry to Philemon and appeal to his kindness and sense of justice." He turned to Timothy and thought for a moment. "Write this:

> Paul, a prisoner of Christ Jesus, and Timothy, our brother, to Philemon, our beloved fellow worker, and to the beloved Apphia, and to Archippus, our fellow soldier, and to the church in your house. Grace to you and peace from God our father and the Lord Jesus Christ.
>
> I thank my God, always making mention of you in my prayers, hearing of your love and faith which you have toward the Lord Jesus, and toward all the holy brothers, so that the fellowship of your faith may operate in a full knowledge of every good thing in you for Jesus Christ.
>
> Therefore, though I am bold enough in Christ to command you to do what I shall ask, rather because of love I entreat you, as an old man and prisoner of Jesus Christ, I entreat you concerning my child, Onesimus, whose father I am in Christ for I brought him into the family of Christ. Formerly he was useless to you; but now he is indeed useful to me and to you. I send him back to you. Receive him as if he were me.
>
> I wanted to keep him to help me in my work for the gospel, but I would do nothing without your consent. I knew that your goodness would come not by way of necessity but by way of willingness. Perhaps he was separated from you for an hour so that you might receive him no longer as a slave, but beyond a slave, as a beloved brother in Christ, which he is to me, and can be to you, both as a person and in the Lord.
>
> If you look on me as your partner in Christ, receive Onesimus as me. And if he wronged you in anything, or owes you for anything, put it to my account. I, Paul, write this promise with my hand: I will repay you, even though I could say that you owe me for your coming to Christ. Yes, brother, that I may have your help in the Lord, set my heart at rest.
>
> Trusting in your obedience, I write to you, knowing that you will do even beyond what I ask.

Also, prepare lodging for me, for I hope through your prayers
that I may be granted a visit to you.

The grace of our Lord Jesus Christ be with your spirit. Amen.

After Paul finished, Timothy asked: "Should you also address the church
at Colossae?"

"Not in this personal letter to Philemon," Paul said. "But yes, we should
commend the Colossians on their progress. Will you and Prisca collaborate
on such a letter, and I will sign it."

Prisca raised a hand in caution: "One among us should escort Onesimus
on the four-day journey to Philemon. Otherwise, someone might identify
him as a slave and hold him in chains for a reward."

"True," Paul said. "Have Tychicus go with him. He knows the country."

Across the city in the artisans' quarter, a silversmith named Demetrius
called a street meeting of his fellow craftsmen who fashioned and sold silver
statuettes of Diana, the mother goddess of nature and fertility. Standing on
a box, Demetrius proclaimed: "You must have seen and heard how this man
Paul tells those who listen to him in the marketplace that gods made by
hand are not gods at all. Thus he discredits our craft, costs us money, and
desecrates our sacred goddess. This is our livelihood. Will we let this foreigner take the bread from our children? No! It is time to act!"

"Great is Diana of the Ephesians!" one young silversmith called out, and
the entire assembly took up the cry, milling about and then marching
through the streets, rousing the entire city to fury. Storming through the
marketplace, the mob seized Gaius and Aristarchus as they preached from
the steps and dragged them to the royal theater, where a crowd was already
climbing into seats, expecting to revel in a bloody killing.

For two hours the mob beat the two captives, until suddenly all eyes turned
toward an official in a toga slowly making his way through the mob to the
stage. The Ephesians recognized Deion, the town clerk, one of their own. In
a pose of calm authority, Deion motioned for silence and began to speak.

"Men, Ephesians, what man is there here who does not know that the city
of the Ephesians is keeper of the temple of the great goddess Diana and of
her statue that fell from heaven? As we know this to be true and undeniable,
it is imperative that you be calm and do nothing rash. These men you seized

have neither robbed the temple nor profaned our goddess. If, indeed, Demetrius or any other artisan here has any claim of damages against anyone, he should take his case to the courts or to the proconsul. For we are in danger now that someone may accuse us of causing a riot. There is no justification for this crowding together. Therefore, I dismiss this assembly."

Bruised and scuffed, Aristarchus and Gaius returned to the academy and told Paul all that had happened. When they finished and left to cleanse themselves, Paul summoned Timothy. "Be warned. The proconsul's guard will come for me tomorrow."

Not the next day, but within the hour a palace guard seized Paul and took him before the magistrate. "You are charged with rebellion against Caesar."

"Who makes the charge?" Paul asked.

"Demetrius and the guild of the silversmiths," the magistrate said, pointing to the company of accusers.

"As a Roman citizen, I am entitled to an immediate trial," Paul said.

"Only the proconsul Capito Canuleius may consider cases of rebellion," the magistrate said. "If he finds you guilty, *ius gladii*, he may order you to be executed."

"I ask to appear before the proconsul at once," Paul said.

"He is in the field with his legion," the magistrate replied and motioned to the commander of the proconsul's palace guard, who led Paul across the street to prison.

Timothy arrived, bringing food and water, to find Paul grim and melancholy. "My life is in peril," he said to Timothy, "but out of this will come my deliverance. I will exalt Christ whether it means my life or death. To me, life is Christ of course; yet death would be a positive gain for me. If I live, that means I shall continue my demanding and fruitful labors. If I depart this life, I will be with Christ. Far better that would be for me. I do not know which I prefer. I am hard-pressed between the two: And yet, to stay alive is a more urgent need for mankind. This much I know for certain, that so long as I have life I shall stand by the faith given me by Christ and by all who hold that faith. Whatever time is left to me, I shall live in a manner worthy of the gospel of Christ."

For a long time both sat in silence, until at last Timothy ventured: "There is good news from Philippi. Epaphroditus brought a gift of five hundred denarii from Lydia, Minerva Mindarus, and others, to be used as you wish."

"Their generosity never fails," Paul said. "Write them at once of my gratitude."

"Epaphroditus also reports three problems: internal dissension, attacks by pagans, and subversion by Judaizers. How shall I respond?"

"Tell them in the letter than I am imprisoned, unjustly, but that the message of Christ cannot be deterred. Then address their problems; you know what to say." After a moment Paul continued; "Timothy, I think it wise to lift their spirits by including the hymn I wrote in Corinth."

"You mean the one that says 'every knee shall bow at the name of Jesus'?"

"Yes, let's sing it now."

As they began to sing, the commander of the palace guard sidled to a place outside Paul's cell door to listen.

"What else shall I write in the letter?" Timothy asked when they had finished.

"Tell them that I long to see them, and that if I live and am freed from prison, I will promptly come for a visit. Lest they doubt my word, notify them that I am sending you to prepare for my visit." After pacing in his cell for a time, he said, "Give me your pen and paper. There is still another message I have for them, and I will write it in my own hand."

> The Lord is near. Do not be anxious about anything, but in everything by prayer and by petitions and by thanksgiving, make known your requests to God. And the peace of God which passeth all understanding will keep your hearts and your minds in Jesus Christ. For the rest, brothers and sisters, whatever is true, whatever honorable, whatever right, whatever pure, whatever lovely, whatever of good report, whatever of virtue and deserving of praise, think on these things. And all things you learned and received and heard and saw in me, practice these things, and the God of peace will be with you.

The proconsul of Ephesus had won his high appointment from the Roman Senate by commanding the army that subdued and subjugated the continuously rebellious Illyrians. Yet a young man, smooth-shaven with black curls carefully barbered, Capito Canuleius kept himself and his palace soldiers always trim and hardened by leading regular military exercises into the rugged country to the east. He was a popular governor, in part because the city prospered, in part because he enforced an official tolerance among the diverse races, trades, and interests of the people he governed, and in greatest part because he regularly brought to his magnificent theater exciting contests between man and beast. Capito loved a good show, and even more he loved being at the center of it.

On court days he presided over a ritual. His household and ranks of soldiers assembled on the raised platform of the tribunal and took their arranged places before the curving pillars behind the high judgment seat. To heighten the drama, court clerks and recorders marched in a body to stand in attendance for the arrival of the famed soldier. When all was ready Capito Canuleius entered, tall and erect in his toga trimmed with gold.

On the morning that Paul appeared before the proconsul, the silversmiths led a mob that filled the pavilion. From the jail Paul was brought forward by a guard to stand on the marble stone of the accused.

"Read out the charge!" Capito commanded the clerk.

"Rebellion against Caesar!" the clerk replied.

Capito saw before him a balding and slightly stooped man with a long face, bulging eyes, and bowed legs, dressed in a worn cloak. With a look of vexation he summoned his clerk, who whispered in his ear.

Then Capito turned to the crowd, gestured toward Paul, and laughed. "Look at this bent old man. Does he look like the leader of a rebellion? Where is his army? His soldiers? His horses? His spears? I judge his arm to be too weak to raise a sword." The crowd laughed with him, and after a time Capito raised his hands for silence. "Only a vengeful ass would have made such a charge against this man. Guards, free the prisoner."

Paul raised his hand. Capito looked at him in surprise. "Does the prisoner have something to say?"

"Yes, Honorable Proconsul. I, too, am a soldier. I am a soldier of God, and I bear his banner of virtue and goodness against the forces of sin and evil. My words are my weapons, my faith my shield, and I battle for the minds and hearts and souls of all who live on this earth."

Upon returning to his academy, Paul immediately washed away the dirt and lice from his week in jail. Cleansed and purified, he strode into the lecture hall and interrupted the recitations.

"Expect to suffer!" he declared, pacing back and forth and surveying the classroom, crowded now with older students filling the benches and new recruits seated at his feet. "Expect prison, chains, floggings by the lash, and beatings with the rod. Pain is our lot, humiliation our prospect. Our suffering is as nothing when we remember the suffering of Christ. As you go forth in your work, know this: Jesus is with you. He is with you in the joy of bringing faith and hope to the lost and downtrodden, and he is with you when your enemies defile you and raise the whip and sword against you."

Leaving the platform he signaled to Timothy and Prisca, who followed him into his private chamber.

"I have bad news," Timothy blurted out. "From Corinth. False prophets are subverting your teachings. The church is in chaos."

"False prophets? Why does Silvanus let them speak?"

"Silvanus left to join Peter and John Mark. He appointed Crispus in his place, but no faction will listen to Crispus."

"My letter — did it not help?"

"Parts did, other parts offended," Timothy said. "You attacked a pillar of the church."

"I attacked a pillar? Who?"

"Quintilianus, the man living with his stepmother," Timothy said. "He is a respected elder. As his father was dying, he asked Quintilianus to care for Leda, the son's young stepmother. Quintilianus has kept his promise to his father, and now plans to marry Leda. And you wrote that he should be expelled and destroyed."

"I must go to Corinth at once," Paul said.

"They may be hostile."

"All the more reason for me to go."

Paul landed in Corinth only to be met with such antagonism that he left after three days. He began by attempting conciliation, but was scorned for weakness. When he tried contesting the factions in strong words, he was ridiculed as blustering. The two false apostles refused to see him. Crispus, weary and ill, could not help. At Paul's request, Stephanas brought together at his house his fellow elders, including Quintilianus, but they spent the evening disputing among themselves. Sick at heart, his mission a failure, Paul told Stephanas, his host, that his visit had been a mistake. He left the next morning.

Upon landing in Ephesus, Paul washed and purified himself at the public bath beside the dock, then went directly to the house of Aquila and Prisca. To her he confided all that had happened to him, unsparing in describing the rejection and humiliation he had suffered in the church he founded and considered among his best. After listening impassively, she said: "Paul, Corinth has lost its way. Give them time."

"Yes, but I must send them a leader."

"In these circumstances I would not try to impose a leader," Prisca said. "Instead, send an emissary, someone who can represent your views with clarity and loyalty, one who is forceful but who possesses the tact and patience that you do not."

"Do you mean Titus?"

"Yes," Prisca said, "Titus is a versatile leader. He must be able to judge how and why the church has gone wrong, and where you may have erred."

"Bring Titus. I shall so instruct him."

Early the next morning Paul left his room and set out for the waterfront. He found the place along the Lysimachus Wall where at times he came to reflect. Looking out to the sea, he concluded that Ephesus had given him the best years of his life. He had lived in comfort in the house of Aquila and Prisca, enjoyed their company, and shared their optimism and goodwill toward all who came their way. By agreement he worked at the loom or the bench when they needed his skills — often enough to earn his keep, but not so often that it hindered his work with the academy and church. His congregation was faithful and devout, if smaller than he hoped for, but the numbers were all he could reasonably expect in a city that worshiped a cultic statue of a woman with sixteen breasts.

Until the silversmiths' riot, he had advanced his mission in peace. In particular he had taken care not to affront the rabbi or dispute with the elders of the synagogue; in too many cities he had provoked influential Jews to have a Roman court silence or banish him. He would never abandon his duty to take the gospel to his brother Jews, but in Ephesus he had at last come to accept that his first responsibility was to serve as apostle to the gentiles — an appointment that came not from Peter but from Christ himself.

By any measure, his mission in Ephesus had succeeded. In three years his *seminarium* had become the center of the Christian movement. All roads led from him. Young disciples he had trained at his academy carried the gospel east to Hierapolis, Colossae, and Laodicea, north to Smyrna, Thyatira, Sardis, Philadelphia, Pergamum, and Troas, south to Miletus and Cos. Once away on their missions, his disciples wrote or returned to seek his counsel on choosing deacons and new ministers. To oversee them as guardians of doctrine and ritual, he had chosen from among them the ones with the greatest merit and most solid judgment; for these overseers he had created a new title, *episcopos*, "bishop." Except in Galatia, the scattered churches he had previously established had succeeded. Philippi, Thessalonica, Beroea — all in Macedonia were thriving, and Corinth surely would be restored in due course.

Ephesus had been good, so successful, so rewarding that at times he thought he might never leave. Here he had traveled less, preached less, suffered less; yet by training and sending out his ministers, he had expanded beyond his highest expectations the reach of Christ's message throughout Asia. He had done well. Given opportunity, he had made the most of it.

Now that his task here was accomplished, it was time to leave. He yearned to be on the road again. He wanted to taste the spray from a plunging bow, to hear the wind in the rigging. Where should he go? First, summer in Macedonia, the promised visit to fair Philippi, then on to Thessalonica and Beroea. That would give Titus time in Corinth to mend the hurt on both sides. Whatever had happened there, Corinth still belonged to him, and he to Corinth. And Phoebe: Every day he longed to see her again.

So, winter in Corinth, and then he would return to Jerusalem again, deliver a contribution from Macedonia and Achaia to Peter and James for the poor Christians of Jerusalem, just as he had promised long ago. That accomplished, he would begin a new mission, this time to Spain, to a new land afar where the cross and the gospel had yet to be borne.

XXXII

REBUILDING

As he set out on the ten-day walk from Macedonia to Corinth, Paul counted himself the most fortunate of men. In Philippi he had been welcomed with warmth and veneration such as had never before experienced. For six weeks he had been celebrated, inspirited by crowds following him in the streets and filling the church hall where he preached daily. In the evenings he, Luke, Timothy, and Aristarchus dined with Lydia, her workers and household, and community leaders she invited in relays to meet her famous guest. Often, after dinner, he and Luke strolled about her quiet garden, conversing about philosophy, logic, history, mathematics, the Greek and Roman methods of governing.

Thessalonians greeted the founder of their church with equal enthusiasm and respect. Jason, aging but still vigorous, proudly described how his congregation had overcome division and doubt, and built a magnificent new church. "It is," he told Paul, "the equal of the church you built in Corinth. And we have a wise and commanding minister, Protagoras, three deacons, ten acolytes, and four hundred and sixty members."

Titus had come with a report on the situation in Corinth: The church was still fractious, still beset by false apostles, but the majority of Christians had come to realize they had wronged Paul and would welcome him back to Corinth at any time. To Paul's surprise, his supporters in Corinth were already collecting contributions for him to take to the poor Jewish Christians in Jerusalem.

All seemed encouraging, but as they neared Corinth, Paul began to worry about what he might find upon reaching the city. One day he would be brimming with confidence and optimism: Stephanas would have dispatched the counterfeit apostles, restored unity to the church, and reinstituted order and dignity to the worship service. The next day would find him in despair, certain that false apostles were prevailing, stirring up more factions that would drive the humble and the innocent out of the church and back into sin and paganism.

Timothy, long experienced in Paul's mercurial bounds from enthusiasm to pessimism and back again, assumed an antipodal role: He would caution Paul when most sanguine, and cheer him up when depressed. By the time they reached Marathon, two days from Corinth, Paul's moods changed hourly. Timothy counseled: "Paul, it cannot be as bad as you fear or as good as you hope for."

And so it turned out to be. Paul arrived in Corinth to find his church still divided but improving. Some in the congregation were returning to services, but benches were only half filled — with each faction sitting by itself. The two false apostles, Jerubaal and Ahaziah, still appeared in the church and now also in the market squares, preening wisdom and collecting money. After earnest talks, first with Titus, then Stephanas, Paul resolved to deal with them first.

The very next morning he rose early at Stephanas' house and walked in the rain to the city offices to find Erastus, who had returned from Ephesus to be again appointed treasurer of Corinth. "Come with me," he told Erastus, and together they walked briskly to the wealthy quarter where the two false apostles had rented a fine house. A servant opened the door. Paul, unannounced, strode in, with Erastus following, continuing through the rooms until he found Jerubaal and Ahaziah at a table spread with baskets of food. Both looked up in surprise at the two strangers.

"I am Paul, a true apostle of God, here by the power of the Lord Jesus Christ to condemn you who have perverted his teachings. I know not whether you are messengers of Satan or simply men of greed. Both are contemptible. As a just man I offer you two choices: Debate me on the scriptures and the gospel of Jesus Christ, both in the church and in the public squares; or leave Achaia and take your 'higher wisdom' to another country."

Once they were outside, Erastus turned to Paul. "I am complimented to be a witness to this bold act, but why did you ask me to go with you?"

"Erastus," Paul said slowly, "have these two imposters paid city taxes on the money they have collected here?"

Erastus pulled at his ear and grinned at Paul. "I do not know. But I will go now and find out."

As soon as Paul returned to the church, he met, one by one, with the most ardent spokesman for each faction, and asked each to summarize the points of difference with the others. As he expected, their points of agreement far exceeded their points of disagreement. Over the next few days he began getting two and then three and then all together, while he led them in prayers for unity and quiet discussions, trying to persuade them that differences are to be expected in the human family, indeed inevitable among strong people. "God himself created differences," he said, "between Moses and his own tribe, between Jew and gentile; but by the grace of the Lord Jesus we are united in faith. We are all equal at the moment of death, and we may, through Christ, be united in God's heavenly kingdom." They listened. Some relented. More did not. Paul steeled himself to show patience, knowing that restoring accord would neither be easy nor quick.

At noon he called his principal staff together. "We need a new minister, one not only able to use authority but never hesitant to do so. So I will call Gaius from Ephesus to take over this church. He cannot travel until spring, so we have three months. In this time, we must all bend to the task. Timothy, the school of deacons and acolytes that you began here disappeared after you left. Bring it back to life. Expand it. Make it a magnet for the young. Titus, Erastus tells me how much you collected for the poor of Jerusalem and stored in his bank for safekeeping. Let us do more. Nothing can energize a lagging congregation like a person-to-person appeal for sacrifice toward a worthy cause. Increase the goal you established, and meet it.

"Aristarchus, you and I will begin tomorrow to preach in the agora. We need new converts. For zeal, the new to Christ have no equal. Sopater, the church building needs a thorough cleaning and refurbishing, and the grounds are full of weeds. Form a special group of members for this purpose, and put them to work. Wash the stone. Paint the front doors. We want everyone who walks by the church to see that something is happening, that improvements are in the making. Stephanas tells me there is an eager young acolyte, Quartus; use him to help you. Tertius, Luke tells me that you are an accomplished scribe. Examine the copy of the Septuagint that was given while I was here before, and the parchments of hymns and prayers we wrote. Report to me in two days on whether they are well preserved; and if not, tell me what should be done." He paced back and forth, hands clasped behind him. "Christ Jesus brought the people of this church together. Now they are adrift. It is up to us to bring them back together, and back to the faith. Time is short. We begin today, this hour."

Paul and his co-workers had arrived on the third day of the week, so Paul had time to organize his team before he delivered his first sermon. In his mind he set three criteria for that appearance. He must have a full church. He must demonstrate calm authority and maintain order and dignity during worship. He must deliver a meaningful sermon.

On the first point, gossip and curiosity would bring many back to hear him. But that might not be sufficient to fill the church, so he asked Iphigenia to mobilize twenty of the most loyal church wives to persuade every other wife in the church to come to the service and bring her husband. "There must be no empty benches," Paul told her.

As to the service, he wondered if the two false apostles would appear in the church. If they did, he would debate them with fact, logic, and solemnity. If they did not appear, he would conduct the service with dispatch and reverence. For his sermon, he decided he would not even mention the problems and differences within the church. This was to be a new start. So he would go back to the basic message that had served him so well here in Corinth at the outset, and so well in other lands.

The first day of the week arrived, the air cold and still, with the low winter sun casting a long shadow of the fine church Paul had built. Many came early. Timothy, observing unobtrusively from a recess behind the altar, moved quietly through a door to the rear chamber where Paul waited. "All but a few benches are already taken," he said. "The church will be filled to overflowing."

"Is there any sign of the two counterfeits?" Paul asked.

"None yet."

"They may be planning to come in during the service so as to disrupt it."

At the appointed hour Paul entered the church from the door near the altar, striding the full length of the right aisle of the nave and down the center aisle to the platform. The crowd murmured and craned heads to look as he made his way.

Raising his hand in blessing, he said: "Grace to you and peace from God our Father and the Lord Jesus Christ." After an extended series of prayers

— of thanksgiving, for the congregation, the church of Corinth, and all churches of Achaia — he called on one older member to read passages from scripture and on a newcomer to lead the singing of a hymn. Then he began his sermon, patterned after his familiar theme: The prophets foretelling the coming of a suffering Messiah of David's line, the birth of Jesus to a virgin, his baptism and revelation as the son of God, his teaching and healing in Judea, his betrayal, crucifixion, and resurrection.

Upon breaking the bread and filling the common cup for communion, he turned to the congregation: "As we here, each and all, share in the pain and suffering of Jesus, and as we, each and all, may be forgiven of wrongdoing and redeemed by faith in Christ Jesus, so now let us all share in these sacraments of bread and wine that bind us together in remembrances of the one who, out of the purest love and compassion, gave his life for each of you, all of you."

At the end of the long day he was satisfied. There had been no disruption, no disputes among factions, no intervention by the false apostles. He had not stirred them with eloquence — he had never been an accomplished orator — but he had delivered the authoritative account of the miracle of Jesus' life and death and what it could mean in their own lives and deaths. He held their attention. He had permitted no one to speak unless called upon. He could see resentment among some, but he restored order and dignity to worship.

Paul was at the church the next day when Erastus came in, his face revealing all. "The two false apostles are gone," he said cheerfully. "They left from the port of Lechaion for Brindisium this morning. One of my tax collectors watched them go aboard just before the boat sailed."

"How did you accomplish this, Erastus?" Paul asked.

"I sent Damas, my most imposing tax collector, to tell them they owed one thousand denarii as the city's share of the money they collected from the Corinthian people. Damas gave them a week to bring in the money, calculating that would give them time to make their escape."

After reflecting for a moment, Paul said: "Erastus, pass the word among the people about what we did."

One noontime, bent over his desk in the chamber at the rear of the church, Paul heard the door open and looked up. Phoebe stood there. With a soft cry of pleasure she ran to him and embraced and kissed him. Leaning back in his arms she frowned, affecting a stern look, and admonished him. "A week you have been here, Paulos, and you have not been to see me." He drew her to him, kissed her, and for a long time held her close.

"Come with me to Stephanas' house," he said. "We will break bread together."

"Better yet, I brought bread, fruit, and wine," she said. "After the rain, the sun blesses the earth with its warmth. So let us go into the garden and rest in the shelter of the wall." Arm in arm, they strolled outside. "I have good news," she said. "For courage in battle our darling little Paulos has been promoted to tribune."

Paul matched her enthusiasm. "Our son a brave soldier! But how did you learn this?"

"From my brother. Alcmaeon is now a magistrate in Lusitania, the farthest province in Spain, and he chanced upon him."

"Let me count the years," Paul said, "he is now . . ."

"Twenty-nine," Phoebe said softly. "Think back, Paulos. Thirty years has it been since the days of our youth brought us only sunshine and flowers and never a care."

Through the afternoon they talked of Tarsus, of their families and friends, and of the joy and passion they shared in young love. "When will you visit me in Cenchreae?" she asked.

The very question tempted Paul, but he knew he must not yield. "I will come to visit you and to speak to your church in Cenchreae. We cannot come together as before, as though husband and wife, Phoebe, for it would violate the rule of conduct that I impose on all unmarried Christians. I cannot break a rule that I require others to follow" — he opened his arms to her — "however great my love and desire for you."

She smiled and opened her arms to him. "So, also, as a Christian, I must obey this rule. My beloved Paulos, we can share our love and yet not be lovers."

At the end of his first month back in Corinth, Paul walked into the church to inspect the work of Sopater's team. To repair a roof beam that had weakened, Sopater and Quartus had recruited boatbuilders idled for the winter. The walls and windows of the church had been cleaned, the wood of the altar polished. Paul was gratified. He had built this church and he was always proud of it, for he had laid down the foundation of faith that made it possible. And the congregation was returning, not as swiftly as he hoped for, but steadily. Walking about, he decided to look in on the small room where the scriptures and communion vessels were stored. When he entered, Tertius leaped up from the table where he was working.

"Tell me what you have found," Paul said.

"The scriptures were barely legible," Tertius said, "so I copied them on new parchment."

Paul nodded his approval and looked more closely. "A fine hand you have, Tertius."

"I have also copied afresh the order of service, and the prayers and hymns you use most often."

Again Paul nodded his approval. "And here," Tertius said, removing the fitted top from a large earthen jar, "here I have stored copies of all your letters that I can find."

"Where did you learn to do this?" Paul asked.

"In Rome, during my three years at the academy of government," Tertius replied. "Archivists tutored us in making and preserving documents."

The ides of March arrived, ending winter rain and gale, bringing forth blossoms in the orchards on the hillsides across the isthmus and opening the sea-lanes. The first boat of the new year arrived from Ephesus, bearing not only Gaius and his favorite horse but also the wise and capable Prisca and her resourceful and enterprising husband, Aquila.

For Paul, it was a welcome and long-awaited day. He was ready, indeed impatient, for Gaius to take over the church and instill a fresh spirit in the congregation. Over the winter in Corinth he had driven himself and his co-workers to resolve differences among members and factions, and to restore their faith; but he had succeeded only in part. It was time, past time, for Corinth to experience a new face, a new voice, a new leader.

To celebrate the arrival of Gaius, Stephanas ordered his servants to prepare a feast at his rambling house, where Paul and his workers were staying. Good meat and fresh bread filled their stomachs and good wine lifted their spirits. After dinner, Aquila went out to visit the overseer who had bought their tentmaking business in Corinth. Paul brought Prisca to a table in the common room. "Prisca, the church in Corinth came close to dissolution," he said, "and I am thankful that you and Aquila came to help Gaius restore all that was lost."

"O Paul," Prisca said quickly, "I have been waiting to tell you before we told the others. We are only passing through Corinth on our way back to Rome."

"To Rome?" Paul sat back in surprise. "You are returning to Rome now? But Jews were barred from working and trading, and most expelled — you among them."

"That was under Claudius," Prisca said. "After Nero became emperor three years ago, Jews began immigrating to Rome again. Our banker sent word that we can now buy back the shop we were forced to sell. So we decided to return." She paused and put her hand on Paul's arm. "We want you to go with us."

Paul shook his head. "You know my rule. I take the gospel only where the name of Christ has never been heard."

"The gospel has been heard in Rome, but by few gentiles," Prisca said. "There it is taught by Jews for Jews."

"I cannot go to Rome now, Prisca. I agreed long ago to help the poor Christians of Jerusalem. The churches of Macedonia and Achaia have already contributed, generously, and I promised to deliver their contributions. I will not break that promise."

"Why, Paul, do you insist on going back to Jerusalem?" Anger blazed in Prisca's eye. "James and Peter and the others there never credit your accomplishments. Instead, they do nothing but disdain and oppose and undermine you."

Paul looked away for a time, then turned back to face her. "Why do I go to Jerusalem, Prisca? The first reason you know. Gentiles have drawn heavily from the great store of spiritual blessings God granted to Jews; therefore, gentiles should pay something back in material worth. The money I collect for Jerusalem is part payment by gentiles against that debt. Second, I go in hope that this least of the apostles may bring unity between Christian and Jew — or die, as Jesus did, for a momentous cause."

Prisca shuddered. "Are you trying to become a martyr? You may succeed, for you will be caught between your sworn enemies — Judaizers on one side, Zadok and the priests of the Sanhedrin on the other. Both will hire assassins the moment you are first seen in the city."

The mention of Zadok startled Paul; not for years had he thought of his former mentor. "All is in God's hands, Prisca."

"But surely God does not expect you to take foolish risks," Prisca said. "Hear me, Paul: Rome is the future; Jerusalem the past. Rome needs a leader. If you establish your gospel of Christianity in Rome, as you did in Antioch and Ephesus and Philippi and Thessalonica and Corinth, it will endure forever."

"I cannot contest the merit of your argument, Prisca. Indeed, it is my plan, after Jerusalem, to go to Rome for a brief time to establish a base for my mission to Spain — as Antioch was my base for Galatia and Ephesus my base for Asia."

Prisca threw up her hands. "So be it. As best we can, Aquila and I will organize a cadre of the faithful in Rome, to be there when you arrive, whenever that is."

"I will sail for Jerusalem in time for Pentecost," he said. "By early summer I will be in Rome."

"If you will not go with Aquila and me now," Prisca said, "will you at least confer on me the status of deacon so that I may speak with your authority before Christians in Rome?"

As Paul hesitated, Prisca said: "I know, how well do I know, that you believe only men can be disciples. You oppose women speaking, yet you appoint them deacons to read scripture — another of your contradictions. If I am to bring anyone to Christ in Rome, I must have your blessing to —"

Paul raised a hand for silence. "I consent, Prisca. I am not always consistent; that I realize. Certainly you have earned the right to be appointed a deacon, and we shall do this tomorrow, and formally, in a ceremony in the church."

Tears filled her eyes. "Why do you weep?" he asked in a brusque voice.

"Because I am happy, and grateful." After sniffing and drying her eyes, she continued: "I have one more request that brought me from Ephesus. Will you write a letter of guidance and exhortation to Christians in Ephesus and the other cities of western Asia? They know you wrote to other churches, and they are jealous. There was never time for you to visit and address them, so let your letter substitute for your person."

Paul began nodding in approval even before she finished. "Certainly we can write to Ephesus and all churches of Asia," he said. "What specific issues are to be addressed?"

"Rather than respond to specific questions, as you did with Chloe's people," Prisca said, "I suggest a broad statement of Christian principles, directed particularly to the newly baptized. Present your vision of God's plan for his people and the place of Jesus in this plan, and then exhort all in these churches to come together as one in commitment to faith and service to Christ Jesus."

"Well said, Prisca. Will you compose a letter that includes these points, and other appropriate issues, and bring it to me? Together you and I will put it in final form."

Prisca smiled. "I have been hoping you would ask me," she said. "So I wrote it on the boat."

Paul sat back. He was surprised but not offended. This was not the first time Prisca had read his thoughts, or anticipated his reaction. "Bring it to me at the church tomorrow," he said.

The first words captured Paul's attention. Prisca's opening sentence, unusually long, conveyed the eternal purpose of God and explicated the breadth of his love for his people and the richness of his gifts. Paul was intrigued to recognize in the writing many of his concepts, but few of his phrases. Altogether it was a compelling letter, organized and composed with unusual skill. At the end he said to her: "If I had written this letter, Prisca, I would consider it among my best. As it is, I will be proud to lend my name to your fine letter as though it were my own."

"You taught me well," she said, her eyes shining with happiness. "It would be good if you would write a passage of your own.

So Paul read the letter again, and began to write:

> I exhort you to walk worthily of your calling, with all humility and meekness, with long-suffering, bearing with one another in love; being eager to keep the unity of the spirit in the bond of peace. There is one body and one spirit, even as you were called in one hope of your calling, one Lord, one faith, one baptism, one God and father of all; he above all and in you all.
>
> Therefore, put off your old life, your former corruption by lust, and become renewed in the spirit of your mind. Put away falsehood. Tell the truth, each to his neighbor, for we are members one

of another. Be angry but do not sin. Do not let the sun go down on your wrath. Give no opportunity to the devil. Let the thief steal no more; rather, let him labor, working with his hands on something useful, that he may have something to give to the one who has need. Let no filthy word come out of your mouth; but say what is good or edifying, as it is suitable for the occasion, that it may grace those hearing you. Do nothing to cause grief to the holy spirit of God, who has marked and sealed you for the day of redemption. Let all bitterness, and anger, and wrath, and tumult, and hurtful words be put away from you, along with all evil things. And be kind to one another, tender-hearted, forgiving one another even as God forgave you in Christ.

Walk in love, even as Christ also loved us, and gave himself for us, in offering and sacrifice to God.

When he finished writing, Paul waited for the ink to dry and pointed to a place in Prisca's composition. "Include this passage here," he said, "and ask Tertius to engross seven copies in his fine hand." He paused. "And send for Tychicus — he is the one most respected in Asia. Direct him to read the letter twice in each of the churches."

"But Paul, Tychicus is in Hierapolis."

"So bring him here," Paul said curtly. "This letter is too important to be entrusted to anyone else."

Alone in the church that afternoon, Paul reflected on how much more rewarding it was to address a positive and uplifting message to young churches than to admonish recalcitrants and correct error. Perhaps with a congregation, as with a child, affirmation was far better than negation in building character. He shook his head in wonder at Prisca; he knew her well, but she could still surprise him with her forthrightness, initiative, and acuity of mind.

Her reasoning on why he should proceed at once to Rome was compelling, and he had wavered, been strongly tempted. He had no doubt that he could continue his mission by preaching the gospel in Rome, and he could also enjoy a personal life. He could bring Phoebe with him, marry her, have children with her, and have her work at his side. After he established his doctrine in the churches of Rome, he and Phoebe could open Spain to Christianity.

In his early travels he could not have had a wife; now that he had succeeded in taking the gospel to so many lands, he could. Certainly Aquila and Prisca had proved how man and wife could work and journey together and serve the Lord with devotion and constancy. Surely he and Phoebe could do as well.

It was an enticing prospect, a happy dream; but at this critical junction in his life it could be only be a dream. He must go to Jerusalem first. He must, as he promised, deliver the collection to Peter and James. And there was the even greater obligation: to make one more valiant attempt to reconcile Christian Jew and Christian gentile. Had not Jesus commanded on the road to Damascus: "I send you to Jew and gentile alike, to turn them from darkness to light."

Once he had made another fervent appeal to his brother Jews in the mother church, once that duty had been met, he could in good conscience sail on to Rome. That was the plan, a good plan, but Prisca's words haunted him. He could not dispel a sense of foreboding, the thought that he might not live to see Rome. A storm might sink his ship. More likely, he could imagine being trapped in a dark alley in Jerusalem, seeing the raised knives of assassins hired by Zadok, or by James. Both had agents sworn to take his life. Prisca's intuition rarely missed the mark. Was he, as she suggested, determined to become a martyr, subconsciously emulating Jesus entering Jerusalem knowing he would be killed?

"If I am soon to die, and so I may," he said aloud, "I must leave a legacy. I possess no goods or gold, but a treasure greater than any other: the message given to me by Christ Jesus to take to the world. I must set forth for mankind the whole of the true gospel for which I have lived and am now prepared to give my life."

XXXIII

RECKONING

At the dock in Lechaion, Paul embraced Prisca and Aquila with warm farewells as they boarded the *Aquarius* for Brindisium. Walking back to Corinth, Paul said, "Tertius, as soon as we return, invite Luke and Phoebe to join us for an important discussion."

"Invite?" Tertius asked in amusement. "Or summon, as you customarily say?"

"Invite is more seemly," Paul said with a smile. "This I have learned over time."

"What shall I tell them is to be discussed?" Tertius asked.

"God and mankind," Paul replied.

As they settled in the leafy garden of the church, Paul's spirits seemed uncommonly serene. "I have decided to write a summary of the doctrine and practice of Christianity," he said, "and I shall need your counsel in this task. My plan, simply, is to compose a treatise that will be both a guide for Christian life and an exposition of God's purpose for mankind."

"A coda?" Luke asked.

"Coda and manifesto," Paul said. "In form I will structure this discourse as a letter to Christians in Rome, but my broader purpose is to present to the world my vision of what Christianity is, how it came to be, and how it is meant to embrace all people. Until now my letters to churches have responded to specific circumstances, but in none have I recorded in full the message given to me by the Lord Jesus. This I now resolve to do." After pausing he added: "As this is my last letter, I intend it to be the most comprehensive of all, and my best."

Phoebe looked at him in alarm: "Why do you speak this way, Paulos?"

"I cannot foresee how Jerusalem will receive me, whether with timbrel and harp or with knife and club," Paul said. "Whatever awaits me there, I shall leave this article of faith as my legacy."

"Prudent and practical," Luke said. "But why do you direct this letter to Rome rather than to Christians in all lands?"

"First, now that my mission in this part of our world is fulfilled, I plan to use Rome as my base for a new mission to Spain. So I want Christians there to know I am coming to them. Second, as Rome is the new center of our civilized world, it is essential that ministers and congregations in Rome have in hand the message that Christ gave me to take to the world."

"Another question," Luke said. "Why, a quarter century after Jesus lived and died, has no one explicated the gospel before this time?"

"Few were qualified," Paul said. "I could have, but my primary mission was to act, to bring people to Christ, organize them into churches, and train leaders to bring others to the faith. I was fifteen years traveling and delivering the gospel before I wrote my first letter — and like the letters that followed, it was ancillary, a device to correct error and exhort the faithful when I could not be present. Now I have reached another turning point in my mission, and I consider this the time and the occasion to reflect, draw on experience, and set down the essence of Christianity."

Facing each in turn, Paul continued: "Tertius, I ask you not only to compose the letter with me, but also to give me your insights about the nature and temperament of the Romans to whom we are writing. Phoebe, you too know Rome. I would like to draw on your wisdom and experience to judge how we can best touch the hearts and minds of men and women not only in Rome but in all nations. Luke, I need your intellect as well as your breadth of knowledge about the beginnings and history of the Christian movement. As you excel in writing, I ask you to help me craft a treatise that will live for generations to come."

"An admonition," Phoebe said. "Ostensibly your letter is to Christians in Rome. Most are Jews; at least they were when I was there as a young woman. Your letters so far were written to gentiles, most of whom had heard you, seen you, knew you. They looked on you as a father, and you could correct them as a father corrects a child."

"What are you telling me?" Paul asked.

"You are a stranger to Rome, an outsider, so you cannot lecture to Christians there. Avoid the didactic, the imperative. Use persuasion. In addressing Jews you must be circumspect about such sensitive issues as the crucifixion, which you contend was a crime by Jewish priests, and circumcision, which you dismiss as meaningless."

Paul turned toward Tertius. "You studied recently in Rome. What do you have to say?"

"Phoebe is right," Tertius replied. "Your name will not command the instant respect it does in Macedonia and Achaia. The churches in Rome are indeed predominantly Jewish. Scripture is read in Hebrew. While sermons are delivered in Greek, content follows closely Jewish ethics and the Law."

"How many were in the congregations?" Paul asked.

"Eight hundred at most, scattered among four churchhouses," Tertius replied. "And this in a city where Jews numbered twenty thousand in the last census."

"Very well," Paul said. "As I address strangers, I must begin by introducing myself. As they are Jews, I must represent myself as an apostle of the gospel as it is taught by Christian Jews."

"What is the difference?" Tertius asked.

"Emphasis. Jews speak more about God; I have spoken more about Jesus. I will tell them I represent both." He turned to Tertius. "Open with compliments and respect, with thanksgiving, and say that as God is my witness, I always include them in my prayers and tell them I will come to them as I have long promised.

"The central theme you all well know: It is faith in Jesus Christ, and not the Law, and not good works, that moves God to accept us. That premise we will iterate and reiterate. In the body of the letter I will begin with an analysis of the human condition and emphasize God's retribution against sinners. So record this, Tertius: God brings down the wrath of heaven against the ungodly and unrighteous. Sinners know they do wrong, for God has shown them what is right. They knew God's will, but did not honor it. Instead they became vain, unreasoning, and foolish. They exchanged the glory of an incorruptible God for images of corruptible man and idols representing birds and animals and reptiles. Therefore God let them remain sinners and follow their lusts. Even their women gave up natural relations for the unnatural; men, forsaking natural relations with women, burned with lust for other men. Men committed shameful acts with other men, and received punishment for their perversion.

"And since these sinners did not acknowledge God, God gave them up to sin. So they filled themselves with all manner of wickedness — evil, covetousness, malice, envy, murderousness, quarrelsomeness. They became gossips, slanderers, God haters, braggarts. They were perfidious, unforgiving, unmerciful, disobedient to parents. Though they know God's decree that everyone practicing such things deserves to die, they not only do them but applaud others doing them."

"What will you say to those who do honor God and give him thanks for their gifts?" Phoebe asked.

"Everlasting life he will give to those who live by faith, and who by proper living and patience seek honor and incorruptibility," Paul said. "And I will say more about those who live by God's Commandments. But this is a warning to those who are selfish and wicked, for he will reward them with anger and wrath, trouble and pain. This to every soul who practices evil, the Jew first and the gentile as well. For God shows no partiality among sinners."

For the next hour Paul discoursed further on sin and retribution, on circumcision and why it caused such internecine warfare among Christians, on why Jews still had to follow the Law but gentiles did not. When he paused for a moment, Luke spoke up: "What do you say is the essence of Christian doctrine?"

"That faith, and only faith, brings God's salvation," Paul replied. "Although the righteousness of God was revealed in the Law and witnessed by the Prophets, it was made manifest in Jesus Christ — for all of us who have faith in him apart from the Law and the Prophets. There is no difference among us: We have all sinned and fallen short of the glory of God. But now we can be justified by the gift of grace from God, and redeemed by Christ Jesus, whom God sent forth as propitiation through faith in his blood."

The next morning, when Tertius brought in a draft of the first day's discussion, Paul seized it eagerly and began to read, holding each page close and squinting his eyes to make out the words. Tertius sat in silence, observing. He saw an old man with poor eyesight, sparse gray curls running from temple to temple, and a bald expanse at the top of his unusually large head. Thin shoulders and a slender neck suggested he was frail, but Tertius knew he was not. Even with his limp, which had become more noticeable in recent months, he never slowed his walk. In recent weeks he had changed, visibly. Since he reunited the church and handed it over to the strong-willed Gaius, Paul's temperament had improved. He was more reasonable, more often ready to listen, not so quick to be offended, more contemplative. He often sat alone for hours, wrinkled forehead resting on his fingertips, meditating. Tertius sensed that his mentor was longing, deeply in his soul, for something, or someone.

Once he finished reading, Paul returned the draft to Tertius. "Much work remains to be done," he said. "First, where are the passages I dictated about Abraham and David?"

"But you are writing to Jews who know the history of Abraham and David," Tertius said.

"All Christians need to be reminded that Abraham and David exemplify faith in God," Paul said. "Second, where is the comment about the meaning of baptism? Third, include in full my account of my own inner struggle against sin. I will repeat what I said yesterday: I am well aware that the Law is spiritual, but I am a creature of flesh and blood sold as a slave to sin. I do not understand my own behavior. I do not act as I mean to, but I do things that I hate. It is not myself acting, but the sin that lives in me. I know of nothing good living in me — in my natural self, that is — for though the will to do what is good is in me, the power to do it is not. The good thing I want to do, I never do; the evil thing I do not want — this is what I do. In my mind I dearly love God's Law, but in my body is a different law that battles against the Law in my mind."

As the four gathered in the afternoon for the second day's discussion, Luke spoke first. "Yesterday we listened to an informed and valuable disquisition. Today I suggest we raise questions, and I have one in particular that no one in Jerusalem can answer: If, from the beginning, God had a plan for sending his son to earth, why did his chosen people reject God's son?"

"No one can ask God to explain his actions," Paul said. "The Prophets tried again and again to show Israel the path to God, but again and again Israel disobeyed and defied God. Yet God never abandoned the people he had chosen; even when they were dispersed into exile or bound into slavery, he always preserved a remnant. Will the Jews' hardening of heart against Jesus lead to their final downfall? God forbid! On the contrary, their failure has brought salvation for the gentiles, one perverse consequence of which is to stir Jews to envy. Therefore, if Israel's loss proved to be a great gain for gentiles, how much greater the gain will be when all are restored to the faith."

"I have a proposal," Phoebe said. "This I know to be true in Cenchreae and Corinth, and presumably also in Rome: Christian Jews resent your insistence that they observe the Law while at the same time you allow gentiles great freedom of conduct. I suggest that in this letter you specify rules of behavior for all who commit to Christ."

Paul opened his arms in a gesture of inclusiveness. "The guiding principle for all is found in Jesus' words: 'Love the Lord thy God with all thy heart and soul and mind, and love thy neighbor as thyself.' For Jew and gentile, let love be genuine. Shrink from evil. Cleave to good. In brotherly love, love fervently. Outdo one another in showing honor. Never flag. Show zeal. Glow with the spirit. Serve the Lord. Rejoice in hope. Endure in affliction. Pray steadfastly and continually. Contribute to the needs of all holy people. Practice hospitality.

"Bless those who persecute you; bless and do not curse them. Rejoice with those who rejoice. Weep with those who weep. Live in harmony with one another. Do not be haughty, but devote yourself to humble tasks. Never be conceited. Repay no one evil with evil; give thought to what is noble for all. If possible, as far as it is in you, seek peace with all others. Never avenge yourself, but leave that to the wrath of God, for it is written, 'Vengeance is mine; I will repay, says the Lord.' If your enemy hungers, feed him. If he thirsts, give him drink, for by so doing you heap burning coals on his head. Do not be overcome with evil, but overcome evil with good."

For the rest of the afternoon Paul discoursed — about the obligations of the strong in faith to help the weak and wavering, how the crucifixion superseded the Mosaic Law, why Israel was able to fall into error yet accomplish so much — while Luke and Phoebe questioned and analyzed the points he made.

The conversation droned on, when suddenly Paul dictated a passage that animated all: "If God is for us, who can be against us? Can anything separate us from the love of Christ? Will hardship, or distress, or persecution, or famine, or hunger, or lack of clothing, or peril, or sword? No! We can conquer all these things through the power of him who loves us. For I am persuaded that neither death, nor life, nor angels, nor rulers, nor powers, nor things present, nor things to come, nor height, nor depth, nor any other thing will be able to separate us from the love of God through Jesus Christ our Lord."

"Eloquent!" Luke exclaimed. "You should close your letter with that moving passage."

"But I have so much more to say," Paul said, with a look of dismay.

"Then I suggest we resume tomorrow," Luke said. "You have given us much to think about."

Tertius worked through the night to pull together a draft of what Paul said and wanted to say. Reading it over, he saw a pattern. The new letter was a compendium of the best of Paul's previous letters, especially those to the Galatians and Corinthians; but the issues were more reasoned than in the Galatian letter, which had been written in anger, and better organized than in the Corinthian letters, which were answers to random questions. He concluded the old man still had his wits; he forgot nothing he had ever dictated or written.

The next day, when Paul read Tertius' second draft, his response was brief: "More cohesive, but yet incomplete." So the four met in the garden for the third day.

As they settled in their chairs Paul said, "So important is this letter that I shall ask Phoebe to deliver it and read it in the Roman churches. As all here know, my trust in you, Phoebe, is second to none; and you, as a deacon of the church, have standing to read before any assembly of Christians."

"Paulos! I am honored!" Phoebe said, her blue eyes shining with delight.

"Now to the task," Paul said.

"A question," Luke said. "As Claudius expelled all Jews from Rome for creating public disturbances over Christ, and as you have been arrested for disturbing the peace and initiating rebellion, how should Christians advocate the gospel peaceably, and what are their obligations to Caesar?"

"Christians should conduct themselves as examples for all citizens," Paul said. "Speak the truth openly; we must never silence ourselves out of fear of a mob. Let everyone be subject to governing authority, for there is no power except from God, and the powers that be are ordained by God. Therefore, he who resists the authorities opposes the ordinances of God. The rulers are not a terror to good conduct, but to bad. If you would have no fear of authority, then do what is good and you receive approval, for he is God's servant for your good. But if you do wrong, be afraid, for he does not bear the sword in vain. He is the servant of God to execute wrath on the wrongdoer."

"Do I hear aright?" Tertius asked. "Do you pledge allegiance to this Caesar? To this murderous Nero?"

"My allegiance is to no man, but only to God," Paul replied. "I am saying simply that I recognize the principle and benefits of authority. Under Caesar's protection I walked his roads and sailed his seas. I also suffered the lash of his praetorian guards and yet was delivered by his proconsul. Whether cruel or benevolent, whether in Rome or the provinces, the authorities serve God as his agents, protecting us from pirate, thief, and barbarian. That is why you should pay taxes to whom tax is due, and honor the one to whom honor is due."

The long and far-ranging discussion of what Paul should write and how he should express it continued until dusk. As they walked away, Paul said to Tertius: "Begin anew. In the opening section offer high praise to Roman Christians. By surviving under Caesar, they merit praise. Present the doctrinal passages in this logical order: The gospel reveals the righteousness of God, his power to grant salvation to everyone who believes, first the Jew, then the gentile. Next, reconciliation to God comes through the death of Christ Jesus. Third, Israel rejected Jesus and the gospel, but in time may see its error and accept Jesus as its savior. After the doctrine, affirm my advice for Christian living, with emphasis on the principles I articulated the first day."

On the morning of the twelfth day of their collaboration, Paul looked up from the latest draft and said: "The main body of the letter is ready. We will close it with certain additions. Emphasize that I write not to instruct Christians in Rome, or correct them in any way, but to refresh their memories about God's plan for Israel, and to offer my reflections drawn from my decades of serving as chief apostle of Christ Jesus to the gentiles."

After a moment he added: "And insert this: Faith guarantees salvation. It is through Jesus Christ, by faith, that we are admitted into God's favor in this life and may reach God's heavenly kingdom after this life. Christ died for the godless. You could hardly find anyone willing to die for someone else, even for someone good. So it is proof of God's love for us that Christ gave his life for all of us who are sinners."

"How should we close the letter?" Tertius asked.

"With personal notes, appropriate greetings, and a brief note that I hope to visit them after Jerusalem, on my way to Spain. Ask them also to pray that I escape my enemies in Jerusalem who would take my life. And say this: I commend to you our sister Phoebe, bearer of this letter, deacon of the church at Cenchreae. Receive her in the Lord as one of God's holy people, and assist her in every way she may need of you, for she is a helper of many Christians, including myself."

Paul put his hand on Tertius' arm. "Cite that it is you, Tertius, who collaborated with me in writing this letter. Your diligence and perseverance made it possible."

The four gathered in the garden one last time. As Phoebe was to read the letter to the churches in Rome, Paul asked her to read it for the authors. By the time she finished, the sun had set and Phoebe was hoarse. Paul instructed Tertius to make one last set of changes, then engross the letter and encase it for the journey.

Paul would permit no one but himself to survey the ships in the harbor at Lechaion and arrange for Phoebe's passage. He then walked to Cenchreae to tell her the plan: The *Vesta*, captained by Bara, a Phoenician Paul had brought into the Way, would sail in five days to Brindisium. From there it would be two hundred and thirty-four miles on the Via Appia to Rome.

As they strolled in her garden Paul asked: "Shall I send one of my ministers with you for your protection on the road?"

"That is not needed," Phoebe said with a smile. "I have traveled alone in Italy, and I am not afraid. Indeed, a woman is safer alone on the Via Appia than she is walking about in Corinth."

"Stephanas will provide money for your journey," Paul said.

"I wish to pay for this myself," Phoebe said.

Her servant brought out meat, bread, fruit, and wine. Together they watched the first full moon of springtime as it rose from the eastern sea, talking of times past, planning their lives ahead.

XXXIV

IMPERILED

With his letter dispatched to Rome, Paul instructed Titus to go at once to Cenchreae and book passage on the next ship for Caesarea. "What is the plan for transporting the money to Jerusalem?" he asked.

"Luke and I will each carry a leather satchel containing gold and silver coins," Titus said. "Sopater, Aristarchus, Secundus, and Trophimus will be our guards. Except for you and Luke, we will all carry weapons."

Paul nodded his assent. "With five in arms, we should be safe."

Finding Timothy in the class for deacons, Paul took him aside. "Corinth needs you, Timothy," he said. "I ask you to remain here for two months to assist Gaius. Then take the boat to Brindisium and meet me in Rome."

After a long silence Timothy looked at Paul in anguish. "I beg you: Let me go with you to Jerusalem. I have never been, and you say this is your last visit."

"Your mission here is too important, Timothy. Gaius needs you to help him bring the church of Corinth back to its former glory. In two months you may leave and meet me in Rome. There you and I will work together again."

With a long face and sigh of resignation, Timothy agreed.

Gaius waited in the church, and for an hour he and Paul walked about the building and grounds, admiring the improvements that Sopater and Quartus and their volunteers had made. The stone had been washed, the roof repaired, the doors painted, and the grounds planted with shrub and tree. "Master the congregation," Paul advised Gaius. "Be quick to hear, slow to anger. Appear to consider even the most foolish notion; the best of your elders will have them. Grant a boon now and then to keep them happy; but on the big issues, use your best judgment, decide, and make it stand. This is your church through the grace of God and by appointment of an apostle of Christ Jesus; those you lead must never doubt that."

He lowered his voice. "I asked Timothy to remain here and help you for two months," Paul said. "He is like a son to me, and I decided I would not risk his life by taking him on this dangerous visit to Jerusalem."

"What is the danger, Paul?"

"From my brother Jews on one side, and my brother Christians on the other. The high priest of the Sanhedrin put a price on my head long ago. The circumcisionists sharpen their knives to slit my throat if they find me alone."

It was late afternoon when Titus returned. "There is no ship bound for Caesarea. The only ship sailing east is the *Cetus*, leaving tomorrow on the evening tide for Antioch."

"Then we sail to Antioch and walk to Jerusalem," Paul said.

"I assumed that would be your decision," Titus said, "so I paid for passage for seven. We are to board tomorrow at dusk."

"Tell everyone to be ready," Paul said.

Paul rose early the next morning and walked briskly to the agora. Around the square he made his way, first saying farewell to shopkeepers he had befriended, then mounting the steps of the colonnade to deliver an impassioned and final testimony to the good news of Christ Jesus. With the sun high, he returned to the church to conduct a last worship and communion service with his disciples, the church elders, and other leaders. To his surprise, the church was full, overflowing. The entire congregation, or so it appeared, had come to pay him homage.

After the service he hurried to Stephanas' house to bundle his cloak and spare sandals. His spirits were high. The outpouring of generosity and brotherly love had confirmed his own sense of accomplishment. He had built Corinth, seen it come close to self-destruction, and returned — against opposition — to rebuild it. Now the congregation was stronger than ever. If there were a prize for steadfastness of purpose, he had won the laurel in Corinth.

A knock came on the door, and a servant told him there was an old man to see him. Paul went out to find Crispus, his defender from his first days, now frail, his walk an unsteady shuffle, his outstretched hand trembling. Paul took his hand and led him gently to a chair. "You should not have left your sickbed to say farewell to me," Paul said in an apologetic voice. "I should have come to you."

"I did not come from my sickbed for that," Crispus croaked, and leaned close. "Don't set foot on the *Cetus*," he whispered. "They are going to kill you."

"Who is going to kill me, Crispus?"

"The elders of the synagogue I once led. They have never forgiven you, Paul. A zealot among them has hired assassins to strike a dagger in your back and throw your body overboard, never to be found."

"How can this be, Crispus? I will have five guards around me."

"I know, and these assassins will kill them, too, and take your bags of money," Crispus said, his voice falling to a croak.

"How do they know our plans?" Paul asked.

Crispus growled like an old lion. "Everybody knows your plans, Paul. Everybody knows about the money you collected to go to Jerusalem. And your man Titus was followed on the docks."

Paul put his hand on the old man's arm. "I know you would not have come were you not certain of this, Crispus."

"Am I certain that I am Crispus? Am I certain that you are Paul? So also am I certain of this plot. It came to me from one I trust. He hates you, like the others, but he is too devout a Jew to have blood on his hands."

"Both views I understand. Crispus, I owe you my life."

Crispus reached out a trembling hand and said: "Do you not know, Paul, that I owe you my life in Christ Jesus?"

As soon as he helped Crispus out to the litter that had brought him, Paul returned to his room. Was this a sign? Was this a warning that he should not go to Jerusalem? Fear he had known many times, but this was different. Enemies were close by, watching, waiting for the chance to end his life. He expected to be in peril in Jerusalem, but not in Corinth. But how could he surrender to threats? Jerusalem was his mission; he must go forward. Had he not just written to the Romans, "If God be for us, who can be against us?" If he believed those words, he must act on those words.

Swiftly Paul walked to Titus' room. "Assemble the traveling party at once," he ordered. When they were together, he led the six into a corner of the courtyard where no servant could hear them. "Say nothing of this to anyone," he said, looking into their solemn faces. "Our lives could depend on it. I have just learned that assassins plot to kill us aboard the *Cetus* and steal the money we have collected for Jerusalem." He raised his hand to silence their gasps. "So we will go another way."

"Then I should demand the captain return the money I paid for our fares," Titus said.

"No," Paul said. "The captain may be part of the plot. So let him and the assassins believe we are coming aboard until the last moment, when they must sail on the tide. Tomorrow, Luke and I, as inconspicuously as we can, will go to another dock and board the first ship departing north for Macedonia. From there we will sail to Troas. The five of you are to wait three days, find a ship for Troas, and bring the collection there. Luke and I will meet you there at the house of Theophilus." Again he raised his hand. "Remember, speak to no one about this."

The plan succeeded. Paul and Luke sailed to Neapolis, waited for a day, then took another ship for Troas. Upon arriving, Paul was relieved to find his five disciples and the collection secured in the strong room of Theophilus.

So warm was Theophilus' welcome, so engaging his nature, so winsome his wife, Erinna, that Paul yielded to their entreaties and consented to remain for a week in Troas to preach every day in the house of Theophilus and in the market squares.

On Paul's last day in the city Theophilus brought together his four sons and their wives, three daughters and their husbands, fourteen grandchildren, and a score of close friends for Paul to lead in worship. All gathered at sunset in a great hall in the upper story of his mansion. As the visitors were to leave the next morning, Paul had much to say. And say it he did. He preached on. And on. At midnight Theophilus ordered his servants to bring oil lamps so that those assembled could see the preacher as well as hear him. Even as the lamps were being lighted and placed about the hall, Paul continued to talk.

The night was warm, the windows open to the breeze from the sea. Eutychus, a youth of fifteen and grandson of Theophilus, was sitting with cousins on the sill of an open window. The preaching made him grow drowsy. Drifting into sleep, he suddenly fell from the window.

His mother and father leaped up and ran down two flights of stairs with Luke close behind. There they found Eutychus lying on the ground, unmoving. Luke felt for his pulse and listened for his breath, but could find neither. His mother and father saw the expression on Luke's face and began weeping and crying out in anguish.

At that moment Paul knelt beside Luke, took the youth in his arms, and held him to his chest, murmuring softly. After a long silence Paul turned to the mother and father: "Do not be alarmed. He lives." Whereupon he lifted the youth in his arms, walked upstairs to the great hall, and laid him on a pillow near the podium. As the mother and father anxiously hovered over their child, Paul began the ritual of breaking bread and preparing wine for communion. After all had shared the symbolic body and blood of Christ, Paul resumed preaching, and talked on and on — until daybreak.

As the room filled with light, Eutychus opened his eyes, looked in surprise at the faces of his mother and father and others bent over him, and rose to his feet. The entire assembly — family, friends, visitors — raised their voices in joy, convinced the youth had been brought back from the dead. Paul closed the service with a fervent prayer of thanksgiving.

After the incident, Paul and his delegation said hurried farewells to their hosts. Theophilus had arranged passage for them on the *Cydnus*, a coaster he owned that would take them as far as Patara. There they would find, in time, a ship bound directly for Caesarea.

Marcus Hatius, the young captain of the *Cydnus*, welcomed them abroad, promising good food for their stomachs and straw mats on deck for their sleeping. "We sail by day and anchor at night," he said. "Our first stop is Assos. With this good wind, we will arrive well before sundown, unload the copper ingots they ordered, and sail on tomorrow to Mytilene."

Luke and the disciples found their assigned mats and lay down to rest after the long and sleepless night. Paul, restless, still charged with energy from his hours of preaching and the revival of the youth, stood up. "Who will walk with me to Assos? It is only thirty miles, a good day's walk. Come, Aristarchus. Let us go together. This is beautiful country for walking."

Entry from the Journal of Luke

In Assos I took the delegation and Marcus the ship captain ashore to a fine inn recommended by Theophilus. There we dined on a haunch of lamb roasted on a spit, leeks freshly pulled from the earth, warm breads, and an abundance of wine. When we returned to the *Cydnus*, Paul and Aristarchus were waiting for us, also in high spirits and eager to boast of the speed of their journey.

The next morning we sailed southward, as in a channel between mountains, the clear ranges of the island of Lesbos at our right and the clouded higher peaks and ridges of the mainland of Mysia at our left, to dock in the city of Mytilene, filled, as always, with philosophers in the temples of learning and revelers on holiday from as far away as Rome.

Finding no cargo in Mytilene, Marcus sailed on the next day toward the lovely island of Chios. As we came near, wind currents from the mountains shifted to and fro, but Marcus nimbly negotiated a narrow passage at the north end of the island and paralleled the coast as the mountains fell away to fertile plains. Entering the fine harbor of the port city of Chios, Marcus dropped the sail and the longboat brought the *Cydnus* to the dock. While the disciples helped the crew bring aboard bags of grain, amphorae of wine, and wicker boxes of dried figs, Paul and I went ashore to find the birthplace of Homer. We found no guide who spoke with convincing authority, so I thought to visit the renowned community of sculptors, but Paul refused to go among stone idols.

The next morning we touched at Samos only long enough to unload the grain, thereby preventing Paul and me from visiting the birthplace of Aesop. From Samos we sailed two miles across to Trogyllium and anchored overnight. As this was only twenty-five miles from Ephesus, Trophimus suggested that it would be good for Paul to go there to say farewell to the Ephesians. But Paul declined, pointing out that he had resolved to be in Jerusalem by Pentecost, thus he could not spend time in Asia. Instead he instructed

Trophimus to go at once to Ephesus and bring the elders to our next port, Miletus, where the *Cydnus* was to arrive the next day. And so Paul will accomplish his purpose of greeting the Ephesians without delaying his journey.

As the *Cydnus* moved slowly under sail toward the second of Miletus' four harbors, Paul stood at the bow with Luke, searching for Trophimus and the elders of Ephesus. They sailed past the docks, crowded and noisy, past the empty theater carved into a hillside, then saw a small group of men gathered on a wide beach framed by a grove of pines, all waving and beckoning. Marcus dispatched Paul, Luke, and Titus to the beach in his longboat.

Stepping ashore, Paul greeted Trophimus, the eight elders, and nine other Christians who had walked all day from Ephesus to see him. So he led them into the shade of the grove, gestured for them to form a semicircle around him, and began his farewell address.

"You yourselves know how I lived among you all the time from the first day that I set foot in Asia, serving the Lord with all humility, and despite the tears and trials caused me by the plots of the Jews. I kept nothing back so long as I believed it to be in your interest. I taught the gospel in public, and from house to house, as it was my duty, earnestly delivering to Jew and to gentile the message of repentance toward God and faith toward our Lord Jesus Christ.

"Now, behold, I am bound by the spirit to go to Jerusalem, not knowing what will befall me there, but hearing from the Holy Spirit in city after city that imprisonment and persecution await me. But I do not hold my life precious if I am permitted to finish the course with joy and complete the mission the Lord Jesus Christ assigned to me — fully to testify to the gospel of the grace of God."

He raised his hands toward them, beseeching. "And now, behold, I know that you all, among whom I went about proclaiming the kingdom, will see my face no more. Therefore, I testify to you on this day when I leave you that my conscience is clear with you, for I never hesitated nor faltered in putting before you the whole of God's purpose.

"Take heed to yourselves and to all the flock, over which the Holy Spirit placed you as overseers, to shepherd the church of God that Jesus purchased through his own blood. For I know this, that after my departure, fierce wolves will come in among you to devour the flock." He paused and fixed a stern eye on one, then another. "From among your own selves will come up men teaching a travesty of God's truth, in order to draw you to themselves.

"Because of this, be watchful, remembering that for three years I did not cease counseling each one of you day and night, often with tears. And now, brothers, I commend you to God and to the word of his grace, who has the power to build you up and to grant you your inheritance among all those who have been sanctified. I have asked no one for silver, or gold, or clothing. You know that with my two hands I earned enough to meet my needs and the needs of those working with me. All this I did as an example, that we should work in this way to help the poor. Remember the words of the Lord Jesus when he said, 'It is more blessed to give than to receive.'"

Paul bowed his head and knelt in prayer, as did the others, and offered thanksgiving to the God who had enabled them to overcome all trials and obstacles to establish the church in Ephesus. After the final "Amen," one by one they came up to him, each embracing him with brotherly love, many weeping at his words that they would not see his face again.

Titus signaled it was time to go, so all the Ephesians went down to the beach with Paul and watched with sad faces and heavy hearts as the *Cydnus* sailed away.

Entry from the Journal of Luke

Of all sorrows, none reaches deeper into the heart than a final farewell to one you love. To know that never again will you see that face, that never again will you hear that voice, whether because of death or distance, brings low the spirit of the strongest of us. So we witnessed as the *Cydnus* moved with the tide from Miletus and the guardians of the church in Ephesus receded across the water. Standing at the stern and apart, Paul raised his hand in one last blessing, then turned and strode to the bow to be alone.

Sails aloft, Marcus set a straight course through the islands and a strong and steady wind shrieking out of the north kept us bounding across the swells of a following sea, so that by nightfall we reached Cos, birthplace of Hippocrates, where we took aboard ten rolls of the lustrous silk cloth the Cosians weave. The next day we reached Rhodes, crossroads of midsea, then on to Patara. There we said farewell to Marcus and his fair *Cydnus*, and found another ship, the *Psamathe*, bound for Phoenicia. The northwest winds of the season bore us swiftly eastward, so that in three days we sighted Cyprus, and in four more days the mountains of Syria rose before us and we put in at Tyre to unload our cargo.

Once the *Psamathe* was made fast to the dock in Tyre, Paul led his delegation to meet the Christians of the city. Jube, Tyre's leader, welcomed the famous visitors and brought together the entire congregation to hear Paul speak. At the end of the service Jube drew Paul aside. "Do not go to Jerusalem," he said. "The Holy Spirit has revealed to me that a terrible fate awaits you there."

"Enemies I have," Paul said, "but my mission for Christ impels me to go. Whatever my fate, I pray the grace of God will be with me."

In a day and a night the cargo of the *Psamathe* was unloaded, and the ship sailed on to the south, stopping one day in Ptolemais, and going the next day to Caesarea, where the voyage ended. There Paul and his disciples were welcomed by Philip the evangelist, minister of the churches in Caesarea and towns surrounding. Once leader of the Hellenists' opposition to Paul, over the years Philip had come to admire Paul for his accomplishments.

Philip's house was modest, but he, his wife, and their four young daughters moved about to make room for Paul and Luke, with the disciples staying with other Christians. At Philip's urging Paul remained in Caesarea for two days to preach the gospel and, with his disciples, counsel the ill and dying. On their last evening, as they dined in the common room of Philip's house, a new guest arrived — a hunchback, shrunken of body but large of head, his cloak threadbare and covered with the dust of the road from Jerusalem. Paul recognized him instantly: Agabus, the dwarf prophet who had come to Barnabas in Antioch to warn of a coming famine.

To Paul, the presence of Agabus was symbolic, a completion of the circle. It was Agabus who had first persuaded Barnabas, and then Paul, to collect money from wealthy Antiochenes to prevent starvation among poor Christian Jews in Jerusalem; now, thirteen years later, Paul was still collecting from those with more, to aid those with less.

Seeing Paul there, Agabus came up to him. Saying nothing, but affecting the way of those who prophesy in mime, using images in action, he carefully unfastened and took the leather belt from around Paul's waist. Still silent, he sat on the floor, methodically bound his own feet, and then contrived to bind his hands. Only then did he speak, his voice yet a guttural and measured rumble. "The Holy Spirit says these things: In Jerusalem the Jews will bind in this way the man whose belt this is, and they will deliver him up into the hands of the pagan rulers."

At first there was silence, broken by Philip: "Paul, heed Agabus. Do not go up to Jerusalem, I beg you. Let the others deliver the collection, while you go on to Rome and continue your mission." With that, the four daughters and other guests joined in, all beseeching him not to enter into the camp of his enemies.

Paul raised his hands for silence. "What are you doing? Your weeping is breaking my heart. For I not only am ready to be bound hand and foot, but also to die in Jerusalem for the name of the Lord Jesus."

Again Philip and the others of Caesarea pleaded with Paul, but he shook his head and all fell silent. Then they heard the rumble of Agabus: "The will of the Lord be done."

XXXV

BESIEGED

The procession that Paul led through the streets of Jerusalem brought wives to their windows and provoked busy men to stop and stare. Not often did they witness such a spectacle: The man Paul, known widely as the young Sanhedrin prosecutor who defected to the Jesus sect, now gray and balding, was striding ahead of an incongruous retinue of strangers. First came a scholar of ample girth in Grecian silks of purest white, then a dark and wiry Jew in rustic cotton, followed by four gentiles in Macedonian dress, two of them unusually tall and crowned with flowing golden hair.

Passing the public market, they walked in train to the upper city and to the house of Mnason, an old Cypriot and early convert to Christianity, now a widower. Philip had gone ahead to arrange for the seven to stay with Mnason, and then to inform James that Paul would visit him at the mother church the next day.

When Philip returned to Mnason's house, Paul was waiting. "What did James say?" Paul asked.

"He welcomes you and all traveling with you to the mother church," Philip said, "and asked that you come at the fourth hour. He will assemble the elders and his disciples to greet you."

"Will Peter be present?" Paul asked.

"No, Peter rarely visits Jerusalem now. Last winter he helped with churches in Antioch."

The old warehouse where the council had met nine years earlier had been torn down and a new churchhouse put up in its place. It was rough stone, whitewashed with lime on the outside; inside, carpenters had built a plain wooden platform, altar, and rows of benches. Entering the nave, Paul felt it looked more like a synagogue than the churches he had built.

He led his delegation to the platform, where all were warmly greeted by James and the elders. Upon Paul's signal, Titus brought the two satchels of gold and silver and presented them to James, prompting murmurs of approval from all. In response James prayed: "As the scriptures tell us, 'Thine, O Lord, is the greatness, and the power, and the glory, and the victory, and the majesty. For all that is in the heaven and in the earth is thine. Thine is the kingdom, O Lord, and thou art exalted as head above all.'" He continued with a prayer of thanksgiving for the generosity of Christians in foreign lands.

After the last amen, James turned to Paul. "This assembly of elders and other brothers who worship in our mother church would hear how the gospel is being received in lands afar."

Paul described his travels by land and sea through Macedonia and Achaia, as well as Galatia and other provinces in Asia; cited one by one the cities where he had taken the message of salvation through Jesus Christ. He enumerated the numbers of souls he had converted in each place, Jew and gentile, and listed the schools he had created for disciples, ministers, and deacons. "All these things we accomplished," he said in conclusion, "by the grace of God and his son Christ Jesus, who sustained us in our mission despite every obstacle and hindrance put in our way by the hand of man."

As Paul took his seat, an elder raised his hand for recognition. "I, Nabal, speak for myself, and for others here, when I say that the works of the apostle Paul affirm and magnify the glory of God. May he long continue his mission in the service of Jesus Christ."

Another hand went up, this one in the congregation. "I am Elihu," he said, addressing Paul. He was young, with a loud voice and many gestures. "You see, Brother, that here in Judea and elsewhere, thousands of Jews have now become believers, and all are zealous in the Law. And they have been informed about you, that you teach Jews to ignore the Law of Moses, and that you tell Jews who live among the gentiles neither to circumcise their children nor to follow the customary practices and traditions."

"Any such charge is totally false," Paul said hotly. "Where are your witnesses to this? Bring them here that I may confront them now! Never have I told any Jew he is not bound by the Law of Moses."

"So you say here to us," Elihu replied with an edge of scorn as he walked toward Paul. "Yet this is what Jews have been told and believe, and when they hear that you have come to Jerusalem, a multitude will gather to confront you." He paused, and affected a voice of reason. "What is to be done? This we propose: We have here four members who have taken a vow. Go with these four and be purified with them and pay their costs of shaving their heads in penitence. Then all shall know that what they have been told about you is not true, that you yourself follow customs and keep the Law."

The proposal was demeaning, intentionally. Paul glanced at James, wondering if his pompous rival might have conspired to humiliate him; James' face was impassive. He knew he must suppress his impulse to dismiss the proposal as unworthy of his standing in the church; but that would surely cause some fools to suspect that the absurd slander might be true. With a casual wave of his hand toward Elihu, he said: "I consent. I know not these four men, but as they are our brothers, I will be purified with them. As to paying for their heads to be shaved, I have today added my own small earnings to the collection given to James for the poor. But I am accustomed to working with my hands, and I will earn the money to pay for all the costs of penance and purification." He turned toward James. "Show me these four penitents."

The next day Paul purified himself, then took the four into the Temple and made a public announcement that in seven days the period of purification would end and offerings would be made on behalf of each man. In the days of waiting, Paul found himself in an unaccustomed state of idleness. Every morning he went alone to the Temple. Afternoons, from the sixth to the tenth hour, he conversed at Mnason's house with Christian Jews who queued to see him. Late in the day he walked about the city with Trophimus or Aristarchus, pointing out significant sites and relating the history of the city.

On the sixth morning of the time of the vow, Paul was alone in the Temple, praying, when he was observed by three Jews on a pilgrimage from Ephesus. One cried out: "Men of Israel, help! This is the man who teaches everywhere against the people of Israel, against the Law, and against this Temple. Even worse, he brought a gentile into the Temple and so defiled this holy place."

The Temple was almost filled with pilgrims, and they broke out in loud shrieks and accusations. Paul shouted in protest — but no one would listen. Temple guards came on the run, heard the cries that their Temple had been profaned, and forced everyone to leave. Guards shut and barred the doors of the Temple; seeing that, some of the angry pilgrims seized Paul, beat him with fists and sticks, and dragged him across Solomon's porch, shouting, "Stone him! Break his neck! Throw his body over the wall!"

Like a windblown forest fire, word spread through the city that the Temple had been defiled. Mobs swarmed through the streets, riots broke out, provoking the commander of the Roman garrison to order troops to restore order. Leading a company of centurions, Claudius Lysias himself raced from Fort Antonia to the porch outside the Temple. The angry Jews, seeing the soldiers and their commander, immediately stopped beating Paul.

Assuming the bloody victim was guilty, Lysias ordered his soldiers: "Bind him." As they were locking Paul in chains, Lysias asked, "Who are you?" Paul gave his name and declared his innocence, but his reply was lost in the shouting and cries for revenge. Exasperated by the noise and emotion of the mob, Lysias commanded: "Take him to the fort."

The mob followed, shouting, "He must die! He must die!" As the soldiers were dragging him up the steps of Fort Antonia, Paul said to the commander: "Is it lawful for me to say something to you?"

"You speak Greek?" Lysias said in astonishment. "Then you are not the Egyptian who started a revolt last month."

"I, an Egyptian?" Paul said. "I am a Jew of Tarsus, of Cilicia, a citizen of no mean city. And I beg you, allow me to speak to these people. I have done them no wrong."

The commander looked at Paul for a moment, then said, "Very well. Speak."

Standing on the steps in chains, Paul raised his hands to signal for attention. "Men, brothers, fathers, now hear my defense to you." When they heard him speaking in the local Hebrew dialect, they listened in silence. "I am a Jew, having been born in Tarsus of Cilicia, but having been brought up in this city at the feet of Gamaliel, and educated strictly according to our ancestral Law, being zealous for God, just as all of you are today. I persecuted those of the Way, even to the point of putting them to death. I bound both men and women of the Way and put them in prison, as the high priest and the entire council of elders in the Sanhedrin will testify. From the high priest I received letters to the elders of the synagogue in Damascus, directing me to arrest those of the Way in Damascus, bind them in chains, and bring back to Jerusalem for trial and punishment."

He surveyed the audience; they were angry, skeptical, but attentive.

"And it happened to me, as I drew near to Damascus on my journey, suddenly, about midday, a great light out of the heaven shone around me, and I fell to the ground, and I heard a voice saying to me, 'Saul, Saul, why do you persecute me?' And I answered, 'Who are you, sir?' And he said to me, 'I am Jesus the Nazarene whom you persecute.'

"Now, my two companions, guards from the Temple, saw the great light and were alarmed; but they did not understand the voice speaking to me. And I said, 'What shall I do, Lord?' And the Lord said to me, 'Rising up, go into Damascus, and there you will be told about all the things appointed to you to do.' But I could not see, having been blinded by the brilliance of the light, so I was led by the hand of the two with me and went into Damascus.

"For three days I sat in an inn in darkness. And then a certain Ananias, a devout Jew of Damascus, came to me and restored my sight, saying, 'You shall be a witness for the righteous one to all men.' And it happened to me, after returning to Jerusalem, while praying in the Temple I fell into a trance and saw Jesus saying to me, 'Hurry. Leave Jerusalem at once, because they will not accept your testimony about me. Go. I will send you to the gentiles afar.'"

At Paul's mention of Jesus appearing to him in the Temple, the mob erupted into shouts — "Rid the earth of this man! He is not fit to live!" Some began ripping their garments, others threw dust into the air and screamed curses. Seeing the mob getting out of control again, Lysias ordered his soldiers to take the prisoner into the fortress. Inside he said to Paul: "You will be whipped until you confess the crime for which they cry out against you."

As Paul was dragged away to the whipping post, his anger rose at the injustice. Not for years had he been flogged, and he would never forget that he had almost died from the illegal beating in Issus. When the soldiers forcibly stretched out his arms around the post and began to tie his hands with leather thongs, he pulled away and confronted the older centurion: "Wait! Is it lawful for you to flog a Roman citizen who has not been brought to trial?"

The centurion immediately went to his commander. "Be aware of what we are about to do, for this man is a Roman."

Lysias walked over to the whipping post and looked at Paul. "Are you a Roman citizen?"

"I am," Paul replied.

Lysias looked in doubt at the bloody and disheveled man in torn robe. "I bought my citizenship with a great sum," he said.

"I was born a citizen," Paul said firmly.

Knowing that they could be punished for violating the rights of a Roman citizen, the soldiers stepped back, and Lysias, fearing he could be reprimanded for putting a Roman in chains before trial, gave a curt order. "Remove the chains."

When Paul was free of the bonds, Lysias said to him, "For your safety you will remain in the fort tonight. As you are a Jew, on the morrow you will go before the court of the Jews. My soldiers will take you to the Sanhedrin so that the high priests may judge the accusations against you."

Paul rose early the next morning to consider his plight. He blamed himself. His closest advisers, an infallible prophet, and his own intuition had warned him that in Jerusalem he might be imprisoned, persecuted, and even executed. Where could he turn for help? Not to his companions at the house of Mnason; five of the six were gentiles. Not to James; his Judaizers considered Paul the enemy. Not to the Sanhedrin; Zadok had sworn vengeance against him. Not to Antonius Felix; Rome's governor colluded with the high priest. Fear, cold and stark, made his throat dry and his knees tremble. But he lifted his eyes to the heavens and said, "I am not alone."

Later in the morning, when the Sanhedrin deputies and guards arrived at the fortress, Lysias issued a stern warning: "This Jew I hand over to you to be examined for laws he may have broken. Be aware: Though he is a Jew, he is also a Roman citizen and therefore under my protection. A company of my soldiers will accompany him to guarantee his safety as he appears before your court."

Standing on the black stone of the accused before the court of the Sanhedrin, Paul looked about. Some faces were different, but the imposing room, the tiers of benches, the sense of imperial judgment, all were the same as when he had been a prosecutor. From an upper tier Zadok, wrinkled and spare, stared at him with his cold black eyes. On a lower tier among the sages was Gamaliel, leaning forward, observing him with a look of grave concern. When the seventy-one members were settled in their places, the court clerk signaled Paul to speak.

"Men, brothers, I have conducted myself toward God in all good conscience to this day."

"Strike him!" came down the order from high on the benches, and a burly bailiff raised his fist and struck Paul in the mouth.

Fierce with anger, Paul shouted: "God will strike you! You are like a whitewashed wall — pure on the outside, dirt on the inside. I know the Law. How can you sit there and claim to judge me according to the Law and then break the Law by ordering a man to strike me?"

The court clerk pointed his finger at Paul. "You revile the high priest of God."

Recovering his poise, Paul said innocently: "Brothers, I did not know he was high priest." In truth, he did not. Paul had never before seen this man, though he knew his name — Ananias, son of the wealthy Nedebaios, who had bought the position for his son some ten years earlier. Subsequently the son was arrested, sent to Rome, and deprived of the office. Through influence he was later reinstated. Thinking he should say something, not to apologize but to recognize priestly authority, Paul looked to the seat of the high priest: "Certainly it is written in the second book of scripture, 'You shall not speak evil of a ruler of your people.'"

Observing that Pharisees still sat apart from Sadducees, Paul remembered how the two rival factions quarreled, frequently and venomously. "Men, brothers, I am a Pharisee, son of Pharisees. It is for our hope in resurrection of the dead that I am on trial."

As Paul expected, he incited the Sadducees, whose doctrine denied the possibility of resurrection. One took the floor to argue: "There is no resurrection, no angel, and no afterlife." The Pharisees rose as a body to shout down the Sadducees, leaving the high priest vainly trying to restore order. Hoping to end the dispute, the chief scribe for the Pharisees stood and raised his hand for silence. "We find nothing evil in this man," he said. "If a spirit spoke to this man, or an angel, let us not fight against God." But the scribe's finding meant nothing to the Sadducees, and the argument broke out again. Lysias, standing outside with his soldiers, had heard enough of the uproar within. Fearing the Jews might tear his citizen-prisoner to pieces, he ordered a centurion to go into the court, bring Paul out, and confine him again in Fort Antonia.

Alone in his cell that night, Paul had a vision of the Lord. "Courage, Paul, for as you have testified for me in Jerusalem, so also will you testify for me in Rome." Thus comforted, that night Paul slept well.

Paul was eating with the soldiers the next morning when a centurion came to him. "A young visitor wishes to speak to you. He will give no name, but claims to know you." Thinking the visitor must be Sopater, the only Jew among his companions, Paul hurried to the door. But it was not Sopater.

"Jonathan! My dear nephew! What a blessing it is for you to visit this old man." After a quick embrace, Paul stepped back to look at Rachel's son. The boy had grown into a virile and handsome youth.

Trying to be casual, Jonathan drew Paul away from the guards. "There is great danger," he said in a low voice. "Within the hour I learned from a friend at court that Zadok, chief counsel to the high priest, plots against your life. At his bidding, a band of forty zealots presented themselves before Ananias himself this morning and swore to this oath: 'We curse ourselves to eat nothing until we kill Paul.' This is Zadok's plan: The high priest will ask Lysias to send you before the Sanhedrin again on the pretense that the court may examine your case more closely. On the way, at the narrow turn of the street behind the old market, these forty men will be waiting in alleys on both sides, all armed with knives and swords. There they will ambush the soldiers, overpower them, and kill you."

Paul looked at his nephew in admiration, knowing that he had put his own life at risk by coming inside the fort. Maintaining outward calm, Paul took Jonathan by the arm and walked over to the centurion, who had been watching them. "Take this young man to your commander," he said, "for he has important information to report."

The centurion, sensing urgency, took Jonathan at once into the quarters of Lysias, who questioned Paul's nephew in private. When Jonathan finished his account of the plot, Lysias said nothing for a moment but reached a swift conclusion: *If these Jews are preparing to assassinate this speech maker in front of Roman soldiers, either they are bigger fools than we had thought, or this man Paul is a more important citizen than we had realized.* Turning to Jonathan, he gave him this order: "Tell no one that you have given me this information. Paul's life, and your life, may depend on that." He summoned the centurion who had brought Jonathan. "Take this young man out by the secret door. I do not want him seen leaving this fort."

At once Lysias summoned his two senior centurions and issued this order: "Get two hundred foot soldiers ready by the third hour of the night to march to Caesarea. With them are to go seventy horsemen, two hundred spearmen, and supply wagons. Provide horses for Paul, and deliver him safely to Felix the governor. Parmenion, you are to command and explain this action to Felix. Julius, you are second in command."

All night the column of Roman soldiers quick-marched, cavalry patrols in front, on the flanks, and guarding the rear; spearmen and foot soldiers arrayed in battle formation around the lone figure on horseback. Some time after midnight they reached the Via Maris, and marched on north to Antipatris, where they camped at the Roman fort. At dawn Parmenion, believing his cohort had brought Paul through the gravest danger, ordered Julius to lead the foot soldiers and spearman back to Jerusalem, in case Paul's escape provoked new riots. The horseman escorted Paul on to Caesarea and through the gates of the fortress of the governor.

Passing through the walls, Paul remembered his first glimpse of this marble city within a city that King Herod had created. He was a youth then, on his way to Jerusalem to enter the school of Gamaliel. He counted: It had been thirty-one years.

Marching his prisoner into the reception court, Parmenion presented Paul to Felix. "Excellency," he said, "this prisoner is Paul, a Roman citizen involved in a dispute about Jewish law that turned into a riot in Jerusalem. Ruffians, hired by Sanhedrin zealots, were plotting to kill him. Since the prisoner is a Roman citizen, he is entitled to military protection until the Sanhedrin brings formal charges against him."

Felix studied Paul's disheveled appearance. "In which province did you become a citizen?"

"Cilicia, Excellency," Paul replied.

"I will hear you fully when your accusers come," Felix said. "Until then, you will be detained here in the palace."

XXXVI

IMPRISONED

From Antioch to Alexandria, the governor of the Roman province of Judea was known to be incompetent, dissolute, cruel, and avaricious. Antonius Felix had been appointed to office only because he was a brother of Pallas, a palace favorite of Claudius' wife, Agrippina; Felix remained in office only because he was the husband of Drusilla, daughter of Herod.

A prisoner in the lavish palace at Caesarea was uncommon, so Felix asked his wife, a Jew, if she could explain why the Jews might plot to kill one of their own. Drusilla told him the story of the prophet Jesus appearing in Galilee many years before and preaching a new order of the Jewish beliefs. "Your prisoner Paul is a leader of the Jewish sect — they are called Christians — that wrongly considers Jesus to be the long-awaited Messiah. Most Jews, like me, consider Paul to be a dangerous heretic."

"If this Paul is so important a leader," Felix said, "then he, or one of his followers, may be willing to buy his freedom."

Drusilla laughed. "Christians are poor," she said.

"Then," Felix said with a smile, "perhaps you Jews will pay me for him."

Five days later the high priest Ananias, seven of his elders, and Tertullus, a hired orator, arrived at the governor's place to present the case against Paul. Felix summoned Paul from his room in the north wing of the palace and ordered the hearing to begin.

Tertullus spoke for the prosecution. "Most excellent Felix, because of you we have long enjoyed peace, and reforms have been made for the people of Judea because of your foresight. We welcome this in every way throughout the land with utmost gratitude. We do not want to take up too much of your valuable time, but I beg you to hear us briefly with your customary graciousness. We find this man pestilent. He stirs up insurrection among Jews throughout the world. He is a ringleader of the Nazarene sect. He even attempted to profane the Temple, so we seized him so that he might be judged according to our Law. But Lysias, the commander of Fort Antonia, came with a great force of soldiers, took him out of our hands, and ordered his accusers to appear before you." He gestured toward Paul, standing at the side under guard. "If you ask this man, you will learn for yourself the truth of our charges."

Felix turned to Paul. "Speak."

"I cheerfully make my defense, Excellency, knowing that for many years you have been a judge over this nation. As you can verify for yourself, it is not more than twelve days since I went up to Jerusalem on my pilgrimage. It is not true that anyone found me disputing in the Temple or stirring up a crowd in the synagogues or anywhere else in the city. They can give no proof of the accusations they make against me now.

"But this I do admit to you: According to the Way, which they call a sect, I worship the God of our ancestors, believing everything laid down according to the Law or written in the Prophets. The Way is not a new or different religion; it is the Judaism of ancient times now fulfilled. I hold the same hope in God that the Pharisees of the Temple hold, that there will be a resurrection of both the righteous and the unrighteous. I do my best always to have a clear conscience toward God and all people.

"I came to Jerusalem after many years to bring alms to the poor of the Way and to offer sacrifices. It was for this reason that I was in the Temple. I was completing the rite of purification, avoiding crowds and making no disturbance. But also in the Temple were Jews from Asia — and they are the ones who should appear before you and make their accusations, if indeed they have anything against me. At least let these who are present say what crime they held against me when I appeared before the Sanhedrin — unless it was the one sentence I called out: 'It is about the resurrection of the dead that I am on trial before you today.'"

Hearing no evidence of crime against Rome, Felix adjourned the hearing and told Paul: "When Lysias the commander comes down, I will decide your case."

After Ananias and his delegation departed for Jerusalem, Felix spoke to the centurion guarding Paul. "Keep this man in custody in the praetorium.

He is free to move about within the palace walls. His friends may visit him and attend to his needs."

Later that same week Felix and Drusilla sent for Paul to come to the pavilion of their living quarters. "I would hear from you on the subject of the one you call Christ Jesus," Felix said.

In reply Paul immediately began a discourse on the Christian's commitment to live a life of truth, honesty, and uprightness and to control his instincts for lust and debauchery. "The time is coming," Paul said, "when God will pass judgment on all who have lived in sin and wickedness."

The mention of God's judgment so frightened Felix that he would listen no more, but said quickly to Paul: "For the present, go. Some time later I will call for you."

As his days of waiting became weeks, and the weeks became months, Paul could do nothing but endure. To be idle, to be barred from preaching, to have no audience of eager followers — this was punishment more painful than any tyrant could have devised for him. He who had walked thousands of miles could now go no more than two hundred paces to the high palace wall. He who had sailed over the limitless blue seas could now only stand in the palace tower and look with longing at distant sails. He who had surrounded himself with disciples and throngs of worshipers now sat alone in his room. He had no book to read, and was forbidden to write.

Visitors he could have. Luke came from time to time, affording the opportunity to converse with a scholarly equal. Then Luke would be off again to Galilee to talk to those who had known Jesus there or had heard him speak. Titus, Trophimus, and Sopater came to ask for instructions. Paul saw no merit in their being idle, so he sent the first to Corinth, the second back to Ephesus, and the third to his home in Beroea.

To Paul's great surprise, a guard came to his quarters one day to say that a man named Peter was at the gate and wanted to see him. Paul greeted his aging adversary with more wariness than warmth. Their conversation began pleasantly, with each describing his successes and disappointments in establishing churches. They agreed that the death of Barnabas had severely hindered the movement. Casually, too casually in Paul's mind, Peter mentioned that he was leaving the next day to organize Rome. And when Peter said that on the way he would go to Galatia to visit his church in Ancyra, Paul could no longer hold his tongue.

"You and James and your conniving agents undermined my churches in Galatia," he said bluntly. "You destroyed everything that Barnabas and I created in Pisidian Antioch and Iconium and Lystra."

Peter leaped to his feet, his weathered cheeks red with anger. "I cannot account for James," he said, "but I absolutely deny that I or any of my following misled your converts and turned them away from the faith." Paul did not believe him; he knew Peter's record of denials. After a perfunctory clasp of hands, Peter left.

Paul's most frequent visitor was Aristarchus, who had volunteered to assist Philip with the churches in Caesarea and along the coast. One afternoon Paul and Aristarchus were walking in the palace gardens when Aristarchus said in a low voice, "Last week, as I was leaving the palace, the bailiff of the governor's court remarked to me that the payment of a substantial fine might set you free. I can find the money, but I am not sure the bailiff can be trusted."

"No more than his governor can be trusted," Paul said. "Felix wants a bribe. He has made that plain, and my answer has been equally plain. A bribe is to free the guilty. I am innocent. No one is to pay a bribe to restore the freedom that is my right."

Unwilling to pay, unable to persuade Felix to summon witnesses and try his case, Paul spent the long days and nights trying to console himself but aching for escape. Often he walked his room through the night like a lion in a cage. Months passed, seasons changed from winter to summer and back again. And still he waited.

At last, after two years, Paul learned from a guard that Felix would soon be replaced. Concerned that a new governor might turn him over to the Sanhedrin, Paul made an impassioned appeal to Felix, concluding: "Use the power all know that you have. Either try my case, or set me free."

Felix refused, yielding to Drusilla.

Porcius Festus, the new governor, was a soldier who had made his reputation countering bands of assassins and terrorists. He knew little about Judea or its people, but he was honest, and his intentions were for the good of the people. Three days after his arrival in the province, Festus rode up from

Caesarea to Jerusalem for his first official appearance in the city. While he was there, Zadok, as chief counsel of the Sanhedrin, outlined to Festus the case against Paul and, with Ananias assenting, asked that the prisoner be transferred to Jerusalem for trial. Festus knew nothing of the Jews' plot to murder Paul. But he replied to Ananias and Zadok, "The man Paul is in custody in Caesarea, and I will soon be returning there. So let those of you in authority come down with me, and if the man has done wrong, let them bring charges."

On the day after he returned to Caesarea, Festus took his seat on the tribunal and ordered Paul to be brought before him. As soon as Paul appeared, Zadok and a phalanx of witnesses who had come down from Jerusalem surrounded him, accusing him of breaking the Law of Moses, of advocating heresy, and of profaning the Temple.

Confronting them all, and facing Zadok eye to eye, Paul said: "You know that I know the Law, and I have in no way committed an offense against the Law or the statutes, or against the Temple, or against the emperor."

Listening to the raucous witnesses and the arguments between Zadok and Paul, Festus realized that no Roman law had been broken. Instead, this prisoner he had inherited was being accused of violating Jewish religious law, and any such violation should obviously be tried by the Jews' own high court. But no Roman citizen could be tried by the Sanhedrin without the consent of the accused. As the new governor, Festus wanted to gain favor with the Jews, so he asked Paul: "Are you willing to go up to Jerusalem and be tried there before me on these charges?"

Paul knew his rights as a Roman citizen, and resolved he must act at once to counter any move by the new governor or the high priest to put him on trial in Jerusalem. Should he go up that road again, he had no doubt that Zadok would either hire assassins to murder him before a trial or contrive a way to execute him after a mockery of a trial. So Paul said: "I am standing before the tribunal of the emperor, and this is where I should be tried, Excellency. I have done no wrong to the Jews, as you surely know. If I had done wrong, or committed any offense punishable by death, I would not refuse to die. But as there is no crime of which they can accuse me, no one has the right to surrender me to them. I appeal to Caesar."

Festus summoned his advisers, listened, then addressed Paul: "You have appealed to Caesar. To Caesar you shall go."

The words filled Paul's soul as a song from heaven. He wanted to shout in exaltation. Once the governor had pronounced that decree, no vengeful high priest could appeal it. Walking back to his room, Paul disciplined himself not to show the exuberance and elation he felt. After more than two years in his palatial prison, he would soon be free. He expected to go to Rome at once. Instead, he was delayed once more.

Two days after Paul made his appeal to Caesar, royal visitors appeared at the governor's palace. King Agrippa II, who held titular responsibility to Rome for Judea, Samaria, and other coastal regions, arrived in pomp and ceremony with Queen Bernice, who was not only Agrippa's wife but his sister as well. Tributes and ceremonies honoring the king and queen fully occupied the new governor and all palace attendants and servants.

In the course of informing King Agrippa about all that was taking place in the province, Festus mentioned the case of Paul. "There is a man here in custody, a Jew who is a Roman citizen, left behind by Felix. On my first official visit to Jerusalem, the chief priests and the elders of the Jews informed me that this prisoner — his name is Paul — had broken their laws, and they demanded I deliver him to them to be punished. I told them that it is not the practice of Roman authorities to hand over a citizen to a subordinate court before the accused has met his accusers face to face and is given the opportunity to defend himself. So the accusers, all Jews, returned here with me and I wasted no time, but took my seat on the tribunal and ordered the man to be brought. When the accusers stood up to speak, they did not charge the man with any of the crimes that I expected. Instead, they had certain points of disagreement with him about their demon worship, and about a certain Jesus, who had died, but whom Paul claimed to live. Being puzzled by the arguments on both sides, I asked the accused if he would be willing to go to Jerusalem to be tried on this issue. But he appealed to Caesar. So I commanded him to be held until I could send him to Caesar."

King Agrippa was himself a Jew, a great-grandson of Herod the Great, and his commission from Caesar entitled him to rights over the Temple in Jerusalem and influence with the Sanhedrin. He listened with great interest to Festus' account, and at the end said: "I am minded to hear the man myself."

"Tomorrow," Festus said, "you shall hear him."

To the sound of trumpets, King Agrippa and Queen Bernice, robed in silks of purple and gold, entered the auditorium of the palace, accepting the acclaim of the assembled tribunes and city officials as they moved in measured steps to their thrones on the dais. Festus, in fine voice, commanded a centurion to bring Paul before the king.

As Paul stood before the thrones, Festus made a formal address. "King Agrippa, and all here present with us, you see before you the man about whom the entire Jewish community has petitioned me, loudly crying out that he should not be allowed to remain alive. But I perceive nothing that would warrant his execution. When he appealed to Caesar, which is his right as a Roman citizen, I decided to send him. But I have nothing definite that I can write to His Imperial Majesty about him. For this reason I brought him before you, King Agrippa, so that you may examine him and guide me with your wisdom in writing to Caesar. For it seems unreasonable to me to send a prisoner to Rome and not state the charges against him."

Agrippa looked directly at Paul, made the slight nod of recognition that is the manner of royalty, and said: "It is allowed for you to speak."

Paul stretched out his hand in blessing and began his defense. "I consider myself fortunate that it is before you, King Agrippa, I am to make my defense today against all the accusations of the Jews, because you are an expert in matters of custom and controversy among the Jews. Therefore I beg of you to listen to me patiently.

"Truly, all the Jews know my way of life from youth, a life spent from the beginning among my own people and in Jerusalem. They have known for a long time, if they would be willing to testify, that I belonged to the strictest sect of our religion, belonged to and lived as a Pharisee. And now I stand here on trial because of my hope in the promise made by God to our ancestors, a promise that our twelve tribes hope to attain, as they earnestly worship day and night. It is for this hope, Your Majesty, that I am accused by Jews. Why is it judged unbelievable by you that God can raise the dead?

"Indeed, I myself was convinced that I ought to do many things against those believing in Jesus of Nazareth. In Jerusalem, acting on the authority of the chief priests, I not only locked up in prison many men and women who followed Jesus, but I also cast my vote against them when they were being condemned to death. By punishing them often in the synagogues, I tried to force them to blaspheme. I was so furious with rage at them that I pursued them even to foreign cities."

As he had on the steps of Fort Antonia, Paul recounted in detail his revelation on the road to Damascus, his recognition that Jesus was the Messiah, and his obedience to Jesus' command to take the gospel to the world. "After that, King Agrippa, I could not disobey the heavenly vision. Instead, I told of my vision first to the Jews of Damascus, then to Jerusalem and all Judea, and also to the gentiles, urging them to repent and turn to God, to live in ways that would make them worthy of repentance. That is why the Jews laid hands on me in the Temple and tried to kill me. But with help from the Lord God, I hold to my position to this day, proclaiming to small and great what the Prophets foretold: By resurrecting the dead, God would bring light to his own chosen people and to the gentiles."

As Paul spoke fervently in his defense, the attendants of the palace listened with awe and rapt attention, but a disbelieving Festus could not contain his dismay. "Paul! You rave! Too much learning has driven you to madness."

But Paul replied calmly: "Festus, Your Excellency, I am not mad. I speak in truth. Indeed, King Agrippa knows about these things, and to him I speak fearlessly. For I am persuaded that nothing I have said comes as a surprise to him. After all, these things were not hidden in a corner." He turned to the throne. "King Agrippa, do you believe in the Prophets? I know you do."

At this Agrippa said to Paul in good humor: "A little more of this, and you might persuade me to become a Christian."

"Little or much more," Paul said, "I will pray to God that not only you, but all those hearing me today, would come to be as I am — except for these bonds as a prisoner."

With this the king rose, and his queen, and they walked with the governor to a private chamber. There Agrippa and Festus talked at length about the case of Paul. At the end, Festus said, "Your Majesty, I can find nothing that warrants the execution of this man, or even keeping him in custody."

The king nodded gravely, and said: "I would release the man if he had not appealed to Caesar."

XXXVII

FINAL VOYAGE

On the day after King Agrippa and his royal party departed, Festus summoned Paul to his private quarters. "The king and I decided that as you appealed to Rome, you will go to Rome, in custody," Festus said. "Once there, you will be handed over to the praetorian guard to be detained until it pleases Caesar to hear your case." Festus paused before he added: "But there is one problem."

Paul held his breath. Would there be still another delay?

"No ship will sail for Rome until spring," Festus said. "With winter so close at hand, few ships risk going to sea at all. However, there is one — a coastal ship out of Adramyttium leaving here in two days to return to its home port. The captain will put in at Myra, and there you might find a ship for Rome. If not, you would be forced to winter there."

Festus sat back in his chair. "Or," he said, opening his hands as if in welcome, "you can remain here in the palace in detention and I will send you directly to Rome on the first ship of the new year."

Paul did not hesitate. Two years of idleness was enough and more than enough. He was not sure he could trust Festus to keep his word; his predecessor had lied. More important, by far, was his longing to be out of this palace, out of Caesarea, out of Judea. He would rather be anywhere on the open sea than being held here in bonds of idleness. "I choose to leave at once, Excellency."

"Then leave you shall," Festus replied, masking his own relief at Paul's answer. Festus had concluded that so long as Paul remained this close to Jerusalem, vengeful Jews would keep trying to assassinate him. If they succeeded, then he as governor would be blamed for not having protected this troublesome citizen.

"These are the conditions for your journey," Festus continued. "You and four other prisoners will be turned over at noon tomorrow to the centurion Julius. He will command the squad of ten other soldiers who will be your guards. All are good men, of the Augustan Cohort, well trained and hardened in battle. I have instructed Julius to take five sets of chains for hands and feet, but not to use them unless necessary. He will afford you some freedom, but you must understand that if you should escape, Julius and one other guard will be put to death."

"I understand and I accept these conditions," Paul said. "Is it permitted for me to take two Christians on the ship with me?"

"Who are these men?" Festus asked.

"The scholar Luke and my disciple Aristarchus, both of Macedon," Paul said. "They have visited me here and are known to your servants."

"You have my consent, but the final decision will be up to the captain. The ship is the *Oeno*, at the main dock nearest the Harbor of Herod."

Paul rose to go, but Festus gestured for him to resume his seat. "Did you know," he asked slowly, "that King Agrippa judged that you could be freed had you not appealed to Caesar?"

"I did not," Paul said, "but I contended from the beginning that I should be freed."

"Yet," Festus said, "except for the protection of Rome, you would have been killed outside the Temple in Jerusalem. And perhaps, except for the guards I assigned for your journey, you could still be killed."

"Excellency," Paul said, "often I have eluded death. You have yet to believe in my God, but he holds power over all, and he is ever by my side."

Against the brute force of a headwind out of the west, the longboat towed the *Oeno* out of the channel and into the open sea. Captain Kronos was a Phoenician, bold enough in good weather but cautious in venturing out so late in the season. He ordered a short sail and a northerly course following the coastline. On the first day they put in at Sidon.

Paul, for the first time of his life, fell ill at sea. Two years of inactivity had softened his body; his legs were so weak that he kept losing his balance on the rolling and pitching deck. Luke knew of medicine that would help. So with Julius' permission, Paul went ashore with Luke to find, among the Christians in Sidon, a physician. They were successful, and brought back herbs to relieve Paul's discomfort.

From Sidon the *Oeno* put to sea again, but the headwind was so strong that Kronos could not sail due west to Myra, so he took the wind on his port beam to reach the lee of Cyprus. Passing Cape Andreas, he changed course to the west, riding the current that flows off the coast of Cilicia and Pamphylia. Two days in the lee of the Taurus Mountains brought the ship again into the open sea. Struggling against new and fiercer headwinds, the *Oeno* tacked day and night, seeming to go nowhere. Paul, much improved, volunteered to stand a watch at the helm. For fifteen days the crew beat westward, until at last the lookout saw the mountains of Lycia and Kronos steered into Myra.

Even before the *Oeno* was made fast, Julius leaped to the dock to find the next ship bound for Rome. There was one, the *Isis*, a large ship out of Alexandria, indeed the biggest ship Julius had ever seen. Her hold was filled with bags of grain, the last of the season's wheat crop from the Nile delta, and her decks were loaded with two hundred and forty-five passengers, all anxious to reach Rome before winter storms closed the seas.

When Julius told Captain Barouk that he was bringing aboard five prisoners, two other passengers, ten soldiers, and himself, he met with protest. "My ship is fully loaded," he said, "but I will speak to my owner, Dairut. He is aboard."

"Summon your owner," Julius ordered.

When Dairut arrived, Julius simply exercised his authority under Caesar to order owner and captain to take his party aboard.

Entry from the Journal of Luke

The *Isis* put to sea on the last day of the tenth month, with the strong winds out of the west persisting. Barouk had plotted his course to beat along the Asian coast to Cnidus, take on food and water there, then sail south, taking the wind off the starboard bow, to Crete, continuing south to near Africa, then beating northwest to the straits between Sicily and the toe of Italy and on to grain warehouses at Puteoli.

The winds being constant against us, we made little headway. With difficulty we finally arrived off Cnidus, but the force of the wind was so strong that Barouk could not maneuver the ship into port, so he headed south. With the wind on the starboard beam, in three days we cleared Cape Salmone, the eastern point of Crete. In the lee of land, we tacked along the coast, finally dropping anchor in the small but for us aptly named harbor, Fair Havens.

As so much time had been lost, winter was upon us, bringing great peril on the seas. Knowing this, Paul elected to speak to Julius and Barouk. "Men," he said, "I can see that sailing on will be so dangerous that you risk losing not only cargo and ship, but also our lives. Winter here, and sail on in the spring." But Barouk and his owner, Dairut, refused, saying the harbor was not a suitable place to spend the winter, and the grain might spoil.

Other passengers then went to Barouk and persuaded him that he should not risk the open sea, but set sail for Phoenix, a larger port a day away on the south coast of Crete. There all could go ashore for the winter. While Barouk hesitated, the skies cleared and a gentle breeze came up from the south. Believing he could easily reach Phoenix in a day, Barouk raised the anchor and began to sail past Crete, holding a course close to shore.

Within hours, the storm wind called Euroclydon struck out of the northeast. The ship was seized as by a mighty force. As we could not head into the wind, Barouk gave way to it and let the ship be driven by the wind. Clinging to the mast in the storm, the lookout saw a small island ahead, which, by good fortune, the storm swept us around, for the helmsman was no longer master of our course. Running in the lee of an island called Clauda, the crew with great difficulty pulled the longboat close to the stern. Two men of courage, working from the longboat, passed ropes under the hull that were then brought up and secured to strengthen the planking. Winds shrieked and waves rose higher. Barouk, fearing the great ship might be swept to the rocks off Syrtia, floated a sea anchor to slow our drift.

Night fell, and in darkness the storm worsened. At last the

morning came, the winds howling without ceasing and the rain beating against us. Barouk, wanting to lighten the ship, ordered the crew to cast the cargo of wheat overboard, and the next day they threw off the loading beam and tackle. Still the Isis sank lower, wallowing in the sea. Neither the sun could be seen by day nor the stars by night. With the tempest pressing hard, all hope of being saved was taken away.

All aboard being hungry and afraid, Paul stood on the deck one morning and gathered around him as many as could hear. "O men," he proclaimed, raising his voice above the storm, "you see, you should have listened to me and not set sail from Crete. We could have avoided this peril and loss. So listen to me now. I exhort you to be cheered, for none of you will die, even though we will lose the ship. For last night there stood by me an angel of God, whom I serve. And the angel said, 'Do not fear, Paul. You must stand before Caesar. And behold, God has granted that all those sailing with you will be saved.' So keep up your courage, men, for I have faith that it will be exactly as I was told. We will run aground on an island."

On the fourteenth night of the storm, as we drifted some-where in the Sea of Adria, about midnight the sailors sensed that we were nearing land. And sounding, they found twenty fathoms. A little farther on they took soundings again and found fifteen fathoms. Fearing that the ship might strike a reef and break apart, the sailors put out four sea anchors and wished for day to come. But some of the crew, seeking to flee the ship for shore, lowered the longboat into the sea, pretending to be preparing to cast anchors from the ship's prow. Seeing this, Paul warned Julius: "Unless these sailors remain to handle the ship, no passenger will be saved." At once Julius turned to a soldier, gave an order, and the sol-dier drew his sword, cut the rope to the longboat, and let it drift away in the storm.

Just before daybreak Paul urged all the passengers to take

food from the last remaining stores, saying, "This is the four-teenth day you have been waiting in anxiety and without food. Therefore, I beg you to take food now, for you will need all your strength to survive. Do as I, and not one of you will lose a hair from your head." And saying this, he took bread, and gave thanks to God in the presence of all, and broke it, and began to eat. Then all took courage from him and they, too, began to eat.

As dawn brought light to the sky, we could see land, great rocks rising above the waves on one side, long lines of breakers, and a wide beach. The helmsman reckoned that he could avoid the reefs and drive the ship up on that beach. At Barouk's order, the crew cut away the sea anchors, the helmsman loosed the lashings from the rudder, and the crew hoisted the mainsail to the wind. At once the wind caught the sail and the *Isis* began to move toward the beach, but then a crosscurrent caught the ship and drove the prow hard into a reef. Held fast at the broken bow, the stern began to suffer pounding by the waves, lifting and falling on the rocks, opening the planking to the sea.

As all knew the ship was lost, the soldiers drew their swords to kill the prisoners so that none could escape. But Julius, determined to save Paul, commanded them to cease. "Cast off your arms!" Julius shouted. "You who can swim, jump overboard and swim to shore. All others, take a plank, anything that will float. Cling to it and the current will take you to land."

And so it was that all aboard the *Isis* reached land.

Their refuge was Malta. The people of the island, presumed to be barbar-ians, were quick to show their kindness and hospitality. They brought dry wood and built the first of many fires to dry and warm the survivors. Paul gathered an armful of brushwood and was putting sticks on the fire when a viper, drawn out by the heat, coiled around his right hand. When the Maltese saw the poisonous snake on Paul's hand, they moved away in fear. "The old one must be a murderer," one shepherd said, "for though he was saved from the sea, justice will not let him live." But Paul simply shook the snake off into the fire and went off for more wood. The natives followed, expecting his hand and arm to swell before he dropped dead. When they saw that he continued to walk about and talk to other survivors, they held him to be a god.

As it happened, the beach where the *Isis* broke apart was on the estate of Publius, chief magistrate of the island. When his farmers came to tell him of the shipwreck, Publius and his servants came to the beach with food, fresh water, and tents against the cold and rain. A man of learning, Publius conversed at length with Paul, Luke, and Aristarchus, then invited them to his house. While they were there, Publius mentioned that his father was in an upper room of the house ill with fever and dysentery. Paul entered, and by praying for the man and laying on hands, cured him. Word of Paul's power spread swiftly through the island, and he spent the winter healing the afflicted of Malta.

At the beginning of March the skies cleared, bringing warm and sunny days that ended Paul's sojourn in Malta. Julius took his prisoners aboard the *Castor and Pollux*, a grain ship out of Alexandria forced to winter in the main harbor of the island. After unloading grain in Syracuse, the ship sailed on to Rhegium. From there a favorable wind from the south took the *Castor and Pollux* along the coast of Italy and into Puteoli, the port for Rome.

News of Paul's miracle at sea had already reached Rome. Publius had sent an account of the wreck of the *Isis* and the survival of all passengers to the senator representing his island. When Prisca and Aquila heard the story at their emporium, she organized a welcoming party; this gathering of excited Christians was waiting when Paul, his fellow prisoners, and their guards reached the Three Taverns on the Appian Way leading into Rome.

Rejoicing, celebrating, calling out to Paul and each other, they crowded around, exalting the prisoner who had saved his captors. Paul embraced each in turn, Prisca, Aquila, Tertius, Epaenetus, Andronicus, Junias, Ampliatus, Urban, Aristobulus, and a score of others. Looking about anxiously for still another familiar face, he took Prisca aside. "Could Phoebe not come?"

"Phoebe is in Cenchreae," Prisca said quietly, taking Paul by the arm. "She waited here for you for a year. Once she learned you were in prison, she came to me in tears, saying you would always know where to find her, in her flower garden that reminded her of you."

"How did the churches of Rome respond to her reading of my letter?"

"The churches not only welcomed her and your letter," Prisca said, "but they invited her back again and again to read it. Before she returned to Cenchreae, she asked Tertius to make a copy for each Roman church. As a keepsake, she took with her the copy you signed." Again Prisca put her hand on Paul's arm. "Gaius sent me a message last month that he had seen Phoebe in Cenchreae. She was wan, dispirited, possibly ill."

Paul buried his head in his hands, whispering, "O God, let me see her once more." After a few moments he turned to Prisca. "Will you send word to Phoebe that I am in Rome at last. As I am a prisoner and cannot go to her, I shall pray that she can come to me here."

"Count it done," Prisca said, and smiled. "Now look to your followers: Everyone here is waiting for you to speak."

With Julius' permission, Paul took a bench from the tavern and, with his guard's assistance, mounted it. Surveying the gathering, he suddenly realized he had not addressed a Christian assembly in three years. After greeting every Christian by name and commending Julius and the guards for their faithful service, he offered thanks for their safe journey. "Take courage from our passage to this place and time. We witnessed the power of wind and wave, but we saw the greater power of the Lord God, for it was his hand that brought us through this peril of the sea. We heard his voice. We believed. When all seemed lost, we held to the faith. And with his loving arms the Lord God brought us to live again, as indeed he will protect all who love him and put their faith in him and in his son Christ Jesus." After Paul's prayer of thanksgiving and a hymn of joy, the strange procession — one stalwart centurion, five prisoners, ten soldiers who had lost their weapons, and a flock of Christians in high spirits — set out to the north on the Appian Way.

Upon reaching Rome, Julius took his prisoners to the praetorian camp and handed them over to the receiving officer for Severus, the praetorian prefect. Only Paul was summoned to appear before Severus. Julius escorted him into the hearing room.

"Of what crime is this man charged?" Severus asked.

"No crime against the state, sir," Julius replied. "In the province of Judea, Jews complained that he violated the Temple of their religion."

"Why was he brought here?" Severus asked. "The Jews who complained should have dealt with him."

"Sir, Paul is a citizen of Rome," Julius said. "The Jews tried to assassinate him, but our commander in Jerusalem rescued him and placed him in the custody of the governor. The Jews demanded his release to them, whereupon Paul, rather than submit to a mock trial and death by execution or assassination, appealed to Caesar."

Severus turned to Paul. "Having appealed to Caesar, you will be detained in Rome until it pleases Caesar to consider your case. As there is no charge of crime against the state, you may live in a dwelling of your own, but you remain a prisoner and will be under guard. You may receive visitors at your dwelling, but you are not to assemble with more than two persons at any time. You may leave your lodging once weekly, accompanied by your guard. Since the complaint is that you caused a riot in the province, you are not to speak in any public place. These are the conditions."

Paul listened, resenting each restriction to his freedom, but accepting the conditions. Surely all would be lifted as soon as he appeared before Caesar.

Outside the room, Paul and Julius stood together for a moment. As it violated military orders for a guard and prisoner to display friendship, Paul simply looked up at the centurion towering above him and said, "May God bless you and keep you, Julius."

"I owe you my life," Julius said, "and that I shall never forget."

At the gate of the camp Prisca and Aquila were waiting to take Paul to their house. Walking along, with soldier and spear close behind, Prisca pointed out the great edifices built by Caesars past and present, but Paul showed no interest. One question consumed his thoughts, and he put it to his hosts: "When will Nero hear my appeal?"

"I have inquired," Prisca said. "Calenus, one of our brother Christians, is a lawyer, and he advises that Severus will first hand your case over to the legal minister for advice."

"How long will that take?" Paul asked.

"There is no guide, Paul. It can be swift, or it can take months." She elected not to tell him that Calenus had warned that it might take many months, even years.

"I would speak with Calenus," Paul said. "Perhaps we can find a way to speed the process."

Paul rose early the next morning to find Aquila and Prisca breaking their fast in their common room. "Consider this," he said to them. "Is it not logical that Nero will be more concerned about the opinion of Jews in Rome than of Jews in Jerusalem? He may well ask Severus, or his legal minister, whether the Jews of Rome complain against me. Why, then, do I not ask Severus' permission to go before the leading Jews of Rome at once and defend myself against any charges they might make to Caesar?"

Aquila put down his cup and smiled. "It shall be done," he said. "We will invite ten or fifteen here to meet you in . . ." he looked at Prisca.

"Two days hence," Prisca said, "at the fifth hour."

When the time came, eighteen leaders crowded into the common room. Paul stood to speak. "Men, brothers, though I did nothing against our people or the customs of our ancestors, I was made a prisoner in Jerusalem and handed over to Roman authorities. After being questioned, the Romans proposed to release me because they found no reason for the death penalty in my case. But my fellow Jews objected, so I was compelled to appeal to Caesar — even though I made no accusation against my own nation. On account of this, then, I asked to see you and speak to you, for it is for the hope of Israel that I am a prisoner."

Zetham, the chief Jew of Rome, rose to reply. "We have received no letters from Judea about you, and none of the brothers coming here has reported or spoken anything evil about you. But we think it fitting to hear from you what you think. All we know about your sect is that it encounters opposition everywhere."

So they set a day to meet again at the house of Prisca and Aquila, and this time even more of the leaders appeared to hear Paul. From morning until evening he talked earnestly of the kingdom of God, quoting from scripture and the Prophets and the Law of Moses, telling of Jesus' teachings and healings and how he had come to fulfill the Law of Moses, and of his crucifixion and resurrection. Some were persuaded by Paul; others turned their faces against him. After a time the leaders began disputing with each other, raising their voices and grinding their teeth. Being unable to agree among themselves, they threw up their hands and moved toward the door to go.

Paul knocked on a table to get their attention. "I have one last thing to say to you," he said. "How aptly did the Holy Spirit speak through the prophet Isaiah to our fathers: 'Go to the people of Israel and say, "You will surely hear, and not understand at all. You will surely see, and not perceive at all. For the hearts of you people have hardened. Your ears are closed, your eyes are shut — lest at any time you see and hear and understand, and be converted."'

"Therefore, let it be known to you that the salvation of God has been sent to the gentiles, and they will hear." The leaders listened quietly, then went away, still disputing among themselves.

After a fortnight of waiting, with no word from Caesar or his ministers, Paul asked Prisca if he might speak with Calenus.

When the lawyer arrived the next morning, Paul was waiting. "I am a captive without cause, a prisoner of circumstance," Paul said. "One word from Caesar, and I am free to take the gospel to Spain. When will Nero hear my appeal? What must I do to come before him and offer my defense? I have committed no crime, yet here I am in chains. Is this Roman justice?"

Calenus thought for a moment, looked about, then beckoned for Paul to follow him into the small courtyard. "I want no servant to hear what I say," he explained. "Paul, this emperor is himself a prisoner of vanity, extravagance, exhibitionism, and cruelty born of fear. Two years ago he contrived the poisoning of his mother, the ambitious Agrippina, because he suspected her of conniving against him. He mocks the dignity of his royal office. What other emperor would run a footrace in the public games, having arranged that all others will fall behind him so that he wins the laurel? He fancies himself a poet, artist, actor, and musician. He dresses in fine raiment and walks about the palace reading his poetry to his ministers and servants. He plays the lyre — poorly I am told — but all applaud. He divorced, then murdered his wife, Octavia, to marry his mistress, Poppaea, but now pleasures himself with young boys — one of whom, Sportus, he ordered to be castrated and dressed in a wedding gown so that he could marry him. It is such obscenities and licentiousness that engage Nero; he shows no interest in affairs of state or empire, leaving it all to Severus or to Seneca, his tutor when he was a youth."

As Paul stood shaking his head in dismay, Calenus put his hand on his shoulder. "I tell you this not to alarm you, but so that you will know that fairness and justice do not apply under this emperor — nor any legal process."

"Is there another path?" Paul asked. "You mention Seneca. He and I were briefly classmates in Tarsus. Would it be prudent to seek his help?"

Calenus stroked his chin, weighing the question. "You do risk offending some minister or functionary, or even Severus," he said, "but Seneca is a man you can trust."

Paul lost no time in searching out and finding Seneca's villa. A servant looked at the soldier standing guard behind him, and disappeared. In minutes he returned to escort Paul to the chamber where Seneca was writing.

They greeted each other as once young classmates would after almost forty years — with curiosity, fragments of remembrance, and respect for the proven merit of the other. "I ask not for your intervention, but for your counsel," Paul said, and summarized all that happened in Jerusalem and since. "So I appealed to Caesar, but Caesar does not deign to hear me. What shall I do to escape this prison without walls?"

"I know your case," Seneca said. "It is one of many, hundreds, that await the emperor's attention." He sighed heavily and opened his hands in helplessness. "There was a time, in young Nero's early days of authority, when I could influence him. However, after I remonstrated with him for murdering his mother and his wife, I lost favor in his eyes. Paulus, I would help your cause if I could, but now any intervention by me would almost certainly antagonize the emperor toward you. You ask my counsel. Wait. Be patient. Endure."

After breaking bread that evening with Prisca and Aquila, Paul told them of his conversation with Seneca. "Patient I am not, but endure I will," Paul said, and looked up at each of them. "As I am to be in custody indefinitely, I shall move from your house. It is humiliating to me to be a guest in your house, requiring the posting of a guard outside your door."

"But we are honored to have you here," Aquila said.

"I am both honored and grateful to you," Paul said, "but so long as I am a prisoner, I wish to be alone."

"Where will you go?" Prisca asked.

"I know not," he said. "Perhaps I should go to the praetorian prison. They detained me. They can keep me."

"No, no," Prisca said. "I know a small house nearby that is empty. We will rent it for you."

"I have no money," Paul said. "Will you permit me to work for you and earn my rent and bread?"

"We owe you for many things," Aquila said. "So let us repay our debt with a stipend for whatever you need."

Prisca raised her hands, entreating. "I beg you, Paul, let us do this for you."

Paul thought for a moment, then said quietly: "Only until I am again free."

In a little mud house in the Jewish quarter, Paul lived a singular life: prisoner, teacher, counselor, apostle. In his one room he had a desk, paper, pens and ink, a chair, a cot, and a lamp — all the material things he needed. In apostolic things he was limited by praetorian restrictions, but he could open the door of his crude hut to any Christian or Jew or unbeliever who came to him.

At first many came to his prison-church — ministers from far-off cities in Italy and Gaul, Christian Jews intrigued by his letter to Rome, scholars engaging him in philosophical debate. Old friends arrived with small gifts: Julius with a packet of ripe dates, Tertius with a book, Aristarchus to read a letter from Lydia in Philippi, reporting all well there and the church continuing to grow. John Mark appeared one day, to reconcile their differences and to tell Paul that Barnabas' last words were of his beloved friend and fellow apostle.

Every afternoon Prisca came with a basket of food from her kitchen and news of their fellow Christians — Onesimus a free man in Colossae and collecting copies of all Paul's letters; Apollos in Alexandria writing a letter to the Hebrews; Peter, Silvanus, and John Mark working together in Rome to establish a new church; and the best news of all, Phoebe recovering, though she was not yet strong enough to sail for Rome.

As the seasons passed, visitors dwindled. Alone, as he often found himself, Paul could only wait, and wait, hoping and praying that Caesar would hear his case and free him from this injustice, give him back his right to speak in public and travel to far countries. In the meantime, he kept his journal. One night he wrote:

Why? I do my best to understand why I was chosen by the Lord God to take the gospel to the world only to be silenced by a cruel and perverse tyrant. Never have I questioned the actions of the Lord, nor shall I now. But wonder I must that the God who sustained me through floggings, stoning, jail-ings, storms, and shipwrecks leaves me now in the greater peril of going mad in a prison of idleness. After two years in Caesarea and three in Rome I waste away, being left to count the hours and rue the numbers of souls I might bring to Christ if only if I were free again.

Is this God's plan to test my faith? If I were sure of that, I could endure. But suppose this imprisonment is not God's doing at all, but the inevitable consequence of my own false pride. Over the years I have come to see that it was not com-passion for the poor that took me to Jerusalem but my own vanity. By collecting from many, I would show my power over my followers; by delivering a fat purse of gold, I would humble the Jerusalem leaders and buy the favor of the Judaizers toward my teaching of the gospel. How foolish I was. Of course James accepted my money; the people were in need. For my generous gift, I expected gratitude, praise from all. Instead I was scorned, slandered, tricked into a demeaning penance, which led to the outcry in the Temple, which led to my near execution, which led to my being imprisoned. What possessed me to think that I, a marked man, could enter Jerusalem with a bag full of money and leave quietly? By that reckless act I may have ended my mis-sion for the Lord Jesus Christ. All needless and profitless, a fool's errand that I would not have undertaken had I listened to the entreaties of those wiser and more farseeing than I. What I convinced myself to be resolution was, I see now, nothing but obstinacy.

O the cost of that folly: idled at the summit of success. Now I may well rot in this dank and dismal prison. Had I not gone to Jerusalem, I would have arrived in Rome more than five years ago, married Phoebe as I planned, and together we would have opened Spain to the Way of Christianity. We might even have found our son . . .

XXXVIII

ROME BURNS

So intent was Paul at his writing that he did not see the strange light streaming through the slit high in the mud brick that formed his prison. Bent over the rough board that served as his table, he dipped the reed into the bronze inkwell beside the oil lamp, inscribed a line, paused for a moment, and wrote again. In time, after closing his eyes to compose his thoughts, he looked up and saw shadows dancing on the hewn beam over his head. At one moment the glow brightened; at the next it dimmed.

That nimbus of radiance could not be the dawn, for that narrow window opened to the west. It could mean but one thing: There was a great fire in the night. With a sense of foreboding, Paul rose from his bench and groped in the dark for the shepherd's staff he kept beside him. Leaning on his stick, he tried to climb on his table to look out through the slit between the stones, but his lame right leg would not support him, and he fell to the bare earth. The pain, though intense, was not more than he could endure. He struggled to his feet, and on his second attempt he succeeded in mounting the table. Gripping the edges of the rough brick, he began to pull himself up, taking care not to fall again. Slowly then, carefully, he stood. Through the gap between the bricks he could see.

All the earth and sky before him was aflame. Not just a block or a quarter, but the whole of creation seemed to be blazing with the fires of hell. In awe, in disbelief, he whispered the words aloud as he watched: "Rome is burning."

He shook his head in wonder. Across this greatest of cities he could see flames, towering pillars of flames, vast tongues of fire leaping and raging into billows and clouds of smoke, blazing embers borne aloft, flying in the hot summer wind and touching with fire the dry thatch of the roofs nearby, the flames spreading to the wooden hovels of the poor near his little house.

As the fire came closer he could hear running footsteps, frantic shouts of men, cries of women and children fleeing this raging storm of flame, fleeing certain death. "O Lord God, hasten their steps," he prayed. "Give wings to their feet and bear them to safety."

As he watched the smoke and flame and listened to the shrieks of terror in the streets, his thoughts turned inward. Flight was for other men. It would not become him to flee now. He had been chosen to persuade men and women to put their faith in Christ. In all his journeys he had made himself the symbol of courage. He could not run away like a frightened child. As a Christian he was bound to accept God's will.

As Paul was bound by faith, so also was he bound by circumstance. He had given his word to the Roman soldiers who guarded him that he would not escape; should he break from prison on this night, whatever the reason, his guards would be punished by death. And though the thick wooden door of his prison might not be barred from the outside, for sometimes the evening guard forgot, Paul was yet bound by age and infirmity. "I walk in pain," he said to himself. "I surely cannot run."

Through the slit in the brick he looked one last time and saw that only a few huts remained standing outside of his prison. He climbed down, certain that he would die within the hour. With a rueful shake of his head, he muttered, "My old bones will be roasted like a red-eyed bull sacrificed on the pagan altars of Asia."

Standing in the gloom, Paul willed the trembling of his hand to cease. Calmly he contemplated the irony of fate. How could it be that after enduring so many painful beatings in the public squares of Galatia and Macedonia, after being left for dead by the roadside in Lystra, after escaping the assassin's knife in Jerusalem time and time again, after surviving earthquake on land and tempest at sea, after a life surrounded by crowds of believers with faith in their souls or enemies with hatred in their hearts — after so full a life how could it be that he was destined to die alone, in prison?

On the bare earth Paul bent his crippled knees to pray. Except for the crackle of the flames outside, all was quiet. As always he began with praise and thanksgiving, then went on to the prayer spoken by Jesus on the mount in Galilee. The ancient words of Moses to Joshua then came to Paul, and he recited them slowly: "Be strong and of a good courage, fear not, nor be afraid of them: for the Lord thy God, he it is that doth go with thee; he will not fail thee, nor forsake thee."

A great peace came over Paul as he calmed his fears. "Thy will be done," he said, over and over. The words brought a stillness of soul, and he was borne by his thoughts onto a sea of tranquility. He resolved to die in grace, to die with courage, to die a man. He closed his mind to the flames outside and put his consciousness deeper and deeper into receptivity, repeating words of faith, hoping, expecting to receive a vision of the heavenly kingdom to come. In the silence Paul felt himself passing quietly from life.

At peace with himself and the world, he fell into a trance and imagined he stood at the threshold of a new life; through drifting mists he could see his mother, opening her arms to him, welcoming him to come with her, when suddenly a loud noise startled him from the depths of his reverie. Vexed by this new sound from the mundane world, Paul tried to dismiss it, telling himself not to be distracted; perhaps it was only a timber falling from a burning building. Again the crashing sound, and something struck the door of his prison. Then he heard someone lift the bar outside his door; when it opened, the suffused brilliance from the fire brought his prison walls out of the darkness.

"Paul! Paul! Come with me quickly!"

It was Julius the centurion, his captor, companion, and stalwart friend. The massive head and shoulders filled the doorway, silhouetted against the flames and smoke roiling through the street outside.

"Julius! Go!" Paul shouted. "Go! Do not be concerned for me. Save yourself. I am prepared to die. It is God's will."

"No! I cannot leave you here. You are my prisoner. By the command of Caesar I am responsible for you."

Roughly Julius seized the old man's shoulder. "Come quickly. The fire is close. Put this cloak over your head — the embers fly. The wind grows stronger with the heat of the flames. Quickly now. Keep your staff in your right hand and hold my arm with the left. I know a narrow alley that may take us to the Tiber if we hasten."

"Good Julius," Paul said, "I will only be your burden. I beg you to leave now while you can escape."

"I, too, know God's will. You will come with me. Now!"

The two looked at each other, prisoner and guard, comrades, and in an instant of understanding Paul knew that Julius' appearance was a sign: God meant him to live; his work on earth was not yet finished. He would go with him.

With a firm grip, the centurion took Paul's frail arm. As they stepped through the door to the street outside, they felt the heat, scorching, intense, and saw the raging fire, angry, dominating, lighting the world. Pulling Paul — half carrying him — Julius hurried along the narrow street only to confront walls of flame on all sides. They retreated. Julius found an alley, then another, and broke through an empty house into a passage to another street. Stepping over twisted, burning bodies, they groped through the smoke; all at once they were again surrounded by flames. Julius stopped, searching about calmly for a path through the fire to the clear road they could see beyond.

"Paul, we must run through the flames. It is the only way. Wrap your cloak tightly."

Julius picked up his prisoner as though he were a crippled child and started running, but the course was blocked. A short distance away stood the skeleton of a house that had already burned; Julius seized a fallen roof beam, struck a mighty blow against the charred timbers of the house, and cleared a path. With Paul in his arms, he raced through the smoking ruins, and this time they broke loose from the flame and embers. Together they made their way to the Tiber, where a great crowd had gathered by the water. Men were shouting, swimming, clinging to debris as they struggled to cross the stream. A boatman, holding out his hand to take money for passage, saw the tunic of a centurion, swept Julius and Paul aboard, and took them across the Tiber. They walked on, making their way slowly through weeping mothers and desperate men, to climb the hill called Janiculum and look east. The Circus Maximus, Palatium and Velia, Aventinus and Velabrum, all quarters of Rome east of the Tiber and south of Quirinalis — all were in flame and ruin.

For a long time Paul and Julius sat in silence, watching the flames and moved to wonder by the vast calamity before them. At last Julius said quietly, "They say at the barracks, Paul, that Nero himself sent his attendants into the streets with torches to start the fire, and then took himself to the Tower of Maecenas, put on the costume of an actor, pranced about as on a stage, and recited poetry."

As Paul watched the burning of the city, his thoughts again turned inward. The Lord God had intervened before, at Philippi and Corinth, in storms at sea; now God had again intervened and sent Julius to rescue him. A feeling of hope and high expectation came over him. Out of this mad Nero's destruction of Rome would come hunger and such disorder among the people that the praetorians would brush his case aside. Thus he would gain his freedom to began another journey for Christianity; he would resume his mission to the world.

From somewhere in the distance a cock crowed, and then another. At sunrise Julius stood up. In his soldier's voice, he said: "Now that you have rested, we will go. Nearby stands a fort and barracks for the guard in this western quarter of the city. I will report that you are alive and hand you over to the commander there."

At the praetorian camp, the burned, the injured, and the helpless gathered in great numbers to clamor at the gate. When the commander of the fort told Julius there was no room in the fort for a prisoner, Paul rejoiced. This, too, was an omen, a sign that he would soon be free.

"Where will you go?" Julius asked.

Paul thought for a moment. "There is nearby, on Bone Street, the house of a Christian merchant, Marcellus Antonius," he said. "I will go there."

"Very well," Julius said. "When Caesar summons, I will find you there."

The two men joined their right hands. "Again you saved my life, good Julius. I shall always be in your debt."

The centurion nodded and turned to walk away, then stopped and turned back to put his hand on the old man's shoulder. "As you saved my life at Malta, Paul, so am I also in your debt."

Elated by his freedom, Paul set out for Bone Street. By good fortune Marcellus was at home and flattered to welcome so prominent a Christian. The cook brought warm goat's milk and bread, figs and almonds. Marcellus led Paul to a room with a sunny window, showed the weary old man a comfortable cot, and moved to withdraw.

"Stay, Marcellus," Paul commanded. "There is work to be done. First, find my disciple Aristarchus and my scribe Tertius. I have need of them. Second, send a messenger to Timothy in Ephesus. Tell him that I am safe, and he is to visit me as soon as he can. Third, dispatch a trusted brother to find Luke — he frequents the Tavern of the Eagle on the Appian Way — and ask him to come immediately. Fourth, have a servant fetch me a writing table, pens, ink, and papyrus. When I have rested for an hour, I shall resume my writing."

Paul woke in the afternoon. He opened his eyes to see Marcellus entering the room, bustling about officiously, ordering one servant to open the curtains, impatiently telling another where to place the writing table, snapping his fingers and waving his hands to tell them to leave.

Alone with Paul, Marcellus could not wait to relate the news of their brothers: Peter, too, had escaped the fire and survived. John Mark and Silvanus were safe with Peter. Prisca and Aquila found refuge in the Jewish quarter of Trastevere. Claudia and Erastus had left the city in haste. Many Christians died in the fire, as did many slaves and shopkeepers. "Do not go about," Marcellus warned, "for hunger and danger rule the streets. All four central granaries burned. Citizen and slave alike beg for bread. A grain ship from Egypt arrived in Puteoli loaded not with wheat but with sand for wrestlers in the forum — and this caused a riot." Lowering his voice, Marcellus added, "They say that Nero's generals are so angry that he burned their fine mansions that they are plotting to kill him and put General Galba on the throne."

Paul tired quickly of Marcellus' gossip, and said he would rest and be alone. Again God had spared his life, and he was certain that God had done so for a purpose. Was it to take the gospel to Spain? If so, with him he would take Phoebe and his best disciples — Prisca and Aquila. None had been more stalwart for the Lord. And Aristarchus, for his courage had never wavered in the worst of the storm. Timothy? How good it would be to have him along, but no. Now that Timothy was bishop for Ephesus and that region of Asia, his duty was there.

If he did journey to Spain, how many good years would he have there? Enough, he hoped, but there could have been more if some of his best years had not been wasted in confinement — and all because of the vengeance of Zadok. He looked at his hand, fist clenched in rage, and stopped. "Be slow to wrath," he admonished himself. All that was past. He could hope to begin a new journey. How good it would be to feel once more the path rising in the hills before him. How he wanted to stand on a deck and admire the lush abundance of a billowing sail, and hear the soft whisper of wave against bow. Lame he was, yes; but strong enough for the next journey. "God made me to endure," he mused with pride.

His thoughts were interrupted by a soft knock on the door, and a slave entered to announce a visitor.

"Is he a soldier?" Paul asked, instantly stricken by fear that he might be taken back to prison.

"No, Master," the servant replied. "He is a citizen who appears to be of the highest class."

Paul followed the slave to the front of the house. There, to his astonishment, stood Seneca. Overcoming his surprise, Paul reached out his hand in welcome.

"Grace and peace," Paul said, as he wondered at the presence of Seneca. Leading his visitor into the garden in the dusk, Paul said, "Three years and more it has been since we last talked." Seneca said nothing until they were seated.

"I bring news from that most knowing of persons — gossip," Seneca said. "More of a fool is this emperor than I thought. He put the torch to a block of old buildings, intending to replace them with pillars of marble commemorating his own triumphs. As we now see, his petty arson has destroyed more than half the city." Seneca paused. "Now he must find a scapegoat — I believe your Hebrew word is *azazel*."

Seneca folded his arms and faced Paul. "Nero will blame the Christians. To divert the common people from their hardship, he has ordered his minister of law to stage a political trial of Christian leaders. The charges will be conspiracy and incendiarism. Some will be put to death. Paulus, I come to warn you that the emperor Nero may begin his executions with Peter. And you."

Paul leaned back in his chair and placed his fingertips together under his chin. He felt more surprise than fear. He had convinced himself that he would be set free; indeed, in that first moment Paul almost raised his hand to scoff at Seneca's warning, as one more of the many threats of death he had heard during his journeys over the years. Yet in the next moment Paul knew this present circumstance differed. He was still Nero's prisoner: Killing was this Caesar's sport. Paul had not anticipated this impulsive act of a despot, but suddenly he could see that the execution of Christians could both satisfy Nero's lust for blood and meet his imperial political purposes. *Be calm*, Paul told himself. In the presence of his fellow Stoic he must display the bravery and equanimity they had both been taught on the porches in Tarsus. In a calm and steady voice, Paul said, "I trust that you have not put yourself in danger by coming here."

Seneca shrugged. "It matters not," he said with a quiet laugh. "One day Nero will ask for my suicide, and I will grant it. Do you remember, Paulus, these words of our tutor, Zagoreos: 'It is within the reach of every man to live nobly, but within no man's power to live long.'"

At the garden gate the two men parted. Paul watched his schoolmate disappear down the street and then slowly walked back to his room. From habit, he sat at his writing desk. Resting his head on his hands, closing his eyes, he attempted to grasp the reality. In his mind he searched urgently for a reason to doubt Seneca's warning, but none could he find. Seneca spoke from knowledge. Out of favor Seneca was with Caesar, but the palace courtiers secretly called on his wisdom and counsel. Seneca came to Paul not merely out of concern, but to show his respect for a peer. It was the brotherhood of the Stoa: There they had learned that reason will triumph over ill fortune. Seneca had come to make certain that Paul would exhibit the composure appropriate to his station before Nero's court. Discipline, courage, acceptance; in these Paul would abide.

He turned to his haven, the pen.

> I have lived for Christ. And always have I known I will die for Christ. But not so soon. Not now. My immediate concern must be not for myself but for the church. When both Peter and I are executed, who will lead the Christian Way? Who will carry to the world the message of faith, the promise of Jesus? Who will know and preserve the true gospel? Who will guide the churches we have built and bind them in unity? To whom will young apostles turn for direction? Who will lead our restless bands of followers toward truth and away from doubt and schism? If I, Paul, am no longer on earth, who will take the light to the gentiles as Jesus commanded me to do? After Peter, who will stand as the rock of the church?

Paul reached for his shepherd's crook and began to pace the floor. Suddenly overcome by a wave of anguish, wanting desperately not to be executed but to live, to breathe, to walk, to marry, to speak, to write to his churches, to teach. For a moment he thought to beseech God to deliver him from this peril. But he stopped himself. "My time has come," he said aloud, in a voice as firm as he could muster. "I know in my soul that I am to be executed. God's will be done."

First, he must write Phoebe: Tell her the truth but fashion a letter that would reflect the splendid memories they shared. Thinking of her, he began to weep. Never again would he see her face, hear the lilt of her voice, feel the soft touch of her hand on his cheek. After a long time he began:

> I, Paul, a man of Tarsus and the world, to my beloved Phoebe, my betrothed and my treasure, keeper of my heart, partner in love and in the fullest measure of life,
>
> I see you now, my beloved, in the garden of our youth, the gentle breeze garlanding with gold the blush of your fair cheeks, rose-lips parted in merry song, soft arms reaching out in the innocence of youthful passion,
>
> I see you now, my beloved, languishing in the white-blossomed bower of our secret cave beneath the green canopy of the tamarisk, weary with love, lying close beside me, murmuring endearments that needed no words,
>
> I see you now, my beloved, the taut sail bearing you far away, and you island-bound and alone, scorning the bold glances of cynics, measuring the days, fighting with tiny hands against the cruel soldier seizing your treasure,
>
> I see you now, my beloved, caught in the magic of the night stars of the eastern sea, the scent of wild jasmine in the evening air, head on my shoulder, hand in mine, the rising moon holding the promise of joy eternal,
>
> I see you now, my beloved, breath stilled at the moment the hooded guard brings down the heavy sword, weeping in sorrow but brushing away the tears knowing that your Paulos savored the full taste of life, cup brimming with joy and good fortune, sunshine and fair winds, overflowing with love given and love received, knowing also that at the last moment of his wonderful life his thoughts will be of you, ever of you.

My beloved, may the peace of God come to you now as it has to me, and may God bless you and keep you in this hour and into eternity.

Paulos

He put out the lamp and sat long in the darkness, wondering at the strange events that had so cruelly ended his every hope and dream.

Early the next morning Paul was awakened by an old slave who told him that a visitor was at Marcellus' door.

"Is he a centurion?" Paul asked.

"No, Master. He is clothed in white linen and carries a tablet of parchment."

Paul hobbled to the door and threw it open.

"Luke!" Paul called out. There standing in the archway was his scholarly comrade of the road, his staunch ally, the beloved physician. There was the broad countenance beaming with good humor, the stocky presence planted firmly on the threshold, the brawny arms reaching out to clasp Paul's shoulders with friendship and affection.

"By good fortune they found you quickly," Paul said, rejoicing. "You are the person I most want to see on this day. Welcome to the house of Marcellus."

"My noble friend, once again the thought we shared bridged the distance between us," Luke said. "I sensed, indeed I knew, that I must come to your side. I was well along the way when your messenger met me on the Via Appia."

As Paul and Luke walked into the garden, the old slave brought food and drink and placed it on a table nearby. Luke did not seat himself on the marble bench, as Paul did, but strolled among the flowers, deep in thought, composing his words.

"The end of the beginning has come," Luke said, his manner grave. "We Christians, we the faithful, have reached a turning point. Our greatest crisis is at hand, Paul, and we must take account of what lies ahead."

"What have you learned?" Paul asked.

Luke sat beside him. "I was with our brothers in Appius when we saw the light in the northern sky that told us of the great fire. You know of Manilius, the palace scribe who follows Christ in secret. Manilius relayed to us in Appius a warning, that the Christian leaders will be executed for starting the fire."

"I, too, was warned," Paul said. "Lucius Seneca himself came here last evening to tell me that Nero has ordered his minister of law to put Peter and me on trial before a public tribunal. And then Nero will order our execution."

There was a long silence, broken by Paul. "Tell me, Luke: Why was I saved from the fire if it is only to be put on the executioner's block to satisfy the momentary need of a mad emperor?"

Luke rose and walked back and forth. "Persecution is an act of fear, Paul. As our followers increase, Nero senses danger. Perhaps he fears that we may become a political force that would challenge his own reign and authority."

"Luke, we Christians are in deed and in fact a political force. We are a kingdom of faith set down in the midst of a kingdom of arms. The ruler is right to concern himself with our growing power. But strange it is that Nero, like other kings throughout history, believes he can put down a revolt by killing the leaders. Can this Caesar not see that invariably a new leader builds on the martyrdom of his predecessors? So it was with Jews, Greeks, Egyptians — and now Romans."

Luke stopped, came close to Paul, and spoke in a whisper.

"You can escape, Paul. A ship sails tomorrow for Spain from Puteoli. It is the *Mistralis*, and the captain is a Christian."

Paul's eyes widened. "A ship to Spain? O my brother Luke, how you tempt me, for long have I dreamed that I will sail for Spain and there find the son I have never seen. It is said that he commands a legion north of Malaca."

"Then you will go?"

"Flee? Not stand up for Christianity?"

"No, that you proceed to carry out your mission," Luke said. "If you do not escape Rome, Paul, who will take the gospel to Spain and Britannia?"

Paul shook his head and uttered a heavy sigh. "In the first hour after Julius rescued me, I was certain that God had set me free from prison, as so many times he did before, so that I might lead an expedition to Spain and the outer reaches of the empire. It seemed so logical." He shook his head. "But now it is not to be."

"Paul, for the sake of the cause it is imperative that you leave this city, and that Peter escape as well."

Paul looked long at his beloved companion of land and sea. "No," he said at last. "Never have I run from danger. It would not be fitting for either Peter or me to flee persecution. A leader cannot be a coward. As I have lived for my beliefs, so must I be prepared to die for my beliefs. And so it is for every Christian. Peter and I must set the example of faith and courage, whatever may be our end."

"All that you say is true and in my mind," Luke said, "yet there is a greater question: What will happen to this movement without you? Next to Jesus himself, no man has so dominated the creation of the Christian churches. I know, for I have spoken with all the apostles and witnessed your enterprise and your successes in city after city. You are our *theologos*, the philosopher who defines and articulates the principles and practices that state what a Christian is and should be. You teach us. You organize our churches. You show the way. You are our leader; our leader you must continue to be."

Paul continued to shake his head. "I will not flee. I cannot hide in a cave or on a mountaintop. To teach and to write I must be free, free to walk among the people, free to live and work among them."

Luke asked: "Without you and Peter, who will lead?"

"Since I first learned of Nero's intentions, I have thought of little else," Paul said. "Our first concern must now be for the churches and for our followers. We must not only put in place the most worthy successor, but we must also establish an orderly process for future succession. From the beginning strife and envy have plagued our churches. We tell the followers of Jesus to follow his example, and to love one another, but the more devout they become, the more they quarrel over the unimportant. Without a shepherd, our Christians will stray like sheep and be devoured by wolves."

"And who is to be the next shepherd, Paul?"

"Luke, I have thought that you yourself may take Peter's place. You have the faith, the gift of persuading, and the commanding presence to be the leader who will take the church forward."

"Were I a Jew, Paul, I could attempt to fill Peter's shoes. But the movement is yet a child, young and fragile. Until this child has reached manhood, only a Jew can serve as parent."

"I thought that might be your answer, and I accept it — although in time Christianity will be more gentile than Jew."

Paul paused to reflect. "Our generation is passing, Luke. Peter is the last survivor of Jesus' inner circle. I never believed that James showed promise as a leader. He was shallow of conviction, and too imprisoned by Hebrew tradition to look kindly upon gentiles coming into his brother's Way. And old John bar Zebedee — ever boastful that he was Jesus' favorite — he never faced a crowd. Nor was John constant in belief. He left Peter's coterie in Jerusalem to join the Essenes and become a pietistic hermit. Then he left the Essenes to seclude himself in Ephesus and write. Andrew was different. Andrew showed great zeal in Achaia, so much so that he was martyred there. Bartholomew journeyed off to India and disappeared. Of the others among the Twelve — plodding Philip, doubting Thomas, Matthew the tax collector — they and the others strayed in faith or weakened in resolution. A poor lot, withal."

Luke laughed. "Perhaps Jesus appointed you, Paul, because it turned out that so few of the Twelve could deliver a sermon or bring in a convert."

Paul did not laugh, or even smile. "That thought has occurred to me more than once," he said. "Upon my first visit to Jerusalem after Damascus I saw clearly that it was Jesus' intention to place responsibility for the growth of the movement on me. So it has been. Peter stood in place; I advanced."

Luke thought for a moment. "Different you and Peter are, yet you became partners."

"Yes, partners in the cause," Paul said. "At first I saw in Simon Peter only weakness, but in time I realized that what I saw as weakness was tolerance, a quality not granted to me. By his sturdiness and patience, the fisherfolk qualities that Jesus must have seen in Peter, this rock of a man soothed the differences between the incestuously proud old apostles who had known Jesus and the new disciples bursting to bear the truth beyond Jerusalem. Peter and I often differed: He would not stand and fight as I did. He let himself be led, or misled, by James. Constancy was not his nature."

Now Paul rose and began to hobble about, continuing his discourse. "In time Peter accepted my proposition that we should liberate Christianity from the narrow minds and petty despots of Jerusalem and take the gospel to other nations. Thus Peter came to Rome — but he did not establish the church here as well as I would have, had I been free."

He turned to Luke. "Peter and I could never have pulled under one yoke. Instead we plowed separate fields."

"That was not by chance," Luke said.

"Of course not," Paul replied. "It was God's plan that he serve the Jews and I the gentiles. But our task is not yet finished. Our past differences mean nothing now. It is imperative that Peter and I appoint the next leader."

"Peter favors Linus the Etruscan," Luke said. "Who is your choice?"

"Not yet have I made a choice," Paul replied. "Steadfast Linus is. He came twice, perhaps thrice, to my prison-house to seek my counsel. Linus could fill the role of dependable caretaker. Clement of Damascus is the rising star of the new generation, that is, of all born after Jesus died. I knew him as a child. Now Clement is both orator and poet, and excels in intellect and authority. He has made his mark as a man of action. But our older disciples may be unwilling to follow so young a leader."

"How will you bring about the succession?"

"As Jesus chose Peter and made it known to the Twelve, so Peter — and I of course — must choose. When we do, Peter will lay his hand on this man's head, and thereby make it known to all that this is the next earthly father of Christianity.

"Luke, find Peter. He and I must meet forthwith, not only to choose the successor but also to create the process for future successions. It is imperative that we avoid the Roman way of succession by murder; we must pass the crown as David did to Solomon. Bring us together at once, for soon both of us may find ourselves in prison and unable to act, or even speak."

"Find Peter I shall, and bear your message I shall," Luke said as he stood to go.

Paul was in the garden that afternoon when the old servant announced that a woman was at the gate. Without a moment's hesitation, he said, "Bring Prisca to me here."

Her wide smile and cheerful words could not hide the truth: She, too, knew what was to come. Paul spent their first hour consoling her and trying to persuade her that she and Aquila should take the good news of Christ Jesus to Spain. "You must go in my stead," he said. She promised they would consider it.

Suddenly Paul stood and hobbled about. "There are important things I must say to you, Prisca." His face stricken, he raised his hands in a gesture of helplessness. "I should have listened when you warned me in Corinth not to go to Jerusalem. Your intuition — that I would be scorned and suspected by my fellow Christians and menaced by Zadok's assassins — turned out to be true. You were right. I was wrong. A stubborn fool I was. My reach for the impossible, to bring Jew and gentile together, was my undoing. One last time, my zeal overruled my judgment."

"Why burden your soul with self-reproach?" Prisca asked. "Zeal was ever in your being. Without your zeal, we would have no Christians in Galatia or any other province in Asia, in Macedonia, or in Achaia. Without your zeal, Jesus' good news for mankind might still be confined within the stone walls of Jerusalem. Indeed, you told me long ago that Jesus chose you, and appeared to you on that road to Damascus, because it was ingrained in your nature to excel above all others and overcome any and all obstacles."

"True," Paul said, "and Jesus told a reluctant Ananias in Damascus, 'I will show him how much he must suffer in my name.' And suffer I have, deservedly, for the naked ambition that drove me to persecute Christians and contrive the Sanhedrin's murder of Stephen." He shook his head. "For the stubbornness that cost the life of Barnabas. He was the best of fellow apostles, the comrade I loved as a brother. No day has passed that I did not regret what I said and did to Barnabas. Now I must suffer yet the worst of punishments: I am denied the opportunity to complete my mission for Christ Jesus."

"Is the lifework of any mortal ever finished, Paul?" Prisca asked. "Surely each of us dreams of greater deeds than God expects of us. Look not at what you failed to do; look instead at all you accomplished, the souls you saved, the churches you built, the hope and the faith your words will instill in generations yet unborn."

"I wanted to accomplish more, Prisca."

"I know," she said, "but perhaps God, in his infinite wisdom, judges it is time for you to rest, time for others of zeal and merit to follow the example you set and carry on, advancing the gospel of Christ to a world yet to be discovered."

With a brusque movement, Paul brought out a fold of papyrus. "I ask you to help me with last things, Prisca. This is my farewell to Phoebe. Will you appoint your most dependable messenger to take it to her?"

"If Aristarchus cannot go, I will deliver it myself," she said.

"I tried to write to Timothy," Paul said, his voice breaking, "but the right words could not break through the sadness that comes from knowing I shall never again see the face of one who is like a son to me. Will you write Timothy for me?"

"Of course. What shall I say?"

"Make it personal, his family as my family, and instructive: Remain true to the gospel as revealed by the Lord to me. Beware of false teachers. Guard against enemies. Expect that all devoted to Christ will be persecuted. Be considerate to widows, elders, and slaves. Be content with little; we enter the world with nothing, and we take nothing into death. Appoint men of impeccable character as bishops — temperate, discreet, courteous, husband of one wife. Follow my teaching, my way of life, my goals, my faith, my perseverance, my love for all. And somewhere in my letter to Timothy, find a place to record this, my final testament:

> The time of my departure is at hand. I have fought the good fight.
> I have finished the course. I have kept the faith.

Tears flowed as Prisca read the scrap of papyrus. "Lastly," Paul said, his voice now strong, "I commend you, Prisca, and Aquila for your stalwart devotion to Christ Jesus, for your open generosity to the church, for your indefatigable spirit of optimism, for your wise counsel to me, much of which I followed, all of which I should have, and for your abiding love for mankind. May the peace of God that passes all understanding be with you now and evermore."

Prisca took Paul by the hand. "For myself, and for all graced by being in your presence, I offer thanksgiving to the Lord God that you, Paul, have been so great a part of my life. Many journeys have you made; now you begin the most momentous of all. May God speed this, your final journey, and crown you with glory as you enter into his heavenly kingdom."

Toward evening, as Paul was writing in his journal, the old servant came to the door of his room and knocked softly. "There is a centurion at the gate," he said. "He gives the name Julius."

XXXIX

CATACOMBS

The trial of Paul and Peter drew vast crowds to the new Circus Neronis and ran for twenty-seven days. The prosecutor, the city prefect Didius Fabricius, opened the series of performances by bringing to the stage a corps of professional informers who swore they witnessed Paul and Peter racing about with torches to set the fires that burned Rome. Each day the two apostles were paraded in chains, to be mocked by palace agents posted in the audience. No evidence was offered, or needed. The verdict had been ordered by Nero even before the trial began. At the end the chief magistrate handed down the sentence: execution for both.

Peter was to be crucified as a criminal. Paul, as a Roman citizen, was to be beheaded. He protested; he asked to be crucified as Jesus had been and as Peter would be. The magistrate refused; Roman law required that a citizen be executed by the sword.

From the circus Paul and Peter were led in chains through the streets to catacombs in the older part of the city and imprisoned there with other enemies of the state. They were fed meager bread and water, and assigned to sleep on ledges cut as tombs for the dead.

In the darkness they waited. And talked, long and often. On Paul's initiative the two rivals reconciled their differences, with Paul accepting Peter's preeminence as Jesus' first choice to head the church, and Peter replying: "Without your zeal and success in bringing so many to Christ, there would be no church." Together they debated and agreed on actions to safeguard the future of the movement. To avoid schisms and maintain the integrity of Christian doctrine, Peter and Paul reaffirmed two policies: Christians must refuse to worship any Caesar or the Roman state, even if it meant death. Teachers of novel doctrine were to be expelled from the church and forbidden to speak before any Christian assembly.

Together they also established the line of succession: Linus to follow Peter as head of the church, then Cletus, then Clement. After Clement, a conclave of bishops would choose the leader by secret ballot. To make certain all Christians would accept the authority of their decisions, Paul inscribed them on parchment that he and Peter signed. By prearrangement, a Christian guard smuggled the archive out of the prison and delivered it to Tertius for copying and distribution to the churches of Rome and the nations afar.

After three months of imprisonment, Nero's soothsayer read the auguries and chose the date for the apostles' execution — the tenth day of the tenth month of the tenth year of Nero's reign.

As he planned, Paul spent his last night in meditation and prayer. Looking back, he counted himself singularly fortunate to have been born a Jew, one of God's chosen, to a mother of affection and spirit who inspired him to excel and to a father with the drive and energy to succeed and provide advantages of position and wealth; a mother and father who had given him a young sister of virtue and character whose courageous son saved his life. With fondness Paul remembered his growing up, the triumph over illness by the ministrations of devoted Alida, the glorious days at the Academy and the Stoa and his delight in exploring new ideas with his Greek and Roman tutors, his mastery of the Law under the guidance of the wise Gamaliel. Yes, he had served the Law with too much zeal; yet had he not done so, he would not have been appointed by Jesus to take the gospel to far lands and people. Surely this was destiny, God's plan from the beginning.

Regrets, yes, he could count many. Had he heeded the signs, he would have foreseen the danger to his mother and found a way to prevent her death. Had he been more grateful by nature, he would have recognized his obligation to his father and found a way to resolve their differences. Had impatience not overcome his judgment during his first visit to Jerusalem after the revelation, he could have formed an alliance with Peter and James and not been exiled for ten years. Had he demonstrated his gratitude to Barnabas, his closest brother in the faith would have lived — and perhaps succeeded Peter as the rock of the church. Good Barnabas, who enhanced his life, rescued him from oblivion, opened the path to Antioch and missions afar, defended him when others would not. Had he not been so stubborn, and so absorbed in himself, he could have married Phoebe and known the blessings of children.

All that was past, the story written, the ending at hand. Weighing his life in balance, he knew he was the most fortunate of mortals. No other man of his time had been so challenged, or been given so extraordinary an opportunity to change the world. He had done his best. He had made a difference. He had expanded the kingdom of God. Were Jesus to appear to him in his last hour, he might say, "Well done, faithful servant of the Lord."

As dawn neared, Paul knelt to pray. "O most merciful and caring Father, help me as I face the morning. Be with me in my last hour and at the moment of death. Sustain my faith. Let not my step falter, or my knee tremble. As you gave me the indefatigable spirit to take the message of Jesus Christ to the world, as you led me to triumph over misfortune and evil, lead me now to face the end of life with courage, resolve, and abiding faith. For the good works I may have accomplished, I ask your blessings. For my sins, I repent. I ask, in the name of Jesus Christ, for your forgiveness. And may your grace and your peace be with me now and to my last moment of life."

The morning of execution arrived, the sky as clear and brilliant as autumn could bring. A company of legionnaires under the command of Julius marched up to the entrance of the catacombs, where a small crowd of Christians and the curious had gathered. Without ceremony Julius accepted Peter and Paul and escorted the two prisoners, side by side, through the Ostian Gate along the Via Laurentina to a place well outside the city walls. When the soldiers halted before marching on to separate sites for execution, Peter turned to Paul and said: "Go in peace, preacher of glad tidings, guide of the just to salvation."

Paul replied: "Peace be with thee, founder of the church, shepherd of the flock of Christ Jesus."

As they prepared to march on, Paul asked Julius to remove the chains so that he might walk free for the last mile of his life. Julius gave the order, and as the smith was breaking the irons, some of the women gathered around Paul in tears. He blessed them, prayed for them, and pronounced a benediction.

His step firm, his face composed, Paul mounted the high scaffold where the executioner, a hooded centurion, waited beside the wooden block with his sword.

"Is your blade sharp, your hand steady, your arm strong?" Paul asked. The hooded swordsman nodded.

Paul raised his right hand to bless his followers, as he had so many times before, and proclaimed for all to hear: "I belong to Jesus Christ. I lived for Jesus Christ. I die now for Jesus Christ. Beyond death, my hope is in Jesus Christ."

EPILOGUE

Entry from the Journal of Tertius

I, Tertius of Macedon, witnessed the execution of Paul.

The sword fell swift and true, and a vivid fountain of crimson blood spurted from the neck of the body, spilling on the paving stones of the Roman road. Many among his followers came forward to dip the hems of their garments in his blood, for they believed that the merest drop would heal the sick, restore sight to the blind, and save their souls.

The severed head of Paul fell from the executioner's high scaffold and bounced once, twice, thrice; and in each place where it touched the earth there came forth a spring of clear and fresh water. Like the words of Paul, these three springs flow and nourish the people of the world.

ACKNOWLEDGMENTS

Curiosity impelled me to write about Paul. When we moved back to New York City in 1962, we took our two boys to St. Thomas Church to enroll them in Sunday school, and there met two persons who would become of consequence to our lives — Father Tom Byrne and Jaqueline Marshall Braxton. These two introduced us to the magnetic power of the words and leaders of the Christian faith, and in time to the letters of Paul.

As a journalist covering politics and national affairs for *Newsweek* magazine, I was intrigued by Paul as a significant public figure of his time. I liked his writing — forceful, imperative. He had vision. He had a message. He conceived and led a campaign to lead the pagan world out of despair and into hope, and he succeeded.

Paul, I learned, changed history. "The birth of Christianity is one of the central dramas in human history," William H. McNeill observed in his 1963 classic *The Rise of the West*. After Jesus' death, "The next great turning point in Christian history focused around the career of St. Paul."

Leadership, and the qualities that make effective leaders, have always interested me. As a soldier during World War II, I observed many leaders, some able, others incompetent. Later I had the good fortune to serve and observe outstanding leaders: in journalism, Henry Luce, Philip Graham, and Osborn Elliott; in public life, Governor Nelson Rockefeller, President Gerald Ford, and Senator Howard Baker.

Ten years ago, after I finished writing about the events and circumstances that brought Gerald Ford into the presidency (*Time and Chance: Gerald Ford's Appointment with History*), I mentioned to Edward L. Burlingame, the wisest of editors, and to Peter Matson, my learned counselor and agent, that I was considering writing a fictional biography of Paul. Both encouraged me and guided me along the way. To both I am deeply grateful.

To begin this project I set out to find out all I could about Paul. First I went to Father Joseph Tylenda, then director of the comprehensive Woodstock Library at Georgetown University, and asked him to show me his existing biographies of Paul. Escorting me through his stacks, he pointed out scores of shelves filled with rows of books interpreting Paul's letters and exploring his theology. Turning aside, he put his hand on an empty shelf. "Here are the books about Paul the man."

Every detail that is known about Paul, I learned, can be assembled in a couple of afternoons. Yet the fragments, like shards of ancient pottery, stir the imagination. The more I studied Paul's life and times, the more I admired his character and qualities of leadership. Paul moved audiences by the content and force of his oratory. He could organize, train deputies, delegate. In his writings he set policy, established processes, and measured results. Zeal, intellect, courage — these qualities he exemplified. He was a consummate ideological activist, the man of thought driven to action.

In researching and writing this account of Paul's life, I am indebted to many, and particularly to the clergy who not only encouraged me but answered all my questions and offered excellent advice: Margaret Graham, Sanford Garner, Charles Minifie, and Stuart Kenworthy. The Reverend Dr. Albert Scariato shared his invaluable scholarship and expertise on Jewish history and early ritual, and pointed out errors in an early version of the manuscript.

For the chronology of Paul's life and significant events, and for the authenticity of his letters, I relied on a masterful reference book by Raymond E. Brown S.S., *An Introduction to the New Testament*. For word-by-word translation of the original Hebrew and Greek texts I turned to *The Interlinear Bible*, by Jay P. Green Jr. The Library of the U.S. Naval Academy provided me essential guidance about first-century sailing ships, practices, and routes.

During the writing, and after, I relied on excellent editors. Patricia Mulcahy showed me how to reduce a sprawling manuscript to manageable size and make it a better story in the process. Robin Dutcher pointed out necessary changes in the penultimate manuscript and instructed me in getting the story ready for publication. To both I am most grateful.

From the beginning, two longtime friends, Jaqueline Braxton and her husband, Christopher Wren, the distinguished foreign correspondent for the *New York Times*, encouraged me in this effort; they also commented constructively on the writing, then intervened to bring this book to publication. To Jaqueline and Chris, I reaffirm my gratitude.

The immediate enthusiasm of publisher Chip Fleischer was a welcome gift, and I am particularly grateful to Chip, to managing editor Kristin Sperber, to Pia Dewey, and to the entire staff at Steerforth Press for their expeditious management of the details of publishing.

Finally, I am indebted to my son Jim for instructing me in the complexities of computers and the Internet, and to my son Scott for coaching me in writing fiction. Most of all, I thank my beloved wife, Cherie, for the constancy of her support for this enterprise and for the wisdom of her comments on the manuscript.

Washington, D.C.
February 26, 2005

A Reader's Guide

APOSTLE PAUL

JAMES CANNON

ZOLAND BOOKS
an imprint of
STEERFORTH PRESS
HANOVER, NEW HAMPSHIRE

1. Without Paul, would Christianity have spread to the world?

2. Why did Jesus select Paul, rather than Peter or another disciple, to take the Good News to the gentiles?

3. Was it better for the cause of Christianity that Paul and Barnabas split up before their second journey? In Antioch and on their first journey the two were clearly complementary — Paul's zeal and creativity combined with Barnabas's common sense and practicality. Did Paul travel and work better alone? Or would he have taught and organized even better had Barnabas been with him to help fend off his enemies within and without the movement?

4. Were Paul's letters written for the ear, that is, to be read aloud, or for the eye, to be read by an individual?

5. What was the thorn in the flesh that afflicted Paul?

6. How can we account for the conflicts in Paul's writings? For example, at one point he says women cannot speak in church; at another he makes women deacons, which qualifies them to speak in church.

7. What would be the first question you would like to ask Paul if you should meet him?